No matter ho[illegible] stop the carir[illegible] her heart, she [illegible]

She liked Mitch Dalton. She liked him very much.

"Why do you love pearls?" He studied her, waiting.

"Everyone knows that a pearl starts with a tiny grain of sand, but to me, it's like faith. We are like that grain of sand, and it's God's grace that can cloak us and make us shine, if we are humble and faithful enough. In the end, it's a thing of true beauty."

"Yes, it certainly is."

He wasn't looking at the pearl, but at her. Somehow his gaze deepened and there he went, feeling too intimate, as if he could see too much. But how could he look past the layers of defense in which she cloaked herself so carefully?

New York Times bestselling author **Jillian Hart** grew up on her family's homestead, where she helped raise cattle, rode horses and scribbled stories in her spare time. After earning her English degree from Whitman College, she worked in travel and advertising before selling her first novel. When Jillian isn't working on her next story, she can be found puttering in her rose garden, curled up with a good book or spending quiet evenings at home with her family.

Multipublished bestselling author **Ruth Logan Herne** loves God, her country, her family, dogs, chocolate and coffee! Married to a very patient man, she lives in an old farmhouse in Upstate New York and thinks possums should leave the cat food alone and snakes should always live outside. There are no exceptions to either rule! Visit Ruth at ruthloganherne.com.

A Soldier for Christmas

New York Times Bestselling Author

Jillian Hart

&

Her Holiday Family

Ruth Logan Herne

ISBN-13: 978-1-335-97116-6

A Soldier for Christmas & Her Holiday Family

This edition published by arrangement with Love Inspired Books.

www.Harlequin.com

Printed in U.S.A.

CONTENTS

A SOLDIER FOR CHRISTMAS

Jillian Hart

To Frank Heidt. Thanks for taking the time to answer my questions about Force Recon. I'll keep your family in my prayers, always.

I wait for the Lord, my soul doth wait,
and in his word do I hope.
—*Psalms* 130:5

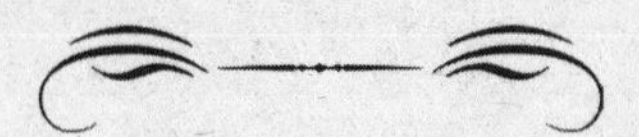

Chapter One

Kelly Logan closed the textbook with a huff and blinked hard to bring the Christian bookstore where she worked into focus.

Math. It was *so* not fair that she, a twenty-four-year-old college student, had to take the required course so she could graduate. She intentionally hadn't thought about quadratic equations since high school, which was six years ago. Hello? Who would want to have to think about this stuff? Unfortunately, she was paying good tuition money to have to think about this stuff. She rubbed her forehead in the hopes that her equation-induced headache would go away.

No such luck. Pain pounded against her temples as though someone was inside her skull, beating her with a mallet. Lovely. She'd been studying algebra for thirty minutes in the quiet lull of a Friday afternoon. Thirty minutes was all it took for her neurotransmitters to quit working in protest. Not that she blamed them. Definitely time for a study break before her head imploded. She leaned a little to the left over the counter to check on the store's only customer, busily browsing in the devotionals display. "Do you need any help, Opal?"

"Any more of your help and I'll break my budget, honey." Elderly Mrs. Opal Finch wandered away from the decorated table with a small book in hand. "I got this one. The one you recommended. I see one of your bosses put up a written recommendation on it, too."

"Katherine has exquisite taste."

Opal slipped the book onto the counter. "Since when have you two steered me wrong? It's such a pretty cover, I couldn't resist."

"Neither could I. I bought it today—payday." Kelly gestured toward the identical small pink book next to her textbooks before she rang up the sale. "I already took a peek at it. The first day's devotion is awesome."

"Wonderful. Are you going to want to see my identification? That new girl did last time I was here."

"Nope, I know your account number by heart."

"That's not what I meant." Opal's merry green eyes sparkled with amusement. "So you can verify my senior citizen discount! It's a hoot, that's what it is, questioning my age. Oh my, it's good for the soul."

"You look eighty-three years young to me," Kelly assured the lovely octogenarian as she scribbled down the purchase on an in-house charge slip.

"Bless you, dear, I surely appreciate that. And I don't need a bag, sweetie. Conservation, you know." She opened her wide paisley-patterned purse, hanging by sturdy straps from her forearm.

Kelly leaned over the counter to slip the book and

receipt into the cavernous purse. "Thanks for coming by. You stop in and tell me how you like the devotional, okay?"

"I most certainly will." Opal snapped her purse shut, her smile beaming and her spirit shining through. "Don't study too hard. An education is important, but don't you forget. There are greater blessings in this life."

In yours, yes. Kelly filed the in-house copy of the charge slip in the till and held back the shadows in her heart. She feared that a happy family may not have been in God's plan for her. Sometimes it was hard to accept, to see the reason why she'd been given the parents she had.

Some days it was all she could do to have faith.

"Kelly, dear," Opal called over her shoulder on the way to the door. "Be sure and tell Katherine good-bye for me. That girl works too much!"

"I'd tell her that, but she won't listen."

The bell over the front door chimed cheerfully as it swung open with a force hard enough to keep the bell tinkling a few extra times.

"Let me hold the door for you, ma'am." A man's rugged baritone sounded as warm as the intense August sunshine, and the bell jingled again as he stepped aside, holding the door wide as Opal passed through.

Something puzzled her. His voice. There was something about it. Kelly couldn't see him well because of the glare of bright sunlight slanting through the open window blinds lining the front of the store.

All she saw of the newcomer was his silhouette cutting through the strong lemony rays of the western sun.

It was a silhouette cut so fine, everything within her stilled, awestruck by the iron-strong impression of his wide-shouldered outline.

"Why, thank you, sir," Opal's genteel alto rang with admiration. "You're a fine gentleman."

"You have a nice afternoon, ma'am." He stepped out of the touch of the light. His shadowed form became substance—a fit, capable soldier dressed in military camouflage, who looked as if he'd just walked off the front page of the newspaper and into the bookstore.

Wow. Definitely, one of the good guys.

"Good afternoon." The soldier removed his hat, the floppy brimmed kind that was camouflage, too, revealing his thick, short jet-black hair. He nodded crisply in her direction.

"Uh. G-good afternoon." Was that really her voice? It sounded as if she had peanut butter stuck in her throat. Totally embarrassing. "Do you need any help?"

"I might. I'll let you know." He stood too far away for her to see the color of his eyes accurately, but his gaze was direct and commanding.

And familiar. There *was* something about him. It wasn't uncommon for soldiers to find their way in here, down from the army base up north.

Could he be a repeat customer? She considered him more carefully. No, she sure didn't think he'd been in before. His face was more rugged than handsome, masculine and distinctive with piercing hazel eyes, a sharp blade of a nose and square granite jaw.

Kelly, you're gawking at the guy. Again, a little embarrassing, so she went in search through her backpack instead. Her aspirin bottle was in there somewhere—

"Hey, I know you. You're Kelly, right? Kelly Logan?" The handsome warrior grinned at her, slow and wide, showing straight, even white teeth. Twin dimples cut into lean, sun-browned cheeks. "South Valley High. You don't remember me, do you?"

Then she recognized the little upward crick in the corner of his mouth, making the left side of his smile higher than the right. Like a video on rewind, time reeled backward and she saw the remembered image of a younger, rangy teenage boy.

"Mitch? From sophomore math class. No, it can't be—" Like a cold spray from the leading edge of an avalanche, she felt the slap and the cold. The past rolled over her, and she deliberately shut out the painful blast and held on to the memories of the man standing before her. The shy honors student who'd let her, the new girl, check her homework answers against his for the entire spring quarter.

"Yep, it's me." A very mature Mitch Dalton strode toward her with a leader's confidence. "How are you?"

"Good." A sweet pang kicked to life in her chest. She remembered the girl she used to be. A girl who had stubbornly clung to the misguided hope that her life would be filled with love—one day. Who had still believed in dreaming. "You have changed in a major way."

"Only on the outside. I'm still a shy nerd down deep."

"You don't look it." She glanced at the pile of textbooks on the counter. She, on the other hand, was still a shy bookish girl—and looked it.

"You haven't changed much." Mitch halted at the edge of the counter, all six feet plus of solid muscle, towering over her. "I would have known you anywhere."

"Why? Because—wait, don't answer that." She saw the girl she'd been, so lost, so alone, in and out of foster care and relatives' homes. She belonged nowhere, and that had been a brand she'd felt as clearly as if it had been in neon, flashing on her forehead. She still did.

Forget the past. Life was easier to manage when she looked forward and not back.

Mitch jammed his big hands on his hips, and the pose merely emphasized his size and strength. "It's been a long time since we sat in Mr. Metzer's advanced algebra class."

"Math. You had to go and remind me of that particular torture. I was lost until you took pity on me and gave me a little help. I wouldn't have passed Algebra Two without you."

"Math's not so bad. I'm planning on getting a math degree after I get out next summer."

"Out of the army?"

"Please. I'm a marine."

"I should have known. The distinctive camouflage outfit gives it away. Not."

His left eyebrow quirked as he glanced down at his uniform and then at his name on his pocket—M. Dalton. "Did you really remember me, or did you just read the tag?"

"You were too far away when you walked in. So, this is what you've been doing since high school?"

"Yep. Being a soldier keeps me busy and out of trouble."

Kelly wasn't fooled. His hazel eyes sparkled with hints of green and gold, and humor drew fine character lines around his mouth. He didn't look as if he caused trouble. No, he looked as if he stopped trouble when it happened. "Are you stationed up north?"

"It's only temporary. I'm here for more training. Then it's back to California, and the desert after that. They keep me pretty busy."

"The desert, as in the Middle East? Like, in combat?"

"That's what soldiers do." His smile faded. He watched her with a serious, unblinking gaze, as if he wanted to change subjects. "How's Joe doing?"

"J-Joe." She froze in shock. Didn't Mitch know what had happened? Her chest clogged tight, as if she were buried under a mountain of snow. She wanted to be anywhere, anywhere but here. Talking about anything, anyone.

It felt as if an eternity had passed, but it had to be only the space between one breath and the next.

Silent, Mitch loomed over her, the surface of the wooden counter standing between them wide as the Grand Canyon. The late-afternoon sun sheened on the polished counter, or maybe it was the pain in her eyes that made it seem so bright. Looking through that glare and up into Mitch's face was tough. It was tougher still to try to talk about her broken dreams. They were too personal.

She'd stopped trusting anyone with those vulnerable places within her when she'd buried Joe.

And that's the way she still wanted it.

She slipped her left hand into her jeans pocket so

he wouldn't see that there was no ring. She could not bring herself to answer him as the seconds stretched out longer and longer and she looked down at the counter, too numb to think of anything to say, even to change the subject.

The truth of the past remained, unyielding and something she could not go back and change. There were a lot of things in her life she would have wanted to be different. A man as forthright and strong as Mitch Dalton wouldn't understand that. Not at all.

The phone jingled, like a sign from above to move on and let go. She had a reason to step away from the tough marine watching her, as if he could see right into her.

"Excuse me," she said to him and turned away to snatch the phone from the cradle. "Corner Christian Books. How can I help you? Oh, hello, Mrs. Brisbane."

Mitch retreated from the counter, captivated by Kelly's warm, sweet voice. It was still the same.

She was not—quiet, yes, sweet, yes, but wounded. So, what had happened?

Years ago, the first time he'd come home on a much-deserved quick break from his Force Recon training, he'd gotten up the courage to ask his mom first about any hometown news. And then about Kelly in particular.

She's marrying that McKaslin boy she's been dating, Mom had said.

Married. That word had struck him like a bullet against a flak jacket and he'd hidden his disappointment. That had been the last time he'd asked about Kelly Logan.

She wasn't married now, whatever had happened.

As he sank into the rows of books, he cast another glance in Kelly's direction. Her gentle tone continued. Clearly she knew and liked the customer who'd called. But this didn't interest him so much as what he could read by simply looking at her. The way she held herself so tightly and defensively, as if she were protecting the deepest places in her heart. The way her smile didn't reach her pretty blue eyes. Sadness clung to the corners of her soft mouth and made her wide almond-shaped eyes look too big in her fragile heart-shaped face.

How much of that sadness had he made worse by putting his foot in his mouth? Troubled, he turned his back, determined to leave thoughts of the woman behind, but they followed him through the long shelves of Bibles and into the Christian fiction rows. He still reeled from the raw pain he'd recognized in Kelly's eyes.

He'd been so wrapped up in his life, in his demanding job and nearly constant deployments, that he'd almost forgotten that heartbreak and tragedy happened off the battlefield, too.

Pain. He hated that she'd been hurt. He hated that he'd been the one to bring up the past. He should have looked at her hand first, the ringless left hand she'd been trying to hide from him, before he'd said anything. Something had happened to her, something painful, and he was sorry about that.

Wasn't pain the result of relationships? He saw it all the time. Marriages failed all around him, it happened to his friends, his team members, marines he barely knew and to his commanding officers.

Between the betrayal when a spouse broke wedding

vows or changed into a different person, and the grief when love ended, he didn't know how anyone could give their hearts at all, ever, knowing the risks. Knowing the pain.

That was why he kept clear of relationships. Not only did he not have much free time to get to know a woman, but he wondered how anyone knew when it was the real thing—the kind of love that lasted, the kind his parents had—or the kind of relationship that ended with devastation.

Either way, it was a lot more risk than he'd felt comfortable with.

So, why was he searching for a view of Kelly? From where he stood, the solid wooden bookshelves blocked the front counter, so he stepped a little to his left until he could see her reflected in the glass like a mirror. Perfect.

He wanted to say it was guilt, of bringing up something painful that had happened with Joe, that made him notice the way the soft fluff of her golden bangs covered her forehead and framed her big, wide eyes. And how the curve of her cheek and jaw looked as smooth as rose petals. Her hair curled past her jawline and fell against the graceful line of her neck to curl against the lace of her blouse's collar.

But that wasn't the truth. Guilt wasn't why he was noticing her. Concern wasn't the only reason he couldn't seem to tear his gaze away. He was interested. He was stationed here for a short stint, that was all, and he wasn't looking for anything serious—that was a scary thought.

No, he wasn't ready for that. He didn't have time for

that. He wasn't a teenaged kid anymore with an innocent crush, and by the look of things, Kelly'd had her heart broken. She probably wasn't looking, either.

He'd come here to find a gift—nothing more—and he'd be smart to get to it. That was the sensible thing to do. He wandered back to the aisle of Bibles, determined to keep his attention focused squarely on his difficult mission: finding a suitable birthday gift.

The rustle of her movements jerked his attention back to her. He was at the end of the row, giving him a perfect view of Kelly. She'd hung up the phone and was circling around the edge of the long front counter. She was keeping her eyes low and intentionally not looking his way, but he kept observing her as he went on with his browsing.

He couldn't say why he watched her as she padded to the far edge of the store. Or why he noticed how elegant she looked in a simple pink cotton blouse and slim khaki pants. It was a mystery. He wanted to attribute it to his training—the marines had trained him well and paid him to observe, but that wasn't it at all. Not truthfully.

He couldn't say why, but he listened to the whisper of her movements and kept listening...even after she'd disappeared from his sight.

Chapter Two

Was it her imagination, or was he watching her?

Kelly slipped the inspirational romance from its spot on the shelf. Her gaze shot between the open book bay to watch the hunky soldier's broad back, which was all she could see of him. Mitch stood with his feet braced apart, browsing through the devotionals display midway across the store.

No, he's not even looking my way, she thought, shaking her head and hurrying back to the cash desk. Besides, he seemed totally absorbed in his browsing as he set down one book and reached for another. He was the only customer in the store, and if he wasn't noticing her, then no one was.

Okay, so she was nuts, but she still felt...*watched.* She remembered the impact of his gaze, and how tangible it had felt. She kept a careful eye on him as she returned to the front.

Although he didn't lift his head or turn in her direction, she felt monitored the entire time it took for her to write Edith Brisbane's name on a slip of paper, rubber-band it to the spine of the book and slip it onto the hold shelf.

I know what the problem is, she realized in the middle of shaking an aspirin tablet onto her palm. *She* was the one noticing *him.*

Who could blame her? He cut a fine figure in his rugged military uniform, and back in high school she'd always had a secret crush on him. He'd always been a truly nice boy. It looked as if time had only improved him.

As she chased the aspirin down with a few swallows from a small bottle of orange soda, her gaze automatically zoomed across the floor to him. Head bent, he had moved on to amble through the gift section of the store, his attention planted firmly on the rows of porcelain jewelry boxes in front of him. There were two inspirational suspense books tucked in one big hand.

When she looked at him, she could hear his gravelly voice asking again, How's Joe doing?

It wasn't his fault, Mitch obviously didn't know what had happened. But that didn't make the raw places within her heart hurt any less.

She was no longer a girl who could dream.

She climbed back onto her stool and debated tackling more of her homework, but she wasn't in the mood to face her math book. She knew that if she sat here trying to solve for x, her attention would just keep drifting over to the impressive warrior. To the past.

What good could come from that?

"Hey, Kelly." Her boss's solemn baritone cut through

her thoughts, spinning her around to face him. Spence McKaslin pushed open the door on the other side of the hold shelf. He emerged from the fluorescent glare of his office, looking gruff, the way he always did when he worked on the accounts. "I'll be in the back going through the new order. Katherine's still out, so if it gets busy, buzz me."

"Sure, but it's been really quiet. Do you want me to start restocking or something?"

"No, we're all caught up. Just watch the front until your dinner break. Study while you can. It could get busy later."

"It never gets busy on a Friday night."

"Don't argue with me, I'm the boss." He gave her an extra-hard glare on his way to the drawers beneath the till, but he didn't fool her.

Spence was strong and stoic and tough, but also one of the kindest men she'd ever met. Her opinion of him had been pretty high ever since he'd hired her, which had saved her from losing her apartment when she'd been laid off from her previous job. Spence would have been her cousin, had things worked out differently with Joe.

A lot of things would have been different if she'd been able to marry Joe.

Feeling as if she'd been sucker-punched, she tried hard not to let the pain show. She didn't know how something so powerful would ever go away, but she did her best to tuck her grief down deep inside. Her gaze strayed to where Mitch still browsed, looking like everything good and noble and strong in the world.

But she also saw memories. And she wanted nothing to do with the past.

Spence grabbed the key ring from its place under the counter and studied her in the assessing way of a good big brother. "Did you manage to fit in lunch today?"

"Well, I ate a granola bar while I was stuck in traffic in the big parking lot on campus."

"I knew it. Take your dinner break at five, and I'll go when you get back," he ordered over his shoulder, already marching away.

Mitch watched the older man pass by the gift section and disappear through a door in the back. It was less than an hour before her dinner break. Interesting. He couldn't say why, but he felt out of his element. And it wasn't because he was in a store full of flowery knickknacks and breakables.

A plan hatched in the back of his mind, and it had nothing to do with his shopping mission.

Kelly remained in his peripheral vision. She made a lovely picture, sitting straight-backed with her head bowed over a book. The math text was still in the stack, so she must be working on another subject. Absorbed in her reading, she tucked a strand of rich honey-blond hair behind her ear, revealing a small pearl earring and her bare left hand.

While he was at home creeping through enemy territory in the rugged mountains of Afghanistan or the deserts of the Middle East, his extensive training did not include what he was about to do.

He kept her in his line of sight as he approached the register. The light from the window seemed to find her and grace her with a golden glow. She kept her head bowed over her book as he approached, but her shoulders stiffened with tension. Telling. But he continued his approach, taking in other details. The soda bottle, her nearly worn-out leather watchband, the pink barrette in her hair that matched the tiny flowers on her blouse. The two sociology textbooks stacked neatly at her left elbow.

He wondered about her life. Did she like being a college student? Did she live on campus in a dorm room or in a nearby apartment? Alone, or with a roommate?

When she looked up from her reading, her smile was cordial but he didn't mistake the sadness, like a shadow, in her dark-blue eyes. He felt a tug of sympathy from his heart. "You look pretty busy," he noted, easing the books onto the counter by her register.

"It's the life of a college student. I have a test on Monday." As she leaned to scan the books, her hair bounced across the side of her face, leaving only a small sliver of her profile visible. "Did you find what you were looking for?"

"I found more." He wasn't talking about the books.

"I do that all the time." Her gaze didn't meet his and her polite smile was too brief. She turned her attention to the cash register. All business.

Okay, he got the signal, but he didn't let it deter him. "How long 'til you get your degree?"

"After this summer, I have two semesters left." She paused to study the cash register and searched for a key.

"It's gotta be slow going, working your way through."

"It's taking twice as long, but at least I don't have a major loan to pay back when I'm done."

"That's one perk of enlisting. My college will be paid for."

At least he wasn't mentioning the past or Joe again, Kelly thought thankfully as she totaled the sale. Her chest was still clogged tight, like the fallout of an avalanche still pressing her down. "Twenty-one ninety-three, please."

Mitch held out his credit card.

When her fingertips caught the other end, she felt a flash, like a shock of static electricity in the air. The sunlight changed to a bright piercing white. The floor rocked beneath her feet. It lasted only for a second. Then the earth steadied, the sunlight turned golden and there was Mitch, unmoved, looking calm and as cool as steel.

That was *so* not a sign from heaven. Just the pieces of what remained of her dreams, longing, in the way faint embers from a fire's flame could glow briefly to life when exposed to air. Her fingers trembled as she swiped his card and plunked it back onto the polished counter between them.

If there was a way to breathe life back into her dreams, she would ask the Lord to show her how. But she didn't bother. Some things really were impossible. "I still can't believe you're a soldier. What happened to your pocket protector?"

"No place for it on this uniform. I love what I do."

"What exactly do you do?"

"Well, I started out at oh-six-hundred with a ten

click—kilometer—run in full gear and spent the day mountain climbing to five thousand feet."

"You get paid to climb mountains?"

"That's not all. I get to do things like scuba dive, parachute, drive around in Humvees and play with explosives." He said it all as if it was no big deal, just in a humble day's work. "Keeps me out of trouble."

"Seems like that would get you *into* trouble."

"Nothing I can't handle."

Wow, Kelly thought, as she bagged the books. He's grown up into quite a man. "See, my day is a piece of cake by comparison."

"Except for the math."

"Oh, you *had* to mention that again. I was trying to forget for a while." She hadn't laughed out loud in a long time. "Where you get paid to do things that you think are fun, I pay out good tuition money to be tortured by algebra."

"I'll be in your boat in eighteen months."

"That's right. That math degree you're going to get." The machine spat out the charge receipt and she held the two-part paper steady while it printed. How her heart ached as those embers of old dreams struggled for life. She tore off the printed receipt and slid it across the counter. "I need your autograph, and then you're free to go, soldier."

"*Free's* a relative term." He grabbed a pen from the cup by the register. "My time's pretty regimented."

"I bet it is. Are you headed back to your base?"

"In a few hours. I'm free until then." He scrawled his signature at the bottom of the slip.

Too bad she'd given up on dreams. She didn't know if she felt relief or regret.

"I hope you enjoy your books." She slipped his receipt into the bag and presented it to him. "I'm glad to see you're doing so well. I wish you luck, Mitch."

"You're letting me go, just like that?"

"Well, what else am I supposed to do? Generally we let customers leave our store. We seldom hold them hostage."

"I'm not talking about other customers. I'm talking about me. We could renew our friendship."

"We were never really friends, you know."

What did that leave him with? Renewing his secret crush on her? He took his bag, but the last thing he wanted to do was leave. She was still the nicest girl he'd ever laid eyes on. He could use a little nice in his world. It wasn't something he saw much of.

"We could be friends now," he suggested with his best grin.

"But you said you were headed back to California." Sweetly, she studied him through her long lashes.

A mass of emotions struck him like shrapnel to his chest. Emotions weren't his realm of expertise, but he felt strong with a fierce steely need he'd never felt before—to protect her, to make her smile, to make her every sadness go away.

Not really in his comfort zone, but a crush was a crush. What was a guy to do?

He tried again. "I'm not leaving for a while. We could still be friends."

"I have enough friends." Her eyebrow crooked up in a challenge.

So, she was giving him a hard time on purpose. "You get a dinner break, right?"

"Now and then they loosen the chains and let me out for a bit." Kelly folded her arms in front of her, considering him.

"You get a dinner break, and I'm hungry for dinner. It's a coincidence."

Kelly couldn't believe how he was just watching her with those intense, commanding hazel eyes of his, so wise and perceptive. She felt the impact as if he could see directly into her. "You're asking me out, aren't you?"

"No, not out. No. Of course not." He held up his free hand, as if he were innocent. Completely guilt-free.

"That's good, because I don't date anymore. I'm sorry."

"That's okay, because I'm not looking for a date. I was asking you to help me out."

"As if a big strong soldier like you needs any help at all?"

"Sure. I need a favor. I'm a lonely marine."

"A lonely marine?" Oh, she was *so* not fooled.

"Sure. It's only dinner." Amusement quirked the left side of his mouth. "C'mon, you gotta eat."

"True, but you probably have better things to do on a Friday evening."

"I can't think of one."

It's gotta be the uniform, she told herself as she assessed him carefully. "They must not let you out much if you think sharing my dinner break is your best option."

"What can I say? I could use a friend. How about it?"

Kelly's heart twisted hard. There was no mistaking the sincerity in his steady gaze. He meant those words. How could she say no? She knew a thing or two about wanting a friend. "You've got a deal."

"Excellent. How do you like your hamburger?"

"With cheese and mayo, no onions and tomatoes."

"I'll be back in an hour. Thanks, Kelly. I'm glad I ran into you."

"I'm glad, too."

He was military-strong *and* nice. What a combo. She couldn't help liking him. Who wouldn't?

She watched him stride away, cutting through the long rays of sunlight and disappearing into the glare. She couldn't help the little sigh that escaped her. The bell jingled and the door swished shut and he was gone.

The dying embers in her heart ached. Be careful, she warned herself, holding on tight to her common sense. A man like Mitch could make her want to believe. And it was the wanting that got her into trouble every time—the longing to belong, to be loved, to know that soft comfort of a loving marriage and family.

"Hey, who was that?" Back from her run to the bank, Katherine, Spence's sister, swished behind the counter. "He looked like a very nice, very solid, very fine young man."

"Oh, that was just a customer."

"No, he was trying to ask you out. I happened to overhear. Accidentally, of course." Katherine leaned against her closed office door, looking as if she'd just received the best news.

That was Katherine. Always wishing for happy endings for other people. "It's not how it looks. We're just friends."

"Right, well, that's the best way to start out. You never know what will develop from there. I'm saying prayers for you. No one deserves a happy ending more than you."

"There are no such things as happy endings." Kelly knew that for an absolute fact. "This isn't a fairy tale. He's only in town for a little while."

"You just never know what the Lord has in store for you. It wasn't fair what happened with Joe."

She had to go and mention it. Kelly swallowed hard, wrestling down painful memories—the weight of them heavy on her heart, along with too many regrets. Too many failures. "Life is like that. It's not fair."

"No, but in the end, good things happen to good people. I believe that." Katherine breezed into her office, sure of her view of the world.

Kelly didn't have the heart to believe. She could not let herself dream. Not even the tiniest of wishes. She was no longer a girl who believed in fairy tales, but a grown woman who kept her feet on the ground.

She had no faith left for dreaming.

Chapter Three

"I think it's gonna be a quiet Friday night." Spence emerged from one of the fiction aisles with a book in hand. "How's the studying coming?"

"I'm less confused, I think. I haven't taken math since high school and I've forgotten just about everything but the basics."

"That's why I use a calculator." Spence nodded toward the front windows. "The soldier who was in here earlier? He's back."

"He is?" It took all her effort to sound unaffected. She turned slowly toward the front, as if she hadn't been of two minds about their upcoming dinner. She squinted through the harsh sunshine that haloed the wide-shouldered man.

She recognized the silhouette striding away from a dusty Jeep, carrying a big take-out bag and a cardboard drink carrier in one hand. The light gave him a golden glow, and he was all might and strength and integrity.

She remembered what he'd said about needing a friend. It had to be a lonely life he'd chosen.

Spence cleared his throat. "I'm glad you're dating again."

Heat crept up her face. She busily set the alarm on her watch, so she wouldn't go over her allotted break time. "It isn't like that, Spence. Really."

"Okay." Like Katherine, he didn't sound as if he believed her. "Go ahead. Have a nice time."

It was Mitch. How could she not have a nice visit? As he strode her way, she beat him to the door. His welcoming smile was lopsided and friendly—definitely a smile that could make a girl dream. "I'm free for half an hour."

"I'm glad they loosened the chains." His shadow fell across her, covering her completely. "Wanna eat across the street? I saw a couple of tables and benches. Okay?"

"Sure. I eat over there all the time."

Walking at his side, she realized that he was bigger and taller than she had thought. He was a big powerful bear of a guy, his field boots thudding against the pavement. She felt safe with him. Comfortable. "Isn't Montana a little landlocked for a marine?"

"It would be, if I worked on a ship. That would be navy."

"But you're training at the army base?"

"I'm doing some advanced mountaineering. They train their Rangers there, and they're letting my platoon climb around on their rocks."

"Advanced mountaineering. That sounds serious."

"We're doing tactical stuff while we're climbing," he explained with a shrug.

"You must be pretty good."

"I haven't fallen yet."

She stopped at his side, at the curb, waiting for the few cars and trucks to pass. "What exactly do you do in the marines?"

"I'm like a scout. It's clear," he said, referring to the traffic and, as he stepped off the curb, laid his free hand on her shoulder. Not exactly guiding her, as much as guarding.

Kelly shivered down to her soul. Nice. Very nice. What girl wouldn't appreciate a soldier's protective presence? They stepped up on the curb together on the other side of the road, and his hand fell away. The world felt a little lonelier.

"How about that table?" She nodded toward the closest picnic table in the park, which was well shaded beneath a pair of broad-leafed maples.

"That'll work," he agreed amicably.

It was hard to keep pace with him as they made their way across the lush, clipped grass. He didn't walk so much as he power walked, even though he was obviously shortening his long-legged pace for her. She had to hurry to keep up with him as he crossed the grass. "How long are you going to be in Montana?"

"I've been here three weeks. I've got five more to go." He set the drinks and food on the table, then pulled out the bench for her. "That means I'll be outta here mid-September."

"And then back to California?"

"Like I said, they keep me busy." Mitch could only nod. He waited while she settled onto the bench, and the breeze brought a faint scent of her vanilla shampoo. The warmth in his chest changed to something sweeter.

She watched him with gentle blue eyes. "I didn't know marines climbed mountains."

"We climb whatever we're ordered to climb." He freed a large cup from the carrier. "I brought orange soda or root beer. The lady picks first."

"I love orange soda. Good guess."

He didn't mention that he'd noticed the pop bottle she'd had on the store counter beside her schoolbooks. He set the cup beside her. Had she figured out that this was a date yet?

"Cheeseburger, as ordered." He handed out the chow. "Do you want to say grace or will you let me?"

"Go for it." She folded her hands, so sincere.

He brimmed with a strange tenderness as he bowed his head together with hers. "Dear Father, thank you for watching over us today. Please bless this food and our renewed friendship. Amen."

"Amen." A renewed friendship, huh? Kelly unclasped her hands and unwrapped her burger. At least he wasn't trying to make this a date. "Why the marines?"

"That's easy." He dug a few ketchup containers out of the bottom of the bag and as the wind caught the empty sack, he anchored it. "My life has a purpose. I make a difference."

"That matters to you." She took a long look at him. "Making a difference matters to me, too."

"When I was a kid, watching the news coverage of

Desert Storm, I was blown away by this segment they did on the marines. They were these powerful men with weapons, and they were taking care of refugees from the fighting. One of the refugees said how amazed he was by these big men. They looked fearsome, but they were also kind."

That pretty much summed it up for her. Kelly blinked and tried to act as if his words hadn't sunk into her heart. He'd grown up and grown well. She only had to look into his clear, expressive eyes to know that he was a very fine man.

Mitch took a big bite of his burger and leaned closer to dig a handful of fries out of the container. "Then it hit me, just how great that was in this world. To be a warrior fierce enough to protect and defend, to stand for what is right. That's honor, in my opinion. And that's how I serve. I do my very best every day."

What on earth did she say to that? She seemed frozen in place. She wasn't breathing. It seemed as if her heart had stopped beating. His gaze met hers, and the honest force of it left her even more paralyzed. The magnitude of his gaze bored into hers like a touch, and she felt the stir of it in her soul, a place where she let no one in. How had he gotten past her defenses?

He grabbed more fries. "How about you?"

"M-me?"

"Sure. Why social work?"

"I didn't tell you that."

"I noticed your textbooks. Are you getting your degree in sociology and a masters in social work?"

"That's the plan. I want to help children. There's a lot of need out there."

"There is." His voice deepened with understanding. There was something about a powerful man who radiated more than just might, but heart, too. "I remember back in high school that you were on your own a lot."

Keep the pain out of your words, she reminded herself. She wasn't willing to confess about the loneliness and the fears of a child growing up the way she did. "I know I can help kids who are in a similar situation. I want to make a difference."

"I'm sure you can." He studied her, his hazel eyes intensified. It was as if he could see the places within her that no one could. "You were in foster care. Is that right?"

"On and off, depending on whether or not my mom was in jail for drugs or if my aunt's bipolar disorder was under control." She forced her gaze from his, breaking contact, but it was too late. She already felt so revealed. "I was lucky. I made it through all right. A lot of kids aren't so fortunate."

"You've done very well for yourself."

"Not by myself."

"By the grace of God?" Mitch waited as Kelly stared toward the far end of the park. There was nothing there, no people to watch, no traffic, nothing but a row of shrubs shivering slightly in the balmy evening breezes. He knew it wasn't the foliage she saw, but the past.

He didn't take for granted one second of his life, especially his childhood with two loving parents in a middle-class suburb. It was a start in life for which he was thankful. "About six years ago, I was training at Coronado when I got the word my dad had had a heart attack. I made it home in time to see him before he went into surgery. I think the good Lord was reminding my family just how lucky we are. We take nothing for granted, not anymore."

"Wise move."

He washed his emotions down with the ice-cold soda. "I've seen enough of the world to know that I wouldn't be who I am without them. It's a blessing to have parents like mine. Remember that favor I mentioned back in the store?"

She dragged a pair of fries through the ketchup container. "I thought this *dinner* was the favor."

"Nope, this is my apology. For sticking my foot in my mouth and bringing up a subject that hurt you."

"You couldn't have known. It's all right." She froze for a moment, and sadness flashed in her eyes again. "What's this favor?"

"I've been trying to find a gift for my mom. No luck. I'm clueless."

"You don't look clueless. And you can't be serious. You look around, you find things and you buy them. It's called shopping. That's how you find a gift. Our store is full of wonderful gifts. Why didn't you say something when you were in before?"

"I wanted to get a look at the jewelry store down the street first."

"Jewelry is always good. We have some lovely gold crosses."

"That's what I got her last Christmas. She has everything else, a mother's ring, more lockets than she can count. A charm bracelet so full of charms there's no room for more. I need help."

"You certainly need something." He was way too charming for her own good, Kelly decided. And she had a hard time saying no to a worthy cause. "When do you need this gift?"

"Her birthday dinner is Sunday night."

"I should have known. A last-minute gift."

"Last minute? What do you mean?" He feigned mock insult. "This is Friday. I have two more days."

Why wasn't she surprised? Kelly took the last bite of her burger. "Okay, what are your parameters?"

"Something unique. Personal. It has to be fairly inexpensive. I'm thinking around a hundred dollars."

"That's not so inexpensive. Have you tried the mall?"

"You're kidding, right? I avoid those at all costs."

"Why is that?"

"No amount of military training can prepare a guy for the conditions that await him in a mall. I'm mall-phobic."

She seriously doubted that. She couldn't imagine Mitch being afraid of anything. "Mall-phobia. I *think* I read about that in my abnormal psychology class."

"Funny. So, you'll help me?"

"It's the least I can do for a friend." *Friend* being the operative word. The beep of her alarm made her jump. Had that much time gone by already? "I've got to go."

"Duty calls."

"Exactly. Did you want to come with me? We can go through the sales books together."

"No time." Disappointment settled like lead inside him. "I've got to be back by twenty hundred hours, and I've got over a two-hour drive ahead of me."

Was it his imagination, or did she look disappointed? Good. Now was the time to set up date number two. "I'm coming back to town on Sunday. How about the two of us get together and put in some serious shopping time?"

"Sunday, then." She folded her empty burger wrapper neatly.

He held the food sack open for her, waiting to toss in his wrapper, crumpled into a ball, after hers. "Where do you want me to pick you up?"

She grabbed one last fry from the tub before she twisted off the bench, graceful and lovely. She backed away, studying him through her long lashes with those big stormy-blue eyes. "The Gray Stone Church on the corner of Glenrose and Cherry Lane. Meet me there. Ten o'clock sharp."

"Meet you there? No, I should pick you up."

"It's not a date, remember?"

Have it your way, pretty lady. He watched her jog away, her hair brushing the back of her shoulders and swinging in time with her gait.

Mitch could only stare, unable to move, waiting as she crossed the street. She was like a vision, awash with light. He remained vigilant until she reached the storefront and disappeared inside.

You're heading to Afghanistan in six weeks, he thought, hardly noticing the crinkling sound the food sacks made when he bunched them and tossed them into the garbage can. What he did was dangerous. He'd learned the value of starting each day without regrets.

If he didn't make the most of this second chance to get to know Kelly, wherever that path might lead, he'd regret it. Six months from now, he'd be shivering on some rock in the border mountains of Afghanistan or belly down on a dune in the Middle East, and he didn't want to be wondering *what if.*

It wasn't only exhaustion weighing her down as she climbed the flight of steps to her apartment. Not the late hour or the dark shadows that fell from the whispering poplars. She felt as if the past clung to her with a tenacious grip tonight, like the stars to the black velvet sky.

Kelly sorted through her key ring as she climbed the outside stairs that brought her to her third-story landing.

In the end, good things happen to good people. I believe that. Katherine's words. They were part of what troubled her tonight and made the shadows so dark, the quiet so deep. Those words haunted her last steps and followed her into the soft pool of illumination from the light over her door. She fitted her key into the deadbolt and turned it with a click. The metallic sound seemed to echo in the chambers of her heart.

Everyone she'd ever depended on had let her down, so it was hard to believe in good things. God never promised that life would be easy or fair. A heart can be broken too much. And she'd learned that every time a heart is broken, it is never the same again.

She withdrew the key and inserted it into the doorknob, turning the knob and shouldering open the door.

Her heavy backpack clunked against the door as she stepped through the fall of porch light and into the dark quiet of the foyer.

Mitch had stirred up some of this uneasiness, too. What a great guy. At least he was only interested in a friendship. How could it be anything else, with him leaving for California and beyond?

She could relax and not worry about him leaving—it was a given. She knew what to expect.

The luminous numbers of her stove's clock cast a green glow bright enough to see by as she pushed the door shut behind her, turned the deadbolt and slipped her keys onto the small table between the door and the hall closet. Her pack made a thump when she set it on the floor.

Hot, stifling air greeted her thanks to keeping off the air conditioning. She headed straight for the living room and unlocked the wide window. Cooler air felt heavenly against her overheated skin. She stood for a moment letting the breeze fan over her. Outside the poplars cast dancing shadows from the streetlights and rustled cheerfully. She pressed her hot forehead to the cooler glass, breathed in the fresh night air and let her feelings and thoughts settle.

Mitch. Just thinking of him brought a smile to her face. He was back at his base by now. This was going to be different—interesting, but different—to have him for a friend.

She was actually looking forward to Sunday.

Chapter Four

Mitch scanned the light-veiled sanctuary, crowded with worshippers and loud with their conversations, searching for Kelly. To find her, he only had to follow the sunshine as it slanted through the glittering panels of stained glass.

Kelly. When he saw her, brushed with golden light and goodness, his heartbeat skipped. The sanctuary, full of light and sound and families getting settled, faded away and only the silence remained. She was sitting in a pew near the middle, her head bowed as if reading.

She hadn't noticed him yet, so he took a moment just to drink in the sight of her. Her honey-gold hair was unbound and framed her heart-shaped face. The lavender summer dress she wore shaped her delicate shoulders and fell in a complimentary sweep to her knees. A book bag slumped on the bench beside her. Matching purple flats hugged her slim feet.

He liked the way she looked, so pure and bright. She made a lovely picture, sitting so straight, with her

Bible open on her lap. It wasn't too much of a hardship to look at her. He eased into the row and onto the pew beside her.

She jumped, and her Bible tumbled onto the polished wood bench between them. "Mitch! You snuck up on me!"

"Hey, I'm no sneak."

"Then what do you call that? You didn't make a sound. That's sneaking in my book." Her eyes twinkled like aquamarines.

Enchanted—he was simply enchanted. *And* she looked glad to see him. What was a helpless guy to do? He shrugged. "Sorry. It's habit, I guess. Didn't mean to scare you."

"You are a scary man, Mitch Dalton." Her smile said the opposite as he rescued her fallen Bible from the bench between them. "Do you have a chance to attend a service when you're overseas?"

"Usually a chaplain holds service every Sunday. I attend whenever I'm in camp." He studied the Bible in his hands. It looked like his, treasured and well-read. He handed it over. "This is some church. It beats a tent hands down."

"A tent, huh?" Her fingertips brushed against his, featherlight and brief.

Wow. Her touch stilled his senses. As if from somewhere far away organ music began, and late worshippers hurried to find seats as the minister stepped up to his podium. The congregation rose.

Kelly stood, and somehow he was on his feet beside her. She was so small and feminine at his side. All he knew was that he liked being with her. Not a comfortable thing for the lone wolf he was. But not bad, either.

She went up on tiptoe to tell him something, and he had to lean so she could manage to whisper in his ear. "I'm wearing my shopping shoes. I hope you can keep up with me."

That was funny. Little did she know what he was capable of doing in a single day. "Bring it on, little lady. I can do anything you can do."

"Be careful. I just might drag you to a mall."

"Hey, we had a no-mall agreement."

"I made no promises, soldier."

Kelly felt as light as air. Happy. She'd been working and studying so hard lately, she was glad she'd agreed to spend this time with Mitch. Besides, it was never a bad thing to have a handsome man—er, *friend*—sit beside you at church.

Mitch. She couldn't help noticing he had a very nice singing voice and yet he didn't attract attention to himself. His voice was quiet and his manner solemn. And he stood powerful and tall. Very masculine.

Not that she was wishing.

As she bowed her head for prayer, she caught sight of the Bible passage on the program. The typed words were the last thing she saw as she closed her eyes and the words from Isaiah emblazoned themselves on her eyelids. "Whether you turn to the right or to the left, your ears will hear a voice behind you saying, 'This is the way, walk in it.'"

It had also been the exact passage from her morning devotional. Coincidence? Probably not.

I'm trying, Lord, to follow where You lead.

But she was so adrift. Even with Mitch at her side. Even in the peace of God's sanctuary with heaven's light falling all around her.

"Whether you turn to the right or to the left, your ears will hear a voice behind you saying, 'This is the way, walk in it.'"

With the minister's message in his heart, Mitch stayed at Kelly's side as they inched patiently down the main aisle. Maybe this was a sign he was on the right path. A new one for him, considering his wariness of long-term relationships. And a strange one, because God's plan for him was thousands of miles away, across an ocean.

Kelly introduced him to the minister, who warmly thanked him for coming. As they followed the departing worshippers down the front steps and out into the bright sunshine, he stayed at Kelly's side, protecting her from any jostling from the crowd.

"Well, soldier, are you ready for your mission? Or do I leave you to survive shopping as best you can?" Her smile was as sweet as spun sugar.

He liked it. "I've already confessed that I'm retail-challenged."

"A big tough guy like you? C'mon, soldier up." She winked, and couldn't help laughing. "I expect a marine to be tougher than that."

"I'll survive with a pretty girl like you watching my six."

"Your six? Oh, I get it. Watching your back. You're

going to need it where I'm taking you. Peril and danger abound."

"I live for danger."

"That makes two of us." Kelly liked the look of worry crinkling his forehead. She guessed he was only halfway kidding her about having mall-phobia. "At ease, sir. I spent some time thinking of a few good ideas for your mom. And we don't have to set foot inside any mall."

"I'm gonna owe you big-time for this."

"No way. What's a little favor between friends?"

Mitch frowned. He had to set the groundwork for date number three. Something gave him a clue that she wouldn't make it easy for him.

He'd just have to wow her so much, she'd want to go out with him again. Maybe even call it a date next time. A man could hope. "You wanna grab a bite first?"

"I didn't think you soldiers took detours when you were on a mission."

"Right, but I'm gonna need fuel. No way can I shop on an empty stomach. Oh, wait. I get it. You don't date. And you're afraid that eating together twice would make it look like we're dating."

"It *could* look that way, but it's not. Right?"

Was that a shadow of fear he saw in her gentle blue eyes? Why would she be afraid? Then in a blink, it was gone.

He stepped off the curb, looking for traffic, but there were no cars headed their way. He fished his keys from his pocket. "Don't even worry. Friends go out to eat together sometimes."

"I just don't want you to get the wrong idea. I know you'll be leaving in a month or so—"

"Exactly, so don't sweat it. We'll do whatever you want."

"I've got the best shop to show you. I really think you'll find what you want there."

"You mean this could be a one-stop deal?"

"It might even be painless."

She was doing her best to thwart his plans for their date. He was going down in flames. Not good. This had to be about Joe. What had happened? What had he done to her? He hadn't known the guy except as a name back in high school.

Whatever had happened, it had sure made Kelly afraid to try dating again. As he unlocked the passenger door, a mild breeze whispered through the maples overhead and shifted the lemony sunshine over them. In the dappled mix of shadows and light he opened the door and took Kelly's hand to help her up.

She dodged him, as if too independent for such a gesture, but he sensed it was something more as she slipped past him. Her cotton dress gave a whispering rustle, and the vanilla fragrance from her shampoo scented the air between them.

Unaware of how she moved him, she climbed into the passenger seat and settled her book bag on the floor at her feet. She sat there in a swirl of lavender summer cotton and dappled sunlight and sweetness. Feelings came to life within his heart and weren't like anything he'd felt before. They were soft and warm, and as soothing as prayer. Tenderness lit him up from the inside out.

He felt every inch of his six-foot-two-inch frame as he closed her door and circled around to his side.

Her smile was calm, her blue eyes bright and friendly. "It's not far from here. If you can pull a U-turn and avoid the traffic jam up the street?"

"Inciting me to break the law, huh?" He winked as he started the engine and belted in. "I'm shocked. A sweet girl like you."

"Ah, the things you don't know about me."

"I'm beginning to get the picture. A hard-working college student who goes to church every Sunday. Yep, you're trouble." He checked the mirrors and the pedestrian traffic before turning sharply out from the curb and down the narrow tree-lined residential street.

Then he saw the sign, allowing U-turns in the wide, turnabout intersection.

"No more trouble than you are, I bet. Sunday service and then dinner at home with your parents."

"Not until six tonight. Until then, I'm a reckless man on the town." A gray tabby cat paraded off the sidewalk about ten yards up the residential street, and he slowed to a stop.

"Yeah, reckless. I see that."

He could feel her gaze like the softest brush against the line of his profile. He'd like to know what she thought about him. Come September he'd be on a bird out of here and he wouldn't be back this way again except for a rare, quick family holiday.

He wanted...he didn't know what he wanted. But he liked being with her.

Once the cat was safely across the street, he hit the gas. A four-way stop was ahead. "Which way?"

"Right. And take the first parking spot you come to."

"It's that easy? I can't believe it." He whipped the Jeep over to the curb and parked. "I just might make it out of this mission without a casualty."

"No casualties, remember? I'm watching your six."

"Then let's do it." He killed the engine and released his seat belt.

Kelly took a deep breath and tried to steady herself, to just breathe. What she couldn't explain was why he'd affected her like this. Why he'd slipped through her defenses as if they were nothing.

She didn't have a clue. He was already out of the Jeep and slamming the door, moving with an easy, latently powerful bearing around the front of the vehicle.

Why was she watching him? Because it was impossible not to. He looked like everything good in the world, honorable and strong. He made the broken places within her heart feel less cracked. He made her laugh and smile.

It was hard not to like him a little more for being a gentleman as he caught the edge of the door when she opened it with his big powerful hand. Golden flecks twinkled in his eyes as he grinned at her. "This might not be a date, but I'm getting the doors for you anyway."

"You're going to spoil me, and then where will I be?"

"You'll be treated the way you deserve." He held out his big hand, palm up and waiting.

She hesitated. He was simply being a gentleman, nothing more, but that's what scared her. There was danger in taking even the first tiny step in leaning on anyone. When you started leaning, you started hoping.

And in the hoping, dreaming.

The pieces of her broken heart ached like shattered bone. Friendship was one thing, but she could get out of the Jeep on her own, thank you very much.

As she tipped off the edge of the seat, his hand shot out, caught her forearm, the tricky guy. His grip was iron-strong and commanding. The warmth of his touch, and the strength of it, rocked through her.

Instead of feeling afraid, peace ebbed into her heart. Even into the broken places.

Her feet hit the concrete sidewalk, jarring her back into reality. Mitch let go, and shut the door with a thump. This gave her the opportunity to step away from him.

That rare, warm peace ebbed away like a tide rolling back out to sea. Although the sun blazed already hot on her shoulders, she shivered, as if with cold.

"I can see the campus from here, just down the street." Mitch pocketed his keys, his movements confident and relaxed as if he hadn't felt a thing. As if this hadn't affected him this way. "Do you live in the dorms?"

Somehow she managed to make her feet carry her forward as though nothing had happened, as though she were perfectly fine. Her voice came as if from far away. "No, the dorms are too expensive. I have a little apartment three blocks from here."

"Any roommates?"

"Just one."

"An apartment sounds good to me. Right now I have the luxury of living in the barracks."

"The luxury?"

"And so much privacy. Not. I'm happier in a hootch—"

"A hootch?"

"A tent—" he supplied, "in a camp somewhere overseas with my team. Give me a cot and I'm home. Better yet, I'd rather be sleeping out in the bush."

"Really, on the ground? You like that?"

"Sure. It's like camping, except for the grenades and C4 explosives. I grew up in these mountains."

"Really? The math whiz I remember from high school didn't look like the outdoors type."

"Looks are deceiving, and I was at an awkward age. Okay, a very awkward age. My dad is a forest ranger. We're gonna take one of these weekends I have free—if I get a whole one free—and hike up into the Bridger Mountains. Spend the night. Camp. Cook river trout over a fire."

"Sounds very rugged. I'm more of a stay-away-from-the-mountains kind of girl."

"You just haven't been properly exposed to the wilderness."

"Where there's no hot water, no plumbing and no electric blankets?"

"Those luxuries are highly overrated. Trust me."

"I'm a little afraid to, with an attitude like that."

When she smiled, sweet as candy, his emotions jumbled into a wedge in his throat. The palm of his left hand still glowed from where he'd taken hold of her arm to help her from the Jeep, and the brightness of her touch remained, calming and terrifying all at once.

Heaven was on his side, because Kelly chose that moment to pause in front of a store window. A striped yellow-and-white awning stretched overhead and he studied the way the hem ruffled in the breeze instead of figuring out what was happening to him.

At the back of his mind, he knew. He had a life, he had a calling, and he had eighteen months left on his contract. So how was this going to work?

"The lady who owns this shop is a good friend of the family—well, of Joe's family." Her voice broke on the sound of Joe's name. "She takes antique gems and resets them in the most beautiful jewelry you've ever seen. I don't know if you'd be interested in something like that for your mom, but Holly's work is so beautiful, it's like giving a little piece of love."

Okay, that was the word he was trying to avoid.

"Do you want to go in and look? Or I have other suggestions. We can just go down the block and there's—"

"No, let's start here." It felt like a definite step on an unknown path in the dark, when there was no light to see by. But he wasn't bothered by the dark.

When he opened the door, he wanted to take her by the hand. But he figured she wasn't ready for that. She breezed past him with a rustle of her cotton dress and the tap of her shoes, and he caught again the scent of vanilla and sweetness.

Impossibly, his heart tightened even more.

Chapter Five

Kelly couldn't help leaning closer against the display case to study the brooch Mitch had taken out of its velvet bed. It was an elegant piece of lacy gold with a baguette-cut ruby looking outrageously fragile against Mitch's broad, callused palm.

Stop looking at the man's hand, Kelly told herself. She was supposed to be concentrating on the beautiful pieces of jewelry, right? Not noticing the deep creases in Mitch's palm. Or how capable his fingers looked. The nicks and cuts and scars marred his sun-browned skin. Such powerful hands he had, just like the rest of him.

She *so* remembered the peace his touch had brought her, when he'd helped her from the Jeep.

"What do you think?" His hazel eyes met hers, and in those green and gold depths she saw glimpses of his big heart. He cared about the people in his life—and he cared about her opinion for some reason.

He's just too perfect. If he wasn't, then she wouldn't feel this turmoil seizing her up. Hard lessons learned ought to be enough to make her step away and stay firmly on the path she believed in. The path where God had placed her over and over again.

Mitch waited for her answer, the delicate and expensive brooch resting rock steady on his palm.

Don't just stand there, Kelly. Say something. Her gaze shot to the other box he'd chosen from among the many in the display cases. Which one did she like better? The dainty necklace shimmered in the sunlight, the delicate swoop of wings and halo around a thumbnail-sized freshwater pearl made her heart stop. "It's a pearl. What can I say?"

"You like pearls?"

She supposed he was looking for a woman's opinion on jewelry. "I think your mom might like the ruby better, though."

"You didn't answer my question."

Which question? Her mind wandered. No matter how hard she tried to stop the caring from creeping into her heart, she couldn't. She liked Mitch Dalton. She liked him very much.

As a friend. She couldn't dare think of him as anything else.

"Why pearls?" He studied her, waiting.

Oh, right. Pay attention, Kelly. "Pearls are so simple and unassuming. Everyone knows that a pearl starts with a tiny grain of sand, but to me, it's like faith. We are like that grain of sand and it's God's grace that can cloak us and make us shine, if we are humble and faithful enough. In the end, it's a thing of true beauty."

"Yes, it certainly is."

He wasn't looking at the pearl. But at her. Somehow his gaze deepened and there he went, somehow feeling too intimate, as if he could see too much. But how could he look past the layers of defense in which she cloaked herself so carefully?

The pieces of her heart stung like salt in a fresh wound, and she felt so vulnerable and wide open. It was Mitch. He made her feel like this. So wouldn't the smartest thing be to head for the door and never look back?

It would be the safest.

"I'll take the ruby," Mitch told Holly, behind the counter. "But could you put the other on hold? I'd like to think about it. Christmas will be here before you know it."

"Sure." Holly gladly set the pearl angel aside and took Mitch's credit card with her over to the cash register.

They were done. Kelly let out a deep breath she wasn't aware she'd been holding. This was how worked up she was. But now Mitch had found his gift, and he'd be heading back to his base.

I'll be back on safe ground.

She probably wouldn't see him again. She didn't want to see him again, right? It wasn't as if she was looking for a man to love—not anymore. Not ever again. It didn't make any sense.

"Mission accomplished." The way he leaned both forearms on the counter, coming in close to her, made her want to hope—past the ache where no hope lived.

How impossible was it to start hoping? And for what?

That kind of hope, that kind of dream, was not meant for her. She thought of what had happened with Joe, and it felt as if the shadows within her lengthened. No, this was her path and she would not step one foot off it.

She cleared the thick emotion from her throat. Somehow she managed some resemblance of a normal smile. "Your mom should love the brooch. I bet she'd love anything as long as it was from you."

"Well, she's biased, being my mom. But you, pretty lady, you saved my bacon."

"Me? I just pointed you in the right direction." Why did her heart flutter in her chest? Maybe it was simply the remnants of that old crush. Maybe. She couldn't let it be anything else.

"I did nothing. You would have done fine by yourself, but I'm glad I could help. I wish your mother a very happy birthday. And you a safe journey back to the base tonight."

She took a step in retreat.

"What? You're leaving me? Just like that?"

"You were the one who said mission accomplished."

"Well, maybe there's another mission scheduled after this one."

"Holly gift wraps, so you're good to go." She took another backward step to the door. "Bye, Mitch."

"Wait." As if he was going to let her escape. She was wrong, his mission wasn't close to being completed. Mitch scribbled his signature on the slip the shop owner slid toward him. "Kelly, don't run off on me."

"I've got to study."

"Flimsy excuse." Done, he dropped the pen but Kelly

was already heaving open the old-fashioned wood-frame door. The cowbell over the door clanked as she tried to evade him.

Emotion struck him hard in the chest, and he remembered the fear he'd seen in her eyes. "Ma'am, could you wrap this for me? I'll be back."

He hardly registered the owner's agreement; he was already out the door and into the blinding burn of daylight. He turned toward Kelly instinctively, as if he could feel the tug of her spirit against his.

She'd gained some distance on him, he had to give her that. She speed walked in those purple sandals as efficiently as if they were cross trainers. The hem of her pretty dress swirled around her slender knees, and her long honey-blond hair swung with her gait, like lustrous liquid gold.

Yeah, she was in definite retreat. What had scared her? He puzzled over that as he bounded after her, cutting around a couple holding hands. She had that strict no-dating outlook on things. Was she bolting because he'd gotten too close? What he needed to know was what had happened with Joe. Otherwise, she was going to run off and he'd never see her again.

Maybe that was as it should be. Maybe it would be best just to let her go. His chest tightened. The tenderness and confused emotions inside him tangled up into an unbreakable knot.

What he did was dangerous. There was no denying it. He'd learned the value of making sure to start each day without regrets. To leave nothing unfinished.

If he let her go, he'd regret it. No doubt about that.

So he continued after her. He could have closed his eyes and found her by heart and by the cadence of her gait. In the reflection of a coffee-shop window he could see her profile, her soft mouth downturned, her chin set with determination. Then her slim shoulders tensed more as if she, too, sensed him behind her. She kept going.

There was a clue, but did he get the hint? No. He kept going. "Kelly? Did I do something wrong?"

"No, you didn't do anything." She spun with a swirl of cotton, stark pain clouding her eyes. "I really do have to study."

"Yeah, but you're running scared, I think. And I want to know why." He towered over her like a bear. "Do I scare you?"

She swiped at a shock of blond hair that fell across her eyes, tucking it delicately behind her ear. He knew she was biding time, trying to think of the right answer—one that was still the truth but not the whole truth, either. She wanted to hold that back, the real reason she was afraid. Maybe because it was too personal or too painful.

But if he wanted to have a chance of seeing her again, then he had to know. He folded his arms over his chest and waited.

She stared long and hard down at the crack in the sidewalk between them. "I know you said you wouldn't mind having a friend, but this doesn't feel like friendship. I don't know, maybe it's just me. But there's something—"

He knew exactly what she meant. It should be a relief that she felt this, too. It wasn't one-sided. But the tangled mess of emotions in his chest clamped tight enough to make him wince. "You know what we can do? Let's find a place to sit down, have lunch and figure this out."

"Figure what out? I don't want to figure anything out."

"Running away from this isn't going to make it go away. Or keep it from happening the next time we get together."

"The next time?"

"See? That's something else we can talk about. There's a taco place right behind you. How about it?"

"No way am I going to let you turn this into a date, Mr. Dalton." Her words were kind, but strangled. He could see the sadness in her honest blue eyes.

He definitely had to know what had hurt her so much. What had that Joe McKaslin done to her? He thought of all the things that went wrong in the world, in relationships, between two people, that caused that much hurt. Hated to think of her exposed to anything like that. "Why? Why can't you date me?"

"I told you right up front. I have a no-dating policy—"

"And I'm asking why. What happened to you?"

"Life. Just like it happens to everyone else." She lifted her chin, as if determined to hold back her secrets and onto what she felt was private. "Surely you've seen enough of life to know what I'm talking about."

"I have." He pushed aside too many images of the world he'd seen up close. Images so far removed from the safe streets of this little college town and luxury unimagined in some of the places he'd been. But young or old, rich or poor, Christian or not, here or in some desperate country, life happened, and there was no stopping the pain that came right along with the living. "This has to do with Joe."

She took a step back, then another, as if wanting distance. "He's at the Mountain View Cemetery. He's buried there."

"I—I'm sorry. I didn't know."

"Now you do." Kelly's chest clogged tight, as if she were buried under a mountain of snow instead of the pieces of her broken dreams.

She left him standing there, in the middle of the sunswept sidewalk, with life teeming all around him. Students from campus were pacing the sidewalks now that the shops were open. People fresh from church were looking for a place to have lunch and discuss the service. Young mothers pushing strollers and young married couples holding hands, their backpacks heavy on their shoulders as they sought out places to sip coffee and study.

Life swirled all around him, and yet he seemed darker than the shadows.

Kelly felt the same shadows in her soul, and she kept on going, woodenly forcing one foot in front of the other until she'd reached the end of the block. When she turned the corner, he was out of her sight.

But, strangely, not out of her heart. She could feel him there, like the shadows.

And the light.

Okay, that wasn't the answer I expected, Mitch thought, still troubled hours later as he helped clear the dishes from the table. He hadn't forgotten the look in Kelly's eyes—not one of grieving as would be expected—but of hopelessness.

He heard the waltzing rhythm of his mom's gait in the kitchen behind him. As he gathered up a stack of dinner plates, he tried to put his thoughts aside. His mother could probably sense that he was thinking about a woman, possibly daughter-in-law material. "Don't even think about asking."

"Why? What was I going to ask?" Barbara Dalton paused in the archway and planted a hand on her hip, but the gleam in her eye clearly said, "Fine, I'll just ask later." "Come out onto the deck. Your father is setting up the ice cream maker."

"This'll only take a minute." Like he was going to leave the dishes for his mom to do. "Go help Dad. Go on."

"Who do you think you are, giving orders?" She hefted the stack out of his hands—she was stronger than she looked. "You might be part of an elite force, Sergeant, but in this house you're still my boy and you'll do as I say."

"Yes, ma'am." He liked it when she pulled rank. He loaded up another pile of serving bowls and joined her in the kitchen, where she was stacking the plates in the dishwasher.

"I love my brooch, Mitch." She beamed as she worked. "Wherever did you find it?"

"A little shop near the university."

"You did good." She studied at him as he went in search of the plastic containers she stored leftovers in. "So, is she a nice girl?"

"What makes you think there is one?"

"Mother's intuition."

"Either way, that's filed under the topic of not-your-business."

"Well, I had to try." Mom went back to loading the dishwasher. "I am praying for you to find someone. I would so love a daughter-in-law to spoil."

"I'm still not going to discuss it." He dug a spatula out of a nearby drawer. "Do you remember Joe McKaslin?"

"He went to high school with you, didn't he?" She rinsed flatware beneath the faucet before plunking them into the basket on the bottom rack. "There was something about him in the local paper years ago. He passed away fighting forest fires."

Wow. No wonder he'd felt Kelly's sadness so powerfully.

"So sad, to lose someone that young," his mom went on. "I worry about you every day. You're the reason behind all this gray hair."

"It looks stunning on you, and you shouldn't worry. I can take care of myself." He dropped the container of leftovers in the fridge. "There. Done. What next?"

"Go take those bowls out to your father." She nodded toward the counter. "He should be about ready to dish up."

"Then leave the dishes, Mom. I'll do them later."

"You'll do no such thing. Now go, before I get out my switch."

He laughed at the joke between them, a threat she'd been using for as long as he could remember and a promise she'd never made good on. He grabbed the bowls and headed to the deck where his dad was fiddling with the lid of the ice cream maker.

Beside him his sister, Suz, a corporate lawyer in Seattle, was out of her area of expertise. "I don't know, Dad. You'll have to ask Mom."

His dad scratched his chin, as if considering the matter. "Maybe Mitch knows."

"He knows nothing," Suz winked at him as he joined them on the deck. "As usual. I'll get Mom."

"Hey now, move aside, Dad." Mitch set the bowls on the patio table and knelt down in front of the ice cream maker. "What's the problem?"

"We'd best wait for your mom. We bust this newfangled thingy of hers, I'll get in trouble." Dad didn't look too worried as he straightened. "It's good to have you home, son."

"It's good to be here for a change."

Memories surrounded him of all the summers Dad had barbecued on the grill and they'd eaten at the patio table, gazing out at the Bridger Mountains. The pool glittered in the sunshine and beyond the freshly mown lawn evergreens seemed to go on forever. Growing up here had been good; maybe the years to come would be even better.

Why was it, miles away and hours later, he could still feel Kelly in his heart? Because, he suspected, there was a chance that she could be his future.

Give it up, Kelly. It's no use. She was *not* into studying, no matter how hard she tried to focus. Kelly slammed the book shut and the sound echoed around the dark house. She was babysitting for one of her regulars, Amy—one of Joe's many cousins—and the little ones were snug in bed. When she checked the clock, she realized Amy and her husband would be home in less than an hour.

Why couldn't she concentrate? That was easy, because of Mitch. He was on her mind. Too much and inexplicably. She rubbed the heel of her hand over her hurting heart. Why did Mitch make her feel again in these broken places?

She had no idea. Aimless, she headed into the kitchen. She put a cup of water in the microwave and while it heated, she fished through her backpack until she found the zipper sandwich bag where she kept her teabags. The cinnamon aroma of the tea comforted her, but who was she trying to fool?

Only herself. There could be no comfort for what troubled her tonight. Everything she wanted with all of her soul—it surrounded her in this homey kitchen with bits of love and family everywhere. Crayon drawings and magnetic alphabet letters were tacked on the refrigerator door. Framed snapshots of the babies hung on the walls and were propped on the windowsill over the sink.

The broken pieces of her dreams and of her heart felt enormous in the comfortable silence of the cozy kitchen. And still, like a survivor beneath an earthquake's rubble, she could feel hope struggling to stay alive in her soul.

Chapter Six

In the middle of reading her assigned sociology chapter, Kelly felt a soft breeze move through her. Awareness flickered to life within her heart, an awareness that was warm and sweet. Highlighter in hand, she looked up over the rail of her top-floor deck, through the rustling, sun-drenched poplar leaves to the street below. A familiar tan Jeep was parked by the curb.

Mitch. Aviator sunglasses hid his eyes and he seemed to gaze along the block. What was he doing here? She hadn't heard from him in a week. She recapped her highlighter and slid out of the plastic deck chair. Remembering how she'd left things between them, part of her was glad to see him, the other part wanted to scrunch down in the chair, hide behind her book and hope he didn't see her.

No such luck. "Hey, Kelly. Are you studying up there?"

"Guilty as charged." She stood, leaving her book open, pages ruffling in the warm breeze.

"It's Saturday evening."

"So? You say that as if it's a bad thing. I like studying." She leaned against the wooden rails. "What are you doing here? And how did you find me?"

"You're listed in the phone book. I know how to read and I am fairly good at finding my way around." He lifted his glasses off his nose enough to meet her gaze. "You went AWOL on me, so I had to hunt you down."

"So, is that a punishable offense?"

"Yep. I've come to impose dinner on you. I hope you like the works, because that's what I got." He withdrew a large pizza box from the back seat. "I'm comin' up."

As if she would want to stop him. "I never say no to a man who comes bearing pizza."

"Lucky me." He piled a cardboard carrier with soda cups and two smaller pizza boxes on top of the one he already carried.

"I like a man who comes prepared."

"Good. I take pizza seriously."

Mitch took one look at her smile, as sunny as the bright summer evening, and the tangle of emotions in his chest yanked so tight he couldn't breathe. She was smiling at him, okay, maybe she was glad to see him… or she really liked pizza, but it was nice to see. As he headed around the small, seventies' apartment building, following the walkways through the mature poplars lining the complex, he spotted Kelly in the open doorway of the top-floor corner unit.

He took in the sweet glint of her dark-blue eyes and her girl-next-door wholesomeness. She looked great with her hair pulled back in a careless ponytail, wearing a light summer T-shirt in the palest shade of blue and comfortable-looking, dark-blue drawstring shorts.

He knew when she'd spotted the flowers because her smile widened. In his enthusiasm, he took the steps two at a time all the way to the top. "I tried calling a couple times, but your line was busy."

"Oh, I was online doing some research at the library. I've got a paper due." She backed into the unit and held the door for him. "I *always* have a paper due, or it seems that way."

She looked nervous. He didn't want that, so he handed her the flowers. "I promise I won't say anything to chase you away this time."

"Deal." She took the bouquet and breathed in the scent of the purple flowers. "I love freesias. How did you know?"

"They just made me think of you. That's a thank you. My mom loved her gift."

"I was glad to help."

He spotted the kitchen straight down the little hallway to the right. Definitely a girl's apartment, he thought as he slid his fragrant load onto the beige-colored counter and nudged a bowl with dried flower stuff aside so the extra-large box would fit. The pepperoni and garlic scent competed with the potpourri. "You haven't eaten yet, have you?"

"No. My shift at the bookstore was over at four-thirty, but I'm waiting for my roommate. We sorta had dinner plans." She joined him in the kitchen and pulled a glass vase from the cabinet beneath the sink. "Do you mind if Lexie joins us?"

"Sure, I'm the one who showed up unannounced."

"Yes, but with pizza and, oh, is that a box of cheesy sticks?" she asked over the rush of the tap water.

"Cheesy sticks and a dessert pizza."

"The blueberry cheesecake swirl one, by chance?"

He nodded confirmation as he removed the drinks from the carrier. "Did I do good?"

"Are you kidding? You did perfect. That's the best pizza in town. Do you mind if we wait? Lexie should be here any minute."

"Sure." He slipped his sunglasses onto the counter. "Pretty nice place you got here."

"Decorated on a budget, but it's home." She unwrapped the flowers and began arranging them in the vase.

He checked out the living area. The furniture was mismatched pieces in different shades of brown and blue, well-worn and comfortable, and aimed at a small wide-screen TV. A sturdy green plastic table sat squarely in the middle of the little deck that looked out over the poplars at the busy street below. A textbook's pages ruffled back and forth in the wind.

"Sit wherever you want," Kelly invited as she arranged the flowers. "How is the mountain-climbing going?"

"I still haven't fallen."

"You must have developed a certain competence at it by now. You said it was an advanced training thing you're doing, right? What's advanced about it?"

"Next week we get to train on glaciers. There's nothing like ice-climbing."

"I haven't ice-climbed in ages." She carried the vase past him to the scarred pine coffee table between a mismatched brown couch and blue striped chair. "Okay, never. It has never occurred to me that people actually climb across mountain glaciers."

"Well, they do if they want to get to the other side."

"Tell me that's not your idea of a joke."

"My sense of humor. It's why no woman will have me."

Oh, I doubt that, Kelly thought as she studied him. She imagined plenty of nice women would definitely consider him a fine catch.

The door opened, and Lexie's voice filled the little foyer. "Kelly? I couldn't believe it! I got the last copy on the shelf—"

Kelly watched her roommate skid to a stop midsentence, stunned by the sight of the guy standing in their living room. Before Lexie could jump to the wrong conclusion, Kelly made it clear. "Mitch and I went to the same high school. He's an old acquaintance, because we were never really friends. I was too shy."

"So was I," Mitch added, slipping his hands into his back pockets, which only emphasized the corded muscles in his arms. "It's good to meet you."

"You, too." Lexie swiped a chunk of wayward black hair behind her ear and looked utterly shocked. "I, uh, am just on my way back out. You two have a nice date—"

"Not a date," Kelly emphasized. "Mitch and I were waiting for you. He brought cheesy sticks. C'mon, let's grab some plates."

His ego was *not* getting a boost. Good thing he was tough, Mitch thought. There was nothing a guy liked better than being a friend, when that wasn't what he had in mind at all.

But it really was, he realized. The least he wanted with Kelly was friendship, and that was a good place to start. He noticed the rental DVD case the roommate was holding. "Is it movie night?"

"You can stay and watch it with us." Kelly offered, handing him a plate over the counter. "Lexie, did you say that you got the last copy?"

"Yeah, of the new romantic comedy that just came out for rent." Lexie still looked uncertain, even as she dumped her backpack and the video case on the edge of the couch. "I bet you're not into romantic comedies, Mitch."

"Not my thing, but I'm up for it."

He really was a nice guy. Kelly knew he probably wasn't jumping for joy to spend his Saturday evening watching a girl movie, but he was here as a friend. He'd come all this way—maybe he really was lonely, just as he'd said last week, when he'd brought burgers for her dinner break.

She was glad he'd come. "This is so much better than what we had planned. Barbecued hot dogs on our hibachi. Thanks, Mitch, for bringing the pizza."

"And the cheesy sticks." Lexie chimed in as she started loading up her plate.

"Any time, ladies."

Yeah, Kelly couldn't help thinking, he was *definitely* one of the good guys.

* * *

Nightfall darkened the dome of the sky as Kelly opened the door. "You were a good sport about the movie."

"It had some funny parts. It was a nice, wholesome movie. It was good for me."

"I doubt that, but thanks for coming. Maybe you'll want to stop by again."

"If that's an invitation, I'll take you up on it. Say, next Saturday night. I'll bring pizza again, if you want."

"My treat since you brought this time. We're friends, remember?"

"All right, then." Somehow, he would survive this friendship thing. He hesitated on the top step. "Same time same place next week?"

"I'd really like that." She trailed him out onto the covered landing. "It's pretty late. You have a long drive back."

"Don't worry about me. I've only been up and going full-bore since oh-five-hundred."

"Your hours seem as long as mine. Except ice-climbing is sadly lacking from my daily workout regime."

"You don't know what you're missing."

"Seeing as I'm more of an indoor girl, I'm more than happy to pass on the glacier-climbing. You really like it?"

"I do." That was an understatement. He started down the steps, slowly, going backward so he could watch Kelly standing in the shower of light from inside the door. "Monday, when you notice the whitecaps on the highest mountains, think of me."

"I'll send a whole bunch of no-slipping prayers your way."

"I'd appreciate it." Mitch stopped at the landing, gazing up the length of steps between them. It was late, he needed to head back but the last thing he wanted to do was to go. "How's the math class?"

"Good, but then I haven't looked at that homework all day. When I crack that book tomorrow, I'll be singing a different tune."

"You having trouble with the class?"

"It's math. Math equals trouble. Wait, you love the subject, so you don't understand delaying torture whenever possible."

"You just don't have the right attitude when it comes to math. You wouldn't happen to have a pen handy?"

"You're not going to look at my homework, are you?" Her brows knitted and made an adorable crinkle between her eyes. "It's late. It's Saturday night. I have a strict no-math policy on Saturday nights."

"You have a lot of strict policies. First no dating, and now no math on certain nights. I'll be back in town tomorrow. Mom's dragging me to church with her and Dad so she can show her friends I really do exist and I'm not a figment of her imagination."

"You don't make it home much, I take it?"

"I've made it home for one Christmas, and about ten days total, and that's after boot camp. I spend ninety-nine percent of my life on a mission or waiting for one. Hey, how about I give you my cell number and my e-mail address? You can call if you want me to stop by. Or just e-mail a question."

"You've got to be kidding. You're busy enough."

"Sure, but I always have time for my friends. And for the thrill of math."

"All right, hotshot, but don't say I didn't warn ya."

"Bring it on. I'm used to a certain amount of hardship."

Kelly darted inside to grab the little spiral notepad by the phone. As she scavenged around the kitchen for a pen, delicate freesias scented the air with incredible sweetness.

"Use mine," Lexie offered, hopping up from the couch to hand over a purple glitter-gel pen. "He's awesome. You should date him."

Kelly shook her head. "Too complicated. He's leaving soon. He's stationed in California. Plus, I'm done with romance."

"Bummer." Lexie returned to the couch where the TV droned the latest local news.

Bummer was an understatement, but that was life.

Kelly stepped out onto the front porch and her gaze found Mitch by feel rather than by sight. He'd retreated to the darker corner of the landing, but he radiated such a strong essence of might and honor that she saw him clearly, even when the twilight shadows hid his features.

She came closer and could just make him out leaning against the railing, his arms crossed over his chest. The embers within her heart breathed to life. Just a flicker, but it was bright and joyful.

This is happiness, she told herself. Mitch was a good friend, the pizza-bringing, kindly, offering-to-help-her-with-her-homework type of friend. Why shouldn't she feel gladdened by that?

Mitch met her halfway, reaching out for the pad and pen. "If I hear you had trouble and you didn't ask me for help, I'm gonna be pretty mad at you."

She wasn't fooled; she spotted the good-natured crook of his grin, even in the shadows. "It's my strict policy never to get someone as big and strong as you mad at me."

"Good policy." His grin widened as he wrote and handed her back the book and pen. "I'll provide the movie next time. Deal?"

"Something PG."

"There's a challenging mission, but lucky for you, I always prevail. Good night, Kelly."

"Night. Drive safe."

He raised one hand in answer, moving down the stairs silently. Not even the bottom step squeaked as he disappeared from her sight, taking the brightness of his presence with him.

In his Jeep, heading north over the moon-drenched Montana landscape, Mitch thought over the evening. Not bad. It had gone much better than he had the right to hope for. Kelly had relaxed around him, especially with her roommate there.

Over pizza consumed at the balcony table, with the rustling trees, the wind and sun, he'd asked questions about college life. About Kelly's life. He learned that she worked full time at the bookstore and supplemented that with babysitting jobs. That she was a straight-A student. She was starting to do extra study for the exams to get into graduate school. And that she daintily picked green peppers off her pizza.

She amazed him. Life had brought her a lot of twists and turns. The image of her standing on the top step, the light from the apartment behind her, the moon's glow falling over her in the dark night, remained. She was pretty determined that all the two of them had in store was friendship.

He considered her side of things. It sounded as if she'd been alone for most of her formative years. And just when she thought she'd found a place to belong and someone to love, it had been ripped from her.

Pretty devastating. No wonder Kelly had given up on dating. On trying to find love again. No wonder the friendship-only thing was so important. He could understand that. He knew what deep losses could do to a person. Closing your heart off kept you from getting too close and feeling too much. It was easier.

But it was no way to live.

Plus the tangled-up emotion in his chest had little to do with friendship feelings. Tonight he'd really felt at home on the couch beside her, with his feet up on the coffee table. He'd enjoyed the simplicity of sitting at her side, and it had felt right. He'd like to spend a lot more evenings just like that. But not as just her friend.

As the highway unrolled before the reach of the Jeep's headlight, Mitch thought how life resembled his limited view. You just couldn't see what was up ahead. Life came with risks and love did, too. You had to give with your whole heart, but you were really just driving in the dark. The turns and obstacles ahead were a mystery, veiled in the night, and you just couldn't know how things would work out.

All you could do was to walk in faith and not hold back.

Chapter Seven

Doom.

Kelly looked up from her textbook and rubbed her tired eyes. The living room came slowly into focus. Two hours of struggling with the mysteries of algebra, mysteries which she had purposefully forgotten over the years, and the truth, as solid as ever, stared her right in the face. The final regular test of the summer quarter was getting closer and she wasn't going to pull an A. She'd be lucky to get a C the way she was going, and that would pull down her entire average.

Definitely doom.

Mitch's kindly spoken words echoed through her mind and right into her heart. *If I hear you had trouble and you didn't ask me for help, I'm gonna be pretty mad at you.*

Since it was a bright late-Monday afternoon, and Mitch was probably out pick-axing his way up a glacier, she opted for an e-mail instead of calling.

It took just a second to type up an outgoing message

to the address he'd given her, as it was only one word: Help! She signed off, including her cell number since she was scheduled to babysit tonight.

The twists God put in a man's path were an amazing thing, Mitch thought as he dialed Kelly's cell number. It had to be no coincidence that he loved math—always had—and that he was in the position to offer her the one thing she'd accept from him—help for her upcoming test. Proof that he was on the right path.

After the third ring, her voice filled the line, dulcet and low as a whisper. "Mitch?"

"Hey, I got your SOS. I would have called you sooner, but we just got in."

"You've been out all day? It's nine o'clock."

"I don't work banker's hours. I'm just lucky I don't have to sleep on the ground tonight. Mountainsides are generally rocky. Not so comfortable. Where are you?"

"Babysitting. Actually, the kids are asleep and so I'm studying, but it's a disaster."

"You've got the right man." He intended to show her that. "What's the problem?"

"If only it were that uncomplicated. I have a test in a week, the last one before finals and it's a big part of my grade. I'm not getting what to do with quadratic equations. It's eluding me."

"Sounds like you're in need of a tutor."

"I am. What are your rates?"

"Barbecue a couple of hot dogs on your hibachi and we'll call it even."

"That's what I had planned for Saturday's dinner."

"I'll come early, we'll get your math crisis figured out before dinner. Sound like a deal?"

"A very good one. How was the ice-climbing?"

"Cold." His chuckle was cut short. There was some noise going on in the background. "Oh, I've gotta go. We've got a surprise field exercise."

"It's almost ten at night."

"Welcome to my world. I'll be at your place, uh, around four-thirty. See ya." The line disconnected.

Kelly sat alone in Amy's living room and stared at the phone, his voice, his words echoing in her head. *Why does he affect me so strongly, Lord?*

No answer came. The brightness Mitch brought to her spirit faded in slow increments with each breath.

And only shadows remained.

Mitch. She couldn't help thinking of him throughout the week. Things would happen that brought him to the forefront of her mind. Driving to work and seeing the highest snowcapped peaks of the Rockies rimming the northwestern horizon, and those glaciers glinting in the hot late-August sun made her wonder if Mitch was out on a snowy peak like those, climbing to his heart's content.

Every time she cracked open her math book or sat in the auditorium class: while she wasn't looking forward to facing a tutoring session, she was glad about her tutor.

Who would have guessed all those years ago that the shy, out-of-place foster girl and the smart, awkward math geek from a middle-class life would wind up being friends? Or that he would be helping her once again?

God worked in funny ways. But she wasn't going to question it. She knew the Lord's hand had been gently guiding them together. Why else would her heart come back to life a little? Why else was she starting to feel a brightness inside her, after Joe's loss had taken it all?

During her shift at the bookstore today, both Katherine and Spence had asked her how things were going with the soldier. Really, they had it all wrong, but when each had asked about him, she started thinking about him all over again. How funny he could be, and how his chuckle rolled like warm joy, low and deep, just the way a friend's laugh should be.

The best part was that she was going to see him in a few minutes. She was running a little early, so she'd have time to get some iced tea made before he came. In a hurry, she whipped into one of the several parking spots in front of her staircase.

Her soul stirred. Strange. She squinted through the windshield to the top landing above. And there, through the shield of poplars swaying in the wind was a silhouette, tall and dependable and waiting for her. Her shining knight—er, tutor.

Like the sunshine streaming through the flickering leaves, her day brightened. She hopped out of the car, bringing her backpack and keys with her. "Hey, stranger. You're early."

"Better than being late." He braced his hands on the rail and leaned, gazing down at her. His smile was wide and friendly, and she knew his eyes were too, behind those aviator sunglasses he wore. He was dressed in jeans again, and a navy-blue T-shirt. "I've only been waiting a few minutes. Are you ready to be put through your paces?"

"Ugh. I knew I was going to regret this. I've been putting off even dealing with anything mathematical all week. It's going to be torture, isn't it?"

"Well, I am a marine. We show no mercy."

"Just my luck." She climbed upward, feeling as light as air. "Lexie wanted me to ask. What movie did you bring?"

"No way. Homework first. Then we'll talk movies."

"Whew, you are demanding." She was close enough to see that there was a military logo on the chest of his T-shirt, and the deep-navy color made his eyes a dark, fathomless green.

Not that she was noticing. "Hey, when you had to get off the phone when we were talking last week—did everything turn out okay?"

"Our CO—commanding officer—thought it would be funny to order us out on a midnight climb."

"In the dark?"

"Well, when you're doing what I do, they don't want you seen. It kind of interferes with the stealthy part of the job. We do a lot of training stuff at night because we do a lot of our missions through the night."

"Missions. That's like what, hanging off cliffs and crossing glaciers? Do you know what?" She unlocked her front door. "I'm starting to suspect that you aren't a normal soldier."

"I told you. I'm like a scout. I do reconnaissance."

"*Like* a scout." Yeah, that was so revealing—not. She opened the door and led the way to the kitchen. "Okay, you keep saying that. You're *like* a scout, but what do you do, exactly? You climb mountains, scuba dive, do amphibious stuff. You're not like Special Forces, are you?"

She feared she knew the answer already.

He shrugged one muscled shoulder, as if it were no big deal. "I'm a Force Recon marine."

Oh, the humble thing was so appealing. Kelly tried to keep her heart still as she took out two cans of soda from the fridge and handed him one. "I don't know what that is. Explain, please."

"Thanks." He popped the top of the can. "We're the elite of the elite. Force Recon is basically the on-the-ground eyes. We patrol enemy territory and act as scouts so our guys know what they're getting into."

"Enemy territory? Like you scout out enemy soldiers?" She took a sip of the icy bubbling cola. It kept her from saying that he looked pretty sane for a crazy person. She tried to imagine how dangerous that had to be. "You need to ice-climb *just* to find out the other side's position? No, you do more than scout, don't you?"

"Yeah. We're pretty big and bad." He shrugged that shoulder again. Apparently that was all he was saying. "Ready to get to it?"

"Math? Sure." Her backpack was still hanging from her shoulder. "We can stay in here, where the air conditioning is, I can turn it up. Sorry." She headed toward the thermostat and adjusted the dial. "Or we can sit outside. Oh, and there's a park a few blocks down."

"The deck is good. I don't want to get too far away from the food."

"I get the hint. Hungry?"

"I could be."

"That's just a hungry man's way of being polite." She grabbed a bag of chips and handed it to him. "Do you like French onion or ranch?"

"Yes."

"I should've known." She grabbed both dip tubs from the fridge and followed him out onto the deck. "Appetizers."

"There's no better." He opened the bag. "Are you ready?"

She tugged her math book out of her pack. It had been a long time since she'd been this happy at heart, especially when it came to algebra.

Mitch's friendship was turning out to be a true blessing in her life.

As Mitch knelt on the deck boards to turn the franks grilling on the hibachi, he could see Kelly's reflection in the large window. She was leaning forward over her plate to scoop her chip through the dip. Her face was turned in profile as she talked with her roommate.

When it came to Kelly, there couldn't be a prettier woman on earth. Not in his opinion. Her golden hair was down today, rippling in the warm breeze and caressing the creamy curves of her face. She wore a sleeveless blouse the exact blue of her eyes, and a black pair of walking shorts and matching shoes. She looked casual and wholesome and womanly all at once.

It really wasn't fair that he was at such a disadvantage.

I hope You know where You're leading me, Lord, because I'm in over my head. He cared for her more than he felt safe admitting, even to himself. He tonged the hot dogs from the grill and onto a plate. "Seconds?"

"It's nice having such first-rate service, thanks." Kelly smiled up at him as she swiped mustard on a bun. "You have great grill skills."

"I've put in a lot of hard practice at the barbecue."

He slid a beef frank onto Lexie's plate before he added the last two to his. Across the table, Kelly was pushing the relish and mustard in his direction. Her fingers were long, slender and delicate, like the rest of her. Her short nails were painted a light pink.

Lexie shoved the tub of deli potato salad closer. "So, Mitch, tell us exactly why you aren't married."

"Because I spend pretty much most of my time on a mission or on standby prepared to head out. It doesn't leave a lot of time for finding a nice lady to marry." He cast a glance sideways at Kelly. "This free time I have—real weekends—is a luxury."

Lexie persisted. "Yeah, but you'd like to get married one day, right?"

"Sure. I just haven't slowed down enough to let a woman catch me and shackle me into matrimony. Yet."

"Shackle?" Kelly questioned with the cute little crinkle at the bridge of her nose.

"That's a totally typical man's answer." Lexie didn't seem too happy with him.

He shrugged, running a line of mustard along both

hot dogs. "Apparently a guy should never joke about the seriousness of marriage in front of women."

"Ya think?" Lexie frowned at him, but her eyes said something different. Like she was on to him.

"Let me try again." He set down the mustard bottle so he could concentrate. He didn't want to get it wrong this time. "I'd like to get married one day. I'm taking my time because I want to find the real thing."

"Real love." Lexie nodded her tentative approval. "Don't we all want to find that?"

I think I already have, he thought. All he had to do was to look at Kelly and his heart did funny things, leaving him feeling exposed and vulnerable.

That just couldn't be good. "Is this how you two spend every Saturday evening?"

"Just about," Kelly answered between dainty bites. "Unless I have a babysitting job."

"But mostly it's a budget meal and a rented movie," Lexie concluded.

"The reality of putting yourself through college." Kelly didn't seem to mind. "On the Saturdays after payday, we splurge and order a pizza."

"You live large. I'm guilty of the same kind of lifestyle." Mitch stole more chips from the bag in the center of the table.

"We're flush. Lexie, remember last January? We were both flat broke from paying tuition, I'd lost my retail job due to layoffs after Christmas, and we couldn't scrape enough money together between the two of us for rent."

"My dad's check was lost in the mail, it really was,

and he was out of the country," Lexie explained, "so we were, like, digging out the pennies from the bottoms of our book bags and purses."

"And on the floor of the car," Kelly added. "Sure, it's funny now, but let's just say there was a big sale on cases of those cups of instant noodles at the discount grocery. It's practically all we ate for three weeks."

"So," Mitch guessed, "you're telling me not to take you out for noodles?"

"Exactly." She laughed. "I'm definitely noodled out."

Her laughter lightened his world. His voice didn't sound like his own as he made a suggestion. "I saw that a couple of good movies were playing down at the old theater. I thought I'd treat you girls to popcorn and a movie. Interested?"

Kelly's gaze met his, and, like a spark to kindling, he felt the impact.

"That would be very nice," she said and her smile moved like sunlight through him.

He had to admit that he cared for her. It wasn't a conscious decision and there wasn't much he could do about it.

With the warm still air and star-studded ebony sky, the August evening felt like a dream. Or, Kelly conceded, maybe it was the man she was walking with. Something about being with Mitch made her world better.

"Are you sure we shouldn't have waited for your roommate?" Mitch asked. "It's dark and she shouldn't be walking alone."

"I have a feeling that guy she ran into at the concession stand has been wanting to date her for a long time. I bet he'll give her a ride home." It was nice of him to be concerned, though, Kelly thought. See? It just went to show what a thoughtful guy he was. "What you did this evening, helping me figure out my math, is a big deal to me. You may have saved my grade point average."

"Well, not yet. The test is tomorrow."

"But now I've nailed every practice test question the prof handed out. I couldn't do one of them before you came today."

"Ah, you could too. You were just getting psyched out about it. I didn't do much."

"It's a lot to me."

"I'm glad I could help." Mitch rewarded her with his charming, lopsided grin, the one that made her spirit light up.

She couldn't remember a nicer thing, simply walking like this at his side. Maybe it's the gorgeous night, she reasoned, the hush of their footsteps on the sidewalk in perfect synchronicity and the quarter-moon peering over the city so that they walked in its platinum glow.

Or, maybe it was the man—wait, correct that—*friend* at her side.

Companionable silence mantled them as they walked down quiet streets. The bright lights of some of the college dorm windows were visible through the trees lining the sidewalk, and, as they turned the corner and crossed the road, the curtained windows of homes stretched for blocks.

Mitch broke the stillness. "I've got only two more weekends left before they drag me back to my base."

"Two more?" She'd known that, of course, but to hear the words out loud hit like a punch.

"Dad and I are going up into the national park next Friday to spend the night. I want to do that before I head out. With this thing going on in the Middle East, I'm gonna be hard core, and I don't know… I might not make it back until I'm discharged eighteen months from now."

She'd known that, so why did it feel as if she were choking on disappointment?

"It'll mean a lot to Dad, and to me, too. But I've got Sunday afternoon free. You're gonna need to take a study break, right?"

She cleared the emotion from her throat, but her voice sounded thick anyway. "Are you kidding? Finals start in a week. I'll be half-comatose. I'll need a serious study break."

"Something fun."

"What does a guy who hangs off of mountains for a living do for *fun?*"

"There's hang gliding."

"Are you serious? I can't do heights."

"How about BASE jumping?"

"*What?* I'd have to be insane, and I'm not there yet."

"Ice-climbing is out?"

"Don't go there, I'm warning you." Although she sounded almost stern, the hint of a dimple at the corners of her mouth showed, even when she was doing her best to keep from grinning.

"All right. How about this: if you get an A on your test, I pick. You get a B or less, then you can pick what we do."

"I'm only agreeing to this because I don't think there's any way that I'll actually pull an A. The only problem is that I have a babysitting gig at six."

Mitch realized they'd stopped in the shadow of her building. There was his Jeep parked a few car lengths up the curb. Disappointment set in. He didn't like the idea of having to leave her. "We'll have you to your babysitting thing on time."

"How about I'll meet you at the city park around noon, and I'll bring my graded test. We'll take it from there."

"The west entrance." He jammed his hand into his jeans pocket and pulled out his keys. Sorting through the ring gave him something to focus on when he really wanted to do nothing more than brush his lips with hers, gently kiss her soft, rosebud mouth so she would know how he felt.

But she wasn't ready for that. She wasn't ready for more.

Yet.

He didn't blame her. He could relate. This was a scary, unknown path. Especially to a marine who was trained to be swift, silent and deadly, but when it came to *this*—matters of the heart—he wasn't so capable.

He walked backward so he could keep her in his sight. "Thanks for a good evening."

"I should be thanking you. Safe journeys, Mitch."

"Night." He could walk away, but he couldn't stop

his tenderness for her that burned like a rocket's glare in the dead of night.

He didn't know where this was leading. He only knew that God was leading him.

He would trust in that.

Chapter Eight

"Are you having fun yet?"

Fun? Kelly studied Mitch over the rim of the giant inner tube she held on to for dear life, although the cool lapping eddy of the river's edge only came to her knees. Fun? That settled it, he was definitely certifiable.

The trouble was, he looked anything but. In running shorts and a military-green tank top, he radiated complete ease and self-assurance as he waded ahead of her into the deeper pull of the current.

I'd have to be crazy to follow him.

She took another step along the rocky river bottom—putting her sanity in serious question.

She squinted through the blinding sunlight bouncing off the wide river's surface at the intrepid man who obviously had no common sense. "This *can't* be your idea of fun."

"You'd better believe it." He stopped waist-deep in the mountain-fed river and took hold of her inner tube.

"That's some death grip you got there. Relax. I won't let anything happen to you."

"Promises, promises." She cast her gaze down river, contemplating all the ways she could drown.

"Don't tell me you're afraid of water, too."

"Okay, I won't tell you." She bit her bottom lip to keep in the squeak of fear that erupted the moment he gave an effortless jerk on her inner tube and kept pulling. Her feet lifted off the rocky riverbed as he drew her through the eddies and directly into the teeth of the current. The force of it seemed to bite like a dog, held on and tried to drag her away. Not the best sensation.

Help? She couldn't seem to make that word come out of her terror-struck mouth. She wasn't aware how it happened, but he was at her side and his steely arm drew her toward him.

Their inner tubes bumped together and she jostled to a stop against him. There she was, in the shelter of his arms, up to her chin in water, protected from the river's tenacious current and shaded from the blinding sun. Safe at his side, her fear trickled away into nothing at all.

Her feet found a firm purchase on the rocks below and a different fear coursed through her as he casually drew her closer still. Somehow she found enough air to breathe in order to speak. "I thought we were going wading or something."

"That'll teach you to jump to conclusions."

"No, it was more like wishful thinking. Clinging to false hopes."

"You do know how to swim, right?" Mitch could feel the way she trembled. Tenderness flowed through him with a force that was greater than the river, greater than anything he'd ever known before.

The emotion sharpened until it ached in his throat. She was so little and fragile and dainty in his arms, and that well of tenderness just kept on brimming. He wished he could hold her close and protect her. Forever.

The question was, would she let him?

He tugged her a little closer, but she seemed to resist. That was his answer, apparently. Okay, he'd work with that.

"I know enough to dog paddle basically." There was that cute furrow again between her eyes. The one he wanted to kiss until her worry went away. He doubted that would make her calmer right now. In time, he thought, although it was tough not being able to take this up a level.

Was it his imagination, or did she cling to him more tightly? His care for her was like nothing he'd ever known before. He longed to be with her in the way mountaintops needed snow, rivers needed the sea. The way night needed the dawn. To feel whole. With a perfect purpose.

Ever since he'd left for boot camp, he'd found a great purpose to his life. One he felt qualified and called to do. But right now, being with Kelly, his whole heart crumpled and fell, changing him forever.

"Don't worry. I'll be right with you," he promised. "I'm qualified in water stuff."

"Water stuff? That makes me feel so much better. *Not.*"

"It should. I'm trained in all sorts of amphibious things. You're in good hands. Ready?"

No, she was *so* not ready. Kelly gave a squeak of fear as she was whisked up onto the seemingly enormous inner tube, which he held safely for her. As aggressively as the current tried, it could not tear her away from Mitch's grip.

This was a very bad idea. Panic roared through her with a quaking iciness, stealing the hot burn from the sun on her face and arms, and drowning out the rush of the river. It wasn't the river that was scaring her now. *That* fear, as great as it was, was nothing compared to the panic threatening to take her over. It was Mitch. Her feelings for him were so strong.

He made it all worse with the gentle brush of heat as he leaned to whisper in her ear. "No worries. I'll keep you safe. Count on me."

It would be so totally tempting to care for him in a way that went beyond friendship, Kelly thought as she clutched the side of the rubber inner tube. Mitch looked like everything trustworthy in the world—he was strong of character and spirit. As a friend, he made her laugh, but he did more than that. He lit up her world.

What could she do about that? She'd stop feeling this way, that's what. She'd hold on tight to her common sense, that's what. At least her panic was in perspective. She studied the roll and hiss of the wide, fast-moving river. Whatever danger it held for her was nothing like the peril of letting herself care too much for this man.

"Just hold on, whatever happens," he advised.

As if any force on earth could possibly be stronger than her grip! If she could lower the panic level enough to speak, she'd tell him that.

"And don't forget to enjoy the ride." He looked way too confident, as if there wasn't a bit of danger.

Help, he was nuts. "I'm not sure about this, Mitch," she choked out. Translation: Let me off.

"That's only because you've never ridden rapids before."

"There's a reason for that."

"Sure, but you'll have the best time, and once you do, you'll want to do it over and over again."

"I seriously doubt I'll suddenly turn that loony."

She wanted to gaze at the shore with longing—if only she could see it. But her stubborn eyes wouldn't look past Mitch. She couldn't see anything but the solid granite lines of his face, the trustworthy honor that burned steadily in his hazel eyes and the unyielding strength as he held her safely against the river's might. His chuckle shot through her like winter thunder.

Every instinct within her shrieked at her to run to higher ground, quick, before he let go, before she was dashed on the rapids that lay ahead like a hungry predator.

But it was too late. Before she could protest, he was pushing her and her inner tube more deeply into the river, toward the hungry, gurgling, dangerous current. The rocky beach floated farther away, and safety with it. The undercurrent grew ferocious, sucking at her feet, which were dangling off the end of the tube. The river's gurgle became a menacing low-throated growl.

Okay, time to get off now.

"M-Mitch?" She couldn't believe it. He'd released his hold on her inner tube. He was letting her go.

While the current sped her away from him, she watched him helplessly. Water sluiced off his sun-browned skin as he hopped onto his tube. He stretched out on the inflated tube with easy confidence, as if nothing rattled him, nothing troubled him, as if he could do anything.

Her feelings for him were absolutely without a doubt way too strong. She clutched the slippery sides of the tube, fighting down panic on many levels, and floated into the jet stream of the current. She sped along so fast that the world whirred by in a blur of green cottonwoods and amber wild grasses dry from the midsummer sun, the green grass of the city park and the clean pure blue of the river.

Her feelings were speeding along too, out of control, just like this inner tube she couldn't stop if she tried—no brakes. The rapids were imminent, she could clearly see the upcoming white crests of water splashing over and around black protrusions of big river rocks. She was going to hit them.

Oh, Lord, don't let me hit them.

God didn't seem to answer—how could He hear her over the roar of the river? And suddenly there was a bump against the back of her inner tube. Mitch had caught up with her. He'd come to save her.

"Fun, right?" His wide, happy smile was a grin of a man who lacked all common sense. "You ain't seen nothing yet. Hold on!"

Hold on? To what? He was nuts. Absolutely nuts.

Her fingers squeaked along the rubber tubing as she tried to get a better grip. The river bucked up like a wild bronco and then bowed back down and up again, whirling her backwards and tossing her up into the air like the worst carnival ride. Suddenly she was spinning toward a fast-approaching hunk of granite that looked very capable of breaking her bones if she rammed into it.

But at the last minute, the white-frothing water steered her to the side of the boulder and with a swoosh rolled her around another. Somewhere behind her Mitch was whooping like a kid on a fair ride, but she couldn't see anything except the swirling water turning to bubbling foam. The rapids tossed her up and down without end, as if trying to shake her bones from her body.

With a last surge of effort, the river reared a final time, tossing her upward with such force that she soared into the hot summer air. Wow, it was like flying. The black ring of rubber shot from beneath her and out of sight and she was falling, gravity-bound, watching the swirling water rising up to meet her in a cool splash of wetness. It was like landing in happiness, then she was sinking deep.

A steely hand caught her forearm and stopped her descent. Mitch's hand, Mitch's touch, his protection as she whooshed to the surface, her pulse pounding with joy. Water sluiced down her face and she drew in a mouthful of air, laughing, as Mitch held her steady, treading water.

"You're right. That was fun." She swiped a wet hank of hair out of her eyes to see him more clearly.

Maybe for the first time. His short dark hair was plastered to his head and seemed to accent the strong high blades of his cheekbones, his straight nose and granite jaw.

But as he gathered her in his arms and helped her ashore, where her inner tube drifted, trapped against the bank, it was his touch that affected her. The shadows within her faded, and there was only light.

"How about another run?" Mitch asked, humor glinting in his hazel eyes because he already knew the answer.

Okay, so he'd been right. "I'll beat you there." She hooked her inner tube and started running along the grassy shore.

Hours later, Mitch took another bite of his hand-dipped ice-cream cone. Walking through the grassy public park with Kelly was pretty nice. "This has to be one of the best things on earth."

"This? An ice-cream cone?" The lowering slant of the sunlight brushed her with bronze. She tipped her head back, scattering the long, damp locks of golden hair. "It *is* good, but it's just an ice-cream cone."

"Are you kidding? This chocolate crust is real dark chocolate. The cone is bakery quality, it doesn't come out of a box. You can't get this just anywhere."

"It's good, sure." She ate her cone by peeling off the thick chocolate layer first, eating it piece by piece. "But there are probably thousands of places that sell something like this or better."

"See, you take it for granted." He resisted the urge to touch the wayward locks whipping in the wind across her face, to feel the silken strands against his palm.

"That's because you can pick up an ice-cream cone all the time. When I'm deployed, I don't get things like this."

"And that makes it one of the best things on earth?" Kelly picked another curve of chocolate off the top of her cone. She was smirking, as if he greatly amused her.

"It's probably not one of the *very* best things, but it goes on my list anyway."

"What list?"

"The one I keep in my head. For nights when I'm with my team and we're hunkered down on some remote mountain in a blizzard, wet to the skin and half-frozen. There's no fire because we don't want the smoke and the flames. No tent, no dry clothes, nothing but a meal in a can. That's when I haul out my list and try to remember all the good things, so it doesn't seem as bad."

"Remembering ice cream is going to make you feel better in a blizzard?"

"Okay, right. I'll save that for the desert list. When it's 123 degrees in the shade, except there is no shade, then I'll remember this afternoon. How the river was cooling—not too cold, just right. The way you laughed when I pulled you up after the rapids. How this feels right now, eating ice cream and walking with you."

"It's the ice cream you'll remember. Not me." She blushed prettily.

Yep, he was hooked. Something more powerful than tenderness filled him up until it felt impossible to breathe. "Oh, I think there's a fair-to-middling chance I'll remember you."

Like he could ever forget.

He caught a dripping edge of his ice cream, but the rich crunchy outside and the melting chocolate center wasn't what filled his senses. "You could write to me, when I'm away. Right?"

"Write to you? Well, I suppose I *could* be persuaded."

"Okay, what'll it take? How about a burger with the works at that stand over there?"

"We just ate ice cream."

"But it's nearly five o'clock. I believe in eating dessert first."

"I believe in eating dessert any time you can." Kelly managed to keep her tone light, although her heart wasn't—not at all. She didn't want to think of him leaving.

"I'm going to miss—" She couldn't quite say the words.

"Yeah, me too." Without words, he understood.

Without words, they walked together, side by side. When he took her hand in his, it was all she could do to hold closed the locks on her already adoring heart.

Could it be true? Was the baby finally asleep?

With the infant snuggled in her arms, Kelly eased the rocking chair to a stop and studied Shannon's sweet cherub's face. Her eyes were closed, her rosebud mouth relaxed, lost in dreams. Her warm weight felt utterly limp as she breathed in a slow, sweet rhythm.

It was amazing someone so small could cry so loud and long, but how could Kelly mind? Holding the little one and rocking her until she calmed was a precious thing. After all, teething, even with all the ways to soothe tender gums, was painful business.

As she carefully rose from the comfy chair, she watched to make sure that the baby didn't stir. With love, she eased Shannon into her snug crib, adorned with the cutest patterned sheets, and dodged the rainbow-colored mobile dangling overhead.

It would be so easy to start dreaming, Kelly thought, standing over the crib, not quite able to take a step away. Already her heart was forming a wish she could not give life to. And it was Mitch's fault for being so wonderful, so everything a girl like her could ever want.

At least she had good control over her heart. The last time she'd made fairy-tale wishes for true love Joe had been taken from her. She'd learned her lesson the hard way too many times. Fairy tales weren't real.

Taking care not to make a sound, she stepped back until she reached the doorway. So far so good. Since the baby didn't stir, Kelly continued on, padding quietly down the hall, past the older child's bedroom door, closed tight while he slept.

She made her way to the kitchen, and she couldn't help the happiness rising up inside her. What a wonderful day she'd had. Not only had she aced her test, thanks to a few extremely important pointers from Mitch last week, but she'd had the best time with him.

Her spirit still felt uplifted as she ran hot soapy water in the sink and started washing up the supper dishes. The faint aroma of frozen pepperoni pizza lingered in the air as she scrubbed the stubborn baked-on cheese off the cookie sheet.

She was rinsing the soap off when a faint electronic tune sounded in the far corner of the room, from her half-unzipped backpack slung over one of the kitchen chairs. Who would be calling her this late? It was after ten. Drying her hands as she went, she snatched her cell phone out of the pack's front pocket.

The ID screen only said Out of Area. Hoping it wasn't her mother trying to get hold of her, she answered tentatively. "Hello?"

"I know it's late." Mitch's baritone sounded short and strained. "I figured you'd still be babysitting."

"Yep, for probably another thirty minutes. You know, I'm still smiling. I had the best day."

"I know you did. Your eyes were shining."

"At first I thought I'd drown, what with all the near-death experiences."

"You didn't even come close to drowning. I wouldn't have let anything happen to you."

"I know. I had complete confidence in you. Otherwise I would have never let you drag me out into the middle of that river in the first place."

Yep, taking a chest full of shrapnel must feel just like this, Mitch thought. Deep, sharp cuts that exposed you clear to the heart. "We have new orders. We're leaving. I wanted to say goodbye."

"Wh-what? I thought you had another two weeks here."

The raw places in his chest seemed to throb, as fresh wounds did when air touched them. "Yeah. Orders change all the time. Believe me, this is not the way I want it, but in thirty minutes, I'll be on a bird out of here."

"Just like that?" In the background there was a faint

scraping sound, like a wooden chair against linoleum. He pictured her clearly sitting down in that graceful way she moved and a crinkle digging in above her nose, the one he liked so much. Her voice became thin and concerned. "It's just so sudden. Is everything all right?"

"We lost a team and we're being brought in to replace them."

"That doesn't sound good. Y-you'll be coming back, r-right?"

He took a deep breath. *Please, Lord, help her to understand this.* He knew she had to be remembering how she'd lost Joe. "Believe me, I fully intend to come back. I've been doing this for a long time. I'm still here."

"But what you do sounds dangerous."

"I can't lie and say it isn't." He wanted to say this right, for Kelly's sake, ignoring the noise and bustle of his team packing up, all business. He was short on time. "We're well-trained and well-equipped. I know how to take care of myself and my team. You don't need to worry about me."

"Maybe I will anyway."

"No way. Put that energy toward something useful. Like acing your math final."

She didn't say anything.

That troubled him. She'd had a lot of people move in and out of her life. She still didn't trust him enough with those stories, but he could guess at what they were based on with what she'd already told him. In and out of foster care. Burying her fiancé. She'd known too much loss.

How did he make her see that he didn't plan on contributing to it? He didn't know. "No one can look ahead and see what's to come, but that's why we have faith, right?"

"Right. Faith is believing in things not seen. In trusting that the Lord will work things out for the good of His faithful."

"Exactly. So have a little faith, okay? In God. And it wouldn't hurt to have some in me, too."

"I already do." Her heart felt heavier with each breath. Her chest tighter. "Y-you have my e-mail address. If you get lonely over there, you're always welcome to drop me a note."

"I get awfully busy. I—" There was a lot of sound in the background. He came back on the line. "I've got to go. I just wish—"

Oh, she, too, wished that he didn't have to go. "Be safe, Mitch."

"I will. Goodbye, Kelly."

I can't take one more goodbye, Lord. There was no way she could make herself say more to him, so she disconnected and sat in the silence and shadows.

By the time the plane had leveled out, the city of Bozeman was nothing but tiny pinpricks of light tossed in the velvety night. Mitch pressed forward against the cold glass window, trying to keep the city in view. Kelly was down there somewhere.

I needed more time with her, Lord. It was tough to wrestle down his frustration. While he believed the Lord caused things to happen for a reason, what good could come of leaving her now?

I didn't have enough time to win her heart. It was

like starting something he'd never have the chance of finishing. Like a loose end, unraveling. In another two weeks, maybe it would have been a different story. Now, he figured he might never know.

The city lights faded to black. The glacier crests of the Rockies below shone luminescent in the moonlight. Emptiness filled him like the wide endless stretch of the night. The gnawing feeling he'd left everything vital behind ate at him.

Kelly would be done with her babysitting job by now. She'd probably be heading home. She'd disconnected without saying goodbye.

That couldn't be a good sign. Not a good one, at all.

So many regrets. He disliked every single one of them.

Images of their afternoon together stuck in his mind. How she'd dazzled him when he'd pulled her up out of the water. He could still hear her laughter. How tender she'd made him feel. How right she'd been in his arms. The vanilla scent of her shampoo.

How could it be that the day wasn't yet over and he already missed her?

This might have been God's leading, but Mitch also knew with absolute certainty that she was his heart's choice.

In the well-lit apartment parking lot, Kelly locked her car door and glanced around the dark vehicles to make sure she was safe. The only movement was the shadows of the trees when the breeze rustled them. She sorted through the keys on the ring as she walked up the sidewalk. High overhead an airplane rumbled. It was a passenger jet from the local airport, not a military plane, but she thought of Mitch heading toward places unknown. Toward dangers unknown. And that made her feel as vulnerable as an exposed nerve.

There was no comfort in the hot, still night as she unlocked the front door and stepped into the darkness. Cool air blew over her as she crept into the kitchen, careful not to make a noise. Lexie was probably asleep by now, she thought as she opened the fridge and pulled out an orange soda.

But there was no comfort from the sugary drink. While the bubbles hissed and popped in the stillness, she curled up in the overstuffed chair in the living room where the moonlight and the glow from the streetlights fell through the window and onto her.

Mitch's words came back to her, rubbing on the exposed nerves in her heart. *I get awfully busy. I—I've got to go.*

In other words, she shouldn't count on him writing to her. She remembered his saying it was rare for him to have much free time. So, he was going to be way too busy to keep in touch. And, in time, too busy to remember her.

And if that made her sad, it wasn't like she was going to admit it. This was just as well—and how things were meant to be. The way she wanted it. She was keeping herself here on the riverbank of life. And she was afraid that if she reached out for those good, rare blessings she wanted, they would be whisked from her grasp.

Just like always.

Just like Joe had been.

Her devotional was in her backpack, and she dug it out. She couldn't remember the morning's passage—it had been such a long day. She felt a craving for the Scripture and flipped to the morning's text.

> I teach you what is for your good, and lead you on the way you should go.

She gazed out at the night stars. Mitch was out there somewhere.

Keep him safe, Lord. He's a good man. Please give him a piece of the happiness You have in store for me.

It was all she had to give him. Mitch had his life, she had hers. That was the way it was. But she would always hold close the memories of their friendship. She would always treasure the chance to have gotten to know such a good man.

Chapter Nine

Kelly sat in a quiet corner of the campus cafeteria in the wash of the early-fall morning sunlight. Outside the sparkling windows other students hurried to their classes. She took a sip of coffee and turned the page of her sociology book.

Deep in the pocket of her backpack, her cell phone began to ring. Probably Amy calling to confirm—or to cancel—babysitting for a few nights this week. Kelly flipped open her phone. It wasn't Amy. She didn't recognize the number, but it wasn't a local one.

She answered it, and popping static filled her ear. "Hello?"

"Can you hear me okay?" asked a deep, familiar baritone that sounded very far away.

No, it couldn't be. "Mitch? Is that you?"

"The one and only. I'm just glad you remember me. It's been a while since I've talked to you."

How did she tell him that the days of September had slipped away like water down a drain, but he had been in her prayers every one of them. "You sound like you're calling from the moon."

"Just about. I feel like I'm in another world. There are no ice-cream cones here."

Oh, he sounded so good—so good and alive and strong…just like Mitch. She closed her eyes, and there he was in her mind's eye that day on the river. Standing waist-deep in water and grinning at her with a challenge. So larger than life and vital, looking as if nothing could hurt him. Of course, she knew that he was as vulnerable as anyone. "I can't believe it. I thought I'd never hear from you again."

"No way. You just try and get rid of me. I thought we were…friends."

"We are." The light in her heart brightened.

"I've got about ten minutes on this card. It has to be early there."

"It's twenty past seven in the morning, but I'm already on campus. Sitting in the cafeteria and trying to get some reading done before class. It's good to hear you. I've been—" Missing you. "—worried about you."

"Hey, I miss you. The guys I hang with aren't nearly as pleasing to the eye. How did the math final go?"

"I pulled an A. Thanks to you, but you don't want to hear about my classes."

"Sure I do. I put you in prayer every night. Even when I'm out with my team doing things I can't tell you about, in places I can't tell you about either. Let's just say you're on my list, Kelly."

"L-list?"

Mitch's chest hitched painfully at the uncertainty in

her voice. Nearly four weeks had passed since he'd left, and yet everything came back in a single heartbeat. The way her honey-blond hair gleamed. The dark-blue strands in her jeweled eyes. How her smile lit up his world.

She was the one. Thousands of miles away and continents apart, mighty affection crashed through him like a tsunami.

Whatever he did, he couldn't let her know. Not yet. The last thing he wanted to do was to scare her. He cleared his throat. "The list of the best things, to get me through. You know: ice-cream cones, riding the rapids, walking in the sunshine with a good friend."

"Right. That list." She sounded relieved, relaxed.

He was glad about that. They were friends now, but in time, he thought they could be more.

Her gentle alto warmed. "You're on my list, too."

"That means a lot. You can't guess how much." He didn't know how to tell her how tough the past weeks had been. It was a different planet where he was, or it seemed that way, where the phone bank was a luxury, and the fact that he'd had a lukewarm shower and hot chow for the first time in three weeks felt like a blessing. So were phone cards. His time was ticking away, and he hated that.

"When you called me before you left last month, you mentioned a team that was l-lost."

He squeezed his eyes shut, briefly, to hold everything in. "Yep. No one died. They were lucky, but there were serious casualties."

"Anyone you knew?"

"Yep. All of 'em. Don't worry. Those guys in 3rd Recon aren't as superior as my platoon."

She heard the catch in his voice. "I suppose you're invincible, huh, Mr. Action Figure?"

"Nope, just very careful. I intend to make it back home. You liked floating the rapids so much, I thought I might make good on my threat to take you mountain-climbing."

"I'm going to hold you to that threat."

His voice rumbled with reassurance. "Then we've got a deal. I'll be here in camp for a bit. They have us training pretty hard, but I'll be able to e-mail."

The line was crackling worse. "Mitch, I can barely hear you."

"Time's up. I've got to—"

There was a click and then nothing.

Be safe, she added silently as she disconnected.

The noise of the cafeteria was increasing around her as more students filed in for a quick breakfast. The tables nearby filled with students who gathered in groups to talk or sit quietly alone with their books and their coffee.

How come Mitch had such a hold on her heart? It took all her effort to turn her attention back to the work before her. She kept going over their conversation, over the sound of his voice. She kept picturing him, so handsome and capable in his camouflage clothing. Her heart gave a tug of admiration.

Careful, Kelly. No dreaming allowed.

Her phone rang again. Foolish seeds of hope sparked

inside her, but it was Amy's number on the ID screen. Life went on as it should—with school, work and babysitting.

She knew better than to hope for more, but she sure wanted to.

Mitch hung up the phone. The hootch around him buzzed with pieces of conversations between other soldiers and loved ones at home, making him feel more alone than ever. Kelly was just so far away.

He tried to picture her in a campus cafeteria, probably lots of tables and chairs, noisy talking and the clatter of flatwear and dishes. She'd said she was reading, but was she studying? Or reading her devotional? He should have asked more questions to fill in the missing pieces.

She'd probably bought a cup of coffee, but anything else? A muffin? A breakfast sandwich? What was she wearing? It could get pretty cool in Bozeman—probably a pair of jeans and one of those feminine cotton blouses she was always wearing. Maybe with a sweater. Was her hair pulled back in a ponytail with those little silken wisps curling around her face, or was it unbound, falling in a long sleek wave past her shoulders?

Not enough time. Not time on the phone and nowhere near enough time with her in Montana. When a man got down to it, there was never enough, not in a life, and he hated this feeling of regret. Of leaving things unfinished. His life had always been tidy, he liked things that way. It's what made him a good Force Recon marine. But the loose ends he'd left when he'd said goodbye to Kelly were ones he feared would unravel with distance.

There's not much I can do from here, he thought.

His way of life was rugged and solitary, and there was no room for much else but his work. It would be simple just to let this go, whatever it was building between him and Kelly. That would be the safest route. That way he wasn't putting anything on the line. But he didn't want to move on from her, not deep down.

As uncertain as the path ahead was, he was committed. He was going to risk it all. She was far away, but he would do what he could.

He'd write her and he'd keep writing her until this tour was over and he was back on American soil.

While the noodles from her box of macaroni and cheese were boiling, Kelly set up her laptop on the dinette table in the eating nook and went online.

Should she be checking her e-mail? No. She had a ton of reading to do, but could she concentrate?

No way. Her conversation with Mitch had been on her mind all day. Of course.

Hearing his voice had done her heart good. Her day had been brighter as she hurried across campus from one class to another, took notes, grabbed a bite to eat on her way to her afternoon shift at the bookstore. Knowing that he hadn't forgotten her, that he still wanted to be friends, meant more than she wanted to admit to herself or to anyone.

She popped up from the table to give the noodles a stir—they were bubbling merrily on medium high—and then returned to study her screen. There was a new e-mail. Already? She couldn't believe her eyes. Her computer screen still looked the same—it wasn't her imagination. There really was an e-mail from Mitch. She opened it and started reading.

Kelly,
No hand-dipped cones here. Chow hall pizza isn't half bad, except there are no cheesy sticks. But no complaining there. It's a step up from the meals in a can I get when we're out. Base camp is basically a lot of tents, but we've got heat most of the time. I'm glad I got hold of you this morning. Good to hear a friendly voice from home. How did your classes go today? The next time you order pizza, eat a slice for me.
Mitch

The stove timer beeped a rhythmic electronic warning, dragging her away from Mitch's note. Already she felt happy as she drained the pasta, measured out the margarine and milk and stirred in the powdered cheese packet. Adding a generous sprinkling of pepper, she stirred until the cheese was warm and melted and dumped it onto a plate. On her way back to the laptop she grabbed a fork and sat down.

After a quick blessing over her food, she reread Mitch's e-mail, wondering what on earth to say back. He would probably be bored by her life; after all, he got to do all kinds of exciting things in a day. Her life was almost as boring as you could get.

She tried to picture living in a large camp of tents, but she could only imagine reruns of a seventies TV show that she'd watched over the years. Maybe it was something like that, sleep in one tent, shower in another, eat in another. If he'd mentioned the blessing of having heat that worked, then he had to be somewhere very cold.

She had no clue what to write. As she munched on her mac and cheese, she gazed out the window at the turning poplar leaves and the sunset blazing purple and magenta across the dome of the darkening sky. What would she say if he was standing in front of her?

Her heart stirred, and she started to type.

Mitch,

You don't know what it means to me that we can keep our friendship going when you're so far away. I get pretty wrapped up with studying—don't be shocked—I'm a little bit of a study-aholic, to use Lexie's term. Between trying to keep my A average and work enough hours to meet my monthly bills, I have about two hours left over in a week for a social life—which is mostly attending a weekly Bible study.

Lexie has been a blessing for a roommate because she tends to drag me places with her, like on Sunday afternoon. We went to the Museum of the Rockies with a couple of her friends and looked at fossils and Native American artifacts.

You're laughing, aren't you? Because that is so not a social life by most people's definition. The college group at church is having a singles' get-together at the town ice cream parlor next Friday night. Lexie has already told me she's meeting me after my shift at the bookstore and dragging me there. Should be fun.

Not only will I have a slice of pizza for you, but I'll make the sacrifice of eating a hand-dipped chocolate ice-cream cone for you, too. I'll suffer, sure, but friendship is worth it.

Blessings to you, and stay safe.

Kelly

P.S. What kind of meals come in a can?

As she polished off her meal, Kelly reread the e-mail, corrected spelling and sent it. It wasn't as if he'd have time to e-mail her for a while, but it felt good to write to him.

Maybe God had placed Mitch on her path because He knew how solitary her life had been since she'd buried Joe. Maybe He knew that Mitch needed a friend too, being so far from home and in danger.

She took comfort in that.

"Hey, I'm off to the library." Lexie burst out of her bedroom in a flurry. "Where did I put my card? I'm losing my mind. That's what I get for majoring in psychology. They say you gravitate toward what you need most, which is apparently therapy for me. Oh, now where did my keys go?"

"Over here." Kelly blinked to bring her eyes into focus, she'd been reading solidly for the past two hours. Night had fallen and the heat had kicked on. The weather was getting colder. She thought of Mitch and hoped that wherever he was, he was keeping warm. She grabbed the ring of keys on the coffee table by her mug of herbal tea and gave them a toss.

Lexie caught them. "Thanks. Oh, and I'd better leave the rent check with you now, or I'll totally forget tomorrow. I've got it written out and everything." She pulled a check out of her pocket and dropped it on the counter. "I'll be back late. Anything you need while I'm out? Okay, I'm gone. See ya!"

Alone once again, Kelly tried to sink into her reading, but no such luck. In theory, her mind should be occupied enough with her studies to completely shove out every last thought of Mitch Dalton.

The practical aspect was a little different. Since she was never going to be able to concentrate properly unless she checked, she popped online while she microwaved another cup of apple cinnamon tea. Like he'd had time to answer her. No, not when she hadn't heard from him in a month. He'd already called, he'd already e-mailed.

She was not going to analyze the fact that she was hoping he'd answered. Apparently, Lexie wasn't the only one in need of therapy.

What she was not going to do was to check. She was going to go on to the library's Web site and do a little preliminary research for her next paper. Then, when she was done, she'd check her e-mail account.

The computer made an electronic bleep. An instant message popped on the screen from Mitchell Dalton. Kelly, got time to type at me?

The light inside her brightened another notch. She started to type.

For you, Mr. Action Figure, sure. I didn't know your extensive scouting skills included the ability to instant message.

She hit Send and waited. In a few moments, his answer popped on the screen.

I know a lot of stuff. So, what's this about a singles' meeting?

Now why would he ask that? she wondered. He was probably interested in the ice cream. She typed, You know the creamery shop downtown?

He answered in an instant. They have the best banana splits.

They do, she agreed. I usually get the chocolate fudge sundae, the one they sprinkle peanuts on top.

His answer shot back, You're killing me. I just had an unrecognizable casserole. It tasted like tuna and creamed potatoes.

Yum, she replied. It puts my mac and cheese to shame.

She left the message to post while she grabbed her steaming cup of water from the microwave. When she returned to the table, Mitch's answer was waiting for her.

You didn't elaborate on the singles' thing. You said you didn't date.

She shook her head in disbelief. Mitch had been blatantly clear about only wanting a friendship with her, as she'd been with him. She typed, It's not a date. It's a church group function.

A singles' function. His reply was almost instant.

I go for the ice cream and fellowship. I don't think I'll ever date again, she wrote.

Why not?

She stared at his question. The fragments of her past began to whisper behind the locked places in her heart. She wanted to silence those whispers, but her fingers were typing the words before she thought them.

Because I've stopped believing that good things are meant for me. She hit Send and waited, watching the cursor blink and feeling the beat of panic pulse through her. That was way too honest, but it was too late to take back the words.

Mitch's answer came immediately. I don't believe that. Not for a single nanosecond.

Old wounds ached like a sore tooth as she steeled her heart and wrote the plain truth. Life isn't a fairy tale—at least my life isn't. End of discussion. You never answered the question in the e-mail I sent. What kind of meals do you get in a can?

Nice try, came his answer, but I'm not gonna let you change the subject like that. What happened with Joe?

Her hands shook as she typed an answer. Two Saturdays ago I went to put flowers on Joe's grave. He's been gone three years now.

Maybe that was being way too honest—for herself and for poor Mitch who was just wanting to hear about the ice cream shop back home.

Then came his unexpected reply. I'm sorry. I know how painful it is to lose someone you care about. If it happens often enough, there comes a time when you can't stand to let anyone else too close. Not one more time.

He knew. Kelly squeezed her eyes shut to hold the emotions inside. How did she answer him? Anything honest she could say would hurt too much.

More words appeared on the screen. I've lost a few buddies over the years. Men I respected and thought of as my brothers. It's never easy to understand why. You had to have been devastated.

Yes, she typed and then stopped. Emotions she'd frozen in place and tucked away seemed to melt like icicles, and the drip of fresh pain made her want to push Mitch away and keep pushing.

The pieces of the truth she'd buried, that she hadn't shared with anyone, lay exposed.

She typed, I was devastated, but some wishes aren't meant to come true. You don't want to hear about that.

He answered, Sure I do.

Just find the words, Kelly. She dug down deep, and found the strength. Prayed for the ability to keep the tears out of her eyes and the sorrow from her heart. She should just tell Mitch, and then he would quit bringing it up. Besides, maybe it would be better for her to release the pain, write it down instead of saying the words out loud.

She began to type. Joe was working as a firefighter. You know the terrible forest fires we had in the national forests a few summers ago?

Yep, they made the national news. Even I read about them. Didn't a couple of fire fighters die over there? One of them was Joe?

* * *

She took a gulp of air as Mitch's question scraped against her exposed, open wounds. Yes, she answered. An unexpected high wind kicked up and trapped him and two other members of his team. This happened eight days before we were to be married.

She hung her head. She couldn't type another word. When she was finally steady enough to wipe at her burning eyes and face the screen, Mitch's answer was there, waiting patiently for her. You must have thought you'd finally had a real home. You lost everything with Joe. I'm sorry for that.

It wasn't meant to be, she typed and hit Send, feeling the shadows in the corners press against the light, against her.

She'd fallen so in love with the idea of being married and of being welcomed into such a warm and loving family. The little girl who'd always felt alone and adrift had finally come home to a husband and a kind extended family. It was her most heartfelt dream.

And to stand in the church sanctuary silent with hope and promises, and to plan, instead of a wedding, a funeral. To tuck away the dreamy wedding gown of silk and lace that Joe's sister had sewn for her and realize that this is how it would always be.

Mitch's answer flashed onto the screen. You're not alone.

How was it that he could know the words she most needed? She felt alone, at heart, at spirit, down to the soul. She knew God cared, that He watched over her, but not even her unerring faith could chase away the loneliness that clung with hungry talons and would not let go.

More of Mitch's reply scrolled across the screen. "Yet it was our weaknesses he carried; it was our sorrows that weighed him down."

She recognized the passage from Isaiah. Those words were a comfort that helped to chase away the memories lying as vulnerable as an exposed root: memories of the little girl she'd been, the child with no stability or security, always wishing for someone to love her, just wanting to fit in, to belong to a real family.

The aftereffects of those memories left a bitter, cutting residue and her throat burned with unfelt emotions. She tried so hard to swallow them down, but they remained like a sticky mass, a tangle of feelings that she could not sort out. It took all of her effort to will the fragments of her past, of her memories, back into the locked room in her soul.

They typed at each other for another twenty minutes before he had to go. With training exercises awaiting him, he signed off, his heart heavy. He could feel the fragments of her broken dreams as sorely as if they were his own.

He missed her with a force so strong, he didn't want to examine it. But as he headed out into the bitter cold, and into the remote base camp of tents, not even the miles between them could break the connection he'd felt with Kelly.

His twisted-tight emotions roiling inside him began to unravel, thread by thread. He wanted to protect her.

He wanted to comfort her. He wanted to make sure she was never alone. That she never hurt like that again. Overwhelming tenderness detonated like a cluster bomb, and he gritted his teeth as the explosion hit. There was no hiding from it. No denying it.

This love for her was as steady as an ocean's current. As steadfast as the northern star. And twice as enduring.

It remained through the day of exercises and all through the night and into each long absorbing day of hard work.

It did not relent.

Chapter Ten

With the light of a new morning, Kelly had nothing but regrets. She'd stirred up feelings that she hadn't intended to. What troubled her most of all was that she trusted Mitch enough to tell him.

It had been easier, sure, since he was so far away, and she hadn't had to actually say the words out loud. But talking about her loss of Joe was one thing. Feeling Mitch's understanding was another.

He was beyond wonderful for having listened to her so politely, when he'd probably expected a much lighter electronic conversation. He'd been way too close, ironically, seeing as he was half a world away. Without seeing her, without so much as hearing her voice, he'd been able to crack her careful defenses. Defenses she hadn't realized were breachable until he'd walked into her life.

There was an e-mail from Mitch.

Kelly,
Glad you let me steal time out of your studies last night.

I didn't really know Joe back in high school. You know he was a year older and ran with a different crowd, but he was a good guy. I am sorry for the grief you've gone through. We lost a team member this past year, he and I met at boot and we were buds. It was like losing a brother. Nothing is quite the same again—it isn't meant to be.

Hang in there. Write me when you get a chance. They keep you pretty busy here, but when you stop moving, you miss home and everyone there. I'm glad we're friends.
Mitch

Kelly took a sip of her coffee, warmed through by his words. Relieved, too. She put aside her cup and started to type.

Mitch,
Talking with you was the best possible study break. I was worried I'd been too personal last night. I'm used to keeping the real painful stuff private. It's just easier to deal with that way. The psychology classes I've taken say otherwise, but it works for me.

I know you've known loss, too. I am sorry about your friend. I imagine, when you eat, sleep, work and train together, that builds an immeasurably strong friendship.

I'm running late this morning, I should not be online but I was glad to see a note from you in my inbox and wanted to say thanks for listening. I'm pretty glad we're friends, too. I've got to go or I'm going to be stuck in the traditional 7:45 a.m. campus traffic jam.

Plus, then I'll get the farthest out parking spot and have a stitch in my side if I have to run to get to class on time. I have a policy on running, jogging or any kind of exercise—I am firmly against it.

Have a great day and stay safe.
Blessings, Kelly

Dear Kelly,
What? A no-exercise policy? That would never work for me. I have more of an exercise-only policy. I've been on the go since 0500 and it's after 2000. One hundred percent of my workday is physical. Did you make it to class on time? Inquiring minds wanna know.
Mitch

Dear Mitch,
I have a strict no-tardy policy to go along with my no-skipping-class policy. I'm sadly scholastically minded. I often sit in the front row, take copious notes and then study my notes that evening.

Scary, I know. I'm lucky my roommate still talks to me. She says I'm way too intense so that's why she hauls me to social events. There's an on-campus thing, Shakespeare in the Grass, that the drama department does, weather permitting. We're going to see The Tempest and then hit the pizza buffet. The play is free and there's a great student discount at the pizza place. So it's a night out that fits a student's budget perfectly.
Keeping you in prayer, Kelly

Hi there, Kelly,

Ice cream and pizza in the same week? See, I'm fishing for information. How did the singles' thing turn out?
Mitch

Dear Mitch,
I had a banana split with extra fudge sauce in your honor. Lexie and I got together with our friends Jessica and Rose. Sadly, the same guys keep coming to these events and no one is actually apparently going to date them, so the singles' thing is a misnomer. Plus, I am, like, three years older than any guy there, since I'm working my way through school so slowly. Jessica and Rose are coming to the play tomorrow, and because these guys overheard us talking, now the entire singles' group is coming. Stay tuned. I'll let you know if this blond perfect-looking dude that really likes Lexie actually talks her into dating. Lexie has a strict no-dating policy too. She thinks guys are untrustworthy.
Sincerely, Kelly

Dearest Kelly,
Hey, I'm trustworthy.
Mitch, the most trustworthy guy ever.

Mitch,
I never said you weren't. Lexie actually gave you two thumbs up, a rare review. I think you won her over with the cheesy sticks.
Blessings, Kelly

Hey, Kelly,
What can I say? Buying cheesy sticks is always the sign of a quality individual. I'm kidding, but there's no way you can tell from here. I've never seen a Shakespeare play. My impression is a stuffy production where guys wear tights. Doesn't sound dignified to me. I prefer something with a lot more action. Hey, is watching Shakespeare better outside or something?
Mitch, the uncultured

Mitch,
You might be able to scale a glacier on a mountain peak or know how to scuba dive and you've probably done that sliding-down-the-rope thing from helicopters, but you don't know excitement until you've experienced Shakespeare. There's a lot of action. If you're ever in this neck of the woods again, and school is in session, I'll drag you to one.

The play we went to this evening starts with a ship that wrecks at sea in a storm, and right when it was supposed to be raining in the play, it really did start to rain. There were cold storm gusts while the characters were getting blown around by the storm in the play. It was really cool, actually, but we were drenched. Lightning started up, and they had to call the production off due to the real tempest. We (the girls) hit the pizza place, stuffed ourselves with pizza and cheesy sticks and talked girl talk until about nine.

How did you spend your Saturday night?
Grace and peace, Kelly

Dearest Kelly,
Cleaning my gun. Then we had a rousing match of chess. I won every match except the championship of the night. It was a close call, but I fell in a brilliant move by Luke after an hour of battle. At least I went down with honor.

Cheesy sticks and pizza? I need details.
Take good care okay? Mitch

Dear Mitch,
We had our pick of every variety of pizza. I make it a policy to have a slice of each kind—the works, the meat supreme, the veggie, the Hawaiian, pepperoni, sausage and pepperoni. You name it. All but the cheese. The owner always boxes up the leftover pizza when the buffet ends and distributes it to the students. He's an alumni and says he gets the student budget thing.

This is why we had cold pizza for breakfast. I went for the straight pepperoni but Lexie prefers the pepperoni and sausage mix for a higher protein breakfast. And guess what we had for lunch after church? You guessed it. Pizza. Enough calories to see me through a long afternoon study session. Do you get Sundays off?
I'm still keeping you in prayer, Kelly

Kelly,
Only in the sense that we're fragged for a mission so this afternoon is prep. I'll be out of range for a while, but I'll e-mail you when I get back. It's rumored we may do that sliding-down-the-rope thing from a helicopter that you mentioned before.

Thanks for your prayers, Mitch

Dearest Mitch,
I know, I have an amazing lack of military vernacular. Keep your head down. Isn't that what they always say in those old war movies? Stay safe.
Sending even more prayers, Kelly

Dearest Kelly,
Count on it. You're in my prayers too.
Mitch

Why did stat class always give her a headache? Because math was involved, that's why.

Kelly rubbed her forehead as she followed the stream of students searching for lunch. Noise from the lounge drifted into the busy corridor and Kelly picked up the concerned voice of a newscaster.

"Today, three marines were injured, when—"

The noise surged around her and drowned out the televised report.

She cut through the student traffic flow to the doorway of the lounge, where students sat with their lunch or books, listening to a cable news network. On the screen in the corner, she could make out a picture of a burning car in a desert-city street before the scene flashed on to other international news.

Mitch was in the mountains and not in the desert, so that news report wasn't in any way about him. But that didn't stop her fear or her worry for him. That was reasonable—he might think he was invincible, but he was wrong. He was not made of titanium.

The roar of the passing students drew her away from the lounge. She wanted to be able to find a table and the longer she stood in the hallway, the less likely that was going to be. She joined the herd moving toward the turnstiles at the cafeteria. The buzz of conversation, the clatter of trays and crunch of the ice machine echoed around her. It had been nearly five hours since Mitch's e-mail, and you'd think she'd stop thinking about him by now, but no.

There he was, front and center. What did she do about that? She cared about him, of course she did. He was a friend. A friend, nothing more, right?

As she grabbed a tray and maneuvered through the crowd toward the beverage dispensers, Mitch remained in her thoughts along with the strength of emotion she'd felt when they were online together. She missed him. It was that simple.

Not only had Mitch slipped beneath her defenses as if they were made of water, but he'd made her care about him. He'd made such an impression, he'd been such a good friend, that she missed having him present in her life.

It was certainly okay to care about a friend, so she shouldn't let it bother her that he was a male friend, right?

She grabbed a large cup and headed to the ice machine. She waited for the guy in front of her to finish. Her chest felt so torn apart, it hurt to breathe. Over the rattle of the ice and the sluice of lemonade into her cup, she tried to stop thinking. Tried to stop feeling.

She grabbed a container of strawberry yogurt and headed for the checkout lines. She chose the shortest one, but it was still a wait. As she inched toward the cashier, she didn't see an available table anywhere. Maybe she'd head outside and find a place in the shade, enjoy the last of the sunshine before it became too freezing to sit outside at all. Maybe she could get a start on her assigned reading. She had a huge paper due soon. *That* was what she should be thinking about—not a man God couldn't mean for her to have.

Mitch was far away preparing for a mission. She had no idea what that would be like, but it couldn't be easy or safe. She remembered how he'd mentioned tough nights sleeping in the elements, or creeping through enemy territory not knowing what waited ahead. How he'd said he needed a friend.

Well, that was what he was going to get.

Focus, man. Mitch crept forward with his team, silent and vigilant, weapon in hand. He heard something.

The clear thin air seemed to make the predawn shadows look like liquid silver hugging the eastern side of the jagged mountain range. Bitter wind sliced across his face as he clenched his right fist and held it close to his chest. The team froze, sinking into the brush. His team members kneeled, facing outward, their backs to one another, defensive.

No sound. Nothing. That was troubling. He waited through long minutes until he heard it again. Mitch exhaled completely before speaking so his whisper would carry no real sound. "Someone's coming."

Every sense alert, reading the shadows, becoming part of the hillside, he waited. Mitch was confident whoever it was would pass on by without noticing his team. With any luck, they might get some scoop on the insurgent force in the area.

Low on the horizon the stars began to wink out as pale-gray light made the landscape stand out in black relief. The inky shadows turned from black to leaden gray, and dark purple brushed the high nearby peaks. Dawn was coming. They waited.

For one brief instant, a single thought pierced his concentration. Kelly. Half a world away, she was sound asleep, safe in her apartment.

The last stars faded as dawn came in its quiet glory. The light did not touch him as he remained motionless in the bitter cold, still waiting.

The cold autumn night temperatures nipped at Kelly's fingers as she fitted the deadbolt key into the door. Her ears were freezing, too, as she hadn't bothered with a hat or mittens for the short trek from the car to the apartment. Not her most brilliant move. What could she say? It had been a seriously busy week.

Shivering, Kelly let the storm blow her inside, fallen leaves raining down behind her as she closed and relocked the door. The air was chilly here too, although definitely not as cold as outside. She shrugged out of her coat.

"Sorry, I turned the heat on as soon as I got home,"

Lexie called from the kitchen. "But as I only got in about five minutes ago, it's still sixty-three degrees in here."

"What is that incredibly amazing aroma?"

"The upscale hot chocolate I love but can't really afford. My mom sent a care package today. Do you want chocolate raspberry, chocolate mint or chocolate hazelnut?"

"The raspberry one, please." Kelly dumped her backpack in the living room, where an opened cardboard box sat in the middle of the coffee table. All kinds of good things were exposed. "Your mom went all out."

"She wanted us to have good study food for midterms coming up. We'll be snacking off that for weeks. Hey, about an hour ago someone called for you." Lexie hit the timer on the microwave. "A certain handsome soldier."

"Mitch? He said he'd e-mail, not call. He's okay, right? He wasn't calling because he was hurt or anything?" She was talking way too fast. "I can't believe I missed his call. Why didn't he try me on my cell?"

"Oh no, he sounded perfectly macho and fine to me." Lexie leaned against the counter and smirked. "He was awfully eager to talk to you. In fact, when I told him you were working until eight, he said he'd call back between eight-thirty and nine. And guess what time it is right now?"

Kelly's gaze flew to the wall clock. "Eight twenty-nine."

He was going to call! Excitement at being able to talk to him had her heading to her room. "If it rings, I'll answer the extension in here."

"I'm glad you and he are *just* friends."

Was that a hint of teasing she heard in Lexie's voice? But the electronic jangle of the phone made her forget Lexie's comment as she dashed the rest of the way down the hallway and into her room. She dove into her reading chair, snatched the receiver from its cradle and realized even as she said it, she was betraying her feelings way too much. "Mitch?"

"Yeah, it's me." His chuckle rumbled, wonderfully masculine and familiar, one of her very favorite sounds. "I'm glad I caught you. I thought for sure Lexie would answer and tell me that I didn't have to call at exactly eight twenty-nine."

Maybe she wasn't the only one who'd missed their friendship. That was nice, wasn't it? She leaned far enough, and stretched the cord so that she could nudge the door closed. "So, you're back all in one piece? No worse for the wear?"

"Well, I don't know about that. There isn't such a thing as a piece-of-cake mission, not on Force Recon, but it went like clockwork. Lasted longer than we thought. It's snowing where I am and hard enough that we're pulling snow-shoveling duty. I'm gonna need snowshoes just to get to the chow tent tonight."

"We haven't had a single flake here yet. What can you tell me about what you've been up to?"

"Not much, seeing as how it's classified, but I can say that I continue to win the best-cup-of-C-4-coffee honor in the team, twelve missions running. Luke thought he came close this time, but there's a talent to it he lacks."

"You're just naturally gifted, huh?" That made him

laugh, warmed her heart, right down to her soul. "First I have to ask. What is C-4 coffee?"

"It sounds like extra-explosive caffeine, doesn't it? Nah, we can't have a fire to cook on, the smoke would definitely give us away, thereby ruining the stealth aspect of our mission. So we light teaspoon hunks of C-4 on fire and cook over the flame. It takes a lot of practice to make that perfect cup of morning coffee."

"You're kidding me, aren't you? You can't cook with explosives. Can you? It doesn't sound sane."

"Now I never said I was sane." That made him laugh. "I'm telling you the truth. It's how we heat our cans out of our MREs, Meals Ready to Eat. It makes whatever is inside the can—no one can tell for sure—taste almost edible. But when you're hungry enough, you don't really care."

"That's why you were so interested in my pizza when we were instant messaging."

"There's a lot of things I miss when I'm over here." Pizza was the least of those things. She'd gone right to the top of his most-missed list. After spending the last two months hunting down terrorists, a physically and mentally tough duty, being able to hear the goodness of her voice was a true luxury. "I'm already running out of things for my warm-thoughts list."

"That sounds serious."

"Yep, I don't want to be forced to head out on my next mission with a diminished list."

"Wow, that would border on a crisis." The smile was in her voice.

Mitch's chest twisted tight. "Help me out, would ya?

You could send me suggestions in e-mail. That way I could fortify my puny list with all kinds of real-life details."

"Trust me, my real life isn't all that splendid."

"Hey, I think so. Besides, I had a long list prepared, and I've gone through it already."

"It must be pretty rough and pretty cold where you are right now. You know I'd be happy to do anything I can for you. Be-because you're such a good friend."

He loved that hitch of emotion in her voice. Yeah, he thought, he had the same problem. He was starting to care way too much for safety's sake. And that was all right with him.

"Friends ought to help each other when they can." Her heart was in her voice.

He liked that. "I'd like to hear about all the good things in your life that shouldn't be taken for granted. For instance, the heat in your apartment."

"It's a lovely thing. You turn on the thermostat and the place warms right up. So, are you sure you want to hear about all the warm blessings in my life? I'll probably bore you."

"Not a chance." Caring like this was nice, but it was also a little like watching a grenade roll toward him, closer and closer, about to go off and there was nowhere to escape. All he could do was brace himself for it to blow.

"Then I'll send you an e-mail every day and tell you about the good things in my life, if you do the same."

"I'll be scarce, but when I'm in, I'll send you my daily compilation. How's that?"

"Perfect."

Yep, that pretty much described how he felt, too.

As they talked through the two hours of his calling card, he couldn't help feeling they became closer with each passing minute. It was nice. Real nice.

Chapter Eleven

It was seriously late, nearly midnight on a Friday night, and they'd been slammed at the bookstore, and closed up nearly an hour later than usual. But Kelly wasn't about to renege on her promise to Mitch.

As her laptop dialed in, she tiptoed around the kitchen and grabbed an orange soda from the fridge and a bag of iced animal cookies Lexie's mom had sent. There was a sticky note on the bag that read, "Kel, eat these please, before I go up another pant size."

Misery loves company, apparently, or at least the diet-challenged. While she munched on an iced elephant, she checked her inbox. There was an e-mail from Mitch.

Dearest Kelly,
Hiya. Here's my list from today. One. Never take a small snowfall for granted. When twelve inches falls in a twelve-hour period, you learn what else to never take for granted.

Two. Your back remaining pain-free and limber.

Three. Food you recognize. They said it was taco-seasoned hamburger, but we were skeptical, as the refried beans looked the same.

Four. Never take for granted sleeping through the night.

What's your list?

Keeping you in prayer, Mitch

That man sure could make her smile. Kelly sipped her soda and sat at the table, trying to stop the memories of their talk last night. He'd had her laughing for nearly an hour solid. He'd said nothing notable, he was simply being Mitch, and she loved his sense of humor.

He made her feel as if she'd been filled with stardust. Even now it was a wonder she didn't glow like the Milky Way.

She started typing.

Mitch,

First on my list. Iced animal cookies. Not great for your warm-things list, but they go perfectly with any hot drink. Coffee. Tea. Cocoa.

Second. Sunshine on your face. It was a perfect late-autumn day today. You know how the mid-afternoon sun gets toasty warm, even though there's a chill in the wind? The air smells woody and morning frost smelled like winter. And all day long there's the crisp crackly frost on the ground.

How am I doing?

Third. The quiet right before midnight. When you've

had a long hard day, and you sit in the shadows and let the peace settle around you. There's a half moon mid-zenith, shining as orange-yellow as a harvest moon. It makes the glacier caps on the mountains shimmer like opals. It's the perfect time for praying. It feels as if the angels are leaning over, listening extra hard.

Tonight, when I say my prayers, I'll put you in them. Be safe.

Your friend, Kelly

Kelly hit Send. And because it *did* feel as if the angels were waiting, she bowed her head and prayed from her heart.

While racking a round into the chamber of his weapon in the base camp's firing pit, Mitch felt a strange tug in his chest. Not like a kick of adrenaline, but this was a slow steady burn like a star winking to life in a twilight sky.

A snowflake brushed his cheek and as he cradled the familiar weight of the MP-5 in both hands, he knew that back home, Kelly was awake and thinking of him.

This relationship thing was still like driving in the dark, but at least he wasn't alone.

Dear Mitch,

Hi. The list of good things continues: Fellowship. The college group at church. We're too old for youth group and too young for the women's groups, the women there are married, and if not, then they are at least adults with real lives. College is that sort of in-between place. So we stick together, firmly bound by worries over our studies, grades, professors and what-are-we-going-to-do-when-we-grow-up kind of things. We had volunteered to help with the autumn harvest festival, which we have for the kids' Sunday-school groups on Halloween, so the kids have a good place to go for that evening. Our group is making the candy bags.

So, picture about twenty college kids sitting around the multi-purpose room talking and stuffing gallon-sized zipper bags with miniature packages of M&Ms and little Snickers and, my personal favorite, Whoppers. Sadly, some of the candy never made it into the bags. Needless to say, we were all extremely sugar-buzzed by suppertime and had to go out and buy more candy to replace what we'd consumed.

I'll keep you in prayer. Stay safe.

Kelly

Dear Kelly,

Hey, I love Snickers and candy corn. I once ate an entire pound bag of them, and Mom had the biggest conniption. I was six, and after zipping around the house full-speed for thirty minutes, I got seriously sick. I learned my lesson. Sadly, I had many such lessons to learn as a little kid.

Mitch

Dear Mitch,

You? I find that hard to believe.

Blessings, Kelly

My Dear Kelly,
Believe it. The most memorable lesson was the coronary I gave my mom when I was four. I climbed the rock wall of the living-room fireplace to the top—all two stories. My little sweaty handprint is still on the cathedral ceiling. I can still hear Mom, over twenty years later, scolding, "Mitchell James Dalton, what are you doing? You get down here right this minute!"
Sending prayers, Mitchell James Dalton

Dear Mitchell James Dalton,
So, you're telling me you were trouble right from the start? And your poor mom. She didn't deserve that.
Kelly

Dearest Kelly,
That's what she says, too. But I always tell her the apple doesn't fall far from the tree.
Mitch

Shivering from the morning cold, Kelly slid into her usual chair in the middle of the auditorium classroom, balanced her to-go cup of coffee on the desktop and lowered her backpack to the floor at her feet.

A glance at the clock over the door told her she had fifteen minutes before class started. Perfect! She'd had such a great time e-mailing back and forth with Mitch over the last few weeks, that she'd been collecting ideas for her list on the walk to campus.

She set her laptop on the desk and started a letter to send later, when she was on break at work.

My Dear Friend Mitch,
Eggnog lattes. I had the very first one of the season from the coffee shop at the corner of campus. Sweet creamy eggnog meets hot soothing coffee. Whoever invented this drink is a certifiable genius. It's perfect on a crisp November morning to warm you clear through, which leads me to the next thing on my list.

Frosty wintry mornings, the kind where white frost has settled everywhere and on everything—tree branches, crisp fallen leaves, car windshields, and it glitters when the sun hits it. Little waves of evaporation rise up from the early-morning streets, and the blades of grass crunch beneath your shoes. The cold burns your face and your breath rises in cloud-like puffs. There's a peaceful joy to walking to your first class on a morning like this—with an eggnog latte.

Kelly paused over the keyboard. It was an odd thing, how different she felt whenever she was thinking about Mitch, or writing to him, or simply hearing his voice. The shadows and difficult memories she hid behind lock and key faded away, and her heart felt whole.

A movement over the top of the screen caught her attention. It was Lexie, on her way to her class down the hall. She dropped into the empty seat next to Kelly. "Hey, roomie. You look studious. Oh, a letter to that soldier of yours. Nice."

"He's not mine. You know that."

"Sure. Just friends. I get it." Lexie rolled her eyes, good-naturedly. "Hey, I saw the note you left on the message board. I'm in. What time do you want a shopping buddy? And what are we shopping for?"

"Your mom's care package inspired me. I want to send something like that to Mitch."

"Great idea. Where is he stationed, do you know?"

"He only said it was a remote base camp, but I think the location is classified."

"Cool. I've never known anyone before who was classified. Ooh, I'll think of a list of stuff while I'm trying not to fall asleep in class. Which I've gotta get to. Adios." She rose, hoisting her backpack onto her shoulder. "How about in front of the library, around eleven?"

"See ya there." One glance at the clock and the students streaming through the doorway told her that she didn't have time to write anymore.

But she was going to start a list of her own, too. He was going to get the most fun care package ever. She hated to think of all the hardships he lived with every day. By choice and by duty, she understood that, but still. It was a sacrifice to be so far from home, and she owed him a little happiness in return for what his friendship had given her.

Just when she'd thought her heart would be as if in shadows forever, Mitch had come along and unknowingly made her feel joy again.

Yep, wherever he was, whatever he was doing, she owed him. Big-time.

The medevac's *whop-whop* faded into the silence of the high-mountain Afghan night and Mitch gave one last thought homeward as he moved out with his now three-man team. Luke had been shot during their ambush.

Not good. His team hadn't been standing still for more than a couple of minutes while they'd loaded up Luke, but already they were all shivering.

"Pick up the pace." They had to put in as much distance as they could as quickly as they could, because the helicopter was like a flashing neon sign to the terrorists, hey, look over here.

At least the storm blowing in would eventually cover their tracks. They had a long hard walk through thigh-deep snow. There was nothing like a fast hike with their packs on their backs to get the blood pumping again.

Kelly. There she was, like a steady candle's flame burning intractably against the dark. Right in his heart, and that light did not fade even as his every thought and his entire focus was on staying alive and completing his mission.

By the time this was over, he was going to forget what warm felt like. But he knew that light would still be burning.

The first frozen pellets of snow tapped off his shoulders. Yeah, it was gonna be a tough night.

With fifteen minutes to spare, Kelly pulled into a spot in the employees' parking behind the store and slid to a careful stop. Gray skies spat freezing drizzle, and a fine coating of ice gleamed on everything.

But did she care? Nope. Her boots skidded as she stood, but she managed to keep her balance as she grabbed her backpack and the huge shopping bag full of Mitch's stuff from behind the seat. It was heavy—she and Lexie had totally blown her budget—but she couldn't wait for him to see all this.

Happiness filled her up and she hardly noticed the drip of ice against the back of her neck as she struggled past the door and into the warmth of the building.

"I'm glad you made it in one piece. It's horrible out there." Katherine looked up from her book, propped open on the lunchroom table before her. She looked elegant, as always, in a slim black blouse and skirt, and her eyes lit up with interest over the bag. "Hey, you've been shopping. Did you get anything good?"

"Lots of stuff, but not for me." She dumped her pack on the floor by the employee closet and set the bag on a corner of the table. "Would you mind if I used one of the empty boxes from yesterday's shipment? I'm sending this to a friend."

"Sure. This wouldn't happen to be for your marine, would it?"

"Oh, he's not my marine." Just saying that aloud made her feel…strange.

"You mean you aren't staying in touch with him?" Katherine peeked into the bag. "We're talking about that drop-dead gorgeous guy with the shoulders of steel, right?"

"That would be the one. We're e-mailing now and then. And he called me."

"Good." Katherine seemed sedate as she rifled through the bag, but there was a subtle glint in her eye.

Kelly didn't miss it or the meaning behind it as she removed her coat. "He's just a friend."

"Right. Of course he is." Katherine didn't look convinced. "Where is he stationed?"

"He's overseas at a base camp. I'm guessing in Afghanistan or somewhere close to there. He said he couldn't say. He's on something called Force Recon."

"Oh, I know what that is. I used to be engaged to a guy whose brother was a Force Recon marine. Those are the real stealthy guys. I know Trevor did everything from deep-ground reconnaissance to counterterrorism. The training is more extensive than for the SEALS, I think. That's like, wow."

Kelly was starting to have the same opinion about the man. "That would be Mitch."

Katherine marked her page and put her book aside. "You know, we don't have a single customer. The weather is keeping everyone away. Why don't we start going through the store? I'm sure there a few things we can find that your marine would like. Some of the Christmas shipments have started to come in, and there's a lot of fun stuff. C'mon."

"He's not my marine." Why did the pieces of her lost dreams seem to ache when she said that? But Katherine apparently wasn't listening, she'd already swept out of the room.

Katherine was right, there was a lot of good stuff. As they sorted through the boxes waiting to be inventoried and shelved, Kelly couldn't get her mind off her boss's words. *Your marine,* she'd called Mitch.

It was really strange, because Lexie had called him *that soldier of yours* earlier this morning. It was like a clue from heaven—except that was totally not possible. No way. It wasn't what she wanted; it wasn't what Mitch wanted. Not rationally, anyway.

But, in truth, her heart longed for more than friendship. The little girl inside her, always alone and wanting to belong, longed, too.

If only there was a way he *could* be my marine, she thought. It was a wish that came from her heart, where she could not afford to start wishing. Only pain came from that.

She'd lost enough. Mitch was her friend. When he was done with his tour of duty and stationed in California, which he called home, he wouldn't be needing a friend. He wouldn't be needing her.

It was best to be practical. It was the only way to protect her heart. She was alone.

And that was how it was meant to be.

But as she sorted through the new stock, which would be perfect for stocking stuffers or a care package, she couldn't help the smallest hope in her heart that wherever he was, he was safe. And, did she dare hope that he was remembering her?

If he'd had a more miserable night, Mitch didn't want to think about it. His turn at watch was over and as he huddled into his sleeping bag and stared at the tarp tied overhead to keep off the falling snow, he shivered hard. Now, if he could only warm up enough to fall asleep, he'd be happy.

Not so easy. The frigid chill from the permafrost he'd bedded down on seeped through the bottom layer of the sleeping bag. He let his mind wander to that summer afternoon with Kelly. It had been hot that day, so hot it warmed to the bones. He tried to remember how that felt, the warm lush green grass, the sunshine so hot and bright it sizzled across the river water onto his skin, but he couldn't visualize it. The images remained in the background, kind of fuzzy and distant.

What he remembered, as clearly as if he were in Montana right now, was Kelly. The rippling sound of her laughter when he'd scooped her out of the river. How good it had felt to have her at his side as they'd walked through the park. She'd looked pretty as could be in the university T-shirt and denim cut-offs she'd worn, and her sneakers had squeaked in the grass, still damp from the river.

He remembered how the sunlight had brushed her with bronze, making her blond hair blow loose ripples and shine like gold. How she'd eaten her dipped cone by peeling off the thick chocolate layer first, eating it in dainty bites.

He tried to imagine her right now, using what she'd told him about her life. Her morning classes would be over. She'd probably be starting her shift at the bookstore. Maybe she'd have an eggnog latte to keep her warm, and she'd be ringing up sales in the store, chatting with the regular customers, or bowed over one of her schoolbooks during the lulls.

While he thought of her, the misery of the frigid cold and the hard day's exhaustion released its hold on him and he slept.

Chapter Twelve

The low squeak of a door startled Kelly out of her thoughts. She looked up from the final printed draft of her research paper. She'd been concentrating so hard, she was surprised to see the gray light of dawn sneaking around the closed blinds and her roommate stumbling in her robe and slippers toward the bathroom.

"How long have you been up?" Lexie asked on a big yawn.

"Since five. I keeled over about one and thought I'd get up early and get this proofed and printed before I left this morning. Ha." At least, it had seemed reasonable in the wee hours of the morning, but in the light of day, not so much. "Not as easy as I thought."

"Tough. I'll be you next week. I've *got* to start the paper that's due." Lexie wandered into the bathroom, yawning.

It was contagious. Kelly stifled a yawn as she spotted a typo and turned to the computer to correct it. The printer she'd set up on the corner of the table whirred and spat out the corrected page. She forged ahead with her reading.

Time kept ticking past and when finally she was satisfied with her printed copy, Lexie was out of the bathroom, hair wrapped in a towel and grabbing a container of yogurt from the fridge. "Kelly, you need any help?"

"No. Ta-da! I'm done." With not a second to spare. She had just enough time to grab a quick shower, pack up and race out the door.

It didn't occur to her until she was bundled up and scraping the thick sheet of ice off her windshield, that she'd forgotten to check her e-mail. Well, it was too late now. She'd faithfully sent an e-mail every day, and she hadn't gotten a response since she'd shipped off the package last week. She'd spent the last six days trying not to think of him. And she'd failed.

And now here she was thinking of him again and feeling confused and turned upside down and vulnerable all at once.

She missed him. As a friend, right?

But, as she circled around to the rear window and began to chip away at the stubborn sheet of ice, she was no longer sure.

No answer.

Mitch swiped his hand over his face. Disappointment hit him like a brick. He'd thought for sure there would be another day's e-mail, sent like all the others. But for some reason she'd skipped the last two days, and now this morning.

Why? *Lord, I'm too far away. You gotta help me*

here, I'm begging. Don't let her start drifting away. Considering his current altitude, he was closer to heaven, but Mitch didn't get a sense that God was hearing him any better for it.

He felt lost as he sent his e-mail. Kelly and her world of brightness and sweetness, of eggnog lattes and studying and college-life groups no longer seemed real at all. One of his best friends had been evacuated to a hospital, and while they'd succeeded in their ambush, they had paid a price.

He'd reread her e-mails, he'd saved every one, listing all the good things in her daily life. But even reading her words didn't make him feel as connected to her as he once had. He wanted to hear her voice. He needed to hear it. But, when he counted ahead to calculate her time, it was about eight o'clock in the morning. She'd probably be seated in her first class, bright-eyed and ready to take copious notes.

He bit back the frustration. He'd try her later, after he hit the rack and got some much-needed sleep. Maybe she would have found his e-mail by then and responded.

"I guess our Christmas rush has officially started." Katherine sounded exhausted as she locked up her till. "I'm going to take my lunch now that we seem to have quieted down for a moment. I'll be in the back. Page me if you get overrun, okay?"

"Are you kidding? It's two o'clock and you've been running since well before I got here." Kelly looked up from where she knelt before the point of purchase displays near the front counter. "You just go put your feet up, get something to eat and relax. You deserve it. Whatever happens up here, I can handle it for a bit. Ava should be coming in any time to help out."

"Yeah. Send that sister of mine back when she gets here, all right?" Katherine grabbed her book from beneath the counter and tapped away in her heels.

Kelly kept stocking. While the sound system played instrumental hymns, she replenished the bookmark display, moving just as fast as she could. The coupons Spence had printed in several of the local church papers had brought in more business than they'd expected. And she still had the card section to get back up to snuff before the next wave of customers hit.

It looked as though there wouldn't be much of a chance to study from here on out. Or, she thought sadly, a chance to log onto her account, using her laptop in the break room, to check her e-mail. Not that Mitch was likely to answer. He was probably busy climbing mountains, rappelling from helicopters, practicing his marksmanship and saving the world. He had important things to do, and she was only a friend. Like a pen pal. Which is exactly what she'd wanted all along. So exactly why did that hurt? Why was she swallowing down a wave of disappointment?

Whatever happened, she could not give in to hoping. Not even a little. So she sent a gentle *friendly* prayer his way.

She would simply have to accept that it was only natural that he would start to drift away. Their friendship was only temporary. He was partway through his tour of duty. By sometime in December, he would be back at his home base in California and he wouldn't need a pen pal after that.

No. She had to simply deal with the fact that as much as she respected Mitch and as much as she liked him, he wasn't hers to keep. As a friend or otherwise. Their lives had gone separate ways and that's how it was meant to be.

She'd known that all along. Mitch would be just another person in her life she would have to say good-bye to. But if she was smart, she could keep him from getting too close. That way, she could be sure that when he did say goodbye for good, he wouldn't be taking a piece of her heart.

It sounded logical, like a good plan. Except the thought of losing Mitch—even as a friend—cracked her heart a little more deeply.

Too late, she thought as she stood, taking the empty boxes with her.

Mitch was glad to be back at camp. He wasn't glad that it was 0500 and he was freezing, but he tried checking e-mail anyway.

No go. No phones with the current storm. They were under whiteout conditions. When they'd be up was anyone's guess. He might as well be based out in the northern tundra for all the good these gadgets were doing him.

Frustration ate at him like the gnawing cold. The heater had conked out again and couldn't keep up with the subzero temps. And he couldn't keep up with his growing frustration.

"C'mon, Dalton." Pierce poked his head in. "We've got PT in five."

"Yeah, I know."

Mitch stood, biting down his frustration. Physical training was just what he needed. It would give him something to focus on. He'd be able to shove out these tangled emotions and struggle with something that was concrete and easier to overcome. He would push harder and harder until every problem and every feeling faded into nothing.

At least, that was the theory. But as he turned his thoughts to the workday ahead, he suspected that all the ways he missed Kelly would remain.

No matter what.

Kelly stumbled through her front door a few minutes after eight-thirty. Her veins were still pulsing adrenaline from her icy drive home. "I can't believe I made it in one piece."

"Whew, I'm glad to see you." Lexie looked up from the couch, where a thick text was open on her lap. The TV droned, volume low, in the background. She capped her highlighter. "There was an emergency broadcast on the road conditions. I'm glad they sent you home early."

"Spence closed the store when we lost power, half the town is out, but it took me forty minutes to drive three miles." She hung up her coat and carted her backpack and computer case into the warm kitchen.

Finally, she thought as she unzipped her laptop. She'd pop online, send her daily list and maybe there'd be a letter from Mitch. And if there wasn't…well, she refused to be disappointed.

But before she could find the phone cord to plug into her computer, the lights blinked. The TV silenced. Darkness washed over them.

"No fears," Lexie said from the pitch-black living room. "I've got a flashlight here *some*where."

There was rustling, the sound of something hitting the floor, and a round beam of light came to life, highlighting Lexie's smile. "I was prepared. With the ice storm and winds, I figured we had a good chance of losing power."

"I can still dial in if there's a dial tone." She checked the line. Yes! It was working. She connected the phone cord and dialed in quickly, before she lost that, too.

"I'll light candles," Lexie said as she rescued the remote control from the floor. "You check for love letters from Mitch."

"They aren't love letters, trust me. Why does everyone have the same misconception?" Kelly knew it irritated her for only one reason—a tiny part of her was wishing for love. And how crazy was that? Insane. Certifiable. She knew better, too. Whatever it took, she would *only* allow friendship-type thoughts and feelings about Mitch.

And that was that.

There was an e-mail from Mitch waiting for her. She couldn't believe it. She had to blink twice just to make sure. His name really was there. He was safe, and he hadn't forgotten her *yet.*

She could hardly breathe past the joy filling her as

she downloaded the document before the phone went out too. Lexie circled around the counter and set a pillar candle on the table. Kelly looked up. "I should get up and help you."

Lexie grinned knowingly. "You should answer Mitch. I take it he wrote?"

"Yeah," she cleared her throat, trying to sound blasé. "I guess he had time to write or something."

Lexie lit a match and set it to the wick. Just as blasé, she said, "Then I guess you should answer him or something."

"Maybe." Kelly didn't want to admit it, but everything within her yearned for the sight of his words.

This was more than simple friendship, a tiny voice at the back of her mind warned her, but she refused to listen. She was already opening the document, devouring his letter.

Dearest Kelly,
I know, I'm finally getting back to you. Hey, your lists are great. You don't know what it means to come in after being out for over a week, and have so many e-mails waiting for me. Here's my list of things:

1. I'll never take a Saturday afternoon relaxing on the couch for granted. I especially miss this luxury after hiking with my team ten clicks with a fifty-pound pack on my back in a high-mountain blizzard.

2. Not having to watch your best buddy get shot.

3. Being warm enough to feel your hands and feet at all times.

4. Going to sleep without having first to set up clay-

more mines and sensors. Each man takes turns at keeping watch, but deep sleep is impossible. You're always listening for the sound of one of the mines going off, meaning your armed enemy is close while you're still in your sleeping bag.

5. Sleeping in a warm place instead of being too cold to fall asleep.

6. Life is uncertain. Never take your friends for granted.

I'll give you a call as soon as I can.

In prayer, Mitch

Wow. Kelly's jaw dropped. She couldn't imagine what Mitch had been through. She reread his words and felt sorrow for his suffering.

"What's wrong?" Lexie turned from lighting a pillar candle on the counter. Light flickered eerily as she hurried over. "Mitch is okay, isn't he?"

"I guess." What did okay mean? She didn't know. "Read this and tell me what you think."

"Mitch won't mind?"

"No, we're really just friends, and he's writing nothing that's private." At least, she didn't think so. Mostly, she couldn't quite believe what her eyes told her, and her heart didn't want to feel. She'd seen enough war movies to be able to fill in the blanks in all that he hadn't said with images of her own. "What do you think?" she asked when Lexie finished reading over her shoulder.

"I'll tell you when my jaw stops dropping. What does Mitch do, anyway? Is he Special Forces?"

"Yeah." Kelly didn't want to get online to answer

him. What if he tried calling? He'd get a busy signal. "I hope his friend is all right."

"Me, too. That puts my day in perspective." Lexie pulled out a chair and sat down. "I'm really glad you sent him that care package. He probably hasn't gotten it yet?"

"Doesn't sound like it." Kelly shrugged, wishing she could do more. So much more. Then she realized it was late where he was. In the wee hours of the morning in his part of the world. He wouldn't be calling, so she tried to get back online, but the modem couldn't get a dial tone.

Just as well. She was no longer a child to believe in fairy tales, but it was nice to know there were good guys in the real world. Very nice.

She shut down her computer and got right to her studies, but her thoughts kept drifting to him. To the radiance he brought to her soul, like starlight on a frosty winter's night.

Mitch shivered in the freezing cold tent and hooked the receiver between his ear and shoulder. While he dialed the last digits of Kelly's home number, he knew chances were good that she wasn't home. She had probably headed straight to work after her morning classes.

As he listened to the first ring and then the second, he figured he'd at least leave a message on her answering machine. He wouldn't try her cell, not when she'd probably be at work.

Sure enough, a recorded message answered. "This is Kelly," came her voice as sweet as the dawn. "And

Lexie," Lexie added. "We're away right now," and Kelly's soft alto piped in, "so please leave a message!"

He waited for the beep. "Hey, Kelly, it's Mitch. I'm bummed that I missed ya. I'll try back."

He hung up, the numbers on his watch showing it was four minutes past four in the morning. He'd gotten up early just to try calling her.

Well, there was nothing to do but to keep at it. He wouldn't stop calling until he reached her. Until he could hear her voice, all heart and goodness, because he needed some of that.

He needed her.

In the silence of Amy's living room, Kelly snapped her book shut, the sound as startling as a gunshot in the sleeping house. The kids were asleep. The scents of crayons and SpaghettiOs lingered pleasantly in the air. With the fire crackling in the hearth, she should feel peaceful. It was a perfect studying climate. But could she concentrate? No.

Lexie had called about an hour ago, while she was clearing supper dishes from the table, to tell her that Mitch had called and left a message. Ever since, she'd been keeping her silent cell phone close just in case Mitch tried again.

She resisted the urge to hop online and check her e-mail account. That would make it obvious, even to herself, how eager she was to hear from Mitch. And if she was going to hold tight to her stance and to her vow to keep her feet on the ground when it came to Mitch, then she couldn't go around acting as if she wanted to fall in love with him, right?

Right.

The living-room walls felt as if they were pressing in on her until she couldn't draw a single breath. She wanted to blame it on studying too hard, but she *always* studied hard. That was no excuse. The real explanation was something she didn't want to think about.

And somehow, she had to make sure she stopped thinking about Mitch and kept every thought of him from her mind. Maybe it was better that he hadn't called. Maybe this was a sign, this pattern of missed communications. Maybe, she thought desperately and with hope, it was a sign from above reminding her she was looking down the wrong fork in the road.

Her cell phone rang. Surely that wasn't a sign, either. She checked the screen—an out of area number. Mitch, her heart hoped wildly before her common sense kicked in and she let it ring a second time. Then a third.

Now she was *definitely* in need of therapy. First she couldn't wait for him to call and now that he probably was, she didn't want to answer the phone. For some reason it felt like a monumental decision as she pressed the button to accept the call, which made no sense at all. At the back of her mind, she worried this could be her mom calling, too. "Hello?"

"K-Kelly." Above the crackle of static in the long-distance line, she heard his voice.

"Mitch." His name was on her lips, as if straight from her heart, and her voice betrayed her. Joy blazed within her. She hadn't realized until this moment how much she'd missed him. How much she'd worried over him. His voice might be her most favorite sound on earth. "I can't believe it. It's really you."

"No imposter this time. You're a difficult lady to get a hold of lately."

"Not as difficult as you are, mister. Are you okay?"

"Right as rain, or maybe I should say snow this time of year. Are you all right? When you answered, you sounded like were hesitant to talk to me. You're not at work, are you? It's okay that I'm calling?"

Please, let it be okay. Mitch gripped the phone tightly.

"Y-yeah, it's absolutely okay, I'm just babysitting. It's just that your number came through as 'out of area' and with an area code I didn't recognize. I was afraid it was my mom using a calling card from jail."

"She does that a lot?"

"No, I'm just always cautious. But you didn't call to hear about that. How is your friend doing?" There was her heart, unmistakable in the warm tones of her voice.

Man, it was good to hear. His chest twisted tight, so strong it was a physical pain that came from missing her. "Haven't heard about Luke yet. He's been flown to a hospital in Germany."

"He must have been hurt pretty badly."

"Y-yeah." He cleared his throat. He'd save thinking about what had happened, seeing his friend shot and defending him while their corpsman worked frantically to save his life, along with the rest of them. Their ambush on the enemy had been a success, and their mission was completed—but at a personal cost. As always. "All we can do is wait. And pray."

"I've been keeping him in my prayers, and Lexie has, too. I let her read your e-mail. Was that all right?"

"Sure."

Emotions tangled emotions like a knotted rope yanked hard, because he had her on the phone, he was listening to the sound of her lovely voice and yet she felt so far away. He closed his eyes, shutting out the officers' hootch and the clatter of the heater working hard in the mountain cold. He fought to bring a picture of her into his mind.

What he saw was her that first day in the bookstore, when she'd been awash in the bright, cheerful light of summer. Her hair had glinted like pure gold and fallen in a soft swoop around her lovely face. Her rosy complexion looked as satin-soft as a rose's petal.

His throat ached as he remembered how dainty and sweet she'd looked in a pale-pink sleeveless blouse. But what he wanted was to see her now. To picture her in the solemn shadows of a November's night, when darkness came early in Montana. He could not picture her. Frustration ate at him.

Kelly's voice interrupted the static on the line. "Lexie said it best. She said that your e-mail put her life in perspective, and I felt the same way. The lists I sent, about all the little unimportant things in my day, probably didn't help you much. It probably seemed trite and disrespectful—"

"No, you couldn't be more wrong." No Kevlar vest could protect him from pain like this. Just the thought of her not writing could nearly do him in. "You have no idea how much I appreciate your lists. So, what's this about your mom?"

"Like I said, you didn't call to hear about my mother."

"I called to hear about you."

There he went, trying to get beneath the appearance of things and into a deeper part of her life where she didn't want him to go. "My mom is out of my life. End of story. Some people say that's harsh, that she deserves a second chance, but the truth is that she's on her six-billionth chance, and I just can't take any more. How is your mom doing?"

"Nice change of subject." He didn't sound upset by it, he sounded amused. "Funny you should mention her. I got a pretty interesting e-mail from her. She wanted to know how long I've been seeing you."

"No, that's not true. She couldn't possibly have thought that. I found her number in the phone book a while back—"

"And why would you do that?"

"Well, it's a surprise. Let's just say I wanted to send you something. As one friend to another, of course."

"Sure." He chuckled, as if he understood perfectly. "I bet Mom didn't see it that way. It's just wishful thinking on her part. It's not me she cares about, she said she wanted a daughter-in-law to spoil. She's never forgiven me for being a difficult kid."

"I know that isn't true. When I told her who I was and that I knew you, she went on and on about what a great man she thinks you are."

"Oh, no," he groaned. "She didn't. Really? Now I

have to disown her. I can't have a mom embarrassing me like that."

She heard straight through his facade to his big heart beneath. He came from a family like this one, she thought, as she looked around the loving home Amy had made here with her husband and kids. Happiness settled in the air like stardust through the windows. A hundred pictures hung on the wall or were mounted in fat photo albums or were overstuffed in a drawer, waiting for framing. Homemade cookies were fresh in a cookie jar on the table, and love and caring seemed to gleam like moonlight on the polished wood.

Did Mitch know how lucky he was? She thought he did. She hoped he did. "I talked to your mom for less than five minutes, but she seemed like a really lovely lady."

"That would be Mom."

Yes, she thought, he knew. She could hear it in his words. "I'm guessing that when you were growing up, she baked your favorite cookies before you had the chance to ask for them. It sounds like she is still your biggest fan."

"Yeah, everyone needs that in their life. I am blessed with my parents, I know I am. I take it that your mom wasn't the kind of mother who ever baked cookies."

"No." The wounds within her began to reopen, whispers of memories that she *had* to silence.

"Or ever baked a birthday cake?"

"Good guess." She steeled her defenses. She could not let him in any deeper. "My birthday is coming up, and between that and the holidays, she often tries to contact me."

"How much longer does she have on her sentence?"

"I honestly don't know. I expect she'll be out by the end of the year." That's all she wanted to say to him. One more word and she would have opened up too far. "Speaking of time, you should be about halfway through your tour, right?"

"Will she look you up?"

"I hope she doesn't." She squeezed her eyes shut, but that didn't diminish the ugly voices of her past, murmuring in her mother's voice. How she wasn't good enough. Like mother, like daughter. How did she silence those memories? "The last time she got out of prison, she showed up pretending to have missed me, but she stole money out of my backpack when I went to make her some coffee. I'd just gotten paid and that cash was my grocery money for two weeks. I didn't have anything to fall back on."

"I'm sorry, Kelly. You've come a long way on your own."

"I'm not alone."

She touched him deeply, Mitch realized, beyond his comfort level and deeper still, where he'd never felt anything like this before. A fierce steely need to protect her anchored him, and he hated the miles that separated them. "When *is* your birthday?"

"In December."

"What day in December?"

"The second."

Okay, he knew what to do. As he checked his watch,

time was ticking away, and he was looking at a hard afternoon of training ahead. But he couldn't hang up yet. He couldn't say goodbye. There was so much he wanted to say, but he was afraid of scaring her off. Afraid of moving too fast. He still didn't know where she stood, if she was moving away from him, or if he could pull her closer.

"Oh, I think I hear the baby." Her heart was showing again. "Let me just whisper, because I don't want to disturb her if she'll fall back to sleep."

He could picture her walking with care down a hallway, to check on a sleeping baby. "Who are you babysitting for tonight?"

"One of the McKaslin cousins, Amy. I've been babysitting for her since Westin, her oldest boy, was three." She paused. "Oh, it looks like little Shannon just needs some comfort. Hello, sweetie. Want me to rub your back? Oh, she's going back to sleep. I was dating Joe then."

"After all this time, they must be like family."

"Family of the heart, that's for sure. Is that what your team members are to you?"

There it was, the depth of her heart in her voice. He felt the distance and the miles melt away. It was a little like being lost in the dark, and she was a beacon lighting the way.

"Like brothers," he confessed. "We spend most of our time together. Sadly, I've got to go before they start without me. But before I do, what are you doing for Thanksgiving?"

"Oh, you're worried that I'll be alone, aren't you?

Well, I've turned down Lexie's offer, and Katherine and Spence's offer and Amy's offer to join them for the holiday. I'm going to volunteer again at the free dinner that the local church charities host, and then I'm taking a meal out to my aunt at the hospital."

"I was going to have my mom invite you, if you weren't doing anything."

"That's really nice. But I'm fine. Thanks. What are you doing?"

"I'll be lucky to be here. There's a rumor we're actually getting real turkeys, but I'll have to see it to believe it. I have to go."

Kelly couldn't believe how hard it was to say goodbye. "You'll call again?"

"Count on it." There was a click and he was gone.

Oh, that man could make her feel—make her come alive—like nobody ever had. And wasn't that the problem?

It was as if he was able to see her bare to the soul, where there were no longer any shields, anything safe to hide behind. That left only the truth—of who she'd been and who she was now—and how much she longed to love again.

Longed to love him.

In the quiet of the living room she slipped her phone back into her pack. And thought of Mitch, so far away. Her heart tugged, impossibly, with emotion she could not let in. *Please, Father, watch over him, keep him safe.*

The rain battered the black windows with renewed fury and the ghosts of the past, of the truths she'd spoken of tonight, seemed to whirl in the air around her.

The heavens opened as rain hailed against the roof, pounding like a thousand bullets.

She hurried down the hall to check again on the baby, but Shannon was still lost in sweet dreams, safe and soundly asleep. Looking like the precious gift she was.

What a dream it would be to have one of her own, and a life like this. Kelly couldn't help hoping, just a little, and it made the loneliness ache. Careful not to disturb the little one, she tiptoed out of the room and wandered back to her school books, which were waiting for her.

Okay, time to buckle down and concentrate on the attainable dreams in her life. She settled down to study, but every neuron in her head seemed focused on Mitch. On the big, mighty, wonderful, kind man he was.

If she closed her eyes and made a wish, it would look just like him. And wasn't that the danger? Dreams weren't meant for her. She knew that for absolute certain. But it was there, anyway. She'd fought so hard not to let a single hope take root, and it had—for a moment—but she'd dared to let in the smallest wish.

And wasn't that the problem? You started small, with the purest, tiniest wish—and before you knew it, that wish bloomed into a full-fledged, all-of-your-heart dream.

I so want him to love me.

There came the wish, the smallest hope, alive inside her. She screwed her eyes shut against the hot blinding tears that rose. The memory of the day at the river, when Mitch had pulled her against him, protecting her from the current…she wished she had laid her cheek against his chest so she would have known how it felt to be held like that by him. She longed for his tenderness as the stars longed for the night.

And it was impossible. She was in someone else's living room, with the cold November night pressing in around her and she was alone.

Always, endlessly, alone with a dream that could not possibly come true.

Chapter Thirteen

Dear Mitch,
I haven't heard from you since last week when you called. I'm keeping you and your friend Luke in my prayers. And sending warm thoughts your way. The first snow of the season fell today—late for Bozeman—but no one is complaining. Here's a list of good things in my day.

One-dollar movie night at the Garland. We watched Pride and Prejudice and ate a vat of fake buttered popcorn. (Lexie says hi.)

Sadly, that was the only good thing in my day.
Sending my very best wishes, Kelly

My Dear Kelly,
What do you mean you only had one good thing in your day? Maybe you should add the bad things, too, because I'm not getting an accurate picture here.

Good things in my day: Word is that Luke is gonna pull through. I'm back from stealthing around, but we're

going right out on another mission. We had recognizable chow today—at least, we think it was chicken.
Sending my prayers, Mitch

Dear Mitch,
I'm so glad for your friend.

The best thing about today was that I recognized everything I ate.

The worst thing about today was that a call came in from the county jail, which Lexie rejected (I wasn't home at the time).

Wherever you are, I hope you're safe and, if not warm, then not too cold.
Keeping you in prayer, Kelly

Dearest Kelly,
I'm sorry about your mom. If I don't get back in time, Happy Thanksgiving. Eat some pie for me.
Always, Mitch

Over the next week, a certain theme had started to emerge in her morning devotional and it was really starting to annoy her. Kelly wished she could take the passage to heart.

> I will turn their mourning into gladness; I will give them comfort and joy instead of sorrow.

This was not helping her stay realistic with her expectations in life.

In the morning quiet of her apartment, she rubbed the pad of her forefinger over the text in her devotional. That is *so* not my life, she thought.

She had to prepare herself for the inevitable, Mitch moving away. And maybe this was it? She'd had no word from him, nothing. The logical side of her brain said that he was busy, that was the nature of his work, to be away from his base camp for days, or for more than a week at a time.

But the totally nonrational side of her knew that goodbyes were inevitable. She was not going to give in to the temptation to believe otherwise. With a thump, she closed the devotional and set it aside. She concentrated on her second cup of coffee on this leisurely holiday morning.

She had the apartment to herself. Lexie had driven home to have Thanksgiving with her parents, and the bookstore was closed today, of course. It was a rare thing to have nothing to do and nowhere to go for an entire morning. She intended to enjoy it while she could.

The trouble was that loneliness seemed to creep into the corners of the apartment like the cold air from outside. Why did her mind automatically switch to thoughts of Mitch? Of the warm, cozy rumble of his baritone, of the comforting brush of his heart against hers when she talked about her past, and of the way his chuckle, so kind and good-natured, chased away the shadows.

She was letting a wish for Mitch's love and a happy life with him take root in her soul. That was wrong, wrong, wrong. The realization sent fear zinging through her veins. What was she going to do about that? It was simple. Don't think about him. Don't go there. That was the only solution.

She took another sip of her coffee. Where did her thoughts go? To the devotional open on the table in front of her—no, of course not. Her thoughts were thousands of miles away with Mitch, wondering if he'd gotten the rumored turkey for his Thanksgiving Day dinner.

You absolutely have to stop thinking about him, Kelly. She sighed, frustrated at herself. This man was already too far into her heart for safety's sake.

Maybe she'd just get online and send him a happy holidays wish. Then she'd be able to get her mind off him, right? It was worth a try.

While her laptop dialed in, she poured another cup of coffee. But the memory of their last talk remained. How close he'd felt, how carefully he'd listened, how he'd somehow made the past less painful, the shadows less dark. That made no sense whatsoever.

An electronic beep from her laptop interrupted her thoughts. She brought her cup with her to the table, attention on the screen, her pulse skipping, because what if that was Mitch?

There, on the instant message screen, was an electronic note from Mitchell Dalton.

Kelly
Happy Thanksgiving. And thanks. That was some care package you sent.
Mitch

Happiness filled her up and buoyed her spirit. She dropped into her chair, already typing.

Mitch
You got it? Great. I thought it might have been sent to Mars by mistake.
Kelly

Kelly
I think I saw Mars stamped on the package. I had to beat off the rest of the guys. Apparently candy corns are a great hit with Force Recon marines. Second only to the candy made in the shape of garbage cans.
Mitch

Mitch
I personally love the bottle-cap ones. Lexie went with me, and we hit every candy counter around the university. I hope you don't get too sugar-buzzed. Katherine contributed the candy canes and the tin of chocolate sugar crunch cookies.
Kelly

Kelly
Thank her for me, would you? I'm vibrating from eating all the candy corns. Apparently I didn't learn my

lesson when I was six. Hey, are you gonna be home for a while?
Mitch

Mitch
I'm here for a few more hours. I'm not needed at the church's kitchen until ten-thirty.
Kelly

Kelly
Then log off and I'll give you a buzz. Deal?
Mitch

Deal. She hit Send and signed off. She was way too happy that he was calling her. But did she try to hold back her heart? No. She didn't have time to try, because the phone rang and she snatched it up before it could ring twice. "Mitch?"

"It's me." Yep, he was hooked, Mitch thought, the instant he heard her voice. He felt every inch of the distance that separated them as he leaned back in the metal chair. "Why the church kitchen? Most folks just want to take it easy, not have to work on Thanksgiving."

"I started the year Joe died, when there was an announcement in the church newsletter asking for volunteers. It sounded better than spending the day with Joe's family or alone with wishes of what could have been. I liked it, actually, so I've done it ever since."

He wasn't surprised. Classic Kelly, he thought, kindness and sincerity and the greater good. That was just another reason why he was falling in love with her. "Your mom hasn't called again?"

"No, thank goodness. I expect she'll try." Her voice went thin. "I try not to think of her, except when I have to. Did you get a nice dinner?"

"We had meat that was supposed to be the rumored turkey. When we slathered it with the pasty gravy, who could tell? It might have been turkey. I'm happy enough with that. You're a long way away. Tell me what you've been up to. What haven't you put in your e-mails?"

"Like with school?"

"Yeah, school, work, social life."

"What social life? Finals are coming up, so I have a close personal relationship with my textbooks. I'm seeing them exclusively."

"Ah. Still not dating, huh?"

She sounded choked. "You like to get right to the point, don't you? I've given up on dating forever."

"There's some poor man somewhere who is probably pretty broken up to hear that."

"I don't think so. In fact, I'm pretty sure there isn't. There can't be."

A spear of sorrow arrowed through him, it was her pain, he realized, and his pain for her. "Why not?"

"It's not meant to be. You said your friend Luke was doing better?"

"Yeah." He understood why she'd changed the subject. He'd gotten too close. He'd noticed that pattern before. She wanted to keep him at a friendly distance, where she felt safe.

Well, fine, but he was going to push that, if not now, then later, because she would always be safe with him.

But he was coming home in about three weeks' time. He had to know where she stood. The last thing he wanted between them was regret.

"Luke's still recovering. He got hurt pretty bad. Are you thinkin' that I might be next?"

"It crossed my mind."

"Don't let it worry you. I won't be. Besides, just living is risky business."

"Yeah, but we're friends. That gives me the prerogative to worry about you."

"Then I'll worry about you and we'll be even."

"What risky things do I do? Oh, I know. You're going to say that I drive."

"Yep, you get in a car every day. That's risky stuff, too." He hated the distance between them, the miles that kept him from reaching out to her and pulling her into his arms and holding her until she believed. Until she could see he had no plans to break her heart. "Is that why you aren't dating? You're afraid of caring about someone and losing them again?"

"Something like that." Her voice sounded sturdy, strong.

But he could feel the waver of emotion; he could feel how vulnerable she was. "The package you sent, it meant a lot."

"Good, because I wanted it to. You helped me when I really needed it." Her tone was friendly, but her heart betrayed her.

At least, he wanted to think it was her heart he felt,

even half a world away. "Are you talking about the little bit of help I gave you on quadratic equations?"

"It made the difference between an A and a B. I know that doesn't sound like very much, but it does to me. I have a four-point grade average, and I'd like it to stay that way, since I'm looking at graduate school next year."

No, this was more than a thank-you. He looked down at the good-sized cardboard box stuffed with candy. Candy shaped like garbage cans, like pop-bottle tops, fruit and people. There was taffy and bubble gum and jawbreakers in every color, gummy bears and gummy worms and long red ropes of still soft and still mealy licorice.

And not only candy, but animal cookies and cheese snacks and gum and the latest military suspense he'd been wanting, cupcakes and Twinkies and packages of beef jerky. At the bottom of the box was an MSU T-shirt, extra-large. She'd sent books of word jumbles and crossword puzzles and a travel-sized chess set.

Not an ordinary care package. He knew, because his mom sent them all the time. Shoeboxes stuffed with homemade brownies, not boxes full of all kinds of stuff that took time and thought to put together. Kelly might say they were friends, but her actions and the emotion in her words said more.

Good to know, since he was walking without cover. Heaven knew he was feeling out of his depth. He was a Force Recon marine, he knew how to be patient, when to wait and when to take a step forward. "You want to go to graduate school there in Bozeman, or are you looking to go somewhere else?"

"I'd like to stay here. I have to be accepted to the program first."

"You will. I believe in you, Kelly."

What on earth could she say to that? Kelly squeezed her eyes shut. Did he have to say those words as if with all the tenderness in his big heart? He made her feel like a new, twinkling star; he also stirred up pain. Like a powerful river's current, scudding along the bottom of the river bed, scraping up raw places and exposing them, the places within her that longed to love again.

But Mitch was right. It hurt too much to let someone in—especially him. What she had to do was stop this, before she'd taken another step on a path leading to where she didn't want to go. How could she let him into her heart any farther? It already hurt too much.

"Mitch, I don't think—" She bit her lips, torn apart by pain. By fear. "I value our *friend*ship, *but—" That's all I can do, she thought.*

"I value you pretty highly, too."

The certainty in his voice frightened her as much as the tenderness in his words. It was a tenderness she could feel as if his emotions were coming right through the long-distance line, too, and into her heart.

I could love him so much. *If* things were different. If I were different.

How did she tell him that?

There was a rustle, as if he'd dropped the phone, and in the background it sounded like men were shouting.

"I gotta go." It was all he said before he hung up, leaving her with an empty line.

What had happened? Was he okay? She tried to banish all the images of war she'd seen on televised news reports and told herself maybe it was a high wind, knocking out the phone connection. It didn't mean something horrible had happened.

She tasted fear as she hung up the phone. Her fingers trembled as she pulled the cup of lukewarm coffee into her hands. Fear for him double-beat through her veins and into her soul.

Please, keep him safe, Lord. It was the only thing she could do for him, so she prayed.

She could not stop the sick cold dread that had followed her all through her day and crept into her like the night's chill. Shivering from the bitter winds and covered with snow, Kelly gratefully turned the deadbolt on her apartment door behind her. The roads had been terribly icy, but she'd made it home safely in one piece.

Her day had been a busy one, but Mitch had stayed in the forefront of her thoughts, where he was still as she shrugged off her coat and hung it over the back of a chair to dry.

She pulled her cell from the pocket. No calls. She knew it hadn't rung, but she had to check anyway. It was another sign that she already cared dangerously too much for this man.

As she turned up the thermostat, she noticed the time. Eight fifty-three. No way was she going to be able to wind down enough to sleep anytime soon. Her mind was spinning with all the horrible possibilities she wouldn't quite let herself imagine—and her stomach was one nauseated knot, as it had been all day.

I'm afraid for him. She couldn't deny it. She'd sent so many prayers skyward, surely every angel in heaven had heard them by now. She dropped her stuff on the floor and sank onto the edge of the couch. What was she going to do? She ached with regret. With all the ways she would never be able to care for this man.

With all the ways she wanted to.

In the silence of the night-dark apartment she fought to keep the past from coming alive. From seeing Joe's coffin, polished black in the funeral home, feeling the shattered pieces of her heart like broken glass shards, impossible to put back together. Her mother's words resonated in her head. "I told you. Didn't I tell you?"

She choked down the rest, forcing the images and sounds and feelings back down behind lock and key. If only she could wipe them away like an eraser over a chalkboard. Life wasn't like that.

To help chase away the shadows and the silence, she clicked on the TV and surfed, looking for something that caught her attention. But what she really wanted was for the phone to ring and Mitch's voice to be on the other end of the line.

She paused over the cable news channels for anything that would possibly concern him, but there was nothing there, and she really didn't expect there to be. He's fine, he's said over and over how well-trained he is. And, she thought, he certainly is a capable man, but that didn't break apart the concern that sat like an iceberg in the middle of her chest.

She didn't need one more sign. Look at how much she was hurting for him. Over him. This is too much, she told herself and buried her face in her hands. She wanted him to be safe with all of her might, but one thing was clear.

She was overinvolved. She cared too much. She *had* to stop ignoring the truth.

I'm in love with him. She was starting to dream, to let hope for a happy life with Mitch begin to grow. And wasn't that the worst mistake ever?

The snowstorm raged and thunder cannoned overhead. She sat unmoving while the darkness at the edge of the lamplight's reach deepened like despair. The phone rang once. Twice.

She leaned far enough over the arm of the couch to read the caller ID on the living-room extension. Out of Area. The same area code Mitch had called from earlier in the day.

Good, he was safe, thank God, that's all she needed to know.

She let it ring.

Chapter Fourteen

It's probably the intensive study week right before finals—that's why Kelly hadn't e-mailed him. Mitch rubbed his hands together in the cold hootch. The heaters had conked out again—they couldn't keep up with the cold. Maybe he'd send another e-mail, just so he would feel as if he'd done something instead of letting her slip away.

He started typing.

My Dear Kelly,
Sorry again that I had to cut our talk short. I know you're busy getting ready for finals, but here's another list. It's the good things I wish for you.

Easy finals that you breeze right through. Ice-free roads wherever you travel. Eggnog lattes steaming hot, every time you need one. I hope you get plenty of time to relax, take time for friends and that you have no regrets.

I'll be out, but I'll keep you in my prayers.
Love and fellowship, Mitch

And, he thought, he'd keep her in his heart. It wasn't enough, he thought as he sent the letter whizzing through cyberspace, but it was *all* he could do.

He'd leave the rest in God's hands.

"Did that poor man call *again?*" There was no mistaking the disapproval in Lexie's voice as she drizzled melted butter over the two heaping bowls of popcorn. "I say the gender is entirely untrustworthy, but there's always an exception to every rule, and I think Mitch is that rare exception. You should date him."

"No way. Especially not him." She didn't mention that she had his latest e-mail on her screen. That she'd gotten online to do some research at the library and what did she do? Check her e-mail just to see his name listed in her inbox.

What did that say? That she'd fallen hard for him. And that was one truth she could hardly admit to, and it was a truth she had to change.

She studied the half dozen e-mails he'd sent, one for every day that had passed since they'd spoken. The first apologizing for hanging up on her, that there had been some kind of attempt to attack their base camp, the second came posted near midnight his time, that they'd successfully tracked down the insurgents, and everyone in camp was safe. And of the remaining four e-mails, each was more concerned than the last. He was reaching out to her.

How did she tell him to stop reaching? To stop pushing? He wanted friendship. And she wanted...well, it was better not to put *that* into words.

"Why especially him?" Lexie wanted to know as she reached for the salt shaker.

"Because that man is a dream."

"Yeah. Duh. He ought to be your dream and you're going to lose this chance with him."

"A chance at what? He's stationed in California. He's just a friend. Here, let me read this." She pointed at the screen for emphasis. "'That you take time for friends.' He wrote that because I'm not emailing him back. He thinks I'm busy. So, we're friends. See? Just friends."

Lexie slipped one of the bowls on the table next to the laptop. She studied the screen doubtfully. "I saw the way he looked at you, and it has *nothing* to do with friendship."

"Exactly what does that mean?"

"Hey, don't get angry at the messenger." Lexie scooped the other bowl from the counter and filled her hand with the fluffy popped corn. "Mitch looks at you like you're a morning star he'd plucked from the sky to dream on. Write him or call him. I mean it, Kelly. He's one of the good guys."

Wasn't that the problem? And why was she so mad at him all of a sudden? Mad that he was so wonderful and perfect, that if he had been anything less than that, she wouldn't be hurting like this. She wouldn't be torn between the past and the present, between the lonely road she'd chosen and everything she was afraid of.

He wasn't hers to keep, but there was love in her heart for him anyway.

"Well, think about it." Lexie settled down on the couch and turned her attention to her schoolbooks.

I don't have to think about it. She knew exactly what had to be done. She hadn't realized how far he'd crept into her heart, but fearing for him showed her exactly how much she cared. She couldn't go back and pretend the interrupted phone call hadn't happened. She couldn't deny how deeply she'd been afraid for him or the breadth of her caring.

But neither could she take one more step on this path. She was in love with him. She didn't *want* to be in love with him because it was going to lead to heartache.

Be sensible, Kelly. She steeled her heart and gathered her defenses. She clicked closed the e-mail screen and typed in the library's address. She had priorities. She had her own goals, goals that would still be within her reach when Mitch was back safely from his tour and in California, where he belonged.

And if that broke her heart, it was only the truth. She'd learned the hard way never to dream.

Being really cold wasn't half-bad, once you got used to it. Mitch gulped down the dregs at the bottom of his C-4 cup of coffee and considered his current problem. He hunkered into his sleeping bag and considered his options.

He had second watch, so there was no sense to going to sleep for an hour, and with so much on his mind and the subzero temps in the small cavelet they'd found for the night, it would take him that long just to shiver himself warm enough to fall asleep.

His real problem was what to do about Kelly. He knew he wouldn't find an e-mail waiting for him when he got back to camp. Had he scared her off with his talk of dating and the future? Well, he'd just wanted to know where he stood and how he could make this work. Surely the good Lord hadn't brought him this far only for heartache.

Next to him Pierce was snoring, sound asleep. The next bag over Mark was writing to his wife. That's what he was thinking of doing too, except he was pretty sure Kelly hadn't written him back. She was moving away from him. He could feel it in his heart, like a light dimming.

Right now, there was nothing he could do about it. Not one thing. He only knew that he wouldn't be able to call her on her birthday like he'd wanted. It would be days before he had the chance to call, and who knew what mission after that? He was losing her.

Or was it already too late?

Lord, I need help on this one. Please. There came no answer in the frigid night.

In the pleasant warmth of the bookstore, with Christmas decorations cheering up the floor and customers shopping to the sound of holiday carols in the background, Kelly *should* have had enough on her mind with ringing up sales, gift-wrapping and helping shoppers.

In theory, she shouldn't have a free brain cell to spare, but she obviously did. And what was she doing with it? Going over her notes in her memory because her first final was cumulative and would be here before she knew it? No, she was thinking of Mitch's last e-mail. The one she'd sworn not to read, and then gone right ahead and read it.

Apparently she needed to ask for more willpower in her prayers tonight.

Kindly Mrs. Finch, her very favorite customer, ambled up to the cash wrap and slid a beautifully illustrated Bible on the counter. "Thank you so very much, young lady, for this wonderful suggestion. It's perfect. My great-granddaughter will treasure it."

"I'm sure she'll treasure you more, Opal. Would you like me to gift wrap this for you?"

"That would be wonderful, dear. I would like the paper with the golden angels."

"It will look really nice, I promise. And there's a coupon on this, so I'll ring it up at the lower price."

"That's good of you. I surely do appreciate the savings."

Kelly grabbed an in-house charge form and a pen. "This will just take a moment to wrap. You could get a cup of hot apple cider and wait in the reading area. That way you can put your feet up and relax."

"I'll do that, then." Opal's smile was as pure as always. "You and I haven't taken time to catch up. You must be working hard at your college studies."

"You know I am." Kelly rang up the sale and presented Opal with her copy of the charge slip. "Finals are coming up. You and I need to compare notes about the devotional."

"Oh, my!" Opal lit up as she slipped the charge slip into her cavernous purse. "It uplifts my spirits every day. Did you get a chance to read today's yet? 'My purpose is that they may be encouraged in heart and united in love.'"

"I did." Kelly was doing her very best not to dwell on it as she found a gift box on one of the lower shelves beneath the register. Time to change the subject. "Your great-granddaughter is hoping to get into MSU, right?"

"Now, don't change the subject, dear. I want to hear all about that handsome soldier who was so sweet on you." Opal looked delighted. "Spence mentioned him the last time I was in. Is he still serving overseas?"

"Yes, he is, and he's not sweet on me. Spence needs a talking-to." There was no venom behind her words; how could she fault Joe's cousin who was always looking out for her? He meant well. He simply didn't understand. "Mitch is only a friend."

"I'm sorry to hear that. He was such a strapping young man." Opal smiled knowingly as she turned away, adding over her shoulder, "Remember, there's more to life than studying. But don't take my advice. Turn to Scripture, dear."

This morning's devotional text popped into her mind. "My purpose is that they may be encouraged in heart and united in love."

Why did that feel so much like *not* a coincidence? Maybe because it couldn't be a sign. She refused to mistake it for one. No matter what. She would not be fooled again.

As she placed a torn-off sheet of the fragile golden-foil angel wrapping paper on the counter, the bell above the door announced another customer. Kelly recognized Holly from the jewelry shop a few blocks down, a close friend of Katherine's. "Hi, Holly, Katherine's in her office. Go right in."

"Actually, I'm here to see you." Holly set the small tasteful gift bag she was carrying on the counter. "This is from Mitch. Happy birthday."

"What?" Kelly stared at the bag, small and dainty. Only one thing could fit in a bag that small—the lovely jewelry that Holly made. "From Mitch?"

"He contacted me from his base. He'd had me hold this for him ever since you two were in my shop last summer." Holly slipped around the corner. "He must really be fond of you."

Mitch. She could only stare, stunned, at his thoughtfulness. He'd remembered her birthday. He'd remembered—no, he'd known at the time how much she'd admired the beautiful jewelry. Surely he hadn't bought the pearl angel she'd liked. No, he hadn't done that. He couldn't have. Because then that would mean *way too much.*

"Open it," Katherine said from her doorway, with a secret smile that said she'd known about this for some time. She disappeared into her office with Holly, but they left the door ajar.

Kelly's hands were shaking. A customer was approaching, shopping basket brimming, and she set the bag on the back counter. She resisted the temptation to glance inside because it would only make the locks around her heart buckle a tiny bit more.

"I'll get this." Spence stepped in with his no-nonsense attitude and stern manner, but there was a hint of a smile at the corners of his mouth as he took over her till. "You go take a break."

"Not until I get Mrs. Finch's Bible gift-wrapped." She stubbornly turned to her work, the gift bag glinting with foil threads of silver and gold.

Mitch. How was she going to keep hold of her senses now? His thoughtfulness touched her in the worst possible places. Her love for him remained, dazzling and enduring even as she fought it.

"Open the gift," Spence told her between ringing up sales. "It's your birthday. It shouldn't be a day of all work and no celebration."

"But that's why I'm here." She folded the last corner on Mrs. Finch's gift and taped it down neatly. "I'll open it later, when we're not so busy."

"What am I going to do with you?" Stern, Spence shook his head and frowned at her, but the concern in his eyes betrayed him.

She didn't know what she was going to do with herself either. She could not let herself start believing in fairy tales and happily ever afters. She was not Cinderella. She would not take a single step off her chosen path, the safe one God had graciously given her to walk. See what heartache came from dreaming? From wishing, just a little?

She secured a generous length of ribbon and made an extravagant bow on Mrs. Finch's package, slipped it into a shopping bag with a few coupons and complimentary sugar-free candy canes, and delivered it to Opal, who was enjoying a cup of apple cider and was pleased with the wrapping.

The store was busy with holiday shoppers, moms toting their babies or pushing strollers, families bursting with secrets as they browsed the store. It was like looking at the pieces of her broken hopes, seeing the happiness around her. The first year losing Joe had broken her to the core, and she had finally, two years after that, come to a numb acceptance.

Deep in her heart, in the secret quiet places only God knew, was the little girl's wish for a real family, a place to belong and someone to cherish with all of her heart. She used to believe God's promise that there would be good in her life. And love, which was the greatest of all.

But here she was, twenty-five today, with plenty of blessings and a calling to do good in this world, and what was she doing? Wishing for more than she deserved. And she knew it. Why? Because at the back of her mind she was waiting for the other shoe to fall. It was her birthday. That could only mean one thing.

"I want to see this gift," Katherine told her, after seeing Holly to the door. "Go into my office if you want some privacy first, but Kelly, this is a big deal."

"No, it's a birthday gift, something thoughtful, but it doesn't mean—"

"It does. You're still in contact with him, right?"

Kelly felt the twist of pain but she swallowed it down. Mitch. Each passing day she'd thought of him. Each day she'd resisted checking her e-mail. How did she explain? She didn't understand it herself. "I'm not dating him. You know that we're just friends."

"That's how it starts, you know."

"How what starts?"

"The real thing. True love. Happily ever after. It starts with being best friends. At least, that's what they tell me. I know, I know, you're going to start arguing with me, and that's okay. As long as you remember that as much as we all wished you could have married Joe and you'll always be a member of our family at heart, you need to move on. Find the blessings God has in store for you."

"Oh, Katherine, please don't break my heart like that." There was the past, the dreaded past, rising up like a tidal wave threatening to pull her into an ocean of feelings she did not want to face. She swallowed past the hopelessness. "Believe me, I have so much in my life to be thankful for. I have enough."

"I know the hard way—it's not enough. Life isn't quite as sweet or as meaningful without someone to love deeply."

Kelly couldn't speak past the emotions in her throat. In her heart. Weighing down her soul. She was hardly aware of Katherine steering her, along with Mitch's gift, into the cozy comfort of the corner office.

What did she do? If she didn't look inside the gift bag, then she wouldn't have to face the truth she'd been afraid of all along. She loved Mitch. He might feel more than friendship for her. Nothing could terrify her more.

Her chest clogged tight, as if buried under the weight of her broken dreams. She couldn't take one more loss. One more goodbye. *I will not step off this path.*

She swiped hot tears from her eyes, feeling as if her spirit was ripping down to the quick. It was fear that filled the cracked places and the wounded places inside her. Terror of being hurt like that again because she'd believed in the impossible.

I cannot believe in this. In what she could never have. Her finger shook as she pulled the small box from the bag. She already knew what she would find as she cradled the jeweler's box in the palm of her hand, but her pulse stalled at the gleam of pearl, and the shimmer of delicate gold that made up the halo and wings of an angel.

A small gift card said, "Here's a guardian angel to watch over you until I get back and can do the job."

Mitch. Did he have any idea what he was doing to her? She was breaking apart, the safeguards she'd built around herself crumbling like clay, exposing the raw, most vulnerable places that longed to believe. The heart of the girl she used to be when she believed in fairy tales and in dreams coming true.

When she'd believed God would find a way one day to give her real love and a place to belong.

Maybe this is your chance. The hope came in the quiet between heartbeats. It came from the deepest parts of her soul. Hope burned like banked embers breathing back to life.

I so want to love this man. What was she going to do? And even if he loved her in return…

No, don't go there. She closed the door on that thought and locked it away. No more wishes. Not one single hope. She replaced the lid on the box, and slipped the box into the gift bag.

If only she could put away the feelings in her heart as easily.

Lord, help take this wish from my heart. Please.

There was no answer. Only the constant slanting fall of the snowflakes outside the window and the faint musical rendition of "Silent Night" from the store's stereo system.

She'd never felt more alone.

Chapter Fifteen

The parking-lot lights beamed a safe path from the pizza parlor all the way to their parked cars. Since her arms were full with the pizza box of leftovers and bags of gifts from her party, Kelly held the door with her shoulder for her friends.

Lexie caught the door handle and helped her, juggling the remains of a cake. "What do you say we hit the ice creamery? We could carpool over. The roads look icy. I've got four-wheel drive."

"Sounds good to me." Jessica commented as she filed outside, zipping her parka snug. "I don't have to hurry home. How about you, Rose?"

"Count me in." Rose brought up the rear, pulling on her mittens.

It had been fairly easy not to have to think about Mitch's gift, which was tucked safely in her backpack's front pocket. But now, with the icy snowflakes brushing her cheeks and the momentary quiet as they all negotiated the icy parking lot without falling, Kelly had a split second where Mitch crowded her mind.

Maybe it was because the greasy, pepperoni tang of warm pizza drifted up through the lid of the pizza box she carried, reminding her of the bright summer night he'd shown up with pizza in hand and had affably watched the romantic comedy Lexie had picked up at the video store.

Just the remembered feeling of being in his presence that day made peace trickle all the way down to her soul. That peace remained through the hour spent at the ice cream shop and into the quiet of her bedroom where she studied, huddled in her flannel pajamas and fleece slippers, while the baseboard heater tried to keep up with the cold seeping in through the window and walls.

Why was she hurting like this? Everything within her ached like a snapped bone, and she couldn't concentrate at all on her studies. As pointless as it was, she took Mitch's gift from her backpack and opened the small box. In the bright reading lamp, the delicate angel's lacey wings and lustrous pearl gown gleamed like a promise.

This was no minor trinket and not a simple gift. This had come from his heart. She rubbed her fingers over the black inked words, written in a delicate script, probably Holly's, but she knew they were Mitch's words. "Here's a guardian angel to watch over you until I get back and can do the job."

Katherine's words from today troubled her. *The real thing. True love. Happily ever after. It starts with being best friends.*

She forced the fears and the whispers from the past aside.

Is there a way, Lord? Could Mitch really be meant for me? Every cell of her being hurt with the wish. In the deepest places within her soul, she wanted to believe. But was it possible?

Losing Joe still had a hold on her. How did she find enough faith to believe that the future could be different? That there were good things waiting for her, good things that wouldn't be jerked from her the minute she reached for them?

The phone rang. When she checked the caller ID, it was Out of Area, from an area code she didn't recognize. It was her birthday, and that was often a day her mom tried to contact her, but what if it was Mitch calling?

"I bet it's Mitch," Lexie called from her room.

I bet it is, too. It would be just like him to call tonight. She lifted the receiver, longing for the warmth of his baritone and a connection to him, and terrified of it at the same time. "Hello?"

There was no crackle on the line, no overseas static. The hesitation was all wrong. She knew who it was before she heard her mother say her name. "Kelly? Is that really my sweet baby?"

I should have had Lexie answer it, Kelly realized, too late. The voices from her past rose up, and there were no defenses strong enough to stop them. Memories she'd held down for so long crashed like a tidal wave, making the past so immediate and vivid she could taste the hollowness and desolation. She knew this was part of her mom's pattern—she'd try to make up and then the pleas for money would start. Then the stealing.

"Mom," she managed to choke out. "You're not supposed to call me. The court said you can't."

"But you're my own little girl."

How many times had she heard that phrase? When she'd been six years old, holding her mom's hair when she was sick from being drunk. When she was ten years old and her mother was high on drugs. When she was twelve years old and they had lost their apartment and were standing in line at a shelter.

Stop it. She squeezed her eyes shut, gritting her teeth, but the images just kept coming. Her mom's anger when Kelly had wanted to live with her aunt Louise. The calls and every attempt to visit whenever Kelly had her life finally leveling out. Her mom arriving uninvited at Joe's funeral and whispering, after the service, "It's just as well he's gone. You might as well learn it now. No one's gonna love you enough to last, girl. You're too much like me."

For once, Kelly broke the pattern and hung up the phone. It was as if all the footholds she'd built to hold up her life buckled and came crashing down. What if her mother was right? That's exactly how it felt. What if every time her life became stable, all it took was her past to knock it down? What if the foundations of her life, her beginnings in life, were not strong enough to support a good future? Whatever the case, Kelly couldn't allow her mother back in her life until the woman made a significant effort to heal.

As time ticked by she placed the jeweler's box into

her backpack. After a while, the dark shadows did not seem so bleak. The memories of the girl she'd been, heart wide open waiting to belong, faded away.

She didn't know how long it was until the phone rang again, and Lexie hurried through the doorway. "We'll just turn off the ringer. Is there anything I can do?"

Kelly shook her head.

"I'll make you some tea. My mom says honey and chamomile tea makes anything a little bit better." Lexie disappeared.

Kelly reached for her Bible. She knew that the Lord worked all things for the good of His faithful. Sometimes it was all she could do to believe, but she held on to her faith with both white-knuckled hands and did not let go.

In the bleak gray of the rugged eastern Afghanistan landscape, Mitch huddled with his team. The spot they'd chosen was well-hidden from the road below, and it offered good protection from the cruel wind whipping down from the glaciered peaks. Hunkered down, they should be undetectable, but he stayed on high alert.

Pierce leaned close, speaking in a voice lower than a whisper. "Not a lot of activity. Doesn't feel right, though."

"Nope. Like we're in the crosshairs." It wasn't a good sign when the hunters felt hunted. He scanned the lower, opposing slope with his gun scope.

Nothing. Maybe it would stay that way. A few more hours, they would radio command, and come dark, extraction. He'd be on a bird out of here.

And then he felt it, as if a steady light in his heart winked out. It was Kelly. She was gone, just like that, and he knew that he'd lost her love. That she had let go of him.

And there was nothing he could do about it.

Hopeless, Kelly opened the window blinds so she could feel the gray light of dawn fall across her face. Exhaustion settled around her like the freezing fog outside, cloaking her, keeping her numb. Her heart beat dully, without feeling, like the deadness that follows a great shock.

Or a great loss.

How can I do this? How can I find the words to tell Mitch goodbye? Rising tears burned in her throat.

Outside the window, freezing fog shrouded the treetops and veiled the sky and mountains from view. Snow mantled the world, clung to the barren poplar limbs, covered the sidewalks and street and rooftops below, and frosted the view like icing on a cake. The gray cold seeped into her soul.

Being alone was the truth of her life. A truth she'd learned to accept the hard way. She didn't want any more lessons teaching her that. The ones she'd had so far had been painful enough. She couldn't go through that loss one more time.

You have to let him go, Kelly. She felt the past whisper. Felt the pain of Joe's loss rising up through the numbness. The wounds within her began to reopen, whispers of memories that she could no longer silence. Joe, who'd come from the black-sheep branch of the

McKaslin family, who'd grown up with his dad in and out of jail, who'd understood. How her greatest fear in life was that her mother was right.

How would Mitch understand?

What if God had already worked a miracle in her life, bringing her on this path instead of into a desperate life like her mother's? What if this was the great good meant for her and there would be nothing more?

Down deep, she knew, if she took one step off this path and risked her heart again, everything would crumble. She'd had that lesson over and over again. Fear clawed through her, sharp-taloned and relentless.

I don't need to hurt like that one more time.

Letting him go was the sensible thing to do. It was the right thing to do, the safest decision. Just do it, Kelly. Stop procrastinating. Do the right thing.

She stared at her computer screen, alone in the apartment, heartsick. How was she going to say goodbye? She had no heart left to feel with. No faith left over to try to believe. Even if he was her dream come true. Even if he was everything wonderful and noble and good she'd ever believed in. Summer felt so far away, with the bright green world and bold sunshine and the rumble of Mitch's laughter as he'd hauled her out of the cool river.

That's how it starts, Katherine's words came back to her. *The real thing. True love. It starts with being best friends.*

She buried her face in her hand and remained perfectly still, letting the past settle down, hoping the memories would release her, but they didn't. There was no solace, no comfort as the heater clicked on, whirring under the curtains, which swayed and billowed. The pain and emptiness of her past was nothing compared to the anguish of this moment without Mitch. And of all the moments to come without him.

She covered her mouth, stopping the sob from escaping. Nothing could stop the grief shattering her soul.

I'm so sorry, Mitch. She was a realist these days, and not a dreamer. She would keep both feet on the ground. Mitch was not hers to keep. Not now. Not ever.

All the prayers in the world wouldn't change it.

Her vision blurred as she placed her trembling fingertips above the keys. Just when she thought she couldn't take another goodbye, here she was, typing that dreaded word that cut like a blade through her soul.

Battle-weary and heartsick, Mitch wasn't at all surprised to see a single e-mail from Kelly waiting for him. He was exhausted, the images on the screen blurred. He scrubbed his eyes and tried to focus.

This could not be good news. He could feel it in his gut, the same way he'd known in the bush deep in enemy territory that things were about to go south.

Retreat would be safer.

He opened the e-mail and felt as he had on the side of the mountain, as if he were caught in a rifle's scope.

Dear Mitch
First of all, I hope you are safe and well. I care about you and I always will, and I want good things for you and your life.

He rubbed his beard, greasy from face paint, and tried to calm the shock settling in his chest. He'd known this was waiting for him. That wasn't what surprised him. It was that she was really doing it, that there was no way to undo this. He was half a world away and it might as well be the whole universe separating them. She was ending it. No, he corrected, feeling the void in his heart. She already had.

I'll always be glad you walked into the bookstore that bright summer day. You have no idea how much I will treasure this time I've spent being your friend, but I have to say goodbye. Although I was touched by it, I can't accept your gift. Finals start next week, and I'm going to be too busy to e-mail, and by the time they're done, you'll be home in California and you'll have no more need for a pen pal, I'm sure, so I'll just say goodbye.
Kelly

Goodbye. He stopped breathing at her words. It took a moment to sink in. She was returning the gift. Pretending all that had ever been between them was a pen-pal thing.

His heart broke, piece by piece, cracking all the way down to his soul. How could she end it like this?

"Dalton." It was Scott, the corpsman, lumbering into the hootch looking as haggard as Mitch felt. "I gotta take a look at your arm."

"It's nothing. Just a little shrapnel."

"After you hit the shower and chow, stop by and let me look at it. You'll need stitches."

"Nah. I'm good." It wasn't the jagged gash or the hunk of metal he'd pulled out of it that was his problem.

"You'd better come, or I'll hunt you down," Scott called over his shoulder on his way out.

The hootch was empty this time of day, and the sounds of other teams training outside faded into the background. Mitch rubbed his forehead with the heel of his hand. How was he going to fix this? Was it possible? It had to be. *Right, Lord?*

No answer. He'd halfway expected one, he thought as he thumbed a calling card from his pocket. How could he have lost so much in a single day? He hauled his overtired body out of the metal chair. It was 0400 in her part of the world. He'd call her after he showered and put some food in his gut. Maybe by then he would have mastered this pain. Maybe by then he would have figured out a way to fix this.

He knew one thing for sure. He would not give up, he would not give in, and he would not go down. Nothing in his life had ever mattered like this. Kelly was his heart's choice.

No matter what.

He prayed to God that he could still be her choice, too.

In the cocoon of the university's library, Kelly chose an empty table next to the stacks. All around her other students were busy studying, reading or researching. She had a few more facts to look up for her term paper, which was due tomorrow. As she unzipped her laptop case, she noticed an ROTC student in his uniform seated two tables over.

Mitch. Her life had been just fine until he'd first walked into the bookstore. From that moment, her life had changed. She hadn't realized it, but coming to know him and fall in love with him had filled a place in her soul she hadn't known was empty. A place that had never been filled before.

It was empty now, like her life. How had he come to mean so much to her? Mitch had become a part of her day. She hadn't realized all the time she'd spent thinking about him, or finding fun things to tell him in e-mails, or looking forward to checking her inbox and seeing his name there.

Every time she'd turned on the TV, she'd checked the news channels. When she saw the reports and footage of the devastation left by car bombings, or reports of the latest military conflict far from home, she knew that Mitch was out there with his men and his weapons and his skills doing his best to protect freedom.

And his gift…the image of his words were etched in her mind. He wanted the job of watching over her.

How had it come to this? How had she let it?

Forget his strength and tenderness. Forget the joy he'd brought to her life. Forget the emotional connection he'd made to her heart.

Forgetting wasn't so easy. Longing filled her, an unstoppable love for Mitch. With every breath she took, it was as if more love filled her up. More affection for him. She couldn't stop it. She wasn't strong enough to stop it.

Take this love for him from my heart, Lord. Please.

There was no answer. Just the one in her heart growing stronger and more true. Right along with the dreams she knew better than to let herself start believing.

In the purposeful activity of the staging area, Mitch shivered in the open air, despite the adrenaline kicking through his veins. He was packed and good to go, except for this one last thing. Impatient, he waited for the satellite phone to connect.

So far away, the line began to ring in Kelly's apartment. He counted the rings above the drone of the prepping helicopters. Two. Three. Four.

C'mon, Kelly, pick up. Gritting his teeth, he waited, his heart dark and empty. Four rings. Five.

He bowed his head. *Please let her answer, Lord. I'm out of time here.*

Six rings. Then an electronic beep. He hung on, he needed to talk to her. He needed this fixed before he went out. Then he heard it, her voice. Her sweet soft voice.

"Please leave a message," was all she said. The gentle sound was like a guiding light in a dark storm, and eased some of the pain down deep.

He scrubbed his hand over his face. Leaving a message was the last thing he wanted. "Kelly, if you're there. Pick up."

Nothing. He knew she was there. Rent down to the soul, he did the only thing left. He told her the truth.

"I'm headed out on a pretty serious mission. I don't know when I'll be back. I just…want to know what I did wrong."

He waited, *feeling* her on the other end, listening to him. He knew what the losses she had suffered could do to a person. He was guilty of some of that himself—closing your heart off and staying distant to keep from getting too close and feeling too much. It was easier.

But it was no way to live. Maybe God had led him to Kelly, because she needed more.

And, Mitch was man enough to admit, he needed more, too.

He cleared the raw emotion from his throat. "You are an awesome blessing in my life, and I—" Love you more than I thought possible, he didn't say, he held back the truth, the frightening truth because he could feel her rejection ready to fall like a thrown grenade.

"Don't forget me." It was all he could say before his throat closed. He loved her. No matter what. And that love, even if she could not return it, remained, not fading, and not budging.

I'll be back, he promised as he handed back the phone, grabbed his MP-5, ready to roll.

Lord, please keep her heart open to me, he prayed. But a cold fear began to gnaw at him. What if there was no way to fix this? What if it was too late?

His future stretched out before him without her, without light. Like the sun going down on his life.

Safe in the warmth of her apartment, Kelly turned away from the answering machine, pressed her face in her hands and fought the bleak, heartbreaking grief. The last hope within her had died.

Letting him go wasn't easy. It *was* the best thing. The safest decision for them both.

But it didn't feel that way. Neither determination, nor distance, nor her own fears could halt the love she felt for him. She feared nothing could.

At least it was over, she thought with relief. She had her path in life, and Mitch had his.

Chapter Sixteen

It was Christmas Eve, and Kelly was thankful she had volunteered to work at the bookstore until closing. It kept her from thinking, and since her thoughts always wandered to Mitch, it was a good thing to keep busy. It was easier to ignore her shattered heart that way.

As she carefully removed the porcelain figurine from the front window display she had a perfect view of the dark parking lot as an SUV pulled off the street and maneuvered through the snow.

Although the snowfall obscured all but the headlights from her sight, the vehicle parked right in front, beneath the filtered glow of the tall security lights. The driver's door open and a booted foot hit the ground. Her pulse jerked to a stop.

That was a military boot, just like Mitch wore. No, it can't be him. She froze, the warmth of the store, the caroling of the sound systems, the frantic bustle of last-minute shoppers faded into nothing.

There was only the sight of the soldier dressed in

camouflage climbing from his vehicle. One look at his wide shoulders and joy speared through her soul.

Mitch. The cry came from the deepest part of her being. In the exact same split second her eyes registered that the man wasn't as tall or as powerfully muscled, and, as he cut through the light crossing in front of the vehicle, he wasn't Mitch.

Disappointment left her arctic cold. The pain of it left her light-headed, but she could not look away from the soldier, who opened the passenger door and helped a woman from the front seat.

Kelly could only stare, captivated, by the sight of the soldier and his wife as they gazed into one another's eyes for a brief moment—a moment that seemed to stretch timelessly—before he turned to lift a baby in a carrier from the back seat. The loving family was straight out of her most secret dreams.

It was like looking at what might have been, what could have been.

What still might be, her heart whispered so strongly.

It can never be, she thought firmly. Hadn't she put all her foolish wishes to rest?

The couple approached the front door, and the soldier released his wife's hand to open it for her. They smiled loving, quiet smiles to one another, clearly bonded in love.

Broken pieces of her dreams were all around her, but she managed to smile at the couple who entered the store and walked past her, hands linked, talking low and warmly to one another.

See how I don't want that at all? She thought as she

took a sheet of bubble wrap and carefully covered the exquisite shepherd with it. Okay, she was just saying that to protect herself. To try to make it true. It was basic psychology. You simply couldn't lose anyone you loved truly, if you refused to love anyone that much.

By the time she'd boxed the figurine, wrapped it and added the purchase to Opal Finch's charge account, Katherine was ringing up the soldier and his wife, who had purchased a blown-glass angel, a last-minute gift.

It took all her strength, but she couldn't stop a great sense of loss from wrapping around her. Wasn't she supposed to be forgetting Mitch? Moving on with her life? She'd prayed and prayed for God to take this love from her heart, but it remained, stubborn and strong no matter what she did to try to get rid of it.

She delivered the gift to Opal, waiting in the reading area where refreshments and Christmas cookies were set out on red-clothed tables. Opal glanced up from chatting with her daughter, and her smile shone warmly. "You are a lifesaver, dear girl. I was at my wit's end when I learned Margie's mother-in-law was coming to town after all."

"I'm glad I could help." Kelly handed the bagged package to Opal's youngest daughter, a lovely middle-age woman with Opal's same smile and gracious manner. "If there's anything else you need, you just let me know. I hope you both have a Merry Christmas."

"I wish you Merry Christmas, too, dear." Opal looked lovely and content as she sipped from her cup of holiday blend tea. "Margie and I have done all our running for the day, and it's a comfort to sit right here and enjoy the decorations. Will I see you at the candle-light service tonight?"

Kelly fetched the teapot, still hot in its cozy, and removed the insulated cover. She leaned to fill Opal's cup. "I'll be there."

"Wonderful. Why, you'll just have to meet my new great-grandbaby. She's just three weeks old, but good as an angel. You make sure and come find us."

"I promise," she vowed as she filled Margie's cup.

If Kelly was given a wish to be fulfilled by the angels on this cold Christmas Eve night, it would be to have a life like Opal's. To be content in her golden years with family she took joy in, and a life behind her in which each and every day had been filled with love, as would all her days to come. Loving Mitch, of course.

Too bad she wasn't the kind of girl who believed in wishes and dreams.

Although how she wanted to.

"Kelly, did you read from your devotional this morning?" Opal asked over the rim of her teacup. "'With the Lord, nothing is impossible.'"

Kelly replaced the teapot on the table. How did she answer that? Some thing *were* impossible, she knew that for certain. "I did read the passage."

"I'm holding out hope for you." Opal's eyes twinkled. "It's the season for miracles, you know."

"I know, and there's more to life than studying. I can't argue with that." Mitch. Why did she think of him and miracles in the same breath?

The store's frantic Christmas Eve rush had thinned ten minutes before closing time. As she pitched in to help Katherine catch up on the gift-wrapping at the front counter, she tried to get her thoughts in the right place. No more thinking of Mitch. End of story.

As she folded and taped the last corner of Mr. Brisbane's gift, Katherine surprised her by withdrawing a small package from her blazer pocket, wrapped in simple gold tissue paper. "I know we're exchanging presents when you come over to dinner tomorrow, but I want you to have this. It will look perfect on your Christmas tree."

Kelly studied the small gift that fitted in the palm of her hand. "Thanks, Katherine. Should I open it now?"

"No, this is definitely something you should open alone. Why don't you do that now? Go. I wanted to let you go earlier, paid of course, as a treat, but who knew we were going to be so busy?"

"I have no one waiting for me at home. I can stay and help you close."

"I'm not doing anything but unplugging the coffeepot, counting down the tills and setting the alarm. That's it. So, go on." Katherine took the gift from Kelly's hand, snapped a gift bag open and dropped it in, and clipped around the long counter. "Go home, Kelly. Merry Christmas."

"Merry Christmas, Katherine." She so loved working for the McKaslins. There was no way she would ever feel lonely in her life, not when she had the blessing of truly nice people in it. There was little to do but to wave goodbye to Opal and her daughter, grab her coat and backpack and trudge out the back door.

Snow fell in a thick veil, scouring her as she fought

her way to her car. Her poor ten-year-old sedan was buried in snow, and by the time she'd swept off the windows and scraped the crusty layer of ice off the glass, her curiosity was getting the best of her. What had Katherine given her?

Huddled in her cold seat, with the defrosters on high fighting at the foggy windshield, she folded back the tissue paper and there, in a bed of gold, lit by the glow of the dash lights, was a small tin soldier. An ornament for her tree.

Her heart broke into a million pieces, and how could that be? It was already broken. Tears struggled to the surface, no matter how hard she blinked to stop them.

I love him so much, she thought, not knowing if she was wishing or, more, if she were praying. She'd lost too many people she'd loved. That was her life, it was not going to change. It was impossible. Right?

Mitch was an elite soldier. Talk about a risky profession. And it wasn't only the fear of him being killed in combat, but the fact that he belonged in California, and that she was safer with him far away.

This was the path God had made for her, and she clung to it with everything she had. It felt as if the ground was crumbling beneath her feet and she was holding on to a fraying rope. Watching it unravel. Watching it snap.

Knowing she about to fall.

With the Lord, nothing is impossible. The text seemed to follow her as she put her car in gear and navigated through the storm. Or was it the fear in her own heart? She tried to banish memories of the lost little girl she'd been, stubbornly clinging to the hope for the happy endings, like those she read in books.

She fought against the memories as she negotiated the icy city, but the images of Christmases past rose up, unbidden and unwanted. The Christmas Eves her mom had come home horribly drunk or high, and the Christmas Eves when she hadn't come home at all.

As a little girl, Kelly would sit in the living room of whatever apartment they'd been in that year, with no glow from a Christmas tree and no presents, and wish on the brightest star in the sky, which she'd thought was the real Christmas Star, for her mom to get well. For a place to belong. To grow up like the princess in the fairy tales and find true love, a good handsome prince—just like Mitch—and a happily ever after.

Even now, there was Mitch. In her thoughts. In her heart. In her soul. Snow fell harder as she eased down the street in front of her apartment building. If she saw a tan Jeep covered with snow along the curb, it had to be her imagination. She pulled into the nearly vacant lot—most students had fled campus for home—and shut off the car.

Snow tapped in big determined flakes, blanketing her windshield. She glanced at the ornament, cloaked in night shadows, and felt the truth bubble to the surface. She still felt like that little girl, deep at heart, alone in the dark, afraid of being alone forever. The little girl feared she wasn't good enough to love. And if something good happened to her, then it wouldn't last.

Now she was an adult with the same fears, fears she'd never faced, and never overcome. Maybe pushing everything down wasn't the best way to deal with them, she knew, but it didn't matter now.

Tucking her heart away, she zipped the soldier ornament into her backpack and stepped out into the freezing storm. The snow tapped loudly, filling the eerie emptiness of the parking lot. Her thoughts drifted to Mitch, always to Mitch. Where was he on this holy night? Was he cold or warm? In hostile territory or home with his family? He'd come back from his last mission safely, right?

Wherever he was, she wished him warm, safe thoughts. She would always love him, no matter what, no matter how far away and how separate their paths in life.

A hunched shadow emerged from around the corner of the building, barely visible through the haze of snowfall.

Alarm coiled through her even before she recognized the woman's voice, the sound from her past, the sound of her fears.

"K-Kelly, my sweet baby? Is that you?" Her mother's thin hair sticking out beneath a worn-looking knitted hat was gray, and her face was marked by time and hard wear. She had that false look of caring on her face.

Kelly took a step back, fighting down the shame and the hurt roiling up out of the shadows of memories. She caught a faint scent of cheap whiskey. Of course her mom was drinking. She knew her mother would never change, and that meant the woman had come for sympathy and to try to steal something to support her other habits. It was the past that hurt so much, the memories and the betrayal. “You have to go back to the shelter, Mom. It’s not that far.”

“But I come all this way. In the cold. Just to see my baby girl.”

“No, Mom. You know you’re supposed to keep away from me.” She felt the weight of the past like an open wound, bleeding and raw. “The court says you have to.”

“But I’m clean.” She swayed as she limped along the snowy walkway. “I brought you a present. Are you gonna let me come in?”

“I don’t want something you stole.” The rank scent of cheap alcohol on the wind was stronger, bringing up memories that cut straight to her spirit. “I’m sorry. You have to go now. Go back where you belong.”

“That is no way to treat your mother. What is wrong with you? No wonder you’re all alone. You think you’re so high and mighty, but go ahead. All that praying won’t change the truth. You’re still the same down deep.”

She knew that her mom was drunk and mean, but logic didn’t rule the heart. Nor did fears nurtured by a lifetime of being alone. Kelly took another step back, whipped her cell phone out of her pocket. “Mom, you aren’t supposed to leave the shelter, I’m sure. So, if you’ll be nice, I’ll call a cab and pay the fare for you. Or I can call the police. It’s up to you.”

“Why, you no good little—”

Before her mother could fly at her, a tall, powerfully shouldered man materialized soundlessly out of the shadows. Coming through the thickly falling snow and shadows, he caught Dora Logan by the upper arm, subduing her. "You heard Kelly. You need to get to a shelter, or you'll be dealing with the cops."

Mitch. His baritone boomed with authority. He radiated honorable strength. That attractive capable masculinity. Just like that, he was in her life again. Towering before her, looking like her best and brightest wish, too good to be true. Sweet longing welled up through her soul.

As her mother left, sputtering curse words that faded as she melted into the darkness, Mitch remained, invincible, at her side. For an instant, she felt as if it was summer again, with sunshine on her face and Mitch's presence like a steady light in her heart.

But then she realized he had to have heard her mom's words. Every last one of them. The damage was done. Her head hung, and in the endless stretch of silence between her and Mitch, she couldn't think of a single thing to say to make this better, to erase the echo of her mother's words. Or the truth of them.

She heard the icy flakes tap against her hood as she stumbled toward the steps. Her throat was one giant knot of misery she couldn't speak past, not even to thank him. For, in saving her, he'd learned the terrible truth of who she was and where she came from.

He now knew that beneath the responsible girl and straight-A student and faithful Christian, she was afraid that she wasn't worthy of being loved. That her past was like a wandering black hole sucking up all the goodness that would ever happen in her life.

She started up the snow-covered stairs, shame sputtering through her.

"Kelly, are you all right?"

She shook her head; she wasn't all right. His question was like a knife piercing deep. She hesitated midstep. "Thank you for—" She couldn't look him in the eye so she stared into the storm where her mom had disappeared. Her throat closed up again. What did she do now?

"C'mon, let's get you out of the cold." Mitch padded towards her like a lone alpha wolf.

She didn't have to look to know how shadows darkened the hazel-green of his eyes or to see the wince of sorrow around his mouth. She felt the emotion in his heart as if it were her own. She didn't want to feel so much, to be too close to anyone. Ever again.

But he was coming ever closer, the nearly silent sound of his boots halted directly behind her. She could feel his affection radiating like the wind against her cheek, and when she heard the faint rustle of his jacket she knew, even before the solid weight of his big hand settled on the dip of her shoulder. Peace trickled into her cracked heart like hope, like mercy. And her love for him flared brightly, like a light burning despite the darkness, a love she could not put out.

His touch remained, firmly guiding her as they ascended the steps together. Helpless to stop him, unable to speak, her hopes gone, she swiped the snow from her face and felt tears burn behind her eyes. Whatever she did, she would not cry. Could not.

She had to face this—face him—with as much dignity as she could muster. She was a pro when it came to pushing shame and hurt down into the rooms of her heart and locking the door. She had to do that now.

He was going to withdraw now—she knew it. He'd seen her in a different light—and he would never see her the same way again. The only thing she could do was to expect his coming rejection and his inevitable departure.

Her fingers fumbled stupidly with her key ring.

"Let me." His words were a gentle fan against her cheek as he leaned closer and took the keys from her.

For Mitch, all it took was one touch to her hand and a supernova of certainty blazed through him. He felt whole. It felt right, having her here at his side. Tenderness brightened in degree and volume until his heart could not hold it all.

As he unlocked the door and held it for her, blocking the worst of the wind-driven cold, he had time to think. He could see why Kelly was so persistent at pushing him away. Well, other than Joe, whose leaving had been accidental, he could see a long line of people in Kelly's life who hadn't had the character or the inner fiber to love her enough to stick by her.

It made sense, he thought, as he followed her into the apartment and closed the door against the driving snow, that she'd lost faith. She felt her heart had been broken too much. A long line of experiences of never belonging, of never having anyone to depend on, might lead you to believe that.

But he was the one man who knew how to stand and fight for what—and who—mattered. He saw now why people risked so much for the chance at real love. For the chance to make a marriage work, despite the uncertainty and the failure rate. He would have no life of any value unless he had her at his side. She gave meaning to his life. To him.

The question was, had he come all this way for nothing? He couldn't see an answer either way, yes or no, as she shrugged out of her snow-flocked parka.

He was used to danger, he was well-trained and prepared to handle any adversity in the field. He risked his life every time he went out on a mission. He spent his life training and working and practicing to be good at what he did. But when it came to Kelly, he was walking along a vulnerable path. No flak jacket existed to protect him from heartbreak if she shot him down.

She held out her hand for her keys. "Th-thank you for coming along when you did." Her voice echoed faintly in the hallway, and she didn't meet his gaze. "I-I'm glad you're back safely."

"Good." Mitch placed her keys in her gloved palm. "I need to know that you care for me. And how much."

What did she do with this man and his constant caring? She wanted to lash out, to say whatever it took to push him back, to put safe distance between her heart and his.

She squared her shoulders and faced all six-feet-two-inches of him. If only there was a way to change the deepest places within her, all the cracks and old wounds, so that she was good enough and whole enough to try to hold a dream again. A part of her wanted to tell him the truth, the part of her that loved him beyond all reason and good sense and with every last bit of her soul.

He padded closer, soundlessly, as stealthy as a stalking wolf, until he towered over her, close enough to touch, one hundred percent good man and noble heart. "Maybe it would help if I went first."

"I don't think that will help at all." All it would do was to shatter her a little deeper. She had no more strength, she was not strong enough to keep the walls around her soul from crashing down.

He took a box out of his pocket and cradled it in his palm. "This is why I'm here. To ask you to be my wife."

Yes, her heart answered. She knew it was impossible, she was too afraid to believe. Her soul ached with dreams yet to be made and wished and to come true.

Step away, Kelly. Right now. Her heart did not want to. Her soul felt ripped apart and she couldn't do it. She wanted to pray for the chance to say yes to this man, to wear his wedding ring and take his name and share his life.

There I go, dreaming again. Believing in fairy tales. She was a realist these days and not a dreamer. She would keep both feet on the ground. Mitch was not hers to keep. Not now. Not ever.

All the prayers in the world wouldn't change it.

Wait, her heart told her. *Only* prayer can change it.

He cradled her chin with his free hand, gazing down at her and in his hazel eyes she could see his soul, full of love for and devotion to her.

Both the little girl she'd been and the woman she was ached to know what real love was like—real love that could last. That could shelter her from the storms of life, that would show her a loving man's tenderness and care.

If only she could have this man to love. If only God could see fit to change her path, change her destiny and give her this one chance. *Please, Lord.* Her entire soul shattered with need.

As if Mitch heard her prayers, he slanted his mouth over hers. Her spirit stilled. Her heart paused. He covered her lips with his in a tender caress.

Her soul sighed. His kiss was like a dream. Sweetness filled her. Like the river whirling over the rapids, the power of it burst through her with the purest force—and there was no way to stop it. She breathed in the brightness. She curled her fingers into his snow-damp shirt and held on to this perfect moment. Where there was no emptiness. No shadows. No pain.

Just the rush of true love swirling up from her soul. Filling the emptiness. Pushing out the shadows. Healing every crack and fissure and broken place inside.

"I know you're afraid of loving and losing again," he said as he pulled an engagement ring of pearls and diamonds from the box he held. "But I want you to know that the love I have for you in my heart is infinite. Nothing can end it. Nothing can diminish it. Not hardship, not distance and not death. The truth is, only God knows what is going happen, but I want you to know I'm committed. I want to walk the rest of my life with you. So, will you marry me?"

She rubbed the heel of her hand over her heart, surprised it was whole. Didn't the Bible tell her to hold on until morning? All sorrows ended, all hurts would heal, and joy would come? She had enough faith, after all, to dream. "I love you with all of my soul. Yes, I will marry you."

"I am so glad." He slipped the ring on her trembling finger. "Because my mother is hoping you'll come to church with us tonight. She's vowed to spoil you. As for me," he brought her into his arms and cradled her to his heart, "I'm going to love you forever."

"That's a promise I'm going to make you keep." She saw the future stretch out before her, full of promise, of family, of loving Mitch.

It was a night of miracles, she thought, as she laid her cheek against his granite chest. It had been a rough journey, but God had seen her through. He had brought her here, to Mitch. She was sure now that there would be more miracles to come.

* * * * *

HER HOLIDAY FAMILY

Ruth Logan Herne

To the real Tina, one of the strongest
and most amazing women I know. God blessed me
the day we crossed paths in Denver, and He has
continued to do so ever since. I love you, Teenster.
And to Terry, Sean, Dan and Ronnie, my siblings
who served when I was too young to understand the
amazing sacrifice they made. Thank you. I love you.
Your dedication is an inspiration to so many!

Acknowledgments

Big thanks to Tony and Debby Giusti, who are always
willing to offer me advice on my military heroes.
Your expertise is invaluable and I'm so grateful!
To Melissa Endlich and Giselle Regus for their
well-tuned advice about how to strengthen Tina and
Max's story. Your advice produced a stronger book
and I thank you! To Natasha Kern, my beloved agent,
a woman with amazing patience and insight.
I am so blessed to be working with you!

To Beth for all of her help and advice
on how to write a better story. To the Seekers, who
are always there, ready to have my back as needed!
To Basel's Restaurant, a fun family-style Greek
restaurant here upstate where I spent eleven years
waiting tables. Real life is the very *best* research.
And to Lakeshore Supply Company, our new local
hardware store: I'm so glad you moved to town!
Charlie Campbell's store came alive because of
your delightful Hamlin and Hilton stores.

For if you forgive others their trespasses,
your heavenly Father will also forgive you.
—*Matthew* 6:14

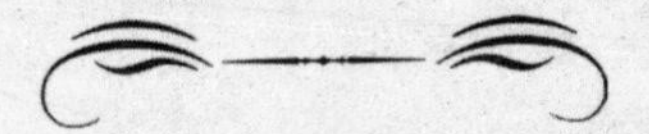

Chapter One

The old familiar voice stopped Tina Martinelli in her tracks as she stepped through the back door of Campbell's Hardware Store late Sunday morning. "I'll do whatever you need, Dad. I'm here to stay."

Max Campbell was here? In Kirkwood Lake?

Max Campbell, her teenage crush. The Campbell son who'd enlisted in the army and had never looked back. Max Campbell, the to-die-for, dark-haired, brown-eyed, adopted Latino son who'd broken countless hearts back in the day? The guy who used to hang out at her neighbor's house, until Pete Sawyer and his girlfriend lost their lives in a tragic late-night boating accident.

She'd never seen Max at the Sawyers' again. Not to visit Pete's parents. Not to offer Pete's little sister, Sherrie, a hug. Abnormally quiet became the new normal.

No more Max, no more Pete, no more parties.

A lot had changed on one warm, dark summer's night.

The wooden back door of Campbell's Hardware swung shut before she could stop it, the friendly squeak announcing her arrival. She did a very feminine mental reassessment before moving forward.

Hair?

Typical elfin crazy.

Nails?

Short and stubby, perfect for a hardware clerk, but not for coming face-to-face with Max Campbell over a decade later.

Makeup?

She hadn't bothered with any. She'd spent her early morning testing a new recipe, something she hoped to use in the not-too-distant future.

"Tina? That you?" The forced heartiness of Charlie Campbell's voice said she had little choice but to move forward, so that's what she did.

"I'm here, Charlie." She strode into the store, shoulders back, chin high, when what she wanted was a thirty-minute makeover. Why hadn't she worn her favorite jeans, the ones that made her feel young, jazzed and totally able to handle whatever life handed out?

Because you were coming to work in a hardware store, and who wears their best jeans to work in a hardware store?

The two men turned in tandem.

Her heart stopped when she locked eyes with Max. She set it right back to beating with a stern internal warning because, despite Max's short, dark hair and dangerously attractive good looks, the guy had left his adoptive family when he'd finished college and hadn't come back since. And that was plain wrong.

"Tina, you remember our son Max, don't you?" Pride

strengthened Charlie's voice, while the effects of his ongoing chemotherapy showed the reality of his current battle with pancreatic cancer. "He's a captain now, but he's come back home for a while."

"For good, Dad." Max's gaze offered assurance tinged with regret, but life taught Tina that assurances often meant little and ended badly. Around Kirkwood Lake the proof was in the pudding, as Jenny Campbell liked to say. And Max had a lot of proving to do.

She stepped forward and extended her hand, wishing her skin was smoother, her nails prettier, her—

He wrapped her hand in a broad, warm clasp, sure and strong but gentle, too.

And then he did the unthinkable.

He noticed her.

His gaze sharpened. His eyes widened. He gripped his other hand around the first, embracing her hand with both of his. "This is little Tina? Little Tina Martinelli? For real?"

The blush started somewhere around her toes and climbed quickly.

Little Tina.

That's what she'd been to him, an awestruck kid stargazing as the wretchedly good-looking youngest Campbell brother broke hearts across the lakeside villages. Max wasn't what you'd call a bad boy…

But no one accused him of being all that good, either.

"It's me." She flashed him a smile, hoping her Italian skin softened the blush, but the frankness of Charlie's grin said it hadn't come close. "I—"

"It's good to see you, Tina."

Warmth. Honesty. Integrity.

His tone and words professed all three, so maybe the army had done him good, but she'd locked down her teenage crush a long time back. Over. Done. Finished. "You, too."

Did he hold her hand a moment too long?

Of course not, he was just being nice.

But when she pulled her hand away, a tiny glint in his eye set her heart beating faster.

Clearly she needed a pacemaker, because she wasn't about to let Max Campbell's inviting smile and good looks tempt her from her newly planned road. Life had offered an unwelcome detour less than four weeks ago, when her popular café burned to the ground on a windswept October night. She'd watched the flames devour ten years of hard work and sacrifice, everything gone in two short hours. It made her heart ache to think how quickly things could change.

"You're working here, Tina?" Max angled his head slightly, and his appreciative look said this was an interesting—and nice—turn of events.

"Tina came on board to help when I got sick," Charlie explained. He indicated the waterfront southwest of them with a thrust of his chin. "She had the nicest little café right over there in Sol Rigby's old mechanics shop. Put a lot of time and money into that place, a bunch of years. Her coffee shop became one of those places folks love to stop at, but it caught fire a few weeks back. The local volunteers did their best to save it, but the sharp north wind and the fire's head start was too much. So

Tina's helping us out while we're waiting for the dust to settle with my treatments."

Concern darkened Max's gaze as he turned her way, as if the loss of her beloved business mattered, as if she mattered.

Don't look like that, Max.

Don't look like you care that my hopes and dreams went up in smoke. That despite how I invested every penny and ounce of energy into building that business, it evaporated in one crazy, flame-filled night. You're not the caring type, remember? When life turns tragic, you tend to disappear. And I've had enough of that to last a lifetime.

Tears pricked her eyes.

She'd been doing better these past few weeks. She could walk past the burned-out building and not shed a tear. Oh, she shed some mental ones each time, but she hadn't cried for real since that first week, when rain or a puff of wind sent the smell of burned-out wood wafting through the village.

"Tina, I'm so sorry." He looked like he wanted to say more, but stopped himself. He appraised her, then stepped back. "You don't mind teaching me stuff, do you? I'm pretty good with a grappling hook or an all-terrain vehicle on caterpillar treads. Put a semiautomatic in my hands and I'm on my game." He made a G.I. Joe–type motion and stance, ready to stand guard for truth, justice and the American way. "But Dad's new computerized cash registers?" He made a face of fear, and the fact that he steered the conversation away from her pain meant he recognized the emotion and cared.

Sure he cares. Like you're a kid sister who just broke her favorite toy. Get hold of yourself, will you? "I'll be glad to show you whatever you need, Max." She shifted her gaze left. "Charlie, are you staying today?"

"Naw." Frustration marred Charlie's normal smile. "The treatments are catching up with me. When Max showed up at the house yesterday and said he was here to run the store for as long as we need him, well, I'll tell you." Charlie slapped a hand on his youngest son's back. "It was a gift from God. I'd just told Jenny we needed someone here to help you and Earl, with the holidays coming up and all. And while I hate that your pretty little restaurant burned—"

The anxious look in the older man's eyes made Tina recognize a timeline she was loathe to see.

"Having you here, and now Max, well…" Charlie breathed deep. "It's easier for me to focus on getting well, knowing the store is in good hands. I know you're not planning to stay in Kirkwood, Tina, but I thank God every night that we've got you here now. I hate having your mother—" he moved his gaze to Max while Tina fought a new lump of throat-tightening emotion "—worrying over me all the time. But you know her, there's no keeping her from it. And while I'm not one to be fussed over, it's good to have her on my side right now."

Old guilt and his new reality gut-stabbed Max.

Time had gone by. Mistakes had been made. No matter how many battles he fought, no matter how many medals the army pinned on his chest, a part of him couldn't move beyond the teenage boy who'd made a grievous error in judgment years ago.

He swallowed hard but kept his face even. "I should have come back sooner, Dad. I know that. But I'm here now, and I'll do everything I can to make things easier for you and Mom. That's if I can keep my mind on hardware with such pretty help." He slanted a glance of pretended innocence Tina's way.

His ruse of humor worked.

Charlie's laugh lightened the moment. Tina looked like she wanted to mop the floor with him, making jokes at a moment of truth, but Max knew his father. Charlie Campbell would be the first to say that getting crazy emotional over must-have treatments and their outcomes wasn't in anyone's best interests.

You could have come back. You chose not to. That one's all on you, soldier.

Max's heart weighed heavy as Charlie picked up his car keys. Ten years of staying away, grabbing for a future because he couldn't face the past. He'd lost time with his mother, his father, his siblings. Time that could never be regained.

Now he was home, determined to make amends and begin again. Charlie and Jenny Campbell had taken in a five-year-old boy, dumped by his mother the week before Christmas, and brought him to their sprawling lakeside home. They'd changed his life that day, given him a second chance not all children get.

He loved them for it. Now? Time to give back. And if reconnecting with his hometown meant facing old wrongs? Then it was about time he manned up and did just that because staying away hadn't fixed anything. Over the years he'd faced enemies on three separate continents. He could handle Kirkwood Lake.

Once his father left the store, Max turned toward Tina.

"Don't you dare break their hearts again, Max Campbell."

He'd come home expecting emotional shrapnel.

Tina's flat-out decree was more like a direct hit at close range. He started to speak, but Tina moved a half step forward, invading his space. "What were you thinking disappearing like that? All those years gone. What were you doing all that time?"

"My job?" He let his inflection say the answer was obvious, but he knew Tina was right. He could have come back. Should have come back. He'd missed weddings, baptisms, anniversaries and holidays. And he'd done it on purpose, because it was easier to face current danger than past lapses in judgment. He got careless and stupid, but he didn't need this drop-dead gorgeous gray-eyed beauty to ream him out over it.

Although he preferred her sass to the tears she'd been fighting minutes before. Tears went hand in hand with high drama. If there was something Max steered clear of, it was high-drama women.

"Your job wasn't 24/7/365." She folded her hands across her chest, leveled him a look and didn't seem at all fazed that he had her by a good seven inches and sixty pounds. Or that he was a munitions expert. Her bravado made him smile inside, but he held back, knowing she wouldn't appreciate his amusement.

"I should have come back. Phone calls weren't enough. I know that now." He'd known it then, too, but it had been easier to stay away. Still, this was *his* personal business, not hers. Fortunately his straightforward admission helped take the wind out of her sails.

Good. He had no intention of being yelled at all day. With the high-volume sales of winter and holiday items upon them, he knew Campbell's Hardware would be cranking. His job was to learn the new aspects of an old business ASAP, shouldering the work his parents did so naturally. "For the moment, if you can take a break from yelling at me, I need to learn as much as I can as quickly as I can to help out. Now we either do this together—" he mimicked her stance and saw her wince as if recognizing her stubbornness "—or we work as separate entities. But, Tina?" He held her gaze, waiting until she blinked in concession to continue.

Only she didn't.

He shrugged that off mentally and stood his ground. "We've got to take care of this for Dad's sake. And Mom's. No matter how you might feel about me. Which means we might have to declare a truce, at least during working hours. Agreed?"

Her expression softened. She stared over his shoulder, sighed, then brought her eyes back to his. "Agreed."

He refused to acknowledge her reluctance. Ten years in the service taught him to pick his battles. He'd seen her face when they'd talked of her business burning. He understood that working side by side with the Campbell prodigal probably hadn't made her short list, and life had done a number on her.

But when she took a deep breath and stuck out her hand again, he realized that Tina Martinelli was made of pretty strong stuff. "Do-over," she instructed.

He smiled, nodded and accepted her hand in his.

"Max, you might not remember me. I'm Tina Martinelli and I'm here to help your parents."

He should resist. He knew it, knew it the minute her eyes locked with his. Held.

But he couldn't and so he gave her hand a light squeeze and smiled. "Well, Tina, I do remember you, but what I remember is a pesky tomboy who whistled louder, ran faster and jumped higher than most of the guys around."

The blush heightened again. Was it because he remembered or because he'd brought up her penchant for sports and winning? Max wasn't sure, but he leaned closer, just enough to punctuate his meaning. "This Tina?" He shook his head, dropped her hand and stepped back. He didn't give her a once-over because he didn't have to. Her face said she understood. "This Tina is a surprise and I can't say I'm sorry to be working with her. Reason enough to clean up and hurry into work each morning."

"Which means we need to set ground rules." She glossed over his compliment as if it hadn't affected her. Max allotted her extra points for that and played along. "Employees are not allowed to fraternize outside of work."

Max frowned. "My parents own this place and I'm going to guarantee they fraternize outside of work. That's how they got to be parents."

She bristled, looking really cute as she did. But he couldn't think of that. There was work to be done so he held up a hand. "You're right. I know you and Earl have been picking up a lot of slack, so my goal is to help you any way I can. If we can keep Mom and Dad from worrying about the store, Dad can focus on getting through his treatments. Getting well."

"Then we share the same objective. Perfect." She gave him a crisp nod as she moved to a stack of holiday-themed boxes. "As long as we keep our focus on that, we shouldn't have any problems."

Saucy and determined, the grown-up Tina wasn't much different than she'd been years ago. He knew he should stop. Let her have the last word. But when she slanted a "keep your distance" look over her shoulder, he couldn't resist. "Working for the government taught me to get around problems efficiently, Tina Martinelli. I expect that might come in handy now and then."

Come in handy?

Not with her, it wouldn't.

Oh, she saw the charm and self-assuredness that had drawn girls to Max back in their youth. Refined now, the charisma was more dangerous, almost volatile. But Tina hadn't spent the last decade pining for her childhood crush. She'd managed to have her heart broken twice since, so Max could flirt and tempt all he wanted. It would do him no good.

Tina was immune.

You want to be immune, but face it, darling. Damp palms say something else entirely.

She shushed the internal warning, but when she leaned in to show Max how to engage cash register functions, the scent of him made her long to draw closer.

She didn't. She ignored the fact that he smelled of sandalwood and soap and total guy, and that the flash of his smile brightened a room.

She didn't need any rooms brightened, thank you. A few LED lightbulbs took care of that in a cost-effective way.

Over the years, she'd shrugged off her teenage attraction to Max as silly adolescent stuff. But today, seeing the straightforward warmth of the hardened but humorous man he'd become?

That might be tough to resist.

Fortunately Tina wasn't in the market for anything in Kirkwood Lake these days. Least of all another broken heart. Been there, done that. Overrated.

She showed him through the layout of the store. His parents had done a complete remodel four years previous, making Max's memories obsolete, and the first thing he noted out loud were the rotational seasonal displays set at four separate locations. "I expect this was my mother's idea."

Tina nodded as she unlocked the front door and officially opened the story for business. "She likes to go to regional conferences that teach how to build sales while keeping overhead in check."

"Always a trick in retail." Max nodded to the first customer in the door, a woman, carrying an older-model chain saw that had seen better days.

"Is Earl here yet?" The look she gave Tina and Max said she didn't put much trust in their abilities.

"No, ma'am," Max told her. "Not 'til noon. But maybe I can help?"

She looked at him, really looked, then formed her mouth into a grim line. "Maxwell Campbell, I do believe you still owe me for some flowers that went missing from my garden about twelve years back. Give or take a summer or two."

Max's grimace said his memory clicked to a younger version of the woman before him. "You're absolutely correct, Mrs. Hyatt. Those would be red roses and I believe they found their way over to Sophie Benedict's house. I'll be happy to make that up to you now with my apologies for the delay. And ask your forgiveness, of course."

The look she settled on him said maybe that was okay, and maybe it wasn't. "How long have you served our country, young man?"

"Over a decade."

Her mouth softened. Her shoulders relaxed. "I'd say we're more than even." She clapped a hand to his shoulder, hometown pride showing in her eyes, her smile. "Welcome home, Max. I expect your parents are most pleased to have you here, and just in time to share the holidays together."

"Yes, ma'am. My mom goes a little bit crazy over Thanksgiving and Christmas, that's for sure. And about that saw?" He dropped his gaze to the chain saw in her arms.

Her face said she was inclined to wait until Earl's arrival nearly three hours later.

"If you bring it to Dad's tool bench, I'd be glad to have a look."

"If you think you can." She didn't try to mask the dubious note in her voice. "It's been a long time since you've worked with your dad."

"True." He led the way to Charlie's well-lit bench and table at the back corner, a popular gathering place for small-town talk and broken tools. "But I remember a thing or two. And working for Uncle Sam taught me a few new tricks. Let's see what's going on." He examined the pieces, then nodded. "We've got a bad clutch. Tina, does Dad carry parts for all models in the back or just current ones?"

His quiet confidence in his abilities lightened Tina's angst. Working for the Campbells helped them and her, but with Charlie out of commission and Earl on limited hours, she'd been fielding a lot of questions with few answers the past two weeks. Maybe having Max around wouldn't be so bad, not if he could actually make sense out of the more difficult hardware inquiries. "I'll check and see. If we have to order it, we won't get it until next Tuesday, Mrs. Hyatt. Is that all right?"

"Tuesday's fine with me. Then would you be able to fix it right away?" she wondered. She hesitated, looking a little uncomfortable, then explained, "I hate to push, knowing what's going on with your dad and all, but I promised my husband I'd get this fixed before wood-cutting season. Once the cold hits, he'll take to the woods for next year's heating supply, but he can't cut without his saw. And with the Festival of Lights coming up, I'm going to have my hands full. I expect you're taking that over for your father, as well?"

Max sent a blank look from her to Tina and back. "Festival of Lights? I'm not following you."

"The annual Christmas lighting event we've been doing for years," Mrs. Hyatt replied. "This year it's the final big event of our bicentennial celebration," she continued. "Your dad heads up the committee, we use the funds raised from the park drive-through to support the women's shelter in Clearwater, and Tina and I handle the food venues with a bunch of volunteers. That money helps stock food pantries all year long. Joe Burns is helping." She ticked off her fingers, listing familiar names. "The Radcliffes, Sawyers and Morgans are all on board, as well. We've got everything planned out, of course, because it starts soon, but no one knows how to do lighting grids as well as Charlie Campbell."

One phrase stood out.

The Sawyers. Pete's family, Tina's neighbors on Upper Lake Road. Pete used to love ditching both his little sister, Sherrie, and Tina. He and Max would take their small boat out and go fishing or girl-watching. When they were young, fishing took precedence. By the time they finished high school?

Partying had replaced fishing for Pete.

Regret speared Max. He shelved it purposely. He'd come back to help and make amends. Right now, helping took precedence, even if it meant coming face-to-face with Pete's family sooner rather than later.

Business owners were taking advantage of today's nice weather to hang festive garland. Town crews had manned a cherry-picker truck to string lights through Main Street trees, and decorated wreaths marked each old-fashioned light pole. Like it or not they were two weeks shy of Thanksgiving and the town was knee-deep in a project that depended on Charlie's calm help and expertise.

"I'll talk to my dad and see what I can do to help. We'll cover it, Mrs. Hyatt. No worries."

Her sigh of relief said he'd answered correctly. "And you're okay with me coming by next Wednesday to pick up the saw?"

"I'll put the part in as soon as it arrives," Max promised. "If there's any delay, we'll give you a call."

"That would be wonderful." She watched as he filled out a tag with her name, gave him her phone number, then smiled, more relaxed than when she came into the store. "I expect you'll both be at the final committee meeting Wednesday night?"

Special ops had prepared Max to tack with the prevailing wind, no matter what the mission. "Absolutely. When and where?"

"We used to have them at my café." The resignation in Tina's tone said her loss rubbed raw. "But Carmen Bianchi said we could meet in her apartment behind Vintage Place instead. Seven o'clock."

"I'll be there," Max promised. "And we'll be ready to implement Dad's action plan, Mrs. Hyatt."

"Good!" Her smile said his confidence appeased her concerns. Which meant he hadn't lost his touch, but if he was coming face-to-face with the Sawyers in a few days, and expected to run this light show thing, he needed to get his mental ducks in a row. Fast.

Max watched Mrs. Hyatt walk out the door, then took the broken saw to the second bench. "I know Dad always puts them in back in the order they come in, but I don't want to forget my promise to her."

"Seeing it is a good reminder," Tina replied. "And the back room is kind of crowded right now anyway." She greeted someone, then waved another pair of customers upstairs to the "country store" shop, another one of his mother's ideas. Fifteen years ago, folks had kind of ridiculed the idea of a home shop in a hardware store, but no one scoffed now. Campbell's "Country Cove" on the second floor did enough winter business to pay the bills and record a profit, a huge plus in northern towns.

When Tina came back to the front, Max indicated the door and Mrs. Hyatt's retreating back with a quick glance. "What have you been doing the past few weeks when customers like that came in? Did you send them elsewhere?"

"Come with me." Tina led him into the back room, threaded a path through the overstock and the glass-cutting corner, then waved toward Charlie's equipment fix-it zone for larger repairs. "This is what Earl's been working on this past week when he was healthy enough to be here."

Max counted eighteen separate tools in various stages of repair. "Are these due to be picked up soon?"

"Tomorrow. That's our regular tool pickup day now."

Tomorrow. Of course Earl was scheduled to work

a one-to-five shift today, but that was a lot of fixing to do before they opened tomorrow morning. "Are the necessary parts available? Have they been delivered?"

"With the exception of Herb Langdon's snowblower, yes. And I called and told him the part was on back order. Earl was out sick this week so all this stuff is here, waiting. Tomorrow morning we'll have a bunch of people coming in to pick up tools that most likely won't be ready."

"So that's why my mother came in yesterday." Max made a face of realization. "Earl was sick."

"And you know your mother. She said it was fine because your brothers took care of keeping Charlie company while she was here, but I could tell she was torn."

"Luke and Seth aren't exactly nursing material." Max respected his older brothers, two decorated county sheriff's deputies, but nursing care wasn't their forte.

"He needs company more than care right now," Tina answered. "And your mom needs to get out now and again. Catch her breath. You know."

Max didn't know any such thing. His mother was the most dedicated and loving person he'd ever met. The thought of her wanting to leave Charlie's side seemed alien. "I expect she'd rather be with Dad. Just in case."

The uncertainty in Tina's expression said he might know tools but he'd just flunked Women 101. And that was somewhat surprising, because Max thought he knew women fairly well. But maybe not Kirkwood Lake women.

Despite Earl's help that afternoon, by the time they locked the doors at five o'clock, there were still three lawn mowers, two leaf blowers, two power-washers and two log-splitters awaiting repair.

Earl held his knit cap in his hand, sheepish. “I shoulda knowed I wasn’t gonna get to all those with Charlie gone, Max. I can come in early tomorrow and help.” He slapped a hand to his head, then shook his head. “No, I’m wrong, Mavis is havin’ some eye thing done tomorrow mornin’ and I promised to drive her. If she breaks the appointment who knows how long it will take to get another. And she’d have my head for puttin’ her off.”

“Oh, those women,” Tina muttered, just out of Earl’s range of hearing.

Max fought a smile and sent Earl off. “I’ll stay late, see what I can do. Thanks for today, though, Earl. It was great working with you.”

“Same here.” Earl made his way to the door, paused, thought, then continued as if he’d never stopped at all. Tina watched him go before she faced Max.

“Do you want me to stay and help? If you show me what to do, I might be able to take some of the pressure off you.”

Assessing the number of tools and the variety of fixes, Max wished that were true, but— “It would take me longer to train you tonight than it would to fix them myself, but I appreciate the offer, Tina. And working with Earl today gave me a refresher course in small-engine repair.” He pointed to a stack of thin books alongside the bench. “I’ve got manuals for each of the models from the internet.” He shrugged, pulled on one of his dad’s sweatshirts from the rack behind the workroom bench and waved her on. "I'll be fine. Not like I haven't pulled double duty in my time."

"If you're sure?"

"I am. I'll call Mom, tell her I'm running late. It's all good."

"All right. I'll open in the morning, so if you need to sleep in, go ahead. I'll have things covered."

"Thanks. I just might do that." He wouldn't, but he appreciated the offer, just the same. In fact, looking at the work spread out before him, he wasn't sure he'd make it home at all, but that was okay. Jenny and Charlie Campbell had rocked him to sleep at night, held him through a phase of unrelenting nightmares and ran him from town to town as he tore up soccer fields across the county. Staying up late to help them out?

Not a big deal at all.

Chapter Two

Tina grabbed the hardware store door handle Monday morning, emotionally sorting through the scene she had just passed. A crew of uniformed firemen, sifting through the remains of her café, searching for evidence of arson. Tina shivered at the thought that anyone would deliberately burn a building, risk harming others and destroy property.

It couldn't be true. Mild crime was unusual here in Kirkwood Lake. Felony crimes like arson? Assault?

Virtually unheard of.

The door swung open beneath her grip, and she stepped in cautiously, looking left and right. Had Max forgotten to lock up? That seemed unlikely for a guy who made his living completing surreptitious missions, but—

"Tina, is that you? I've got coffee back here. Come get some. If you drink coffee, that is."

"I owned a café. I live on coffee. Gimme." She reached for the cup as she entered the back room, then stopped, surprised. "Max. They're all done. Every last one."

The array of broken equipment had been put back together, each one tagged with the owner's name and the cost of repair. They formed a pretty line along Charlie's back-room bench, then marched across the work floor, ready to be loaded into vehicles from the rear loading dock. There would be no reckoning with angry customers, no putting folks off, no begging for more time, hoping people understood business limitations brought on by Charlie's illness. "I can't believe this." Tina turned in a full circle, then stopped when she faced Max again. "You stayed all night."

"Not the first time I've stayed late somewhere. Won't be the last." He brushed off the sacrifice like it was no big deal, and that almost made her like him. She'd had enough of guys who promised one thing, then did another. Max's casual treatment of his sacrifice for his family touched too many of those empty-promise buttons. He directed his attention to the coffee cup. "I wasn't sure what you like, so I got flavored creamers and regular. And sugar. And artificial sugar."

"Covering all the bases." The fact that he'd gone the distance for his parents surprised her. And that he'd provided for her despite his lack of sleep? Downright sweet of him. "Max, this is so nice. Thank you."

"You're welcome."

He hesitated a moment, coffee in hand, as if wanting to say something. Tina prodded him as she stirred hazelnut creamer into her cup. "And?"

His next words surprised her. Because it was old

news or because the sympathy in Max's voice rang with quiet sincerity? Maybe both.

"I didn't realize your parents were gone, Tina." His gaze showed regret. "I'm truly sorry."

Max's years away had wrought lots of local change. Losing her parents had become a big part of that "new normal." She sighed. "Me, too."

"And your aunt owns The Pelican's Nest now?" He sipped his coffee and shifted his attention to the east window. The steep peak of the restaurant profile was just visible beyond the parking lot. "I would have thought they'd leave it to you. Or give it to you. Something for all those years of work you put in."

"Well. They didn't."

"Because?"

She didn't want to talk about this. She didn't want to rehash old Martinelli news the whole town already knew. But Tina knew if she didn't answer, he'd just ask his parents. It wasn't like anything stayed a secret in a small town. "My aunt and uncle were in a position to buy in. They promised to let me manage the business. My father had developed a bad heart, a combination of genetics and smoking, and he needed to step down. Mom and Dad moved to Florida to escape the tough winters and my uncle booted me to the curb."

"He fired you?"

"Yes."

"Oh, man."

He was feeling sorry for her, and the expression on his face said he couldn't understand family acting like that, treating each other that way. Well.

Neither could she. “It was a long time ago.”

“Yes. But then you opened a café there.” He indicated the burned-out shell visible through the west-facing window. “With their restaurant right here.” He turned back toward the window facing the parking lot and whistled lightly. “Gutsy.”

Tina made a face. “Gutsy, yes. And maybe a little mean.”

“Mean?” He put away a handful of small tools as he scrunched his forehead. “How can that be mean?”

“Because as my business grew, their customers dwindled,” Tina admitted. “And that made my uncle grumpier than usual, and he was pretty miserable already. That couldn’t have been fun for Aunt Laura and Ryan.”

He raised one absolutely gorgeous brow at the mention of her cousin’s name.

“My cousin. Their only child. And now my uncle’s dead, my aunt’s running the place on her own with half the help she needs, and raising a kid who’s hanging with a rough bunch from Clearwater. So maybe if I hadn’t been bullheaded and put my café right under their noses…”

“Where your success would be painfully obvious…”

She frowned. “Exactly. Maybe things would be different. Maybe we could actually be like a normal family. Like yours.”

“Ah.”

“You have so much to be grateful for, Max.”

His face said he knew that.

“So staying away, leaving your parents and brothers

and sisters, shrugging them all off…" She set her coffee cup down and faced him. "I don't get it. I'd give anything to have a family. My parents are gone, my mom died two years after my dad, I've got no brothers or sisters, and my one aunt won't acknowledge me if we pass on the street. I'd trade places with you in a heartbeat."

Sympathy deepened his expression. "You know, I never thought of family in terms of temporary until Mom called me with Dad's prognosis. Reality smacked me upside the head and said *head home, soldier.* But you're right, Tina. I've got a lot to make up for, but standing and talking won't do anything but put me to sleep this morning. I'm going to pull the last of those Christmas displays out of the shed and bring them in. I promised Mom we'd get them into place today."

He wanted a change of subject. So did she. She turned, flipped the Closed sign to Open and turned the key in the door. "Bring 'em in, Max. I'll be happy to help."

"Thank you, Tina. I'd appreciate it."

He was playing nice

His generosity rankled Tina more. After seeing investigators comb through the cold morning rubble of her beloved business, discussing her family's casual disregard for each other was more unwelcome than usual. But Max would know nothing about that, because Campbells looked out for one another.

She took care of a handful of customers while Max built a Christmas lights display case in their seasonal corner. Once he had it firmly in place, she helped stock the wide range of holiday lighting kits.

"Doesn't it seem early to be putting out Christmas stuff?"

Tina gaped at him, then laughed. "You've been in the army too long. The stores start shelving Christmas items as soon as their back-to-school displays are depleted. By mid-September, most places are stocked, lit up and ready to roll with holiday sales."

"And Thanksgiving gets lost in the shuffle." Max's lament surprised her, because it was a feeling they shared.

"I love Thanksgiving," she admitted. "I love the simplicity, the warmth, the food. Of course, I'm Italian, why wouldn't I love the food?" The look she sent him made him smile, but his grin turned to understanding when she added, "The whole idea of an entire country, praying their thanks to God, regardless of faith. I just love it."

"You know, it's funny." Max eased a hip onto the sales counter as he grabbed a bottle of water. "When you're in the field on holidays, most of the guys seem to feel the loss of Thanksgiving more than any other."

"More than Christmas?"

"Yeah. I might be wrong." He shrugged, thinking. "Most soldiers get stuff at Christmas. Even the ones who don't have family are hooked up with agencies that send care packages to deployed soldiers. But on Thanksgiving, there's nothing but memories of what was. What could have been. What might be again. *If* you make it back. Maybe it was just me." He stood, stretched and tossed his bottle into the recycling tote. "But I don't think so."

She'd never thought of it that way. She'd helped on Wounded Warrior projects, she'd arranged pickups for the Vietnam Veterans thrift shops, but she'd never thought about how lonely Thanksgiving must be when you're thousands of miles away from anything American. "Hey, if you need to catch some sleep, head home. I've got this. Earl will be here in an hour and we'll be all set."

"I'll leave once Earl's here," Max answered. He rolled his shoulders, stretched once more, and she did her best to ignore the amazing muscle definition formed by long years in the armed services. He moved to the front of the store. "I'm going to use the Cat to level the parking-lot stone. I can see where the water's been puddling, and that won't get any better once the snow hits."

"Good."

"And when I come back in, can you give me the low-down on this festival thing we talked about yesterday? There's not much time left, and I work better with a plan in my head."

"From the looks of that back room, you do pretty well without a plan, too." She didn't say how she'd dreaded facing disappointed customers today, their expected equipment lying unfixed in the back room.

He shot her a grin over his shoulder. "Let's see if they work before giving me too much credit."

"You tested them, right?"

He ignored her question and kept on walking. Was he laughing? At her?

She finished the Christmas lights display as a customer arrived to pick up one of the newly fixed lawn mowers. When they wheeled their repaired machine out the back door, she felt a stab of pride. It might not be a big deal that Chuck Beadle was going to be able to give his yard a last mowing it didn't really need, but it was important that their efforts to maintain Charlie and Jenny's business as he fought his battle with cancer were successful. And without Max, it wouldn't have happened, so she needed to give credit where credit was due.

Her cell phone signaled an incoming call. She pulled it out, saw the realty office number and picked up quickly. "Myra, good morning."

"Hey, good morning to you, Tina! I'm emailing you a short list of potential sites for your café if you're still thinking of Spencerport as your go-to place."

"I am," she replied. "That or Brockport." She'd done her homework and these Erie Canal locations in Western New York had lots of potential. "They both have proximity to the expressway, and they're on main-feeder corridor to other towns. What I want is a west-side-of-the-road location and a drive-through for those a.m. customers."

"Did you have a drive-through in Kirkwood?" Myra asked.

"I was lakefront, so no, I didn't. And we're a destination spot, not a commuter town, so it's a different configuration."

"Won't you miss the water?"

Miss the water?

Yeah, absolutely. But if she wasn't willing to sacrifice something to change things up, nothing would ever happen, and that option didn't cut it anymore. The time for change was here. Now. "Not if I have a view of the canal," she promised. "Or at least proximity to it so folks can grab a cuppa, head for the canal walkway and stroll along the banks watching the boats. Those villages are a walker's dream, so no. I won't miss the water."

It was an outright lie. She knew it, and she was pretty sure Myra's silence said she recognized Tina's resignation, but was kind enough not to call her on it.

Tina loved the water. She loved taking her little boat out on calm summer days. Dropping a line just off the docks outside the Kirkwood Lodge where perch and bass gathered in the heat of summer. She'd caught her share of fish that way, a sweet respite from work. Private time, time to think. And pray. And dream.

But her dreams were gone now. Ruined.

She promised Myra she'd look at the property listings in the email and get back to her. Another customer walked in, then another, and pretty soon she was too busy to think about smoldering dreams and ruined hopes. She'd promised herself she'd never get mired in the past again. She meant to keep that promise.

"I brought Beezer in to keep you company," Jenny Campbell announced as she came through the back door of the shop a little later. "And I'm going to drag Max home to catch some sleep. I think that's a good trade, don't you, Tina?"

"Leave the dog and take Max?" Tina sent Max a

look that said she approved fully. “I think I’m getting the better end of this deal.”

“Hey, Beeze.” As Tina moved their way, Max squatted low and gave the aging golden retriever a long belly rub the dog loved. “You missing the action, old boy?”

“He is.” Jenny tipped a mock frown down to the beloved pet. “I reminded him that his master is sick and good dogs stay by their master’s side.”

“They do in books,” Tina agreed. “But Beeze was raised in town. He likes to check out the hustle and bustle of the shop.”

“He’s restless if he’s home too much,” Jenny admitted. “When I let him out, he starts prowling the yard as if looking for a way down to the village. I’m afraid he’ll wander close to the road and won’t hear a car coming around the bend.”

“Well, he can keep an eye on Tina if I’m heading home.” Max grabbed his bomber jacket from the back hook as Earl finished up with a customer. The thought of a few hours of sleep sounded real good now. “You guys will be okay?”

“Tina will boss me around, and I’ll answer any fix-it questions that arise.” Earl’s wry tone said he was only partially kidding. “Same old, same old.”

“Women are bossy creatures.” Max smiled at the older man, then turned his attention to Tina. “We never did talk about the festival thing. My bad. It got busy and—”

“Max, we can’t expect you to do the festival, too.” Jenny frowned as she caught the gist of the conversation. "That's not fair. You came home to have time with Dad. If we keep you working day and night, then—"

"We'll make time for both, I promise. I managed to run a unit with a lot of guys and barely got my hands dirty, Mom. I'm good at delegating. But first I need to know what's going on." He turned back to Tina. "I don't suppose you have time to come over tonight and go over things? That way we could have Mom and Dad's input, too."

"You can have supper with us." Jenny's face said inviting Tina to supper made everything better. Max wasn't so sure Tina would agree now that he was on hand, but she'd been civil all day, and that was a sweet improvement. Of course they'd been busy from the moment they unlocked the doors, so maybe the key to keeping Tina happy was keeping her busy.

"I'll come over once we close up," Tina promised. "And I'll bring Beeze along. That way he's got the best of both worlds."

"Thank you, Tina." When Jenny gave Tina a big old hug, Max realized their relationship had grown close over his years away. His mother's next words confirmed it.

"I don't know what we'd do without you." Jenny's voice stopped short of saying she wanted Tina to stay right here in Kirkwood, but the inflection was clear.

Tina winked as she headed for the register area. "Back at ya. Gotta go. Mrs. Lana is here for her leaf blower, and last night's killing frost means she'll be really glad to have it back, especially with snow in the late-week forecast."

"I love this." Max stopped at the back door and swept the town center a long, slow look of appreciation. "The old town buildings. The lake. The decorations that look like an old New England village. Now that I'm home and see it all again, I realize how much I missed it."

Jenny looped her arm through his as they went through the back doorway. "Always something to miss, no matter where we are. But I'm glad you're here, that I don't have to run down the coast to see you. As fun as that is, I prefer having you home for a while. And I'm making your favorite dinner, so once you've gotten some sleep, I intend to fatten you up."

"A mother's prerogative." Max yawned as he moved toward his upgraded sports car. "It feels good to be home."

Tina watched him pull away from inside the store.

He drove a muscle car, a total chick magnet. He flashed those big brown eyes and that smile like it was nothing, nothing at all. And every now and again he'd watch her, as if appraising.

Was he comparing the old her with the new?

And if so, what did he see? And why did it matter to her?

Sherrie Morgan breezed through the front door a few minutes later. "The promised cold snap has arrived," she noted as the screen door bumped shut behind her. "And tell me if the 4-1-1 is right. Max Campbell is back and unattached? Girlfriend, this is not news anyone should keep to themselves unless, of course, one really, truly wants to keep it to herself?"

Tina retrieved the last repaired lawn mower and cautioned Sherrie with a look. "He is back, yes, to help his parents. Sherrie, come on, you know the situation. They're delighted to have him here and I'm pleased to have someone with hardware knowledge on hand. I was totally in over my head last week. But you know Max as well as anyone. Here today, gone tomorrow."

"Oh. Ouch. Unfair." Sherrie picked out three boxes of Christmas lights, paused, then added a fourth to her stack. "He was eighteen," Sherrie reminded her. "And people react to sadness differently. I think back to that day, losing Pete and Amy, and for years I kept wondering what I could have done differently. If I'd been less pesky, less bothersome, would they have stayed at home? Hung out by the campfire? Maybe knowing there'd be a kid sister around later pushed them to take the boat out. Have some romantic boyfriend/girlfriend time."

"Sherrie—"

"I know it wasn't my fault." Sherrie brushed off Tina's protest with a shrug. "I'm all grown up now, I know people make choices every day, and that I was just a normal kid, pestering her big brother and wishing I was as pretty as Amy with her long blond hair and those big blue eyes. And then they were gone, and it left such a hole. But just because Max didn't come around doesn't make him a bad person, Tina. He might have been older than us, but he was still a kid who'd just lost his best friend. And that couldn't have been easy."

Sherrie's argument made perfect sense, but Sherrie hadn't done a decade-long disappearing act after college. Max had. And Tina was done with capricious men, even if her heart managed to skip a beat every time Max walked into a room. Clearly hearts knew nothing and were not to be trusted. End of story.

"So you're working together." Sherrie ended the sentence on a note of question, hunting for an informational update. Tina gave her a look that said nothing interesting was happening. Or would happen.

"Of necessity. Jenny and Charlie need help. Max and I are available. Simple math, one plus one and all that."

"Except you had a crush on him all through high school," Sherrie mused as she pulled out her debit card. "Honey, when God plants your dream right in front of you, I think it's an invitation to grab hold. See where life leads."

"I know exactly where my life is heading, thanks." Tina patted the thin stack of computer printouts. "These are possible café sites near the Erie Canal. Not so far away that I can't visit, but far enough to wipe the slate clean, Sherrie. And that's something I desperately need. A new beginning, a fresh start."

"And you've prayed about this, chatted it up with God, right?"

"I think the fire was a good sign that my time in Kirkwood has come to a close," Tina told her while ignoring the fact she'd done no such thing. A thin ribbon of guilt tweaked her. "If you're looking for signs, that one was pretty direct."

Sherrie tucked her debit card back into her purse once Tina ran it through, but refused to be dissuaded. "If someone did set that fire, that's no message from

God, Tina. That's a depraved act of humanity and shouldn't go unpunished. And folks around here rebuild after disaster all the time. Look what happened after the floods last year. And those blizzards that took out three old barns? We're rebuilders. We don't give up. And I don't even want to think about you being more than two hours away. We've been besties forever, so yes, selfishly, I want you here when my baby comes. Babies should have their godmothers close by, don't you think?"

"You're pregnant?" Delight coursed through Tina. Sherrie and her husband had been hoping for a child for years. With two sad outcomes behind them, a well-set pregnancy seemed almost impossible. But a tiny prick of envy niggled the rise of joy, because Tina had thought her life would be on a similar track by now. Married. A cute kid or two. Maybe a dog like Beezer, loving and easygoing. Surging happiness displaced the twinge of envy, and she grabbed her best friend in a big hug. "Tell me when."

"In less than five months," Sherrie said. "We kept it quiet until we were far enough along to be more confident, so in four and a half months, I'll need your help. But you can't help me if you're so far away."

Sherrie was right. She'd be little help from that distance, and starting a new business took a level of dedication that went beyond the norm. She remembered her early days with the café, long, tedious days, keeping overhead down while working to build business up. That meant lots of personal man-hours.

Was she ready to do that again?

The morning's image cropped up once more, the firemen, sifting through the ashes, their movements kicking up the smell of old, wet, burned wood, a hunk of ugly set in the middle of the season of light.

What if this person was targeting her personally?

She knew the investigators were checking out Sol Rigby to see if he had a reason to torch his own place, but Tina doubted that. Sol was frugal, and he didn't look well-off, but Tina was pretty sure the old guy was doing okay financially. Which meant he had no reason to want insurance money.

The realization that they would investigate her hit hard. They would check her financials, and while not great, they weren't bad, either. And no way would she do such a thing.

But clearly the investigators thought someone had purposely burned down her place. The question was who? And why?

"I know the arson investigators talked to your aunt today. And I know this because Jim was with them," Sherrie offered as if she'd read where her thoughts had wandered. "He didn't repeat anything that was said, but he said it was a tough interview."

"My café hurt her business."

Sherrie nodded. "Which might be motive enough to get it out of the way."

"Aunt Laura would never do that. Rocco, maybe." Memories of her uncle's temperamental tirades hit hard, but Rocco was gone, and Laura wasn't the hurtful type. She was more mouse than lion and Rocco had taken advantage of that for years. "I know they're in a tight spot. Rocco didn't believe in life insurance so Laura and Ryan got left with nothing but a failing business and a stack of bills."

"Well, he wasn't the sort to look out for his family," Sherrie replied. "Which means Laura's trying to run the place alone because Ryan is no help. Jim said that bunch of boys from Clearwater are a tough group. They're old enough to drive and he's sneaking out to hang out with them. Laura's so busy trying to do things on her own, no one's watching the kid. And that means trouble's on the way."

Talking about this made Tina tired. She'd run the scenario through her head countless times, and had come up with nothing good. All the more reason to start anew somewhere else. She hated drama and avoided it at all costs, but burned-out businesses came with their own spectacle of tragedy.

"Right now let's focus on this baby. Do we know if it's a boy or a girl?"

"A boy." Sheer delight said Sherrie was more than okay with the change of subject. "We found out today. Jim wanted to be surprised, but I said uh-uh. I wanted to know so I can give him the coolest little kid bedroom ever."

"And Jim said, 'Whatever you want, honey.'"

"Exactly!" Sherrie laughed and moved outside where Earl was loading the snowblower into the back of her pickup truck. "We'll talk soon. Don't make any rash moves, okay?"

"I won't. I promise."

"See you later."

Excitement colored everything about Sherrie today. Her tone, her face, her eyes. And Tina was overjoyed for her friend. She understood the struggles Sherrie had faced, and now she'd pray for a happy ending, a beautiful healthy baby boy for Sherrie and Jim to hold and feed and do all that other stuff one must do with babies.

She and Sherrie had grown up together. Their family homes had been right next to each other. They'd shared classes together, dance instructors and soccer teams. She'd been Sherrie's maid of honor five years ago, and Sherrie had a rose chiffon bridesmaid dress collecting dust in her closet from Tina's short-lived engagement a few years after that. Evan Veltre had decided tall, buxom and raven-haired was more his style. Dumping her mid-engagement made her previous boyfriend's infidelity seem mild by comparison. At least they hadn't been engaged when the blonde caught his eye.

A niggle of sensibility tweaked her.

Had she been hurrying the process, wanting to fall in love? Had she been trying to fit the guy, rather than letting God's timing take charge?

The pinch of common sense was nudged by a twinge of guilt. She did like to make her own path, chart her own course, a charge-ahead kind of woman in many ways. Sherrie had asked if she'd turned to prayer.

She hadn't, not really. Was she too busy, too independent to trust God?

Beezer whined and pawed the door, ready to go. Tina drew a breath, switched off the lights, activated the alarm and went out the door with the big, gold dog ambling alongside her.

Wind tunneled down Main Street, tumbling the last of autumn's leaves. They scurried along the street, pushed by the stiff breeze, gathering in curves and hollows.

Soon it would snow. And they'd continue to decorate the town in beautiful light, a beacon of Christmas hope and cheer. And once again she'd spend Christmas alone, no family, no beloved, no kids.

Beezer pushed his head up under her arm.

He wanted her to pet him. Talk to him. So she did just that on the drive to the Campbell house, happy that no one could see her talking with the big yellow dog, but more glad of his trusting company.

If nothing else crazy occurred in her life this year, she was determined to get herself a dog. Maybe.

Beezer yipped softly, as if telling her she didn't need another dog, she could still share him. If she stayed.

And there was the crux of the problem. A big part of Tina didn't want to stay and face past failures anymore.

Chapter Three

"Hey, Beeze." Max swung down from the elevated boathouse as Tina rounded the corner of the Campbell house at half past six. He looked sports-channel-commercial-friendly in easy-cut jeans and a long-sleeved Pittsburgh Pirates sweatshirt.

"Did you keep an eye on things, old fella?" He stooped and ruffled the dog's neck, rubbing Beeze's favorite spot beneath the wide collar. "All good?" He looked up at her as he asked the question, and the sight of him, caring for the aging dog, looking all sweet and concerned and amazingly good-looking…

She took three seconds to put her heart back in normal sinus rhythm mode. "Everything went fine. Dozens of happy customers picking up their tools and buying fixer-upper stuff to get ready for the holidays." She frowned as Beeze headed for the water, though she knew she had nothing to worry about. Beeze was a country dog and his daily swim was an old habit now. "He'll smell like wet dog all night."

"I'll put him on the porch. Dad's gotten sensitive to smells. The chemo, I guess. He says nothing smells right anymore."

"Will it get better when he's done?"

Max's expression said he wasn't sure anything would get better, ever. Seeing that, her heart softened more.

"Hope so." Max headed for the house. "Come on in. Beeze will join us once he's done with his swim."

Tina knew that. She'd spent an increasing amount of time at the Campbell house over the past decade. Charlie and Jen were good at taking in strays, and when her family had fallen apart, they'd jumped right in. She'd spent holidays here, preserved food with Jenny during the summer, and when Seth Campbell spotted her café on fire a few weeks back from his house across the road, he'd called 9-1-1 and his parents.

They'd helped her then.

She'd help them now. And she'd have done it for no pay, but Charlie wouldn't hear of it. A true fatherly type, he understood cash was finite in a week-to-week existence, and he insisted on paying her for her time. "You know, if you're too tired, we can go over this stuff in the morning. I know you've had a long day."

"Except we could really use the light guy's take on all this." Max's nod toward the door said Charlie's input was key.

"Is he up to it?"

"Let's ask him." Max swung the porch door wide and waited while she stepped in. The smell of roast chicken chased away any pale arguments she might have raised about staying for dinner. She used to grab quick food as she prepared orders at the café. She'd never worried about cooking or grocery shopping at home because she ate on the job. Now?

Truth to tell, she'd been barely eating at all. The realization smacked her upside the head as she crossed to Charlie's big recliner. "Hey, there. We had a great day today, thanks to Max's overnight efforts."

"Yeah?" Charlie's smile was a thin portrait of the one they knew so well. Tiredness dogged his eyes. "Max and Earl got all that stuff fixed?"

"We did. And how about we have you move into the living room, Dad, because when Beeze comes in from the lake, he's going to smell pretty bad. I'll leave him outside for a while, but then I'll tuck him on the porch. If that's all right."

"I can towel him off when he's done with his swim," Tina added. "Then he can curl up by the heater. He and I are used to this routine."

"Are you now?" Max lobbed an old towel her way from the stack they kept inside the back door. "You're elected, then. Need a hand, Dad?"

"I wouldn't mind one." Charlie huffed as he pressed his hands against the wide arms of the chair. He pushed down hard, but paused midway to catch his breath.

Max didn't fuss, he didn't act the least bit concerned or surprised, which told her he was skilled at pretense, and that wasn't something women put in the plus column. She'd had her share of guys who pretended to be happy. Never again. Still, his calm demeanor and strong arm beneath his father's elbow allowed Charlie the extra support he needed, and Max's matter-of-fact manner kept the moment drama-free. "Do you want to eat at the table or in the family room? There's an eight-o'clock game on ESPN."

"Who'd you say was playing?"

Tina sucked a breath. Charlie Campbell knew sports like no other. He loved catching games on TV, and he'd installed a TV in the hardware store so he could catch Pittsburgh throughout both seasons, baseball and football. He'd been celebrating their growing success all year. Before chemotherapy muddled his mind, Charlie would never forget what game was on, who'd scored the most points or who landed on the disabled list.

But he had.

He passed a hand across his forehead as he settled into the firm family-room chair. "They said I might forget stuff."

"It appears they were right," Max teased. "But Dad, that's normal for chemo. And it all comes back later."

Charlie stared at Max, stared right at him with a look that said too much, but then he shrugged, playing along. "That'll be good."

Tina's heart sank. For just a moment, she read the realization in Max's eyes, his face-off with the grim reality of a new timeline, but then he leaned in, hugged his father and backed off. "I'll bring you a tray, okay?"

Charlie's face paled further, and Tina hadn't thought that was possible. She touched Max's arm to draw his attention to "Plan B." "Or Charlie and I could just sit and talk while you guys eat," she offered brightly. "I'll fill him in on store stuff and pick his brain about the festival of lights."

"Since I want to be in on that conversation, I bet Mom won't mind if we hold off supper for a few minutes while we figure this out. Great idea, Tina."

His praise warmed her. His expression said he recognized her ploy and approved. It was clear that Charlie didn't want food, and despite the great smells emanating from Jenny Campbell's kitchen, Tina didn't mind waiting. Not if it helped Charlie.

Max set a side chair alongside Tina's in the family room and took a seat. She pulled a notebook and pen out of her purse. "Charlie, can you give us a quick overview of your normal festival timeline? Max has offered to help, but he hasn't been here since this tradition started."

Ouch. Salt in the wound... Max angled her a look she ignored.

"I've got some notes on my laptop. I'll have Mom get you the file," Charlie promised Max, but then added, "Thing is, I go my own way most times, and your mother told me I should write stuff down, but I was stubborn—"

A distinct cough from the kitchen said Jenny heard and agreed.

"So some of this I just roll with as it happens."

"Tell me those parts, Dad, then I can roll with it in your place."

Charlie explained the contracted light display in the park and the circle of lights surrounding the lake supplied by year-round home-owners and lakeshore businesses. A few cottage owners came back in December, too, solely to set up light displays at their summer homes. "The *Kirkwood Lady* takes dinner cruises around the lake after Thanksgiving," he added. "It only holds three dozen diners, so it gets booked up fast, but it's a sight to see, the boat, all lit up, circling the lake, surrounded by Christmas lights."

The image painted a pretty picture. The big boat, all decked out, surrounded by a ring of lights, trolling the lake's perimeter.

Max had been raised on the water. He'd learned how to fish, catch bait, water-ski and swim, all along the shores of Kirkwood Lake. But since the Sawyer family tragedy, and with the exception of army-related maneuvers, he'd purposely stayed on land. Losing his best friend, knowing what led up to that tragic night and how he might have prevented the heartbreak that followed, spoiled the beauty of lakeshore living.

As Tina jotted down information about the contracted lighting company, Charlie's eyes drifted shut.

"Supper's ready." Jenny walked into the room, saw Charlie and didn't hide the look of concern quite quick enough.

"We tuckered him out." Tina stood, leaned over, kissed Charlie's forehead, then moved toward the kitchen as if Charlie's slumber was the most natural thing in the world.

It wasn't, and Max felt funny leaving his father sleeping in the chair, worn from the influx of medications. He hesitated and remained seated. "I could just sit with him while he sleeps."

Jenny shifted her attention from son to husband and back, then she crossed the room, took Max's arm and drew him up. "He'd feel bad if you skipped eating, and the smell of food doesn't sit well with him now, so come to the kitchen, eat with us, and then you can sit with him. The doctors told us to expect this, all of this." The wave of her hand included Charlie's tiredness, his lack of appetite, aversion to smells and the loss of hair. "Though telling us didn't prepare me for the reality of watching him struggle." She hugged Max's arm as they moved into the kitchen he'd loved as a youth. "We'll take each day as it comes. I'm so glad you're here to help out, Max. I truly don't know what I would have done without you. Just having you at the store with Tina has taken such a load off his mind. Last night was the first peaceful night's sleep he's had since his diagnosis a few weeks ago. I can't tell you how happy that makes me."

Her affirmation confirmed two things for Max. First, he'd made the right decision in coming home. Second? He'd waited far too long, and if God allowed do-overs Max would be at the front of the line, begging. But for now he'd do what he could, when he could, making things easier for his parents. Yes, it meant he'd have to face the past—

And sooner or later he'd run into someone from the Sawyer family. Wanting to take charge of the situation, he decided to make the trip to the Sawyer house a priority. Knock on the door, walk in and talk to Pete's parents. Would they hate him for not stopping Pete from taking the boat that night?

Maybe. And they'd be justified in feeling that way. But owning his part in his friend's accident was the right move to make. And way overdue.

* * *

"That was amazing." Tina glanced at the messed-up dinner table and made a face. "I think I ate half that pan of chicken and biscuits. Which means you two didn't get enough, and while that should make me feel guilty, I'm too happy and full to apologize properly."

"Not eating right lately?"

Max's question made her squirm because she wasn't looking for sympathy or someone to watch over her. She'd just been downright hungry and Jenny was a great cook.

Downright hungry? I'd go with ravenous. Quick, there's one last biscuit. Don't let it get away!

"You don't know this, but we had a fire once, Tina, a long time ago." Jenny leaned forward, hands folded. "Charlie and I were newlyweds, living in an apartment in Clearwater. We were saving like crazy to buy a house of our own. Our oldest son, Marcus, was a baby and we'd broken the smoke alarm. I meant to buy a new one, but it was winter, Marcus had a bad cold and I didn't get out to the stores.

"A space heater in the apartment below us caught fire. Dad was working for the town, and he'd been called in to run the road plows. Marcus woke up to eat." She frowned, glanced down and clenched her hands tighter. "I wouldn't have known there was a fire if that baby hadn't been hungry. What if he hadn't woken up? Already the smoke was coming through the vents and the heat ducts. I grabbed Marcus and a big coat and some blankets for him, and we got outside, but for weeks afterward, all Dad and I could think was what if he hadn't woken up? There was no smoke detector, and we knew it. I could barely live with myself, Tina, imagining what-ifs. I couldn't eat and I don't think I slept for more than minutes at a time. It was crazy."

Tina had been doing exactly the same thing. Not eating, barely sleeping. But she'd spent so long pretending everything was okay in her world that having someone—even Jenny Campbell, mother extraordinaire—recognize her weaknesses seemed to put her at risk.

"For once Marcus's demanding personality did us some good." Max's joke eased the moment, but Jenny didn't let it go. She reached a hand over to Tina's and said, "Charlie and I will support whatever decisions you make, but we want you to know how much we love having you in Kirkwood. We'll do whatever it takes to help you reestablish your business if you decide to do that here. Now, I know you're thinking of starting over elsewhere, so I'm not saying this to pressure you," she added as she stood. "But we wanted you to know we're on your side, Tina."

Jenny's promise of help during this time of personal struggle should have made Tina feel good.

It didn't.

She didn't want to be torn. She didn't want to weigh options or decisions or pros and cons. She didn't want to talk to God about it, or waste more time than was absolutely necessary.

She just wanted to leave. Put it all behind her and go, brushing the dust of her family-less hometown off her feet like Jesus directed the disciples to do. She didn't want to think about broken engagements, loss of family and burned-out businesses. She wanted a clean slate, a new beginning.

Alone? You really want to start all over, someplace else? Absolutely alone?

Jenny's sincerity made Tina's decision to pull up stakes and leave town seem less inviting.

Beezer whined at the door. Jenny started to turn, but Tina raised her hand. "I promised Max I'd towel him off when he was ready to come in. I'll get him, Jenny."

"Thank you. I'm so distracted lately that I'm afraid I'll forget to take care of him while I'm helping Dad."

Tina grabbed her hoodie and went out the front porch door. She toweled Beezer off, then brought him into the warmth of the enclosed porch. "Here you go, old buddy." She switched the radiant heater on and laid one of Beeze's favorite worn blankets on the floor.

"You *have* done this before."

Approval softened the deep timbre of Max's tone. He stepped down onto the porch and reached low to pet Beezer. "He was little more than a pup when I joined the service."

"Yup."

"He's gotten old."

"That'll happen." She couldn't sugarcoat things for him. Sure, he was devoted to the service, to making rank, to moving up, but he'd stayed away on purpose. And that was inexcusable.

"I wish I'd been here."

His honest admission defused her resentment. She

expected him to make excuses, to launch a well-prepared defensive explaining his choices and lauding his service.

He did no such thing. He just sank down onto the floor and petted the old dog's head silently.

She didn't know what to say, what to do. He'd surprised her. She'd spent years wishing she had a family like this, a family that clung together through thick and thin, while Max had brushed them off.

But she hadn't expected outright, blatant honesty. Hearing his regret said she might have been too harsh in her initial assessment.

"Do you have a dog, Tina?"

She'd never had any pets. Why was that? she wondered, seeing the love bond reignite between Max and Beeze. "I don't, no."

"But you're so good with him." Max tipped his head back and looked at her, and there it was again, that glimmer of assessment, appraisal. "Like you're born to love animals."

"I get my share of loving when I come over here," she told him. She stood, gathered her purse and slung it over her shoulder crosswise. "That's plenty. It's tough to give an animal all the love and care it needs when you're working all the time."

His nod said he understood.

His eyes said something different altogether.

But no matter what Max thought, Tina understood the motivations behind her singular actions. When everything you've ever loved…or thought you loved…went away, alone was just plain better.

* * *

Max's cell phone buzzed him awake in the middle of the night. He answered it quietly, not wanting to disturb his parents, but knowing it must be important for his brother Seth to place a call at that hour. "What's up? Do you need help? I can be there in five minutes."

"Only if you break all the speed limits, and yes, I need you here. Now."

Max was half-ready before his brother placed the request. "Are you okay? Is it the babies? What's going on?"

"My family's fine," Seth assured him.

Max breathed a sigh of relief. Seth's wife, Gianna, had given birth to fraternal twins in early summer. Mikey and Bella were the sweetest things God ever put on the planet, and he'd felt a fierce shot of protective love when he'd met them for the first time the week before.

"Someone was snooping around the remains of Tina's place on the water, then cut through the pass between the church and the hardware store. I'd just finished feeding Mikey and saw a flash of movement at the edge of the light. I don't think he or she knows they've been spotted."

"I'm on my way."

Max bolted for the car once he'd quietly closed the kitchen door to the side entrance. He started the engine, backed out of his parents' drive slowly, then picked up speed as he cruised toward the village at the northern point of Kirkwood Lake. In town, he drove past the hardware store as if it was perfectly normal for traffic to pass through Kirkwood in the middle of the night. He turned right onto Overlook Drive, passed Seth's house deliberately, then let the car glide to a silent stop. He turned the engine off, slipped from the driver's seat and leaned the door shut. If anyone was still around, he didn't want to ruin the false sense of security he'd just created.

His eyes adjusted to the darkness quickly. He spotted Seth's unmoving frame at the far edge of his carriage-style garage. Max walked around the garage, hoping Seth recognized his maneuver. When Seth melded back into the shadows on the far side of the angled garage, Max knew he understood. They met up on the farthest, darkest edge of the building. "Have you seen him again?"

Seth shook his head. "No. But I've been watching to see if he came back."

"Was he at the hardware store? Do you think someone's trying to break in? Or set another fire?"

Backlit by the outside house lights, Max couldn't see Seth's face, but he read the consternation in his tone. "I'm not sure. It seemed the original intent was to find something in the ashes of the café."

"This person was crawling through a roped-off crime scene?"

"Yes."

Max could only think of one reason why anyone would grope their way through the ashes of Tina's cafe in the middle of the night: to find something that might incriminate them. "Man? Woman? Child?"

"No way to tell. Too far and too dark. But whoever it was moved quick and light."

"Probably a woman or a kid."

"I hate to think either," Seth admitted, "but that was my gut reaction, too."

"I'll go the long way around the store, circling the outside of the church and the cemetery behind," Max said. He clicked his watch to mark time. "In four minutes you come around the front to the back entrance of Dad's store. I'll flash my pen from the edge of the cemetery woods. And we'll go in together."

"You packing?" Seth wondered aloud.

"Always." Skill with handguns had become intrinsic to Max years ago. Going through life armed and ready was second nature now.

"Just don't shoot me, okay?"

"It *is* dark," Max whispered as he slipped along the back of the garage, then into the shadows of the tree-lined street. Strewn leaves would have marked his presence on a dry night, but the late-day rain silenced his movement. He slipped along the front edge of the graveyard, then through the forested southern border. If this person was targeting area businesses to burn, or searching to remove incriminating evidence, Max was going to make sure he or she didn't get any farther than Dad's hardware store parking lot. Unless they'd already made their way home, wherever that was, and in that case, they'd let the authorities figure it out. Right now, with Seth covering his back, Max knew he was in the driver's seat.

"Stop right there."

Max froze.

"I've already called the police, and if you move, I'll—"

"Tina?" He turned, hands up, and peered into the trees. "Where are you?" he whispered. "What do you think you're doing?"

"Max?"

If there'd been time or if he was sure she wasn't pointing a gun at his back, he'd have banged his head against one of the nearby trees in frustration. As it was, he held perfectly still until he made out her shape—well, half her shape—behind one of the sprawling maples planted nearly eighty years before. For one split second he wondered if it had been Tina that Seth had spotted in the rubble…but it couldn't have been.

Could it?

Why would Tina be snooping around the ruins of her burned-out café, the place she loved so much?

She's pretty anxious to leave this town behind. Anxiety can push people to do things they'd never do normally.

"I saw someone," she whispered as she crept through the trees.

Tina lived in an upstairs apartment on Overlook Drive, kitty-corner from Seth's house. Her front windows overlooked Kirkwood Lake and Main Street. At this point, Max was actually surprised they hadn't been joined by a cast of thousands, which was just as likely as having four people roaming Main Street in Kirkwood in the dead of night. "What did you see?"

"Someone moving around the timbers of the café."

"And do you make it a habit of being up in the middle of the night, checking out Main Street?"

"I didn't used to," she retorted, and he didn't have to listen hard to hear the sting in her voice. "I used to sleep soundly. And then someone burned down my business, and I'm lucky I sleep at all. And at this point, the three hours I got tonight will probably be it, because how can I crawl back into bed and fall asleep after all this?"

Jenny's words rushed back, how she'd lost sleep and her appetite in the aftermath of an accidental fire as a young mother. How much worse must it be to think you were targeted?

Tina pointed west toward Seth's house. "I woke up and saw Seth's lights on. I worried that one of the babies might be sick. When he came creeping outside, I knew something was up. I looked further and saw something. Someone," she corrected herself, "moving through the remains of the café."

"Doesn't anyone sleep around here anymore?" Seth's voice entered the conversation from the near side of the church parking lot.

"It appears not." Max decided the time for subterfuge was over. He flicked the flashlight of his cell phone on. "Tina saw someone, too."

"She did, huh?" Seth moved forward, frowned, then yawned. "Well, between the three of us, we've managed to give away any tiny advantage we might have had. Max, did you see anything?"

"Other than Tina? No."

He directed the light toward her. She flushed.

"Me, neither. So whoever it was didn't hang around

tonight, but I don't like that he or she hightailed it up here toward Dad's store when he thought he'd been spotted."

"Me, neither. I could start sleeping here. Add an ounce of Fort Bragg protection to the local mix."

"Mom would go crazy with that. And Dad would worry, and the last thing we want to do is make Dad worry."

"No argument there. So what do we do?"

"For now, go home." Tina offered the suggestion as she turned back toward Overlook Drive. "Although the likelihood of getting more sleep is pretty much impossible now."

"Because?" Max left the comment open-ended, hoping for the right answer. She supplied it, and wasted no time doing it.

"There's only one reason someone would be poking around the ashes of my hard work," she answered quickly, and he read the thick emotion in her voice. "And that's because they're looking for evidence that puts them at the scene of the fire. Which means the supposition of arson just became a reality in my head."

Chapter Four

She looked like someone had just stolen her best friend, her favorite toy and her puppy all at once. A sheen of tears brightened her eyes, and Max resisted the pull for sympathy until her chin quivered.

That did it.

He reached out and gathered her in for a hug. Tina's expression reflected the very emotions his mother had shared over supper. Fear. Questioning. Guilt. Remorse.

Not eating.

Not sleeping.

Barely existing.

He hugged her close, letting her cry against his shoulder. He heard Seth slip off into the shadows, retracing his steps back home. When the tears paused, he looped an arm around her shoulders and headed for the sidewalk.

"Where are we going?"

"I'm walking you home."

"This is the long way," she whispered, then scrubbed

the arm of her sweatshirt across her face, total tomboy. "No tissues."

"I see that." He quirked a tiny smile down to her. "Could've asked me, you know."

"You carry tissues in your pocket?"

"No. But you could have asked."

Her smile said she was feeling better. She moved a step ahead and waved him off. "I can find my own way home. You don't have to walk me, Max."

He pulled her right back by his side and reestablished that arm around her shoulders. "I do. First, if there's someone lurking in the shadows, I can't exactly leave you alone to discover them, can I?"

"Well, no, I suppose not, but you don't need to put your arm around me."

"Wrong again. If anyone sees us, we want them to think we're taking a leisurely romantic stroll around town, not staking out felonious criminals."

"At four forty-five in the morning?"

"Last I knew there was no clock on romance, Tina. It is what it is."

"I actually prefer folks assuming we're on a clandestine mission than star-crossed lovers, Max. In this town, the latter gets you into a lot more trouble. Everyone knows and rarely forgets. Take it from the voice of experience." She paused and he did, too, looking down. "Fishbowl romance isn't fun."

"The joys of small-town living." He walked her past his car and to her door. "I'll see you at nine, okay? But if you do fall asleep and want to sleep in, that's fine. Earl's in early and we can handle things."

"I might, then. Thank you, Max."

She looked up at him. Met his gaze.

Maybe it was the flicker of fresh-washed moonlight now that the rain had passed. Maybe it was the way the soft night breeze lifted the short tendrils of her hair, dancing them around her face. Or the way her mouth parted slightly, looking up, as if wanting to say more…

Do more.

He breathed deep, holding her gaze, wondering what it would be like to lean closer. Touch his mouth to hers. See what Tina Martinelli was all about.

"Max, you want coffee?" Seth's rather loud attempt at whispering effectively ended the moment. "I figured it's late enough, we might as well start the day."

Tina stepped back.

So did Max.

And as Seth lumbered out of the shadows of his Dutch Colonial across the street, the sound of a car squealing east on Main Street said someone had just made a quick getaway, and in a tiny, quiet town like Kirkwood, the noise stood out. Blocked by trees and houses, they couldn't make out the car, or even ascertain where it had been parked, but that told Max two things: one, the car hadn't looked out of place, or Seth would have noticed it. Therefore the car was a regular visitor to this end of town.

And two, that they were on the right track in circling around the small business center of Main Street, Kirkwood Lake, because someone was up to no good.

The question was who?

He turned back toward Tina.

She'd paled at the sound of the car, and he didn't have to explain the car's presence or rapid retreat. The stark look of her face said she got it.

But wished she didn't.

"We'll figure this out," he promised. "In the meantime, you could always come stay at the house. Mom would love the company, and you wouldn't be alone."

Her jaw jutted, stubborn. "I've gotten used to being alone. And Seth's right there, across the street. Most people don't want to mess with a county sheriff if they can avoid it."

"But your apartment backs up to the cemetery and the woods leading to the highway," Max argued. "And Seth has to sleep now and again, although with two babies, that's a trick in itself." He didn't add that someone had torched the business not far from Seth's home, clearly not worried about a sleeping sheriff's deputy.

"I thank God for their grandmothers every day," Seth droned, yawning. "Shift work has proven to be a marvelous thing. But Max is right, Tina. Most arsonists target something. In this case it's either you—"

Max hated the stark look that came into her eyes as she glanced south toward the burned-out building.

"—Sol Rigby or the town. Sol's out on Log Cabin Road, and it's pretty tricky to get to his cabin without being seen. If it's the town, then this guy could strike again anytime. We took precautions on Gianna's business and the hardware store with increased security cameras and alarms, but that doesn't mean he can't get around those to start a fire. But what if he's targeting you personally, Tina?" Seth crossed his arms and stared her down, and instead of getting mad like she'd have done with Max, she looked resigned. "How do we keep you safe?"

"Right now, all I want is to be warm," she retorted. She pulled her hoodie tighter and moved toward the side door leading up to her apartment. "We'll discuss this later. Whoever it is has left for the night, and I can't think straight on little sleep and no coffee. Good night, guys."

She slipped into the side door, locked it, and Max and Seth waited until they saw her light blink on upstairs.

Max turned toward Seth. "I don't like this."

"Me, either."

"We're caught in the middle, not knowing what's really going on until we get to scene two, which is usually another fire."

"And no one wants that."

"But figuring this out with three diverse directions will take legwork."

"I'm calling the fire chief and the arson investigation squad once we're at first light," Seth assured him. "I don't know what this guy—"

"Or woman."

Seth acknowledged that with a nod. "What he or she was looking for, but the team will want to comb things carefully again before they can clean that mess up. Which means the eyesore of a burned-out building might be around for a while unless the investigators feel confident that they've got everything they need.

Not exactly the draw for the Christmas light festival we hoped for. By the way." Seth pulled the storm door open and let Max move into the house ahead of him. "Do you need help with the festival stuff? I know everything's gotten kind of dumped on you, and it's your own stupid fault for staying away so long, but you are my kid brother and I'll help. If I have to."

Max started to laugh, realized the house was still mostly asleep, stifled the instinct and shook his head. "You take care of babies, that cute wife, your various new Italian relations and your job. Plus guarding the town. I can handle the lights."

His words sounded braver than he felt, but he'd put the lighting array folders into his car the night before so he wouldn't forget them this morning. If he grabbed some slow minutes at the hardware store today, he'd go through the schematics and get an idea of how the lake-wide show worked.

He'd tackled some pretty impressive jobs overseas. He'd learned to blend, build and dismantle secretive missions on a moment's notice. But those had been on the down-low. If he messed up no one but he and his team knew, and they were trained to improvise on a moment's notice.

Not one of those clandestine missions made him as nervous as the possibility of messing up Christmas for an entire town. If for no other reason than to make up for times he was a jerk as a teenager, Max wanted this festival to go right. It was the least he could do. And with the upcoming committee meeting, he'd be face-to-face with folks from his past, including Pete's mom. Truth to tell, he wasn't sure how to handle that.

"Max!" Mary Sawyer claimed a hug the moment she laid eyes on Max the next night. The embrace felt good…and bad all at once. The mix of emotions tunneled Max back in time. The Sawyers' beachfront yard, the campfire, the bottle Pete had paid a college guy to buy. If he'd put a stop to Pete's foolishness then, would Mary Sawyer's son and his girlfriend be alive now?

"It's so good to see you." Mary's warm voice softened his flashback. "Look at you! All grown up, and so handsome. We're so proud of you, Max." She gripped his arm in a show of support and affection. "I hope your mother's told you that. Every summer we put up honor flags along Main Street, remembering our men and women in the service, and I make sure yours is right there, dead center, for everyone to see. Welcome home, Max."

His heart churned.

Seeing Pete's mom, being wrapped in her motherly embrace, felt like old times. But Max was a trained army officer. He'd stayed alive doing clandestine work because he knew better than to wallow in false security. Mary Sawyer was gushing over him because she remembered the good times…

And because she didn't know the whole truth. Only three people knew the full extent of what happened that hot August night, and two of them were gone.

Guilt climbed his spine, then tightened his neck. Several other committee members came through Carmen

Bianchi's door just then, including Tina. One of them called Mary's name. She patted his cheek and moved off to talk with an unhappy-looking woman. Max didn't recognize her, but within two minutes of opening the meeting, he realized that if he was marking friend and foe, this woman would be firmly in the latter column.

"There's no way that can work," she insisted when Tina went through Charlie's basic plan. "You don't know me, Max Campbell, but I've been on this committee for eight years, and I can't believe we don't have a more detailed description of what goes where than that." She pointed to the folder of papers Max laid out on the table of Carmen's living room. "We have to have everything constructed and ready to go in a week. I don't see that happening."

"We've got a contract with Holiday Lighting out of Buffalo, Georgia." Mary Sawyer sent Georgia Palmeteer a calming look. "They take care of the park display. The town does the Main Street lighting, same as always, and Max will oversee the rest. Most folks do their own thing, so it's not like he even has all that much to do. I think he'll do just fine." She beamed a smile his way, and once again the thought of what should have been broadsided him. He needed to come clean, and he needed to do it soon because enduring her understandable wrath was far better than letting a nice woman like Mrs. Sawyer think he was a great guy.

Aren't you a great guy?

Now? Yes.

Back then? No.

Pete and Amy's accident was a long time ago. You

were a kid. Look at the facts, man. Your buddy had a wild streak those last couple of years. It wasn't your job to look after him.

Max knew better. They'd been friends a long time. Pete was like a brother to him, and if there was one thing Campbell brothers did well, it was take care of one another. When they weren't beating on each other, that is.

"We've left the majority of a massive fund-raiser in the hands of someone who doesn't write down what needs to be done," retorted Georgia. "That's plain carelessness."

"Oh, Georgia, really." Mary rolled her eyes. "It's gone fine every single year. Why are you all up in arms over this?"

"We Palmeteers like things done right," she snapped, and her pretentious tone said she didn't think all too much of Mary Sawyer's more casual attitude. "Leaving things to chance is for amateurs. Folks pay good money to come here for the drive through the park and the Main Street Festival. I, for one, don't take that lightly."

"Having Max on board offers us an opportunity for change," Tina remarked.

The committee shifted their attention to her.

"Max and the guys might not do everything exactly the way Charlie would have done it, but as long as we have everything lit and beautiful, what difference does it make?"

"Because we like things the way they are, young lady." Georgia's clipped tone said she didn't appreciate being brought to task by someone half her age.

"With an aging population, it's probably good for us to get used to change now and again," offered Carmen Bianchi as she rolled an old-fashioned tea cart into the room. "As the younger generation takes over, we have two options, to compromise and trust them to lead the way or give up. And I never give up on anything so, Max Campbell, you have my vote." She smiled at Max and indicated the cart with a dip of her chin. "I know this isn't as fancy as what we used to get at Tina's café, but Tina did the baking so we know that part is wonderful."

"Well, that's another thing," Georgia groused as she bustled to be first at the portable coffee setup. "Tina's done the majority of food for the park vendors and for our 'Christmas on Main Street' day. How are we going to manage this with her business gone? I say we tap into The Pelican's Nest restaurant and see if Laura will help with food. I mean, it seems silly not to ask her with Tina's place out for the count."

Georgia's careless words stabbed Tina's gut.

She'd half-expected someone to come up with this idea, and it wasn't a surprise that it was the town supervisor's ill-tempered sister, but to have her spout it here, in front of the whole committee, without putting it on the agenda or checking with her... She felt blindsided, and rightfully so. It wasn't as if the entire town didn't know her broken family history and the animosity Rocco had shown her for years.

Mary Sawyer turned toward Tina. "What do you think, Tina? County health laws say we need to produce food in a certified kitchen, so we can't just cook up a storm at home. Liability rules prevent that. How can we set this up?"

"We have a couple of options," Tina replied. She felt Max's gaze, but kept her attention focused on the other committee members as they helped themselves to coffee and cake. "Certainly we can ask Laura to help. We've done that in the past and, if you remember, Rocco made it clear he wasn't about to undercut his business by feeding folks in the street."

Several nods said they all remembered Rocco's mean-spirited replies.

"But with Rocco gone, Laura might be more willing to help. Who would like to ask her?"

No one spoke up, but then Carmen Bianchi raised a hand. "I will, dear. No harm in trying, I always say, and I don't know Laura so there's no hard feelings either way."

"Thank you, Carmen." Tina smiled at the aging Italian woman and quietly thanked God for bringing Carmen Bianchi and Gianna Costanza to town the year before. The two expert seamstresses had brought a thriving business and warm, open hearts to Main Street, a definite plus for the popular village.

"With or without Laura's help, we'll be fine," she went on, and when a couple of people raised skeptical brows, she met their unspoken concerns head-on. "I haven't been spending these four weeks with my head in the sand. Piper Harrison has offered the use of their kitchen at the McKinney Farms Dairy store. And Lacey Barrett has done the same at the apple farm across from the Campbell house on Lower Lake Road. If we set up the heated tent on Main Street like we always do, we can have food prepped at either or both of those locations, and we can do on-site cooking/grilling right in the food tent like we've done in the past."

"That would work just fine," Mary announced. "Tina, thank you for making those arrangements. And I know the fire department is excited to be manning the grill as always."

"Perfect." Tina smiled at her, glad that her legwork had defused the situation. "And—"

"Well, that's another thing," Georgia interrupted with a tart glance to Carmen's east-facing window. "How in the name of all that's good and holy are we going to have a pretty, sweet, inviting Christmas festival with the mess from Tina's fire just sitting there, getting wetter, soggier, smellier and sloppier every day?"

Tina's heart froze, the very heart that had built a thriving business over years of hard work and sweat equity. It didn't matter that she felt the same way. To have Georgia throw it up in her face in a sneering, I'm-better-than-everybody way cut deep.

"It may not be a problem."

Attention shifted to Max. He splayed his hands, clearly comfortable with taking charge as he stood and moved toward the group. "The investigation into the fire is still incomplete. I know the arson squad feels the need to comb through the remains of Tina's coffee shop to find clues about who would do this kind of thing, but I also know they've slated the comb-through for tomorrow. After that, we should be able to schedule the big equipment for demolition and removal."

"They can get it done that quickly?" Mary Sawyer looked impressed.

"The change in the weather is pushing them," Max told her. "And they know the town needs to put a sad piece of history behind them and move on."

"But what if he strikes again?" wondered Jason Radcliffe, another committee member. "I've been a volunteer fireman for years. Arson is rarely a single-crime event. How do we protect the town and the festival? I can't pretend I'm not concerned about that."

"Me, too."

Again all eyes turned to Max, and Tina had to give it to him. His squared-off, rugged but calm stance said he'd do whatever it took to get the job done. And when he smiled at Georgia Palmeteer, Tina was afraid the older woman might keel over on the spot. Clearly her sour temper didn't make her immune to Max's dark good looks and take-charge style.

"But that's why the squad wants to get this done. If there's evidence to be found at the scene, they might be able to make an arrest before the festival and that would put an end to our concerns."

"Oh, it would!" Georgia nodded as if Max was the smartest—*and cutest*—thing on the planet.

"It would be a relief," Carmen agreed. "The thought that someone could destroy another person's hopes and dreams is a shock in such a wonderful town."

Her words provided the balm to close the meeting peacefully. As Tina tugged her coat from the row of hooks inside Carmen's kitchen door, strong hands reached over hers, withdrew the coat and held it open for her to put on.

"Thank you, Max."

He frowned at the coat, then her. "It's too cold for this jacket."

"I only have to go up the hill to get home." She tugged her coat sleeves down over her hands to avoid the deepening chill. "And it wasn't this bad when I headed down here. I must have missed the weather report that said arctic air was nose-diving into Kirkwood Lake."

"Lows in the twenties," Max advised. He turned toward Carmen and gave her a big hug. "You did great. Thank you for hosting the meeting and for your vote of confidence. I wasn't sure which way things would go right then, but your words tipped the scales. I'm grateful."

"Well, it's much ado about nothing," Carmen replied. "When folks don't have big things to concern themselves with, they pay too much attention to little things."

Her words hit home with Max.

Self-satisfaction wasn't an easy lesson learned. He'd learned to like himself in the service, and had earned his share of respect and responsibility along the way, but he'd had a hard time wrapping his head around what he needed versus what he wanted.

He needed to be forgiven. That might or might not happen, but he couldn't be back in town and walk in the shadow of old lies and live with himself. Which meant he needed to set things straight with the Sawyers, a task he'd do as soon as time allowed.

On top of that?

He longed to belong somewhere. To be part of something calm and quiet. He'd done the gung-ho thing to the best of his ability, but seeing his father's decline and his mother's worry showed him a dark mirror image. He'd let shame keep him at bay for too long. His unexplained absence hurt his parents and his family. He would never do that to anyone again. "Thanks again, Carmen. I'm going to see Tina home—"

"Are not."

Max ignored her and continued, "Then I'm going to set up camp at the hardware store, but I'm going to leave my car stashed behind Seth's place."

"You're baiting a trap." Approval laced Carmen's comment. "Gianna told me what Seth and Tina saw last night." Carmen directed her gaze toward the window that faced Tina's burned-out shop. "It's creepy to think someone was out there, snooping around in the dead of night while I was sleeping. What do you think he was hunting for?"

Max shrugged. "I'm not sure. But once word gets around that the arson investigators are going to go through the site, the perp is likely to come back for whatever he lost."

"So you guys are going on watch patrol, hoping you've tempted him or her out?"

"That's why I mentioned the time limit at the meeting," Max admitted. "This way word gets around, folks will yak it up, and the arsonist might show up."

"Unless I was the arsonist and you just warned me off," Tina countered, looking straight at Max, and the look on her face said she was voicing her own personal concerns. "Maybe I wanted out of town so badly I torched my own business."

"Tina, that's ridiculous," Carmen spouted. "Anyone in their right mind—"

"I expect it's what a few people might be thinking," Tina continued. "And I know the arson team investigated me."

Max put a hand to Tina's face, her cheek. He left it there, trained his gaze on hers and uttered one short sentence. "You didn't do it."

Her chin quivered.

She firmed it and pulled back, but the coat hooks got in her way.

"They have to investigate everyone, Tina," he continued. His low, level voice helped calm her frayed nerve endings. "That's the job of the arson squad. But we all know you would never do such a thing, so you need to relax. Shove off the urge to take offense, let the investigators do their job and keep helping me at the hardware store so I don't mess up Dad's business. And maybe we'll catch whoever it was you and Seth saw last night."

"You believe me."

Max's wry expression said that was about the stupidest thing he'd ever heard. "Woman, I never doubted it for a minute. No real coffee lover destroys a crazy-expensive espresso machine. It just isn't done."

He meant it.

He meant every single word even though people used insurance fraud to pad their budgets far too often. "I do love my coffee," she admitted. And then she smiled up at him, and he smiled down at her, and for just a moment there was no Carmen, there was no divisive meeting, there were no worries, there was just Max's smile, warm and soothing, the kind of smile a girl could lose herself in for oh…say…forever?

A rush of cold air changed the course of her thoughts as Max pulled Carmen's door open. They hurried through, closed the door, then headed up the sloped incline of Overlook Drive toward Tina's apartment.

Cold, biting wind didn't allow casual conversation, and when a strong gust tunneled down Overlook, Max grabbed hold of Tina's arm, gaining leverage for both of them.

And then he didn't let go.

Her heart did one of those weird flippy things girls talk about all the time, like it used to when she watched Max from afar fifteen years before.

Stop it, heart. Stop it right now!

Her pulse refused to listen. The grip of his hand on her arm, the solidity of him, the intrinsic soldier effect, combined to make her heart jump into a full-fledged tarantella.

Working side by side with him taught her something new. Max had changed in his time away. He was still crazy attractive, the kind of dream date any girl would want, but he was more now. He'd grown up to be a man of honor and strong character. Suddenly the two past relationships she had thought might end in happily-ever-after paled beside the valor of the U.S. soldier escorting her home. Did that make her fickle? Or stupid?

I'd go with smart, her conscience advised.

Tina wasn't so sure about that. She'd almost married one guy and had thought about it again with the other. So…not smart.

Wrong. The mental scolding came through loud and clear as they approached Tina's door. *Why is it okay to notice Max has grown up and not realize you've done the same thing? Every princess kisses a toad or two. That's how we find Mr. Right. Eventually. And let me take you back to Sherrie's bit of advice... Have you given this to God? Prayed about it?*

She'd done no such thing, and the realization shamed her.

"We're here, we didn't blow away. And wear a warmer coat tomorrow. Please." Max added the last word when she frowned up at him, and the look he gave her, now that they were in the sheltered alcove of her door, said he wasn't just being bossy. He was concerned.

Her heart didn't flip this time.

It softened under his warm look of entreaty, as if her comfort mattered. From somewhere deep inside, an old feeling dredged up, a fledgling feeling of something good and warm and holy.

His gaze flitted to her mouth, then back to her eyes, wondering.

She stepped back into the doorway.

She'd put her heart on the line twice before. And even though it was no longer baseball season, every American understood the "three strikes and you're out" rule. Right now—

She paused, gazing up at Max, and realized she

wasn't sure what she wanted right now, because when Max Campbell was around?

Her thoughts muddled.

"You did mention that you weren't seeing anyone." Max smiled down at her and touched one chilled finger to her cheek.

"And I have no intention of seeing anyone." She held his gaze, refusing to back down or step forward. "My short timeline says we need to leave things uncomplicated. We're coworkers." She squared her shoulders and raised her chin. "And that's only until I move away. I can't afford to get involved, I have a serious disregard for broken hearts and I'll be gone soon. The hardware store is slower in winter. That will give you time to train someone else to step in."

"They won't be as pretty," Max observed, but he took a step back.

And the minute he did? She wished he hadn't.

He glanced up. "Head in, get warm. I'll watch until your lights come on, then I'm circling around as if I'm leaving. That way if anyone's watching, they'll have the false assurance that I'm gone and Seth's on duty in Clearwater."

"Is he?"

"No. He's staked out inside the vestibule of the church. Reverend Smith was more than happy to give him a warm place for his watch."

"The reverend and his wife are good people." She thought the world of the Smiths, a wonderful couple. They seemed so strong, solid and peaceful in their faith.

Sometimes she sat in the back of church, feeling like an imposter. Did she believe in God?

Yes.

Did she trust Him to take charge of her life, lead the way?

No.

Isn't that why He gave her two arms, two legs and a working brain? So she could run her life her own way?

How's that been working out for you lately? You might want to rethink that whole trust-in-God thing. Just a suggestion. She silenced the internal rebuke, but hadn't Sherrie been telling her that same thing lately? To put God in charge, play Him on the front line and not leave Him on the bench?

The very thought required courage she didn't have. "Be careful tonight."

"Will do. And remind me to order some kind of coffee service for the hardware store. It's crazy not to have a coffeemaker there."

Tina read what Max didn't say, that he felt funny patronizing her aunt's business when things were bad between them. She nodded, then paused. "I'll bring over my one-cup system. You buy the pods. But in the meantime, I'm okay with grabbing coffee from Aunt Laura's place. I think she could use the business and I'm pretty tired of having bad feelings surrounding me. Know what I mean?"

Max mentally counted her request as superachievement number one.

He knew exactly what she meant. He read it in her

eyes. Old regrets wore on the soul, never a good thing. "I'll do that. Good night, Tina."

"Good night, Max."

He crossed to Seth's place once Tina's lights blinked on, then took his car for a short spin. He returned the back way, slid into a parking spot behind Seth's garage and wound his way through the trees to below the hardware store. From the shelter of an alcove he could watch the ruins of Tina's store.

His brother Luke, another deputy sheriff who lived farther down the east side of Kirkwood Lake, would take over the watch in two hours, allowing Max time to sleep. And Zach Harrison, a New York State Trooper who lived next to the McKinney Farm on the upper west side of Kirkwood Lake, had agreed to relieve Seth. They'd set up a schedule between them, knowing manpower was tight on their combined forces, but also aware of an arsonist's typical time frame. The emotional "high" of a fire wore off quick, and most arson-lovers struck again fairly soon. Seth, Luke, Zach and Max had decided among themselves that it wasn't going to happen on their watch.

And that was the beauty of a small town like Kirkwood, especially one front-loaded with a good share of first responders. The arsonist had used the element of surprise to his advantage when they'd torched Tina's café.

They refused to allow him or her to have that advantage again.

Chapter Five

Tina lugged the coffeemaker into the hardware store early the next morning. She assumed she'd lie awake half the night, thinking about fire and arson and being alone.

She didn't. For the first time in weeks she fell into a sound sleep quickly and slept through the night. Why?

Because Max was watching over things.

When he's here, her conscience chided.

The sage advice hit home. Life taught her to tread carefully now. She had no desire for another broken heart or to be the object of conversation in their small town. She'd been there, done that.

It wasn't a bit fun.

First, falling for Max would be a game changer and she was done with games.

Second, she knew his style. When the going got tough? Max did his own thing. She'd seen that with the Sawyers, then with his family. And how anyone could take a wonderful family like the Campbells for granted…

Reason enough to run scared right there.

She was leaving, anyway. And even if she wasn't ready to wipe the dust of her hometown off her heels, it would take more than Max's word to convince her he was back in Kirkwood to stay. He'd traveled the world, gone on secret missions, played G.I. Joe to the max. The likelihood of Max setting up house in their quaint, sleepy, lakeside hometown?

Thin. And Tina was done with thin promises and broken dreams. She set up the coffeemaker, filled the water dispenser, then hesitated, caught between her bravado from the previous night and the cold light of morning.

She'd told Max that she wanted to mend things with her aunt. Had she meant it?

Yes. But could she do it?

She sighed, made a face and walked to the front window. To the right lay the church, white wood and stone, a sweet country remembrance of putting God first, a lesson she needed to embrace more often.

To the left and slightly uphill was The Pelican's Nest, the lakeshore eatery her parents had owned for decades. She'd taken her first steps there. She'd learned how to read there. She'd had her first kiss there, on the back steps of the kitchen, when Brady Davis dared her to kiss him.

Afterward, she couldn't for the life of her figure out what all the fuss was about. A few years later, watching Max Campbell date girl after girl, she got a clue.

It wasn't the kiss—in fact it had very little to do with the kiss. It was the person you were kissing that made all the difference.

She glanced at the clock, saw she had plenty of time, then walked out the door and across the street to the restaurant entrance.

It felt odd walking through the front door. She'd always breezed in and out of the kitchen entrance, laughing, talking, working, her days and nights filled with school and The Pelican's Nest.

She hauled in a deep breath, pulled open the door and strode in.

Two customers she didn't know glanced up from the counter, nodded and went back to their coffee. Just two customers in the whole place, at prime breakfast time on a weekday morning.

"Can I help you?" Laura turned, saw Tina and stopped.

Tina took advantage of the surprise and moved forward as if everything was all right. "Can I have three coffees to go, Aunt Laura?"

"Of course." Laura half stammered the words. A pinched look said she wasn't sure what to say or what to do so Tina helped once again.

"I need room for cream and sugar in two of them. And if you have fresh Danish or coffee cake on hand, that would be nice, too."

"Three of them?"

"Sure. Any mix will do. We'll share."

An awkward silence ensued while Laura put the order together. There was no typical morning smell of sizzling bacon or rich French toast grilling alongside eggs over easy. Tina recognized the coffee cake as a recipe her mother had perfected two decades ago, a buttery-rich cinnamon concoction with melt-in-your-mouth texture. Tina's love of pastry making came from her mother, her love of restaurants from her father, and her stubborn nature had been a combo package. As Laura wrapped the square hunks of cake, she thought of the family they'd been so long ago.

Where had that gone? Why had it ended?

Illness, then greed. Her father's weakening condition pushed him to sell. Rocco's greed put her out on the street. But Aunt Laura…

"I'm sorry, Tina." Laura paused from the simple task. She bit her lip, then squared her shoulders and looked up. Met Tina's gaze. "So sorry. Losing your coffee shop like that, after all the work you did."

Tina stood silent, unsure what to say. There was so much more to be sorry for, their histories intertwined, then butting heads.

"No matter what went on before, it broke my heart to see it happen."

Sincerity laced her words. For the first time in a lot of years, Tina felt the grace of sympathetic family, and it pricked emotions she'd thought long-buried. "Mine, too. Thanks, Aunt Laura."

Laura nestled the drinks into a tray, bagged the wrapped cake squares, added plastic forks and napkins and set the bag alongside the drinks. For just a moment she faltered, as if not sure how to charge Tina, but Tina pulled a twenty from her pocket and handed it over without waiting for a total.

Laura drew a breath, hit the register keys, then handed Tina's change back.

Tina wanted to tip her, tell her to keep the change, but she understood the restaurant business like few others. First, you never tip the owner. It just wasn't done.

Second?

Laura would be insulted. Tina knew her well enough to understand the awkward dynamics between support and charity. Support wasn't a bad thing.

Charity?

Martinelli pride would fight that, tooth and nail.

She lifted the bag in one hand and the drink tray in the other. "Thank you." She turned to go, but Laura called her name softly. She turned back. "Yes?"

"You were busy over there."

Tina didn't deny it. "Yes."

"I could use some of that here." Laura glanced around the diner, and her expression said the lack of business was customary. Tina was restaurant-savvy enough to hear a death knell when it rang in front of her. Aunt Laura was going to lose The Pelican's Nest.

"Well, your competition's pretty much gone," Tina remarked. "Maybe things will pick up."

Laura frowned, and Tina had the strongest urge to hug the older woman.

She resisted.

"I want business to pick up, but not at your expense, Tina."

Not at Tina's expense?

Laura's words dredged up raw feelings.

She hadn't worried about Tina's expense when she

turned her out on the street, no job, no family and no college education shoring her up. She hadn't worried when Tina worked night and day a block away, building a cozy, inviting enterprise, the kind of place The Pelican's Nest used to be, in the shadow of her aunt and uncle's business.

She and Rocco had taken Tina to court, tying up time and a legal defense that took years to pay off at fifty dollars a month, saying she violated the non-competition clause of the sale agreement. Even though they were planning to move south, her parents had agreed not to open another restaurant within eight miles of The Pelican's Nest for at least ten years, a common practice in the sale of a family business.

The judge threw the case out, but not until Tina had wasted time and finances fighting the pointless suit. As the judge pointed out, Laura and Rocco had made the agreement with Tina's parents.

Not with Tina.

And that was that.

But they had to know that fighting a court proceeding was a huge setback for a young person trying to set up their own business. Which is exactly why they'd done it. But now, with Rocco gone, maybe Laura saw things differently. Tina hoped and prayed it was so. "I'd like them to find whoever set that fire and lock them away for a good, long time. Although maybe the fire was my cue to go elsewhere. Start over." She lifted the tray and the bag of baked goods. "To everything there is a season…" She left the quote open-ended deliberately. It had always been one of her father's favorites, and Laura was his younger sister.

"And a time to every purpose under the heaven." Laura finished the popular Ecclesiastes saying and nodded. "It's a lesson I should have learned a long time ago."

"Maybe now's the time." Tina moved to the door and smiled when one of the customers got up and opened it for her. "Thanks."

"Don't mention it, miss."

She started through the door, then stopped. Turned back. "Aunt Laura?"

"Yes?"

Tina's heart stammered in her chest. Old emotions fought for a place, but she shoved the negative feelings back where they belonged. "I could use your help."

"Help?"

Tina would have to be blind to miss the uncertainty and surprise in her aunt's eyes. She stepped back in and nodded. "The festival. I always did the baking for the vendor booths, but I've got no ovens now. Piper and Lacey both offered their baking areas, but they're not close enough for me to manage the baking and the running to keep fresh supplies going. Do you think I could do it here? In the restaurant kitchen?"

Her aunt's face brightened, but then she hesitated, looking embarrassed. "I don't have supplies, Tina. Or money for them."

"That's all covered under my budget," Tina assured her. "All I need is baking space. And I know your ovens aren't geared for major baking, but they'd work fine in a pinch. If you don't mind."

She'd extended an olive branch. Would her aunt take it?

Laura glanced toward the kitchen, then back to Tina. "I think it's a great idea, Tina."

Tina released a breath she didn't know she was holding. "Me, too. I'll have to come over here early."

"Can I help?"

"Sure, I'll—"

"I missed the bus again."

A young voice interrupted the moment. Tina turned and spotted Ryan, her fourteen-year-old cousin. He didn't notice her at first. His gaze was trained on his mother, his expression sullen and defensive. A bad combo.

"I got you up." Laura stared hard at the boy, then the clock. "You were in the shower when I left."

"I fell back asleep. So sue me."

Hairs rose along the back of Tina's neck. The boy's profile, the gruff tone, all reminded her of Rocco, and that tweaked a host of bad memories.

But then he turned more fully.

Ryan didn't look anything like Rocco from the front. Seeing him up close for the first time in a few years, he was the spitting image of her father, Gino Martinelli, in his younger days. Realizing that, she pushed aside her assumptions and said, "Ryan, you need a ride? I'll run you over to school."

He turned, surprised, then paled when he recognized her.

"Tina, could you?" Laura turned, her voice appreciative.

"No." Ryan's quick refusal drew the interest of one of the guys sitting at the counter.

"Well, you have to get to school and I can't take you," Laura reminded him. "In case you haven't noticed, I have a business to run."

Ryan glanced around, as if searching for a third option.

"I'll run him over, Laura." The older man at the counter stood, stretched and yawned. "I've got to go home and catch some shut-eye before the next shift, and it's on my way. Come on, Ryan, let's get you an education so you don't end up working two jobs to make ends meet like I do."

"Thanks, Bert."

The older guy shrugged and waved. Ryan followed him out the door, but he turned and looked at Tina again before he left, like he couldn't believe she was standing in his mother's restaurant, talking.

He'd been a preschooler when she got tossed, and Rocco made sure that lines were drawn in the sand, with Tina on one side and the D'Allesandros on the other. She'd just blurred that line by coming over, asking for help, and maybe with a little more time they could erase the line altogether.

She'd like that.

Max strode into the hardware store just before nine. He'd left the house early to fulfill his end of the bargain. He'd driven to Clearwater, the small city tucked at the southern tip of Kirkwood Lake, stopped by the Walmart there and grabbed four boxes of varied one-cup coffee pods. Turning the corner into the back room, he saw that Tina had remembered to cart her brewer down to the store.

His coffee-loving heart leaped in approval.

And when he noted the steaming hot coffee and cake from her aunt's restaurant, he wanted to hug her. Draw her close and tell her he was proud of her. But if he did that with two customers and Earl in the store, he'd create a groundswell of small-town conversation neither one wanted or needed.

He grabbed the third coffee, took a sip, moved out front and smiled his thanks to her over the brim. "Perfect, Tina."

Her expression said she understood he was praising her for more than the coffee, and the slight flush of her cheeks said he'd scored points in the good guy column.

Good.

He'd decided last night that he enjoyed gaining points with Tina Martinelli, and if he stopped to examine it, he might wonder why. But when she handed him a wrapped piece of tender apple cake, it became obviously clear.

Fresh.

Funny.

Beautiful.

Cryptic but kind, and she loved little kids, small animals and his family.

His heart opened wider, and he'd have loved time to explore these feelings, but the day flew by with little time to chat or flirt, and he was on watch duty again that night, so by the time they closed up shop, he needed to have his car disappear as if he'd gone home—

And then slip back into town like he'd done the night before.

"Are you guys working the same game plan tonight?" Tina asked softly as he turned the key in the back door lock.

"We are."

"Do you want supper first?"

"You asking me out, Tina?" He turned, grinning, and her rise of color said she wasn't—and yet, she was. "What have you got in mind?"

"I did a stew thing in the slow-cooker, and there's plenty. But you probably want to get home and see your dad."

"Mom just texted that he's sleeping and she's going over to Luke's to help Rainey make some new kind of tres leches cake thing. So I'm free."

"Rainey's tres leches cakes are the best things on the planet," Tina said.

"I don't know," Max mused. "I heard something from my brother Seth about a sweet potato pecan pie that's won the hearts of the entire lakeshore. And that's saying something because that's a fair piece of geography, Tina."

"I'll have to remember to thank Seth for the kind words."

"Don't be too nice to him. It'll go to his head. Now." He stopped and braced one hand on either side of the door, effectively trapping her between him and the hardware store entry. "You're really inviting me to dinner?"

"Crock-Pot stew isn't fancy enough to be called dinner."

"Supper, then."

"Supper works."

"Then let's do this." He motioned to her car. "I'll bring my car up and after we eat I'll noticeably leave your place. Then I'll circle around back again."

Tina nodded, moved toward the steps, then paused. "Thank you for doing this, Max. The whole stakeout thing. I know it's not your fight—"

"My parents love you to pieces, so it is my fight," he corrected her. "You might be family by attrition and I'm Campbell by adoption, but if there's one thing about us Campbells, we take care of our own. I'll meet you at your place."

He parked on the street in front of Tina's apartment, leaving the car in plain sight. When he followed her up the stairs to her apartment, he was pleasantly surprised. "Retro chic. I'm kind of surprised and intrigued. Where's June Cleaver hiding?"

Tina laughed and brought two plates over to the small enamel-clad table. "Necessity. I had no money, and the antique and cooperative shops had lots of this fun retro stuff really cheap, so I decided I'd go with it."

"These old bowls." Max lifted one of the pale blue Pyrex bowls into the air. "Grandma Campbell had these. And these cabinets look like the ones in Aunt Maude's old place over in Jamison."

"Cute, right?" His appreciation deepened Tina's

smile. "I figured if I had to live in an apartment, I wanted it as fun and homey as I could get it."

"You've achieved your goal. Can I help with anything?"

"You're doing enough standing guard into the dark of night. Sit and eat."

Max didn't have to be asked twice. "You made bread?"

"Nope, bought it when I ran out at lunchtime. Rainey's got a nice baked-goods section over at the McKinney Farms Dairy store, and it's only five minutes away. I figured it would go well with stew."

"Beyond wonderful."

She turned.

Her chin tilted up. She met his gaze, and he knew the second the compliment registered, that the words were meant for her, not the bread, because her eyes brightened and she looked embarrassed.

"But—" he sat down, reached over and sliced a couple of thick hunks off the loaf of freshly warmed bread "—you warned me off, so I'm trying to keep my compliments to myself, to stay calm, cool and slightly detached. How'd I do today?" He asked the question as if wondering how his job performance was going, quick and casual.

"You got an A on detachment and a B-on cool." She sat in the chair opposite him and offered the grades as if the assessment was the least personal thing ever.

"A B-?" Max shook his head. "On my worst day I couldn't get a B-. No way, no how."

"Are you protesting your grade?" She set the ladle down, then looked surprised and pleased when he reached across the small table and took her hand in his for grace.

He gave her fingers a gentle squeeze. "Naw, no protest. The bad grade just gives me incentive to try harder. Be cooler. Although I'm not sure that's even attainable."

She laughed.

It felt good to see it, good to watch her relax. Smile. Joke around. From what he'd gleaned in his short time home, Tina hadn't had a lot to laugh about these past few years, and that was wrong by any standard. He held her hand lightly and offered a simple prayer, a soldier's grace, and when he was done, he held her hand just long enough to make her work to extract it.

She scolded him with a look that made him grin, and then they shared a hot, delicious meal in a walk-up apartment decked out in second-hand 1950s motif, and he loved every minute of it.

He wanted to linger but the clock forced him to leave.

She walked him to the door, then stayed back a few feet, creating distance. But Max hadn't served in the army for over a decade without achieving some off-the-battlefield skills.

He noted the distance with his gaze, then drew his eyes up. Met hers. "Nice ploy, but if I wanted to kiss you, I'd cross that three feet of space and just do it, Tina."

"Which either means you don't want to, or you're being a gentleman and respecting my request to keep our lives uncomplicated." She sent him a pert smile. "Excellent."

"Except—" he opened the door to the stairway, then turned, smiling "—Uncle Sam trained me well. I *like* things complicated. Creates a challenge. But tonight?" He pulled a dark knit hat onto his head, and matching leather gloves from the pockets of his black leather jacket. "Duty calls."

He started down the stairs, mentally counting them as he went. If she called his name before step number ten, he'd won a major battle.

If she stayed silent?

Well, that meant there was more work to be done than he'd thought. He stepped down quickly, leaving it up to God and Tina. *One, two, three, four...*

Total silence followed him from above.

Five, six, seven, eight...

"Max?"

He stopped, turned and had to keep from power-fisting the air. "Yes?"

"Thank you." Her gaze scanned his cold-weather gear and the village beyond the first-floor entry window. "Like I mentioned before, this means a lot to me."

"You're welcome." He didn't wink, tease or do anything else. There was no need to. By calling his name, interrupting his departure, she'd shown her mix of feelings. She liked him and wished she didn't.

Would she hate him when she found out the truth about Pete and Amy? Their deaths affected her best friend, their family, the entire neighborhood, the town. And he had *known* Pete and Amy had been drinking and hadn't stopped them from going out.

Maybe the better question was this: Why wouldn't she hate him?

He glanced up as he swung open the driver's-side

door. She waved from the window, and the sight of her, backlit and centered in the white-framed pane, made his heart yearn for that kind of send-off on a regular basis.

Blessed be the peacemakers, for they shall be called children of God. That's what he wanted now. To be a different kind of peacemaker here at home. Twinkle lights blinked on throughout the town. By next week, everything would be fully decorated. They'd open the Festival of Lights with a prayerful ceremony on the church green, and then they'd "throw" the switch, lighting up the lake, the town, the park.

Right now, with the sweetness of the newly erected church manger and the decorated, lighted businesses flanking Main Street, a sweet surge of the blessed holiday engulfed him. Yes, they were lit up a little early with Thanksgiving still days off, but as he tucked his car away and slipped through the cemetery paths to take up his watch station, the sweet lights celebrating Christ's birth welcomed him home.

Chapter Six

Whoever had been combing the ashes of the café had either found what they were looking for or smelled a trap. Either way, nothing came of the men's combined maneuvers.

Jason and Cory Radcliffe stopped into the hardware store at closing time. "Tina, can we talk to you out back before you head out?"

"Sure." She led the firemen into the back room, then turned. "Bad news?"

Jason shrugged. "Well, not good news. We've done what we can, the arson squad has gathered their evidence, they know an accelerant was used, but there's no real indication of who did this and the site's dangerous. We've ordered the excavation equipment. They're going to clean the site tomorrow."

Clean the site.

It sounded so simple. Matter-of-fact. A decade of work, hopes and dreams purposely destroyed, then scooped away.

Her heart ached, but it was the right thing to do. She knew that. Still.

She didn't want to be on hand to see it happen, but that couldn't be helped. "I appreciate you letting me know, guys. Thank you."

They didn't look the least bit comfortable accepting her thanks, and when they were gone, Max cornered her at the register. "Cleanup time?"

"You were listening?" Her tone scolded. Her look followed suit.

He pointed a finger at himself and made a face that said of course he was. "Covert operator. That's what I do, Tina."

A tiny smile escaped as she accepted his pronouncement. "That doesn't exactly rank you higher on the trustworthy scale. Snooping is unattractive."

"Snooping's for amateurs. I was on an information-gathering mission. Highly professional. And I needed to be close by in case they made you cry."

"They didn't."

He smiled. "I know. Because I was right outside the door."

A tiny part of her heart stretched, thinking of Max watching out for her again. "Then you know they're excavating tomorrow."

"An empty lot can be considered a fresh palette."

It could.

And yet the thought of big equipment sweeping up the remnants of her life in Kirkwood bit deep. "It's got to be done," she admitted. "I just hate the thought of being around to watch it happen."

"Then we'll find something else to do," Max said as he locked the door "The weather's supposed to be fairly nice tomorrow, according to my mother. But for now, come with me."

Max crooked a thumb toward his Mustang. Tina grabbed her purse and warm jacket, then followed him to the door. "Come with you where?"

He pointed to the passenger seat. "You did supper last night. My turn."

"Max, I—"

"Don't disappoint my mother. She's been simmering red sauce and meatballs and made me promise to bring you. You can't insult a woman who spent half the afternoon cooking, can you?"

"You don't play fair."

His smile agreed as he backed the car around. "All's fair in love and war."

"Well, as long as we're at war. Okay, then."

He laughed, but as they pulled out of the hardware store parking lot, two big rigs rounded the corner of Main Street. A huge loader with a bucket and a large dump truck chugged down the road, then parked along the edge of her burned-out café.

The sight of them reignited Tina's internal reasons for leaving. Enough was enough.

But then Max hit the car radio. Christmas lyrics filled the air, the perfect accent to the growing number of decorated houses leading out of the village. The bright sight of her old, familiar town filled her with nostalgia.

She thought she wanted new, fresh and bright. But

how much would she miss the familiarity of her hometown once she made the move?

Her phone vibrated an incoming text from Sherrie. I know U R busy but could use help with nursery. Ideas?

She had tons of ideas. Ones she'd imagined for herself as she watched her biological clock tick for years. The thought of happily-ever-afters and cute kids had filled her with anticipation. In her quest for the American dream of marriage and two-point-four kids, had she hurried things? Charging ahead and regretting at leisure had always been part of her profile. Had she done that in matters of the heart?

Maybe. But she needed to think more on that tomorrow. With Christmas music playing, and Max easing the smooth ride around lakeshore curves, she focused on answering Sherrie.

Tons, she texted back. Call me later, we'll make a plan.

Thank you! Sherrie's return text was immediate, which meant she was waiting, hoping Tina would help. Was Sherrie feeling pushed to hurry because Tina was leaving? They'd been best friends, always together, for over two decades. The idea of being too busy or too far away to be a true help to Sherrie seemed wrong.

"Max! Tina! Perfect timing!" Jenny's voice caroled a welcome as Max tugged open the side door a few minutes later. "Dad was just saying he could use some company."

Beeze padded their way, tail wagging, as if wondering how they got through the day at work without him.

He pushed his big, golden head beneath Tina's arm, knowing she'd give him a thorough welcome.

"I'm going to wash up and get rid of the remnants of changing oil and replacing hoses," Max announced. He reached down to pet Beeze. Tina looked up. Met his gaze. And when he smiled as if seeing her with the dog, in his mother's kitchen, made him happy, her heart tipped into overdrive again. "Back in a few minutes."

"Okay."

She helped Jenny finish things up while Charlie sat nearby, talking over the events of the day, and by the time Max returned, supper was on the table and Beeze had been relegated to the front porch.

"I'm not all that hungry, but I'll sit with you." Charlie pulled out the chair where he usually sat. "As long as none of you pester me about eating."

"The smells aren't bothering you?" Tina asked.

"Not as much, no."

"Good." Tina beamed at him, happy to see him looking more at ease.

Jenny's sigh said she'd follow his direction about not fussing, but wasn't thrilled with his pronouncement, and Max just grinned and said, "More for me, Dad. Leftovers tomorrow. I'm okay with that."

"Earl will be thrilled, too." Tina held a forkful of pasta aloft and breathed deep. "I could live on pasta. Cooked any way, anytime. Short women should not have this kind of affinity for carbs. And the oven-roasted broccoli is perfection, Jenny. Thank you."

"I grabbed the broccoli right across the street at Barrett's Orchards," Jenny told her. "I love having all their fresh produce so handy."

"Lacey's apple fritters aren't anything to wave off casually, either," Max noted. "We did some racing through those orchards when we were kids," he added. "It was a great place to grow up. The farm on one side of the house, the lake on the other."

"Isn't it funny to have people live in the same area, but have such different experiences?" Tina observed as she twirled more spaghetti onto her fork.

"As in?"

She indicated the village north of them with a wave. "Living in town had its upsides, and I helped at the restaurant a lot, but there were no games of hide-and-seek in the orchard, or grabbing a boat and taking off to fish when they were biting. Not until I bought my own, anyway."

"You like to fish?" Max looked surprised when Tina nodded.

"Love it. That's how I kept my sanity running the café all these years. Some days I'd just grab my little rowboat with its pricey trolling motor and cruise the docks, looking for bass and perch."

"I haven't had fried jack perch in over a year," Charlie lamented.

"It's late for perch, isn't it?" Max glanced from the calendar to Charlie and Tina.

"You can find them here or there if the weather's good and the wind is from the south-southwest," Charlie said.

"Do you want to go out, Dad?" Max stopped eating

and faced his father. "They're calling for a nice day tomorrow. Sunny. Wind out of the south. I can grab a few hours off and take you around the lake. We could catch enough for a family fish fry between us."

"I'll go out with you when I'm feeling better," Charlie replied. "But the thought of eating fresh perch sounds mighty good. As long as you boys don't mind cooking it in the garage. The smell might be a little tough, otherwise."

"That's what the old stove is for," Max declared. He looked at Tina.

Something in his expression said he'd do this, but could use help. Which was just plain silly because a guy like Max didn't need help with anything. With tomorrow's decent weather forecast, one last day on the water sounded good to Tina. And better than watching her business being swept away. "Max and I can go out tomorrow if Jenny can come down to the hardware store and spell us."

Charlie's face brightened, and when Jenny saw that, she agreed wholeheartedly. "I'd be glad to get out of this house for a little bit," she declared. She sent Charlie a teasing smile. "I think Dad is tired of me fussing over him, so he'd be relieved to have me gone, and I'd get to see how things are going at the store."

"It's a date." Max met Tina's gaze across the table and grinned, and she had no trouble reading that smile or the double entendre of his word choice. "Me. Tina. Worms. And a boat."

"Good." Jenny met Charlie's smile with one of her own. "Then we can have a nice fish fry on Saturday night. Unless you're too tired to have a crowd around, Charlie?"

"Not if there's fish on the menu," he declared, and for just a minute he sounded like the Charlie of old. Strong. Determined. Decisive.

Tina met Max's eyes across the table and read the "gotcha" look he aimed her way. She couldn't wiggle out of a fishing date with Max, not with Charlie's hopes up.

And the thought of hanging out with Max on the water, handling smelly worms and flapping fish, could prove interesting. Tina was at home in two places: a kitchen and a boat. So if Max thought he was being altruistic by going fishing with her, he had a lot to learn. She might have messed up in the old boyfriend department, but when it came to fish, Tina Martinelli knew her way around Kirkwood Lake.

The unseasonable warmth tempted multiple boats onto the late-season water the next day, anglers wanting one last spin before packing things up for the winter.

Temptation wasn't goading Max into the boat. Love for his father was. He gassed up the motor, checked the anchor and loaded supplies. Fishing poles, bait, tackle, life jackets, compass, a cooler for fish and one for sandwiches, and a thermos of coffee.

He eyed the lake, appraising.

He didn't fear the water after losing Pete. He hated it. Big difference. But the only way to make his father's fish fry a reality was with fish. And there weren't too many jack perch hanging out on shore. He tucked two flotation devices beneath the backseat, and wished he'd thought to do the same before Pete and Amy went cruising that night. If they'd been sober, with the right equipment, would they be here now, living life?

His heart ached, but his mind went straight to God. *I know what I need to do, Lord. I'm not shirking this confrontation, I'm just busy with stuff on this side of the lake. I'll make it a point to go see the Sawyers once things are settled with Dad. And the store. And the lighting gig. And if anyone tells You that small towns don't come with their own share of drama, well, they're wrong. But I'll go see Mary and Ray. Soon.*

Tina's approach pushed his thoughts into actions.

"We could have used my boat." She settled onto the seat of Charlie's much bigger rig and made a face at Max. "It's not the size of the boat—"

"It's the heart of the fisherman," Max finished one of Charlie's favorite sayings, but went on, "That didn't stop Dad from buying this, did it?"

"Well, with a crew like yours, I suppose a bigger boat could be deemed a necessity."

Max eased the boat away from the dock, turned it around and headed toward deeper water. "But here is where I give in to your expertise. I know the big perch usually seek deeper water in fall, but do you know any hot spots?"

"Warrenton Point with today's breeze, at the end of the longest docks. If not there, then the off side of the west curve, just north of Kirkwood Lodge."

"She can talk the talk," Max teased as he aimed for Warrenton. "But can she back up the talk with action?"

"Time will tell."

He revved the motor, steering the boat through open water. As they drew closer to the point, Max decreased his speed, then idled the engine. His intent was to have a successful trip for his father.

Fish weren't always cooperative and that was a reality every fisherman faced, but today the fish were fighting to be caught.

They brought in eighteen good-size jack perch in the first forty minutes, evenly split. "I will never cast an aspersion about your fishing abilities again," Max noted as he reeled in number eighteen. "I forgot how nice this can be when you troll into a good school of fish."

"Not much time for fishing in the army?"

What should he say? The truth, that he avoided the water purposely? No. "Lack of time, lack of desire." He stared out across the lake, looking at the long, sweeping curve of the west shore, but seeing Pete's face. Hearing Pete's laugh. He sighed. "And busy working my way up. That didn't leave too much time to kick back and do much of anything, actually."

"Those captain's bars say you've done all right," Tina noted as she shifted her line to the other side of the boat. "And it can't be easy to give that all up. Doesn't it become ingrained? The love of adventure, the joy of service?"

"It does." Max rebaited his line, then cast it toward the docks on the opposite side of Tina's rod. "But I faced a few enemies these past few years that wanted me dead. And I decided it would be a shame to have that happen when I'd never been gutsy enough to move outside of my military comfort zone."

* * *

Outside his military comfort zone? Tina frowned as she studied a slight shift in the wave patterns.

"Most people don't describe hand grenades, snipers, IEDs and long desert tours as comfort zones. Doing so either makes you odd or oddly exciting." Tina paused and adjusted the angle of her rod. "And I'm not exactly sure how to classify you yet, so I find that more than a little disturbing. An unusual predicament for me."

His smile rewarded her. "I think I like disturbing you, and let's just say when you do a job well, it's easy to get caught in a rut. I wanted to change things up. When Mom called me about Dad's diagnosis, I realized I might be running out of time, and that was stupid on my part."

"They don't think you're stupid." Tina left enough bite in her tone to let Max know she wasn't quite as convinced.

"Well, they love me."

She frowned and reeled her line in as she acknowledged his comment. "They do. And we've fished this out or they've moved off. Let's try the lodge."

"Your wish is my command."

He stowed his line, backed the boat away from the point, then aimed west into the late-day sun. "Gorgeous day."

"And possible snow tomorrow, so it's good we took the time to do this now. I don't ice fish. Not even for Charlie."

"Do you think he's going to make it, Tina?"

The question took her by surprise.

Her heart paused. Her breath caught, because the look Max gave her over his shoulder said he'd read the reality of Charlie's condition and wanted her truthful answer.

She looked off over the lake and shrugged off tears. "No."

Max nodded as if she'd confirmed what he already knew, and Tina realized that despite their close parent-child relationship, he might have trouble discussing this with Jenny. Jenny believed heart and soul that with God, all things were possible.

Tina believed that, too, but she'd watched her parents die, seen her best friend's family suffer through the loss of their son, and she knew that while God wanted his people healthy and happy, the human body was a frail vessel.

Max pulled into a deep-water crevice off the end of the lodge. He stood, turned and grabbed his pole, but not before Tina saw the anguish in his eyes.

She wanted to cry. She wanted to give him hope. She wanted his father to be healthy and happy and ready to rock more grandbabies on his knee, show them how to build a campfire and take them trolling through migrating swans and geese in the boat.

Charlie's timeline said that wasn't likely to happen.

Max pulled himself up. He drew a breath, then slanted her a look that said more than words as he jutted his chin toward her pole. "Let's get this show on the road, woman. These fish won't catch themselves, and there's a bunch of Campbells coming for supper tomorrow night."

His words said he was ready to deal with whatever came his way, as long as Charlie Campbell got his fried perch dinner. Tina figured if the fish didn't cooperate, Max would dive into the water with a net to make sure there was plenty of food. If this was to be Charlie's last perch dinner, Max would see it was a great one. Tina was certain of that.

"Forty-two fish?" Jenny hugged Max and Tina in turn, and Charlie looked suitably impressed when they lugged the cooler full of fish up into the front yard of the Campbell house. "That's amazing."

"Well, our little Tina knows her way around the lake," Max drawled. His grin said he was proud of her, and the combination of Jenny's surprise, Charlie's joy and Max's pride made her feel like she could handle anything. Even in Kirkwood Lake. That realization felt good and surprising all at once.

"I'll clean fish," Max announced, and he set up the old fish-cleaning table that Charlie kept stored in the boathouse. "Do we want to order pizza and wings for supper? I should have these guys filleted and on ice just in time to catch the Thursday-night game. You up for that, Dad?"

"Could be." Was it the sight of the fresh fish or the thought of a football game that brightened his father's eyes? Max wasn't sure, but it felt good.

"I'll turn on the floodlights," Jenny told him. "It's getting dark soon and I don't want you cutting yourself."

"Thanks, Mom."

"I can help." Tina moved over to the small table and pulled up a stool. "I know how to fillet perch."

Max handed her an extra knife. "Don't expect me to say no. There are eighty-four little fillets here, and that's a lot of skin-zipping and slicing."

"It is."

"I'm ordering the pizza to be ready at game time. Is that okay?" Jenny called from the house.

"Perfect. And if some of those wings are Buffalo-style, you'll make me very happy," Max called back.

"Is there another kind, darling?"

Max laughed, because raising five boys and two daughters had schooled his mother on the intrinsic differences. Cass and Addie liked the country-sweet wings with a hint of fire.

The Campbell boys had always tussled for the hotter side of life from early on. Maybe that was what pushed him into the service, the "let's best each other" guy-speak he'd grown accustomed to as a kid.

Now?

He was all right with tough, but he yearned for more. He longed for a chance to be all the things his father had been to him. A kind and giving man, a loving dad, a humor-filled confidant.

"Tina, I ordered hot wings for you, too. With extra blue cheese. I hope that's okay?" Jenny's voice cut through the thinning light from the far side of the screened porch.

"Perfect. Thank you!"

"Hot wings?" Max sent a look of interest her way as he zipped through the motions of cleaning fish.

"Mmm-hmm."

"Skilled fisherwoman?"

She grinned at the full cooler. "So it would seem."

"And you clean up well."

"I do what I can."

He leaned over, forcing her to look up. Meet his gaze. She did but his proximity made her look nervous. Max decided he liked making Tina Martinelli nervous. And while his head cautioned him to sit back and be quiet, his heart pushed him forward. She sent him a mock-frown as if interrupting her focus was a terrible thing. "What?"

"I think I'm falling for you, Tina. And I'm not too sure what to do about that because you're determined to go and I'm intent on staying."

Her mouth opened. Her eyes went wide, as if the last topic of conversation she expected over a pile of perch was a declaration of affection. A declaration he probably shouldn't make because Max understood the rigors of fall-out, and when folks found out what he did, or rather what he didn't do, people's respect for him was likely to nosedive. But spending the day with Tina, talking, fishing, trolling the lake for the first time since Pete and Amy's accident...

He felt like he was home, finally.

"You're not like anyone else, you're the prettiest thing ever and your fighting spirit makes me feel like I can fix things. Old wrongs, cranky motors and rusted-out tools."

"Max—"

"Well, now, I didn't say all that to interrupt your

work, and I don't intend to eat pizza and wings while I'm smelling like fish, so we've got to hustle if we're going to have cleanup time, but..." He drawled the last, leaned back in his seat and let his eyes underscore his words. "I just thought you should know."

He'd silenced her.

He decided that might be a good thing to remember for future reference, because strong women like Tina didn't do quiet all that well.

"You don't play fair, Max."

"I thought we ascertained that in the car last night."

Her frown said she remembered their conversation.

"Except I'm ready to be done with war, which brings us back to the first part of the saying."

"And I'm not a game player. Ever. Toying with people's hearts and emotions doesn't make the short list especially since my heart's been run ragged the past few years."

The guard in her tone said she'd erected boundaries for good reason. "Tell me something I don't know." He zip-skinned another fish, like Charlie had taught him years before. "Women tend to be a confusing bunch, if not downright crazy." She bristled and that made him grin. "But not you. And when I asked myself, 'Why is that? What makes Tina Marie Martinelli different?' I knew right off what the answer was. Because she's honest."

She darted a look at him that said he should stop, not go any further.

"Forthright."

"There's a compliment and a half for you."

"Faith-filled."

Her jaw softened. Her eyes did, too.

"And when I'm not with her, she's all I can think about."

Her chin faltered.

Her eyes went wet with unshed tears. "Don't mess with me, Max Campbell." Her voice came out in a tight whisper.

"Two things you should know about me, Tina Marie."

She met his look with her jaw set and her mouth firm, determined and ready to clean his clock if needed. And he decided that riling Tina was a new kind of fun. He liked it, but he held her attention with a straight-on look. "I don't mess with anyone. I talk straight, I shoot straight and I mean what I say every time."

Her throat convulsed, reading his meaning. Hearing his pledge. "And the second thing?"

"I'd like three kids, but I could be talked into four. Under the right set of circumstances, of course."

Her smile started small and grew. She ducked her chin, picked up her filleting knife and growled. "This is how you court a girl, Max? Over a mess of fish and a sharp knife?"

"Whatever works, Tina." He grinned and got back to the fish, but not before winking at her. "Whatever works."

Chapter Seven

Gone.

Tina stared at the vacant lot the next morning, under a cold, leaden sky.

The burned-out shell had been razed and carted away. The concrete deck remained, but the cute garage sale tables and chairs she'd bought, sanded and painted in bright shore-tones of blue, green and yellow had been toted off, as well.

Regret hit her. She'd meant to keep them, to put them in storage, tuck them away. They'd been safe from the fire because they'd been out on the broad, concrete deck. They could have been spared destruction, but she hadn't said anything to the work crew and now they were gone.

Scorch marks marred the concrete, but the lot itself was scraped to the thick cement slab, the footprint of a building she'd loved.

Emotion pushed her forward. The weather had turned seasonal again, with a sharp wind off Lake Erie.

Yesterday's transient warmth had been an anomaly, a flashback of Indian summer. Today?

Reality set in. Her business was gone, the lot swept clean and the unseasonable warmth had been jack-knifed east by a Canadian clipper system that promised Thanksgiving snow.

She pictured the jazzy, retro tables she'd stained and stenciled. The fun, mismatched chairs. The cool espresso machine, the bank of syrups. The double-sided deep sink, the rotating convection oven that baked sixteen pies at once. The five-seat counter, small but friendly, and the locals who used to frequent it throughout the year.

"Hey."

Max's voice hailed her.

She turned, fighting the rise of sadness. She wasn't generally overly emotional, but since the fire, it seemed like she couldn't grab hold of her feelings. She didn't like this new normal. It left her vulnerable, an emotion Tina abhorred. "Different, right?"

His gaze appraised her, and his expression changed from wondering to "handle with care."

She made a face and dug her toe into the loose dirt alongside the scraped-clean slab. "I didn't think it would affect me like this."

Max nodded.

"I hated seeing it all burned-out, such a mess, but this seems so final."

"Only as final as you make it, Tina."

Redo? Restart? Begin again? Here?

One look at Max said the idea was tempting. But she

wasn't about to jump into rash decisions, not ever again. She hauled in a breath and smiled when he held out a coffee. "I thought this might taste good."

"It's morning and it's coffee, so one-plus-one." She paused and sipped, then smiled. "You made me a mocha?"

"Mocha latte. And yes." He slanted the lake a quick look, reminding her of their fishing excursion the previous day. "You've got hidden talents. So do I."

"It's delightful."

"I agree," he said, but he wasn't looking at the coffee cup when he said it.

A slow blush curled up from somewhere around her toes, so she changed the subject. "I wanted to thank you for yesterday." She turned and started walking toward the hardware store. "For using the fishing trip to keep me out of town while they worked here."

He shrugged one shoulder. "I got the girl for the whole afternoon, the first fishing trip I've had in years, and the makings of a great dinner. I was in the winner's circle on all counts."

"You're a thoughtful man, Max."

"I've improved in that department," he corrected her. "And it took a while, but I'm educable, Tina. I do have a shot of bad news, though."

"Charlie?" Apprehensive, she turned quickly and banged square into his arm. He steadied her with his free hand…and then didn't let go.

"No, he's holding his own." He waved west of Main Street to Upper Lake Road with his other hand. "The company that was contracted to do the park lights backed out today."

"No."

His grim expression said yes. "They called the house phone this morning and left a message. I tried contacting them, but got no answer, so I called a guy in Buffalo to check it out. The company bellied-up this week."

"Max." This was the kind of thing that could put the committee over the top. With less than a week to go before the Festival of Lights officially opened how could they possibly fix the situation? "What are we going to do?"

"I'm not sure. The Christmas on Main Street part is all set between the town and the business owners. And the home-owners do their own thing around the lake to give us the circle of light. The living Nativity will be set up for the two weekends before Christmas, with people taking rotations for playing the parts of the family, angels and shepherds in the cold. But the park..." His dark expression said he understood what a huge loss that was to the town fund-raising. "The park drive-through is a big draw and a financial plus for the women's shelter."

"There's got to be someone else to hire."

"Not at this late date," he reminded her. "And if this company dumped a bunch of contracts, then there are other places scrambling for services. I'll check around today, but it doesn't seem likely."

"I can't imagine facing Georgia Palmeteer with this news." Tina matched his frown. "She'll eat us alive."

"We'll keep it to ourselves while I check out other possibilities, but if I haven't come up with something by tomorrow, we'll have to inform the committee," Max replied. "And my dad."

"Do you want me to tell them?"

Max looped his arm around her shoulders, an arm that seemed to know she'd gotten chilled standing at the shore. "No, I'll do it. But first I'm going to see if I can't put some form of Plan B into action. It's always better to deliver bad news with an alternative action plan in place."

"You learned that in the army."

He let go of her, opened the back door of the hardware store, unlocked the inner door and let her precede him as he laughed. "I learned that being Jenny Campbell's son. When your mother's nickname is 'Hurricane Jenny' you grow up realizing she's a force to be reckoned with and act accordingly. Which means unconventional measures became a way of life."

She acknowledged the truth in his words. His mother had always been the "get 'er done" type the woman folks approached if they needed advice or something accomplished. And Jenny herself was handy with power tools and the softer side of home decor, so her expertise had helped people for decades.

But how were they going to decorate a drive-through park with no Christmas lights?

That posed a tough question with the annual festival looming.

"I asked Mrs. Thurgood to join us tonight," Jenny whispered as Tina hooked her jacket that evening.

"She's not as strong as she was last year, and I thought an old-fashioned fish dinner might be nice for her."

"I'll go sit with her," Tina replied. "I miss our wise little chats when she'd come in for coffee."

She purposely hadn't driven to the Campbell house with Max. If she let him drive, he'd have to take her home later, and no way was she setting herself up for more romantic moments. She had enough on her plate right now, didn't she?

I think Max is a pretty nice addition to that plate, her conscience scolded. *You might want to think twice about holding him off. Remember that old window/door thing? When God closes a door, somewhere He opens a window? Why can't that be here? Now? Maybe Max is your destiny and you're too stubborn to see it.*

Max was amazing, she admitted to herself as she crossed the room to see Mrs. Thurgood. But—life was confusing right now. And she didn't do confusing all that well, it seemed.

Because you can't control the confusion, her conscience tweaked one more time. *You like to set the rules, run the show.*

The truth in the reminder made her wince internally.

Let go, and let God. Follow the path. Trust, Tina. That's what it comes down to. Trust.

She'd weigh her internal struggles later, after a night of Campbell fun, a night that might be Charlie Campbell's last fresh-caught family fish fry. No way in the world would she let worry spoil that. She sank down next to Mrs. Thurgood, a sweet old gal who lived in a filled-to-the-brim house outside of town. She reached out and patted the elderly woman's knee. "Mrs. Thurgood, how are you? I don't get to see you all that often now."

The old woman gave her a hug, an embrace that seemed weaker than the last time she'd seen her. "I miss that café! It was like a home away from home, without the clutter, of course. To stop in there or mosey next door to the vintage store and see Carmen and Gianna, well, that just made my day," she exclaimed. "But my driving days are over according to the DMV—though I can't imagine staying cooped up in my place all winter, hoping for a ride to town."

It seemed life's changes weren't just surrounding Tina. Reading the look on the old woman's face, Tina understood that Mrs. Thurgood was facing her own dragons of adjustment. But then Mrs. Thurgood blessed her with a bright smile and said, "I'm thinking of renting that apartment right below you, actually."

"Really?" Tina knew the first-floor tenants in her building had bought a place closer to Clearwater and were scheduled to move. "Mrs. Thurgood, I'd love it if we were neighbors."

"Me, too. It would be just the ticket, I think." Her words said one thing. Her face said she hated the thought of moving. She looked up just then, and her face broke into a wide smile. "Max Campbell. Come give an old woman a hug!"

Max did just that, and the gentle way he embraced their elderly friend showed the tough, rugged soldier's big heart. "You look wonderful, Mrs. Thurgood."

"Oh, you!" She blushed in delight, and gripped his hands in hers. "It's so nice to have you back, helping with everything. You are a blessing to your family, and this town, and I'm so glad you're here, Max!"

A slight grimace darkened Max's face. Why? Tina wondered. Guilt over being away? Staying away?

But then he smiled and squeezed Mrs. Thurgood's hands gently. "It's good to be home."

"Any luck?" Seth drew a chair up alongside the couch and kept his voice low as he addressed Max. "On the search for lights?"

"No. There aren't lights to beg, borrow or steal in a three-state radius unless we're willing to pay retail and foot the bill."

"Georgia Palmeteer will eat you alive," Seth told him, and in typical brother fashion, he sounded kind of excited about that idea.

"What's gone wrong?" Mrs. Thurgood grasped Max's hand. "What's got you worried about Georgia, Max? Maybe I can help."

Max sent her a rueful look. "Only if you've got a barn full of Christmas lights we can use for the park."

She perked up instantly. "As a matter of fact, I do!"

Seth stared at her.

So did Max.

"You've got Christmas decorations, Mrs. Thurgood?" Tina broke the silence and leaned closer. "I'll help you put them up in your new place if you'd like."

"Oh, no, no, dear, not like that, that's not it at all," the old woman exclaimed. "You know how I can never throw anything away?"

Tina had heard stories about the packed clutter of the old woman's home, but had never visited. "I've heard."

"Well, my husband and son had a thing for Christmas—they just loved it! We collected all sorts of fun things over the years, and George and Butch put everything they had into building great big displays. Once George passed away, Butch kept on buying, right up until he went to war. I didn't have the heart to tell him no," she confessed, "so the barn is chock full of outdoor Christmas decorations. Now, they're kind of old-fashioned-looking, but I'm sure that barn is jam-packed with lots of fun stuff you can use in the park."

Tina looked at Max.

Max returned the gaze.

"If we use Mrs. Thurgood's stash of Christmas lights—" Max began.

"And have people donate any extra lights they may have—" Tina added.

"We can use Dad's emergency backup generators from the store." He looked downright hopeful at the thought. "We might be able to do this, Tina."

"Come out to the house tomorrow," Mrs. Thurgood urged him. "You can use anything you find. If George and Butch were here, they'd be glad I found a home for this stuff at long last."

Max gave her another hug. "I'll do that. Seth, you free tomorrow?"

"No, but Luke is, and there's nothing he'd like better than to help you."

Luke made a face at Seth but shrugged assent as he drew closer. "Count me in as long as Rainey's mother can watch the kids. I'll give her a call."

"Can we do it first thing?" Tina wondered. "Before

church, maybe? Because we've got to open the hardware store midday."

"Is there electric in the barn, Mrs. Thurgood? Does it have lights?" Max asked.

She nodded. "Sure does, and far as I know they work fine. I haven't been in there in a good many years," she told them, "so there's maybe the odd critter or two as well, but not too many with a tight roof and no food. Critters like food, so I make sure there's none lying about. An old lady on her own can't be too careful."

From what Tina had heard, careful didn't apply in all aspects of Mrs. Thurgood's life, but the eccentric old woman had been a constant support for Tina's business. She'd shared recipes, insight and time, and her visits to the café had been a welcome respite. "Is 8:00 a.m. good?" She raised an eyebrow to Max.

He nodded. "I'll pick up Luke and meet you there. Mrs. Thurgood, you might have just saved Christmas for the town."

She brightened noticeably. "Well, good! And if Butch was still here, he'd be right alongside you, stringing lights and hanging holly. He loved Christmas so much." She sat forward and aimed her gaze back to Max. "George and I just loved that boy, being our only child and all. When George passed on, it was just me and Butch, getting things done. I didn't want him to join the service, but he had a mind of his own and then I lost him. I lost a part of me that day the army came calling, a part of me that cared about foolish stuff. I decided then and there I'd put folks first, and I've done it, too. My house might be in a sad state of repair, but my soul smiles at the name of Jesus."

Max held her hand. "I believe you." He turned his attention toward the dining room. "Do you feel up to filling your own plate, or can I fill one for you?"

"Since getting up isn't as easy these days, I'd be obliged, Max Campbell, and I do love your mother's tartar sauce with my fish."

"I'm on it."

Max went to get her food, and Tina bent closer. "You're an amazing woman, Mrs. Thurgood." She gave the older woman's arm a gentle squeeze. "I wanted you to know that."

"Well, thank you, but I'm common enough," she argued lightly. "I do prefer everyday people, though, Tina. The simple folks, the kind I run with. I look at my friend Charlie, there—" she jutted her chin across the wide room "—and I'm just plain sad to see him so ill at his age, but for myself, honey?" She reached a thin-skinned pale hand to Tina. "I won't mind goin' home when the time comes. Seeing my husband. Hugging Butch. It's been a long time gone."

An old mother's lament, but brave and true despite her eccentricities. Tina would miss her bright-eyed initiatives when God called the aging woman home. How blessed she'd been to know her and her quaint wisdom for so much of her life.

"Paydirt."

Luke nodded and sent Max a look of pure surprise the next morning. "It's organized."

"It is that!" Mrs. Thurgood bustled into the sprawling barn after she'd grabbed a mismatched tangle of coat, boots and hat. "The barn wasn't my domain, so I've left it alone. Butch had a nice little apartment over the garage, just the right size for someone on their own, and doing this Christmas stuff for folks was something he and his dad loved. If you look over there—" she pointed to a long group of shelves by the far door "—that's where Butch kept most of the stuff. He had a love for electric from early on, and he took courses in high school at the cooperative place in Clearwater, so he had a fine hand with wiring. 'Course, things were simple back then, not all fancy-schmancy like they have now, but sometimes that simple stuff is more Christmasy than all the electric doodads they've got out today."

"Is that Rudolph?" Luke asked, looking up into the hay loft.

"And all of his friends!" declared Mrs. Thurgood. "With Santa and his sleigh parked on that end." She pointed left of center, and sure enough, Tina spotted a full-size wooden sleigh with a wooden Santa sitting front and center in plain sight, an amazing find.

Max whistled.

Tina grabbed Mrs. Thurgood's arm when the older woman slipped on an uneven surface. "You really don't mind us using this stuff?"

"Mind?" Mrs. Thurgood snorted as if that was the silliest thing she'd ever heard. "Why should I mind? Butch would be sad to think his hard work sat gathering dust all these years. No, you guys load it up and use what you need. I can't say we've got enough for the whole park, but we've got enough to make a difference."

"I'll say." Max slung an arm around the old woman's shoulders and gave her a half hug while he set a plan in motion. "I'll get Dad's trailer and gather all this stuff tomorrow. We'll start rigging the park right away. I can't tell you how grateful I am, Mrs. Thurgood."

"That's what friends are for, Max Campbell." She gave him a big old hug and smiled. "Glad to help."

"Are you as amazed as I am?" Max muttered to Tina and Luke as they approached their vehicles a few minutes later.

"Astonished. I think she's got more than half a park full of classic Christmas decorations in there, totally vintage and yet timeless," Tina declared.

"Vintage." Max rolled the word around on his tongue, thinking.

"Right." Tina opened her car door and turned. "You know, dated but sweet. An upgrade from *junk*."

"Thanks for the dictionary lesson, but I got that part. I mean, *vintage* is how we can get this all taken care of. We put out a call for any old-fashioned or classic Christmas decorations we can borrow to line the park drive."

"That could work," Luke agreed as he opened the door to his SUV. "If everyone pitches in, we can set up great displays in plenty of time."

"A Vintage Kirkwood Christmas!" Tina grabbed Max's hands. "Max, that might be brilliant."

"Well, it is or it isn't, but knowing we'll have half the park set with Mrs. Thurgood's collection puts me at ease," he admitted. "And I bet the town would get behind something like this."

"Let's notify the committee of the change in plans." Tina ticked off her fingers. "I'll do that so you can focus on planning. I'll put an announcement on Facebook, and I bet Hose Company 2 would let us use their lighted sign to ask for donations."

"I'll call Bill Ripley over at the fire hall, too," Luke said. "Between their ladder truck and the town equipment, we should be able to get this squared away in time for the lighting ceremony Wednesday night."

"Perfect."

Max turned toward Tina as Luke started the engine. He wrapped big, strong arms around her and hugged her close, grinning. "We might have actually nailed this thing. Nice work, Martinelli."

The slight buzz of an incoming text on his burner phone alerted Max as he climbed the church steps a short while later. The army was contacting him.

He stepped into the anteroom of the church entry, pulled out the phone and scanned the coded message. Rocking to 'Need You Now.' Love Lady A!!!

Translation: You're needed down South.

Max keyed back Concert tickets unavailable.

He was on their payroll for six more weeks. He'd left Fort Bragg knowing he might be called back, hoping it wouldn't happen because his parents needed him here. His commander understood the situation in Kirkwood, and only a serious emergency would push him to request Max's services, which meant if this current situation deteriorated, he could be called into action.

For how long?

That was anybody's guess, but now, with his father's condition, the holidays and his responsibilities here, assuming an instant new identity didn't make the short list. And how would he explain this to Tina? He'd left town once and hadn't returned for ten years. If he disappeared into the night on army business, how would she feel? Would she ever learn to trust him?

A new text buzzed in. Front row filled. Balcony seating options.

Which meant they'd covered the situation for now. But Max knew the drill. With international tensions mounting, anything could happen in that length of time. And probably would.

Chapter Eight

"While I'm very sorry to do this, I'm going to have to withdraw the permission certificate for the drive-through part of the Festival of Lights." Town Supervisor Ron Palmeteer didn't look the least bit sorry when he faced off with Max that afternoon. The self-serving politician seemed oddly confident about the confrontation. Max's guard went on high alert.

"On what grounds?" he asked. His easy tone let Ron be the instigator, a practiced tactic.

The store was busy, but nothing Tina and Earl couldn't handle for a few minutes, and having the rug pulled out from under this long-established Christmas project wasn't something Max would leave unchallenged.

The supervisor kept his voice low, as if hoping other customers wouldn't hear, but the well-heeled bully wasn't going to get his way on Max's watch. Not if Max could help it. "In order for me to sign off, we'd need a licensed electrician to lay out the schematic and oversee the displays."

"And what else?"

Palmeteer frowned. "I think that's quite enough, don't you? With just a few days to get ready, there's no way your hodgepodge of donated lights can handle six weeks of wear and tear. Your father's expertise wasn't lost on any of us, but with him out of the picture, and the contracted company pulling out, we've got to let the park thing slide."

"Oh, I think we'll be okay." Max kept his voice at normal volume. His father had told him enough about the supervisor to suspect the man's motives weren't exactly altruistic. Ron had led a drive to access the lakefront property owned by McKinney Farms, just west of the village. His ploy failed, but revealed his true colors: the supervisor wanted Kirkwood to become more upscale and exclusive, a getaway destination spot geared toward the financially secure. For the moment, Ron was in charge, but Max wasn't about to let him mess with the town's sweet devotion to Christmas. Not if he could help it.

The town supervisor sputtered. His reaction drew curious shoppers closer.

"We won't be okay," hissed Ron. His eyes narrowed. His jaw went tight. Clearly he came into the store ready to do battle. But why? Max wondered.

Charlie and Jenny entered the hardware store just then.

Palmeteer's dark expression said the supervisor hadn't been able to muscle Charlie Campbell about anything, ever, but he wasn't above trying to gain leverage on Charlie's son. Well, that wasn't about to happen.

"Charlie! How are you doing?"

The customer's greeting stalled the Campbells' progress, but realization broadsided Max. His sick father was about to walk into a confrontation he knew nothing about and it was all Max's fault for not telling him about Holiday Lighting's demise.

"Hanging in there," Charlie replied with practiced ease. "I just wanted to swing by and see how things were going while Jen does some rearranging upstairs. Then Beeze and I are heading home for the afternoon." Jenny kissed his cheek before she hurried upstairs to the housewares shop. As soon as she did, Charlie moved beyond the stairway and faced Ron and Max, his face grim. "Problem?"

Max shook his head. "Nope."

"Yes."

Charlie gave the supervisor a look that said he'd wait him out, but not with any level of patience.

"Your son takes casual regard in brushing off fire code. Fortunately for the welfare of the populace, we take it much more seriously at the town offices."

Charlie turned to Max and hooked a thumb at Palmeteer. "You got any clue what he's talking about?"

"The park lights for the festival."

"From Holiday Lighting in Buffalo?"

Palmeteer whistled lightly between his teeth. "You didn't tell him? The entire committee knows that Holiday left us high and dry, but you didn't bother telling the committee chairperson?"

Max ignored the supervisor and faced his father, but the look on Charlie's face showed disappointment. Disappointment in Max? In the situation? Probably both, deservedly.

He waded in. "Holiday backed out of their contract two days ago. They filed for bankruptcy and protection, so the money for the down payment on their services was lost. I waited to tell everyone—" he shot a dark look at Ron Palmeteer "—because Tina and I wanted to come up with an alternative plan. Which we did this morning. Mrs. Thurgood and others have donated a hefty supply of vintage Christmas lights and decorations for us to use in the park. We'll start setting them up tomorrow."

"We *won't* do that because we have no certified electrical contractor on-site," the supervisor countered.

"Chad Bartolo is certified, and he works for the town. I'm sure he'd be glad to—"

"Not gonna happen," declared Ron, looking pleased to shoot down the idea. "There's no money in the budget to pay overtime for frivolity. The town council would laugh me out of a job if I approved something like that."

Charlie's face went tight, and Max figured the supervisor was lucky that Charlie Campbell was a man of peace. "I'm not dead yet, and if the job needs overseeing, I'll do it," Charlie announced. "We aren't canceling the park. The kids love it and people come from all over to see it. And you know the Clearwater Women's Shelter counts on the money we raise. It's crucial for them."

"Your health won't allow you to oversee weeks of an outdoor lighting display." The supervisor stressed the word *health*, as if Charlie needed any reminding, but when Charlie opened his mouth in rebuttal, Max held up a hand.

"He won't need to. I'm here."

Palmeteer sighed, loud and overdone, as if he had better things to do than stand around and argue with simple laborers. "As I said—"

Max flipped open his wallet and withdrew a card. "If the U.S. government allows me to oversee multimillion-dollar projects, I expect they'll okay me to cover six weeks of Christmas park duty."

"Well, I—" Palmeteer backtracked, clearly at a loss.

"The number's right there." Max pointed to the lower right side of the card. "I'm sure they'd love to talk to you."

The stout, middle-aged man huffed, tossed the card onto the counter and strode out of the store, leaving looks of interest in his wake.

Max turned to Charlie, wishing he'd said something sooner. "Dad, I'm sorry. I should have told you."

Charlie glared at him, and Max couldn't remember the last time his father had looked that angry. Charlie turned and walked out through the back of the store without a word, leaving Max to deal with customers.

Jenny came into the front of the store a few minutes later. "I was upstairs for ten minutes and the world imploded. What happened?"

"I messed up. Big-time." He explained the situation to his mother. When he got done beating himself up, she gave him a big hug, but it didn't help much. He'd come home to help his father, and managed to insult the best guy on the planet by keeping this from him. "I can't believe I did that."

"Max, you stumbled into the middle of an ongoing tug-of-war between the people who would like to see Kirkwood Lake become a go-to resort area for Buffalo and Erie, and those that like the eclectic mix we've enjoyed for a century. Most folks at this end of the lake like our mix of rural, vacation and tourism, and don't want to upset that balance with high-scale development. Your father and Ron don't see eye to eye, and you happened to be in the middle of it."

"I should have told him, though." Max had read the look on his father's face, the expression that said he was tired of being protected and overlooked. And after forty years as a leader in this end of the county, he was right. Max should have gone to him first.

"Max, this is a Christmas lights display, not a peace treaty." Jenny's expression said he should go easier on himself. "Let's be sensible here. Yes, your father wants to know everything that's going on, but if we forget something or don't want to worry him, he'll deal with it. I'd rather have him focused on getting well and gaining strength than wrangling with Ron Palmeteer."

"Well, that's because you're trying to protect him, too." Max wasn't sure if his mother's blessing counted for very much right now, because Charlie got annoyed with her attentiveness on a semi-regular basis.

Jenny sighed, glanced around the now-quiet store and faced Max. "They say there are stages you go through when you fight a tough diagnosis and prognosis like Dad's."

Max swallowed hard, not sure he wanted to hear this but knowing he needed to pay attention.

"Acceptance is the last stage. Dad hasn't gotten there yet."

"But he seems so calm." Max mentally drew up the times he'd shared with his father over the past few weeks, and while Charlie seemed tired and worn from the treatments, he hadn't seemed overly stressed.

Because he's protecting you. He's protecting everyone. Like he's always done, advised Max's conscience. *Putting others first has always been his motto. It's what makes him Charlie.* "He's pretending to be calm so we don't worry."

"Yes." Jenny put her hand on his arm, the hand that bore a wedding ring from over forty years before. "But part of that pretending is to still feel like he's in charge of something, and he's lost the chance to run the store, run the festival, run his life." She made a face of dismay. "Your dad is used to running things, helping folks, being sought after for advice. To suddenly have everything taken away because he's fighting for his life seems wrong to him."

"So to have us going overboard being nice isn't in his best interests."

"Exactly."

"I'll talk to him tonight. And maybe he can help me plan some kind of schematic for this whole park thing. He's got an eye for it. I don't."

"But Tina said you flashed that card at Ron as if you were some sort of electrical genius."

Max shrugged as he slipped the card back into

his wallet. "I can find my way around a fuse box as needed."

Jenny stared at him, then pointed a finger toward the wallet as he tucked it away. "What kind of card was that, Max?"

Max grinned. "A special one."

"And if Ron had taken the number and called?"

"He'd have been told that my electrical expertise has been essential to the safety of the country."

"And if someone called them about excavating a bridge?"

"They'd find out that my bridge-building expertise was essential to the safety of the country."

Jenny studied him, his face, his gaze, and then she grabbed him into a hug, a hug that said she was happy to have him home. "What exactly have you been doing all these years, Max?"

He returned the hug and whispered, "Whatever they asked me to do, Mom."

She held him long seconds before letting him go. She lifted an armload of light boxes she wanted for a Country Cove display and moved toward the stairs. Halfway there she paused. Looked back. "You hang on to that card, you hear? A card like that can come in real handy, son."

She was right. There'd been many a time when someone called that number to check on Max's story, and the caller was always reassured that Max was exactly who they needed him to be.

So far, the army's strategy had worked well. Max wanted that to hold true in his hometown, because no matter what else happened, Max was getting those Christmas lights up and running. And hopefully Uncle Sam wouldn't need him before that happened.

A few hours later, as he pulled into his parents' driveway, he spotted a lone figure standing on the shoreline. Tall and broad-shouldered, Charlie faced the lake he'd known all his life, his bald head covered by a snug winter hat, his arms crossed. He turned, saw Max approaching and shifted his attention back to the water. Max had never seen his father look this sad, this aggrieved before, as if joy itself had been sucked out of him.

"I'm sorry, Dad." Max stepped in front of the man who'd taught him so much, the father who exampled the very best way of being a man, honor bound and family-oriented, and met his gaze. "I messed up and I won't do it again."

Charlie's mouth went tight. "You didn't mess up." His voice was gruff, almost harsh, totally unlike the Charlie Campbell Max knew so well. "You're doing just fine, and I shouldn't take my frustration out on you. Or your mother, or your brothers, or—" He paused, looking beyond Max, his expression seeking, then he pressed his lips into a firm line and brought his attention back to Max. "I'm dying."

Max's heart gripped. His throat went tight. For the life of him, he couldn't muster words past the sudden lump in his throat, and he couldn't look his beloved father in the eye and pretend, so he stood perfectly still and blinked an acknowledgment.

"And I'm not sure how to handle that," Charlie continued. He waved a hand at his body. "All the pills, the

IVs, the treatments. They're stopgaps, Max, ways to gain me some time, time with you." He smiled at Max and in that smile, Max saw the first glimmer of acceptance in his father's eyes. "And your brothers and sisters. Time with the kids. I just didn't expect this to come so soon."

"We never do."

Charlie nodded. "That's right. And I don't know what to say, what to do, how to help your mother."

"Can't that be our job?" Max supposed. "After all you guys have done, I think it's okay to let us step in. Take a turn."

"I'm willing enough to share the tasks, but seeing Mom bustling around, all full of hope, trying to keep me on the straight and narrow so I get better..." He hauled in a deep breath, his forehead creased. "I don't think I'll be getting better, Max, but I'm scared to let her down."

"You've never let me down, Charlie Campbell, not one day in your life, so if you've got something to share with me, I expect you to do it." Jenny's voice made them both turn, and the look on her face, the raw acceptance, told Max it was time to slip away.

"I'll leave you guys to settle this, but I want to tell both of you that God couldn't have sent me better parents." He faced them, knowing he'd been blessed beyond belief, and maybe far beyond what he deserved. "If I knew where my birth mother was, I'd send her a thank-you note for dumping me because God put me here, with you guys, and all the craziness of being a Campbell, and I—" Max stepped forward and embraced them both in a hug, a hug that filled Jenny's eyes with tears and made Charlie look damp-eyed, too "—will never be able to repay all you've done for me. For us." He jutted his chin toward the house that sheltered seven kids, four born to be Campbells, three brought by the grace of God. "I love you guys."

He left them to sort through the emotion of the moment. Charlie's acceptance and Jenny's awareness.

His heart crushed at the thought of losing his father, a town patriarch, the man whose kindly example and strong stance said so much. A man of faith and vigor, who knew how to apply both to life. But it was also strengthened by that example, the pledge of a man who saw a job and completed it to the best of his ability. Always.

And that was a quality Charlie Campbell passed on to Max.

Early the next morning, Jenny handed Max a steaming mug of coffee. "Before you say anything or offer an argument, I'm working at the store today," she announced in her "don't argue with me" signature voice. "Jack and Kim are bringing the boys down from Buffalo. They're going to cut a Christmas tree at Wojzaks Farm, then hang out with Dad. You're going to be tied up stringing lights in the park all day, so I'm working with Tina and Earl."

"Perfect."

She stared at him, then laid a cool hand against Max's forehead. "No fever."

"Nope."

"Headache?"

He smiled, remembering her old game. "No, I'm fine. Just ready to let you live your life the way you should. I probably should have realized that as soon as I got back home."

She accepted that, hugged him and ruffled his hair. "I figured you'd catch on sooner or later. And if Dad shows up at the park to help..."

"Close my mouth and let him."

"Bingo. You're a quick study, Max Campbell."

"After a while, things start to sink in. Seth and Luke are helping in the park. We've also got a bunch of guys on the committee and two from the Highway Department."

"Ron Palmeteer approved that?"

"They took vacation days so they didn't need to get approval," Max told her. "Just a group of guys wanting to get something done. We're meeting at nine."

"And I'm ordering Chinese for supper tonight, enough for everyone, so we'll have a big old Campbell supper."

She was turned toward the sink so Max couldn't see his mother's face, but her voice hitched on the last word. He knew that choked sound meant tears.

Max didn't want to look, because as strong as his father was, Jenny Campbell was the driving force behind this family. And in all the years he'd known and loved her, she'd never fallen apart. Oh, she'd cried now and then, mostly when she was spittin' mad or watching some sappy movie she'd seen half a dozen times before, but she rarely caved.

The crack in her voice said she was caving now. Max

stepped up behind her. Stubborn, reminding him of another woman he knew, she kept her chin down, as if buttering a bagel had taken on momentous importance.

He put his hands on her shoulders. "Hey."

The shoulders shook.

Max turned her around and drew her into his arms, a role reversal that felt wrong and right all at once. "Hey, it's okay."

"None of it's okay," she whispered, and the harshness of her tone surprised him. "He's insisting on coming into town for the lighting ceremony on Wednesday. The doctors said no crowds, don't risk infection, and he's willing to ignore all that, the stubborn old coot." She sniffled. He glanced around hunting for tissues, saw none and grabbed a paper towel for her. She blotted her face and waved the toweling around. "I know why he's doing it. I know he's facing choices, choices I have to let him make, but I feel so helpless. I question everything I do. Part of me wants to break down, the other part wants to beat up on someone, and I can't fall apart because he needs me to be strong and stoic."

"You're the definition of *strong*, Mom." Max hugged her tighter. "But it's okay to want to beat on something now and again. With a houseful of boys, I think it's a family tradition, right up there with mistletoe and eggnog from McKinney's Dairy store."

"Oh, Max." She hugged him, blotted her eyes and blew her nose, then scowled. "I'm sorry. I shouldn't have dumped on you, it's just the thought of trying to act normal when nothing's normal..."

"Death is as normal as birth," Max reminded her. "Just not as celebrated."

She looked up at him, considering his words, then patted his cheek. "You've done all right, Maxwell."

"I had help." He leaned down and kissed her cheek, wishing he could make this better, knowing he couldn't. And on that note— "Mom, you know I'm not really out of the army until the first of January, right?"

"Yes."

"And there's always the possibility they may call me if necessary."

"They need you, Max?"

"Not at the moment," he hedged. "But they warned me they might."

She moved closer and studied him. "Are you sure about leaving the army? Are you doing this because of our situation here, or because you're ready to move on?"

"Both. So the timing is perfect. But I can't turn my back on a command if it comes."

"So if you disappear in the dark of night…"

"Know that I'll wrap it up and get back here as quick as I can," he promised. "Because this is where I want to be."

She reached out and hugged him, hugged him hard. "I love you, Max. I've loved you since that day we picked you up at Social Services and brought you home."

"You gave me cinnamon rolls and hot chocolate and let me try eggnog that first Christmas, and it's been a love affair ever since." He hugged her back. "Thank you for coming for me that day. For saying yes when that phone call came saying they had a little boy waiting."

"Timing," she assured him with a smile. "Luke had just moved into his own room and having a noisy little brother to pester him helped to keep him humble. It was the least I could do. Do you want a bagel before you take off?"

He shook his head as he grabbed his to-go cup of coffee. "I'll catch food later. We're supposed to get rain tonight, so if we nail this park setup today, I can relax with Dad a little. That ranks higher than stringing lights in trees."

"I'll see you tonight. I love you, Max."

He smiled from the door. "Feeling's mutual."

Tina parked her car just south of where the light crew was working, opened her back hatch, stuck two fingers into her mouth and gave a sharp whistle. Seth Campbell turned first. "You've done that ever since you were a kid."

She laughed as she withdrew a large drink tray filled with steaming coffees and hot chocolate. "Warm drinks, guys. Break time."

She didn't have to tell them twice. And when she pulled out a box filled with sandwiches, chips and a box of her fresh-baked cookies, the words of approval made the expense and time worthwhile.

"Tina, you rock."

"I owe you, Martinelli."

"You want flowers this spring, I will come and plant you a garden, Miss Tina!" Bert Conroy held up his ham-and-swiss on grilled rye and grinned. "This is one happy landscaper right now."

Tina glanced around and tried to not look like she was hunting for Max, but Luke laughed at her. "Max had to run to Dad's store for a few things. Or to check out the pretty girl working there. You must have just missed him."

She almost pouted, and if there was one thing Tina Marie Martinelli never did, it was pout. But knowing she'd missed Max by a hair while she was ordering sandwiches at the deli made her almost succumb.

A car engine cruised up the road behind them, and when Tina turned, Max was pulling into the parking space south of hers. His grin?

Wonderful.

The look in his eyes that said he was happy, surprised and quite possibly downright delighted to see her?

Better yet.

Their eyes met. Locked. And stayed locked.

"Aw, look how cute they are." Luke made a gagging noise. Total guy.

"Hey, it wasn't that long ago that you were doing the same thing," said Seth, "so I'd zip it if I was you."

"Look who's talking," countered Luke.

"Except I'm not the one teasing a guy who's packing heat and highly skilled in combat maneuvers," Seth shot back. "Which makes me the smart one. Or should I say still the smart one. Not like that's a big surprise."

The guys laughed, and when Max walked over and grabbed Tina in a big hug, they hooted approval.

"Max."

"My way of saying thank-you for the sandwiches,"

he told her as he reached into the box. "I'm excited to see food. And you."

"You said food first. I could take offense."

He waved his wrapped sandwich toward the gathered men. "Audience intimidation. The pretty girl is always first."

"Any pretty girl?" she asked out loud.

This time he stopped, faced her and smiled. "Nope. Just one."

She blushed as the guys groaned, then she smiled up at him, reading the emotion behind his fun words, seeing the warmth and camaraderie. He grabbed a coffee eagerly, added cream and sugar, and snugged the lid down before sipping it. "Perfect. And I knew you were doing this because my mother ratted you out. She thought it was funny and not exactly a surprise that you came here midday, while, in *her* words—" he stressed the pronoun for emphasis "—I was making an excuse to stop by the hardware store and see you."

"Great minds think alike." Looking up, she found herself lost in the depths of his dark brown eyes, the didn't-bother-shaving-to-work-in-the-woods-rough chin and the hint of curl returning around his neckline.

"They do." He chucked her on the arm, noted the time and wolfed his sandwich in record time. "Channel Seven says the rain's moving in by four, and I want all systems checked and ready to roll before then. And—"

A noise interrupted him.

His attention shifted to the southern end of the park road. He turned, caught Seth's eye and called Luke's name softly. His brothers followed the direction of his gaze and watched as Charlie and their oldest brother, Jack, pulled up in Jack's SUV. Dressed in outdoor work attire, the two Campbell additions came ready to help.

Mixed emotions ruled the moment, until Seth tossed his coffee cup into the trash bag Tina brought, strode forward and gripped his father's hand in a firm show of support. "Now we'll get something done!"

Charlie grinned.

Jack's face said he was just doing what he was told, and Luke and Max moved forward in welcome.

Tina shifted her attention to the other workers.

Their expressions told a story of empathy and understanding, but not one of those burly guys made a big deal about having Charlie on-site. No, sir, they shouted out welcomes as if it was any old day, asked advice and then got back to the business of decorating a town park.

An artist might have been able to capture the rare combination of broad emotions of those precious moments, but Tina was no artist, so she pulled out her cell phone to record the moment. The Campbells, making the best of a rough situation, like always.

"Hey, you're not dressed for this damp chill." Max motioned her toward the car. "And if my father catches you sloughing off on company payroll, he's liable to get upset."

Charlie laughed and moved down the road at a steady pace. "Let's see what you've got here. If we can get this hodgepodge of lights looking like something decent before the end of the day, I'll sleep well tonight."

"Me, too." Max waved to her but stayed by his father's side, attentive to Charlie's advice. Tina raised her phone and snapped a series of pictures, the Campbell boys walking with their dad, all eyes turned on him, soaking up his wisdom.

It would be a day to remember. A day to cherish, and her pictures would help re-create the memory.

She climbed into the car, turned it around and headed to the village below. The town's efforts might not have the grandeur a professional lighting crew would have supplied, but little kids wouldn't notice any of that. All they'd see were lights, bright lights, twinkle lights, chaser lights. And they'd be happy.

With Thanksgiving three days away, and the circle of lights slated to blink on at dusk on Wednesday, having this job done would mean kudos for Max and the Campbells.

And the look of satisfaction on Charlie's face, to work with four of his sons at one time?

Priceless.

Chapter Nine

Go time.

Max and Bert Conroy had run a preliminary light test midafternoon. They'd held their breaths, thrown the switch and the world did not implode. *Then.*

Now, if they got the same result tonight, when the village and shoreline blinked on around five-thirty, he'd breathe a whole lot easier. And if nothing major went awry in the next six weeks?

Max might consider doing this again next year.

"I made you coffee." Tina clamped a lid on his to-go cup, then slipped into her heavy coat. "Two sugars, two creams."

"I like having my own personal barista. I could get used to this." He smiled across the top of the cup and when she rolled her eyes at him, he glanced around. "Where's yours?"

"No time, I'll get one later. You've got to be—"

"Here." Max took a sip of the coffee, then handed her the plastic travel mug. "We'll share."

"We will not."

He made a face at her. "You'll have supper with me, but you won't share my coffee? That's ridiculous, Tina."

"I'm simply abiding by our nonfraternizing rules. So should you."

"I believe I already cited the impossibility of that. And besides—" he waited until she looked up "—the army saw to it that my skill set is breaking rules. Which brings us back to the 'all's fair in love and war' discussion."

"I'm not discussing any such thing," she chided. "And we need to get over to the town square, ASAP. Once Reverend Smith is done with the prayer service, you've got to be ready to hit the switch. You can't be late. You're, like, the vice-president in charge of Christmas lights, a VIP around here during the holiday season."

"I'm not going without you. And don't worry, I've got it covered. Make your coffee. It only takes a minute."

"Which is about what you have," she grumbled, but she brewed a quick cup, fixed it and snapped a lid on tight. "Okay. We're good to go."

He held the door open, locked it behind her, then let her precede him down the front steps.

The street and the white-frosted green milled with people. Old, young, tall and small, the diversity made this lighting ceremony a wide-ranging event. He reached out and grabbed Tina's free hand when he descended the steps, then tugged her around the back way, behind the church. "This gains us some serious leverage because fighting through that crowd would mean talking to folks, and we're skating close on time as is." They moved across the back church parking lot, through the lower end of the cemetery, then into the park square opposite Seth's house. "Done, with ninety seconds to spare."

"Not bad." She sipped her coffee and smiled up at him. "I'm impressed, soldier."

He started to smile, but Ray and Mary Sawyer approached from one side, with Sherrie and her husband, Jim, behind them. From the other side of the street, Seth and Gianna worked their way across the green with Charlie and Jenny. Seth carried Bella, bundled from head to toe in a bright pink fleece snowsuit with teddy-bear ears. Mikey was dressed in a brown version, but he stubbornly kept grabbing his hood and yanking down, giving his petite mother a hard time. Seth's adopted daughter, Tori, and Carmen Bianchi flanked Gianna, and the sight of his brother's growing family and the Sawyers drove the sharp difference home.

Seth was here with his family, a spirit of joy abounding.

Pete would never have that chance.

"Max! Tina. We're so excited about all this." Mary grinned up at Ray, then added, "The thought of a new baby, our first grandchild, Christmas, the lights..."

"Grandson," added Ray, clearly proud. "Peter James Morgan, named for his Uncle Pete—"

Max's heart strangled.

"And next year this time, little Pete will be here with us." Mary pressed a kiss to Sherrie's cheek, clearly delighted. "I'm just crazy excited to think of it!"

Nearly fifteen years they'd waited for this new chance at happiness. Fifteen years without their oldest son. A decade and a half of an empty chair, Pete's laugh silenced by an early grave.

Guilt clutched Max and refused to let go.

Why hadn't he said something? Why had he stormed off, letting Pete make the final decision?

You know why. You didn't want to be a third wheel, and you felt like Pete would rather be alone with Amy than have a buddy hanging about, especially a buddy that didn't want to drink with them.

Reverend Smith keyed his microphone. The gathered crowd went quiet, waiting.

The reverend smiled at the crowd, letting his gaze wander and linger here and there. When he got to the growing group of Campbells and Sawyers, he paused. Not a long pause, but enough to tell Max that the aging rector recognized the moment.

He knows. Or at least suspects. And why wouldn't he? Max realized. The reverend had officiated at Pete's funeral. He'd watched Pete and Max grow up, he knew their families, their friends. Maybe ministers came especially equipped with guilt meters, or as least a heightened awareness of human reactions.

The reverend looked at him, straight at him, and his gentle gaze said the time was right, the time was now.

But then he launched into a sweet story of Christmas, of Christ as light. With the wind unpredictable, each person had brought a penlight or a cell phone with a flashlight device, and when the reverend called for them to turn on their little lights, hundreds of tiny beams filled the night.

"You've heard it said that it is better to light one candle than to curse the darkness." The reverend motioned toward the sprinkling of lights surrounding the decorated gazebo in the town square. "For the next six weeks, let us make sure our lights, the light of Christ within us, shine as brightly as our town and lake shines during this blessed and joyous Christmas season. And now, may the Lord bless thee, and keep thee: May the Lord make His face shine upon thee, and be gracious unto thee: May He lift up His countenance upon thee, and give thee peace."

A chorus of "Amen" resounded to the old benediction from the book of Numbers, and as Tina nudged Max forward to hit the switch, he balked. Smiling at his father, Charlie Campbell nodded and moved through the crowd.

The doctors had warned Charlie to avoid infection, to stay out of crowds, to lay low, but as his father threaded his way to the gazebo, he paused and shook every hand offered. If this was going to be Charlie's last Christmas in Kirkwood, he seemed determined to make it a good one.

He drew up alongside the reverend, reached out, shook his pastor's hand and then hit the switch.

Main Street was flooded with light; beautiful, warm, holiday light.

Set to timers, other banks of lights blinked on around them. The village, the circle of homes surrounding the lake, the businesses, all decked out.

And when the park switch was thrown, a collective gasp filled the air.

Vintage yet timeless, the depth of light along Park Drive would thrill every carload of people who came to see the beautiful displays.

"Amazing." Tina hugged Max's arm and smiled up at him.

"I'm pretty psyched that it all came together," he admitted.

She shook her head. "Not the lights, although I have to say I think they're the best ever. You, Max. You're amazing."

She meant it. He read the truth of her emotions in her eyes, the smile she aimed at him. And despite what he needed to face once and for all, Tina's shining approval made it feel possible.

The crowd didn't linger long. A brisk west wind promised deepening cold and most likely snow by morning, but as folks headed home, greetings of the season echoed around him, making him feel like he could handle anything, anything at all.

Even the truth.

"Uh-oh."

Max followed the direction of Tina's gaze and paused a few minutes later. "Uh-oh, what? I don't get it."

"The restaurant." She indicated the people heading toward The Pelican's Nest. "Look at the stream of people going in there."

"That's bad?" The confusion in his voice said he wasn't following her, but then Max had never worked in the food industry. A rush like this, without the proper staff?

Crushing from a restaurant perspective. "I've got to go help them." She darted across the street and moved quickly up the sidewalk to the far side of her parents' old business.

"Me, too."

She ducked behind several cars and turned as she pulled open the back door. "What does a soldier know about restaurants?"

"I can clear tables and do dishes. And you might be surprised by the wealth of things I know, Tina."

"I already am and find it more than a little intimidating," she whispered, then breezed into the restaurant kitchen as if she belonged there.

Laura looked shell-shocked by the growing crowd. Ryan's expression alternated from nervous to strained. Han, the Vietnamese cook who'd worked for her parents years before, looked stressed, as well. Tina tossed her coat onto the pegged rack alongside the back door and grabbed two aprons from the bin. She tossed one to Max and donned the other. "We're here to help. Laura, you want kitchen or tables?"

Gratitude and surprise softened Laura's expression. "I'll help the girls out front. You and Han can cover this. Max, I—"

"Dishes." He moved to the large commercial machine, slid the first filled rack of dishes into place and locked it down. "Uncle Sam makes sure everyone knows how to operate one of these babies."

Laura hurried out. Ryan's worried gaze went from

Tina to Max then back again before he followed his mother into the front of the restaurant.

Han assessed the new situation, grinned and pointed to the stack of orders. "You prep, like old times, eh?"

"Will do."

She bustled around the kitchen, laying plates, starting orders, doling out specials Han had prepared earlier in the day. Wednesday-night pasta specials were a standing tradition in Western New York, and Han had prepped accordingly. Tina prayed that lots of folks would want rigatoni and meatballs tonight. That would take a load of work off the minimal staff.

She put a new kettle of water on to precook more pasta, glanced around, and asked, "Garlic bread?"

Han made a face. "No more."

"No more tonight? Or you don't serve it anymore?"

"No more, anymore. Too much money."

Her father's garlic bread, a Martinelli tradition, the bad-for-your-waistline deliciousness that brought throngs of folks to The Pelican's Nest every Wednesday. Great sauce, al dente pasta and Gino's warm, buttery garlic bread, dusted with fresh basil.

If she was running this place, the last thing she'd drop would be the Italian staples that set the "Nest" apart from other lakeside restaurants. With their family diner atmosphere, steeped in Italian traditions, they'd provided family dining experiences at reasonable cost.

Her parents hadn't gotten rich off the place, but they'd done okay, and shouldn't that be enough?

Rocco's image came back to her, gruff and scowling, grumbling over money and costs all the time. How hard it must have been for Laura to live with him, deal with his outbursts.

Unexpected sympathy welled within her, but she couldn't dwell on that now. The three waitresses and Laura kept sliding fresh orders onto the wheel, and as Han moved them to the hanging bar over the grill, she'd prep the plate, drop fries or pull potatoes, and let Han finish the order from his spot. Max alternated between rolling dishes through their cycle and cutting fresh lemons and veggies for tomorrow's specials. The old kitchen radio added background inspiration. Old hymns blended with new Christmas carols, the jovial tones adding to the familiar atmosphere.

By eight o'clock the crowd had dwindled to a few dawdling diners, enjoying a few minutes of quiet before going out into the cold.

Laura came into the kitchen, faced Tina and Max and promptly burst into tears.

"Hey!" Tina moved forward, not sure what to do. She looked back at Han.

He shrugged, just as confused.

"Laura, I—"

"Thank you."

Tina paused as Laura grabbed some tissues from a box behind her, mopped her face and took a deep breath.

"Are you okay?"

Laura faced Tina more fully and offered a watery smile. "I'm fine. That's the first time we've been busy like that in over a year. It felt—wonderful!"

"I love a rush," Tina admitted. "The adrenaline gets going, and pretty soon you've got a rhythm of food and orders and checkouts and seating and if all goes well, it's like a well-oiled machine."

"And when it doesn't, chaos erupts." Laura breathed a sigh of relief. "No chaos tonight, thanks to you guys. And you." She smiled at Han, then wrapped Ryan in a hug as he carried another bus pan of dishes into the kitchen. He looked embarrassed and slightly worried, unsure what to make of this kitchen scene.

Tina couldn't blame him. For years he'd been told to avoid her and now she was standing in his mother's kitchen, filling orders. "Great job tonight, Ryan."

He ducked his chin.

Laura looked like she wanted to reprimand him, but Max changed the subject. "So is this the norm? When folks come to town for the lights or the lighting ceremony? Because I'm beginning to see why the light gig is so important if it pumps local businesses like it did tonight."

"Well." Laura shifted a sympathetic look to Tina. "It was always busy during the light festival and the opening ceremony, but it was especially busy tonight because Tina's café is gone."

"True enough." Tina made a face, then sighed. "But I have to say, this was a lot of fun, Laura. Working with Han again. Pumping orders. It felt like old times."

The middle-aged Asian cook grinned. "Is very good, no?"

"Is very good, yes!" Tina laughed at him, sharing an old joke, wondering why it felt so good to work with Han and Laura again.

Sweet memories of what had been? Or longing for what could be?

"Well." She peeled off her apron, tossed it into the appropriate bin and stretched. "I'm heading out. This was fun, and if you need help the next few weeks, Laura, I'd be glad to step in. I'll be right across the street at the hardware store, and if the light show brings folks like it generally does, the extra help might come in handy."

"You'd be over here every night?" Ryan's sharp surprise said he might look like his grandfather, but he had a measure of his father's rudeness.

"Ryan!"

"The busy ones, anyway." Tina kept her voice level and met the boy's frustrated gaze.

"Hey, I'm not the one that called her names and shook his fist out the window for years," Ryan defended himself. "Now Dad's gone and all of a sudden she's like our new best friend? What's up with that, Mom?"

Laura stared at him, mouth open. She started to speak, but he turned and rushed out of the kitchen. The slap of the back door said he was gone.

"Tina, I—"

Tina raised a hand to stop her. "Laura, it's time we all moved beyond the past. I'm sure Ryan heard a lot of stuff over the years. He's young. He'll sort things out in his head soon enough. But in the meantime, you have a business to run and I don't mind helping you. You're my father's sister. He loved you. My mother loved you. And I won't pretend it didn't feel nice—and weird—to be here again." She shrugged. "Can't we just take it a day at a time? I'll come over and help as needed, and we'll all take a breath. Okay?"

"I'd like that, Tina. And if you want to use our ovens for anything—"

"Like pies tomorrow morning?" She'd noticed the empty dessert cooler, and the thought of opening a restaurant on Thanksgiving with no pie seemed alien.

Laura inhaled. "You'd do that?"

"I miss not doing it, so yes. I'll be here by six."

"I'll meet you and make coffee," Laura promised. Her eyes brightened. "Tina, thank you. I don't know what other words to use because *thank you* doesn't seem like enough."

Tina jerked a thumb toward the window, where a side view of the church spire reached up into the trees. "Forgive us our trespasses as we forgive those who trespass against us. I forgot that for a while, Laura. But I won't forget again. I promise."

"I'm so happy." Han grinned but kept cleaning the grill, getting ready for closing time. "I will serve the best turkey tomorrow with the best pie. A true Thanksgiving meal!"

"And while I'd love to wash dishes nightly, I must bestow the honor on someone else, although I hate to miss all the fun," Max teased as he took their jackets off the peg rack and held Tina's out. She started to reach for it, read his droll expression and slipped her arms into the sleeves, allowing him to help her.

And when he rested his hands on her shoulders as if they belonged there?

It felt like they did.

He grabbed his leather gloves and opened the kitchen door. “Laura, Han, it’s been real.”

Han grinned her way. “Very real with Miss Tina here!”

“Thank you, Max. We’re grateful.” Laura included Han in her statement, and the Vietnamese cook nodded.

“It is our pleasure to have you back here.”

Han’s words touched Tina’s heart because she felt exactly the same way. It had been a pleasure to jump in, work with Han, run the kitchen she’d known for years.

A thread of hope unfurled inside her.

She paused outside and looked back, studying the lakeside eatery from the sidewalk.

“You missed this place.”

“You think?” She turned his way and lifted her eyes to his.

“I *know*.” He stressed the verb purposely. “It was written all over you tonight. You jumped in like you belonged there, and watching you work, throwing those orders?” He shifted his attention to the restaurant, then brought it back to her. “You fit, Tina.”

“I do.” She shrugged, and started to move away. “Well. I did.”

He laid an arm around her shoulders, slowing her down. “Still do. You can pretend otherwise, but I know what I saw.”

He was right. She knew it the moment she took her place to Han’s left, like a dance she’d practiced and performed for years.

Working with Han, hearing the hustle and bustle of

the waitresses and Laura, the customers, the clang of dishes as Ryan bussed tables…

She'd missed all that by working alone. The downside of being a one-man band was that you were a one-man band. The flow of a busy, well-coordinated restaurant, like she'd experienced tonight?

That's what she'd been raised to do, and she hadn't realized how much she missed it until just now. "Well, I was raised there."

"There's that," Max mused. "And your inherent kitchen skills. All that baking I've heard so much about—"

"I love baking."

"Can't prove it by me," Max retorted. "We've worked together for over a week and I've seen two measly cookies. Kind of lame, Tina."

She laughed, and it felt good to laugh. They got to her door, and she swung about, surprised. "That's the first time I've passed the café site without getting emotional. I didn't even realize we'd gone by."

"The company, perhaps?" Max bumped shoulders with her, a friendly gesture.

"Indubitably," she joked back, then looked up.

His eyes…

Dark and questing, smiling and wondering.

He glanced down at her mouth, then waited interminable seconds, for what? Her to move toward him?

She did.

Would he ask permission? Would he—

The warmth of his lips gave her the answer. His arms wrapped around her, tugging her close. The cool texture of his collar brushed her cheek, a contrast to the warmth of his mouth.

He smelled like leather, dish soap and fresh lemons, a delightful mingling of scents in the chill of a Christmas-lit night.

Perfect.

Max's singular thought fit the moment.

Holding Tina, working with Tina, kissing Tina?

Perfect.

He pulled her close when they ended the kiss and tried to level his breathing.

No use. Being with Tina meant a ramped-up heart rate and accelerated breathing, which meant being without her, even for a little while, would equate a new low. "Well."

She pulled back, frowning, as if about to scold him, but then she smiled, put her hands up around his neck and whispered, "Do-over."

Like the day they met. *Met again*, Max corrected himself as he languished in one more kiss. When he finally let her go, he dropped his forehead to hers and smiled. "I didn't think we could improve on the first one," he whispered, his forehead warm while the cold air chilled his cheeks. "But amazingly, we did."

Her smile curved her cheeks beneath his. He pulled her into a warm, long hug, the kind of embrace he wanted to enjoy forever. Here, in Kirkwood, with the past behind them and the future ripe with possibilities.

"Go in." He palmed her cheeks with his gloves,

smiled and gave her one last kiss. "I'll see you tomorrow. Mom said you're bringing pie for Thanksgiving."

"I am if I can get my mind off kissing you. That might be my morning downfall, Max Campbell."

He grinned wider. "Worth the risk. I can always buy a pie. Finding a Tina?" He raised his shoulders and his eyebrows, hands splayed. "Much more difficult."

He watched her go in, waited for her lights to blink on, then strode to his car parked back at the hardware store.

He had one final coat of paint to apply to the café tables he'd rescued from the fire site before they cleared the mess away. The chairs were done, and the lustrous satin finish said summer in bright tones of yellow, green and blue. The alert from command meant he needed to be ready at a moment's notice. He didn't want anything left undone if he got called to duty.

He started the car, eased away from the building, then paused at the road, considering. He could go straight home and get ready for Thanksgiving when all the family would gather at the Campbell homestead. Or he could head to the far side of the lake and see the Sawyers.

Now? The day before Thanksgiving? Are you nuts?

He swallowed hard.

He'd been called worse. But hearing the reverend tonight, seeing his gaze sweep their families, the thought of possibly being called up and leaving things unsettled much longer gnawed at him.

He turned right and aimed the car for the western

shore. He passed Tina's place and pictured her inside the vintage-style rooms.

She'd looked tired and energized tonight, a fun combination, deepened by facing the shadows of her past. Standing in the lighted doorway, kissing Tina, he knew he could do no less.

He pulled into the Sawyer driveway about five minutes later. He got out of the car, shut the door and walked onto their porch. He knocked lightly, hoping they weren't asleep, and when Mary Sawyer came to the door wearing an apron, he realized his foolishness.

No one hosting Thanksgiving got to bed early on Wednesday evening. She swung open the door. "Max! What a surprise, come in! What's happened? Is there something wrong with the light display in the park?"

He shook his head as Ray took his place alongside his wife. "You need help, Max?"

He paused, swallowing hard around the lump in his throat, while two of the nicest people in the world faced him, and said, "I came to apologize for Pete's death. I know it's too little, too late, but I can't see you guys all the time without you knowing the truth. Pete's death was my fault."

Mary's face paled, then crumpled. She reached out a hand to him. "Max, no. It was an accident."

Ray grabbed his arm and pulled him into the living room. "Sit down, Max. What's this all about?"

Altruistic, even at a moment like this, but that shouldn't surprise Max. The Sawyers had raised their children with strength, expectations and loving care. Warmth was their benchmark. He tried again as Mary and Ray sat, facing him. "Pete and I were together that night. Earlier in the evening. I'd come over and then Amy showed up. She'd gotten out of work early and wanted to surprise Pete."

"Right." Mary nodded. "And you went home before they took the boat out. Max, we knew that. Sherrie and Tina saw you before I took them to the amusement park for the reduced ride night."

That wasn't a big surprise. Tina and Sherrie loved to spy on him and Pete back then, a pair of pesky tomboys, cute and annoying.

The thought of the tough kid Tina was then and the strong woman she'd become pushed him on. "I left because Pete had been drinking. He paid Cody Feltner to stop at the liquor store in Clearwater and hook him up. Cody dropped it off sometime that afternoon. By the time I left to go home, Pete and Amy were already pretty wasted."

He stared down, twisting his hands, then brought his gaze up. "I'm so sorry. I shouldn't have left. I should have called you guys. I should have taken the keys to the boat. I should have done something other than go home mad because my best friend was behaving like an idiot." His throat went tight. Simple breathing was getting harder to do, facing these good people and telling them he could have saved their son and Amy and didn't do it. He hauled in a breath and manned up. Met their eyes. "I came to apologize for what I didn't do that night. If I'd made other choices, Pete and Amy might still be alive. I'm so sorry." His voice cracked. His jaw hurt. "So terribly sorry. Please forgive me."

Ray's face swam before him, an ill-defined image of sorrow and angst.

"Oh, Max." Mary moved forward, knelt before him and took his hands. "Max Campbell, did you think we didn't know that Pete and Amy were drinking? Did you think we blamed you?"

"I—"

"Max, we'd pushed Pete into therapy a few weeks before the accident," Ray told him. "We saw what was happening, and with college coming up, we knew Pete's drinking was out of control. We were scared to death to have him go off to college, with no rules or regulations. He was mad at us for interfering. For weeks we didn't leave him alone in the house. One of us was always here, making sure he didn't drink."

"But that night we knew Amy was working, we knew you were coming over and we'd gotten tickets for the girls to go to Darien Lake," Mary explained. "We'd promised them, and it felt wrong to keep breaking our promises to Sherrie because we had to stand guard with Pete."

Ray rubbed a hand through his thinning hair. "I was on ambulance duty. I got a call for an emergency in Warrenton and Mary had the girls at Darien. Then that call was followed by a second call, and I was gone hours longer than I expected. When I got home, Pete, Amy and the boat were gone."

"Max." Mary wrapped her hands around his. "This wasn't your fault. And it took a long time for us to realize it wasn't our fault, either. Kids don't always make good decisions, and when you add addictions into the mix?" She frowned, her blue eyes clouded with sadness. "We loved our son. We still do. But Pete knew better than to drink like that, he knew better than to take the boat out under the influence, and those two choices led to tragedy. It wasn't your fault."

"But—"

"If you pave life's roads with unanswered questions, you have a real hard time finding the answers, Max." Ray crossed the space between them and sat down next to him. "You've carried this for a lot of years. Too many. And despite Pete's mistakes, I believe God forgives the foolishness of children. I believe I'll see my son in heaven, and that we'll be reunited. We'll gather at the throne of the Most High and be together. But Pete would be the last person to want you to feel guilty. He loved you, in spite of his behavior before he died. And that's the Pete we remember, the one who loved his friends and family before he became an alcoholic."

Max's heart went tight.

Then it loosened.

They didn't hate him. They didn't blame him. They knew about Pete's choices and even with that, Mary and Ray couldn't protect him 24/7.

"There is no forgiveness needed." Mary's firm tone highlighted her words. "We loved you then, we love you now, and we knew how badly Pete's death affected you. But never in my wildest dreams did I realize you lugged this guilt around. Guilt like this isn't of God, Max. God loves. He sees. He knows. He forgives. I don't want you to spend one more minute blaming yourself. Heaven knows such a thing never crossed our minds."

Ray swiped a hand to his eyes.

Mary made no pretense of not crying. She grabbed Max in an embrace that felt good, and long overdue…

"Thank you."

He stood. Mary and Ray stood also, and instead of reaching for his hand, Pete's dad pulled him into a big, long hug. "You're a good man, Max. And I'm proud to know you. And to work with you. And if you settle down here now that you're leaving the service, there will always be a place at our table for you. I hope you know that."

He did. *Now.* He returned the hug, grabbed his gloves and moved toward the door. Almost there, he turned. "I'm sorry for coming so late. I just had to get over here. See you. Talk to you."

"I'm glad you did." Ray clapped a hand to Max's shoulder. "Very glad. I wish we'd had this conversation ten years ago. But at least we've had it now."

"Yes."

A kitchen buzzer alerted Mary to Thanksgiving chores. She turned, surprised. "I've got pies in the oven. Good thing I set that timer, because I forgot all about them!"

Max gave her one last hug. She patted his face and hurried to the broad kitchen overlooking the lakefront.

Ray opened the door. "Thank you, Max. For being Pete's friend all those years, for being a good soldier, for being on hand now that Charlie needs you. I'm proud of you, son."

He extended a hand to Max.

Max took it, and when Ray Sawyer shook his hand, weight tumbled from Max's shoulders.

They didn't hate him.

They knew Pete was in trouble, and even with their diligence, Pete managed to get hold of alcohol and get drunk.

Foolishness of youth.

Ray's words made sense to Max, now that he was older. He couldn't see that clearly as a teen. All he'd known was the guilt of walking out on his friend, leaving him there with Amy and the bottle.

He paused at the car, looking out over the lake. Clouds had nipped the earlier starlight, but merry lights circled the expanse of water, and the brilliance of the decked-out village called to him.

His father had started this beautiful tradition years ago. He'd spearheaded the committee, the planning and then the implementation, all to bring the joy of Christmas and the light of Christ to people.

Max drew a deep breath, drinking in the beauty of reflected light, and knowing, at long last, he was exactly where he needed to be. Home, in Kirkwood Lake.

He climbed into the driver's seat, backed out of the Sawyer driveway and aimed for the eastern shore. He'd spend tomorrow with his family, surrounded by Campbells and Campbell friends, sharing the first family-themed holiday he'd allowed himself in over ten years.

And he'd have Tina there, by his side, laughing. Talking.

Kissing?

The thought of that made him smile.

He shouldn't feel this way after so short a time. His brain knew that, but his heart wasn't listening. His heart thought being with Tina Martinelli was the best thing that ever happened to him, and now...if he could just get her to hang around a while...he might be able to convince her heart of the very same thing.

And he had every intention of doing just that.

His burner phone buzzed as he pulled the car into his parents' driveway. He walked into the house and read the message. Casting Crowns concert in Erie phenomenal! Faves: Set me Free and East to West. Wish you were here!

His heart sank. He knew the drill: the coded message meant he'd be heading out of the country to go free someone. A hostage? A prisoner? Man, woman, child? No way of knowing until he was briefed. He understood time was crucial and he couldn't stop by the village and make explanations to Tina about why he was about to disappear into the night.

Accepting orders had been easier when he was tucked in the military net of Fort Bragg. A summons like this was expected there. Now?

He had to go. He knew that. But a part of him ached to stay right there in Kirkwood Lake, enjoying Thanksgiving with his family and Tina.

Maybe next year.

He swallowed a sigh and texted back: Love that album, especially While You Were Sleeping.

That meant he'd be on the red-eye as expected. He scribbled a note to his mother, and walked back out the door.

He longed to stay and be part of the festivities, to take his place at the table with everyone else. Share this first beautiful holiday with Tina, thanking God for so many blessings. His time with his father, his time with Tina.

He'd told her that Thanksgiving was tough on soldiers. He'd meant it. Leaving his childhood home right now was one of the hardest things he'd ever done, but he had no choice. Not yet, anyway.

They'd booked him a flight out of Erie. With clear roads he had just enough time to get there and board.

He got back in the car, headed south and grabbed I-86.

And just like that, he was gone.

Chapter Ten

Giddy anticipation lightened Tina's step as she set three pies into the backseat of her car at noon on Thanksgiving. She'd baked fourteen pies in the restaurant kitchen, enough to get them through three busy days of customers. With the success of the park light display in full swing, the *Kirkwood Lady* decked out in brilliant splendor for her cruises around the lake and the influx of customers in the lighted village each evening, preparation was key. Helping Laura made her feel better, like the happy ending to a made-for-TV Christmas movie, where everything comes out all right in the end.

She carried two pies into the Campbell house, ready to celebrate a grand if subdued Thanksgiving with all the Campbell kids in town for the first time in several years. Charlie's illness made for a command performance, but at least they were all here.

She stepped into the kitchen and was immediately grabbed by Max's younger sister, Addie. "It's Thanksgiving for certain. Tina's here and we've got pie!"

"A bunch of them." Tina handed the first pie to Addie, the second one to Cass, Max's other sister, and gave each Campbell daughter a quick half hug. "Can you guys set these on the small sideboard, please? I've got to go grab the caramel Dutch apple from the car."

"I say we take a detour to the fork drawer, grab what we need and follow the sage advice of 'Life's short. Eat dessert first,'" joked Cass.

"I'm in." Addie pulled the pecan/sweet potato pie closer and breathed deep. "Reason enough right here to move back to Kirkwood and have Tina as a roomie. As long as you cook and bake like this we'd be the perfect match, because none of my mother's cooking skills rubbed off on me."

"I had a special request to make that one again." Tina waved toward the pie in Addie's hands as she moved back down the side stairs. "Seth talked it up, and I promised Max he could try it."

"But Max isn't here."

Tina stopped on the short stairway and turned. She shifted her attention from Addie to Cass and back again. "Not here?"

Cass shrugged Max's absence off, which meant Tina was doing a great job of hiding her disappointment. "He got called back."

"Called back?" That couldn't be right. Why would Max get called back into service? He was done, wasn't he? Or at least on leave because of his father's deteriorating condition until his official time was over.

"That's what we're assuming, anyway." Addie's expression said she wasn't all too sure of anything. "Mom said he left a note saying he'd get back as soon as he could and not to worry."

"Which means we probably should worry," added Cass, but then she made a face that said worry and Max went hand in hand. "But this is Max we're talking about, and he always goes his own way."

"And comes out of it with barely a scratch," Addie said as she moved toward the dining room. "Nice trick."

"Tina!" Jenny bustled into the great-smelling kitchen as the girls moved off to the dining room. "You brought the most delicious pies, thank you! Come in, dear, let me take your coat."

Tina hesitated, breathed deep and tried to smile. "I've got to go grab the apple pie. I'll be right back."

"Wonderful," Jenny went on. "I'd really hoped to have everyone here for the first time in years, but Max's call-up changed things. So now my hope is we can re-gather with all the family at Christmas as long as Max is done saving the world."

Saving the world.

Doing his job.

Tina swallowed the lump of disappointment that had taken up residence in her throat.

Max was gone. Without a word. Without a mention. Just…

Gone.

I'm here to stay, home for good, he'd told her.

Not true, obviously.

He'd lied.

Like so many others in the past, people who'd made

promises they hadn't kept. Max had pulled out all the stops to tip her heart in silly, gleeful directions, then left.

She walked to the car feeling partially shell-shocked and habitually stupid. She'd suspected from the beginning, hadn't she? She'd held back from the get-go because she knew Max, and she should be experienced enough to avoid bad-ending entanglements.

She'd messed up, and she didn't want to go back inside and pretend everything was all right. She didn't want to put her game face on and go through a family-filled afternoon that reminded her of how lame her family relationships were. She wanted to jump into the car and drive hard and fast—with the pie, of course—grab a fork and eat the whole thing with a pint of ice cream and watch stupid, lame happily-ever-after movies while she cried.

Except that would make Charlie and Jenny sad.

She didn't do any such thing, because inside the quaint lakeside Colonial was a family who loved her, minus one. A family celebrating what might be their last Thanksgiving with Charlie. A family grounded in faith and love. No matter that Max had done his typical "here today, gone tomorrow" vanishing act while grabbing her heart in his short stint home.

Her fault.

She'd watched him do the same thing from a distance as a teen. She'd longed from afar then, but should have learned her lesson over the years.

For whatever reason, choice, destiny, fate or Providence, the movie-style happily-ever-after eluded her in matters of the heart.

Serving coffee was different, Tina realized as she strode back toward the house, determined to put on a good front.

With coffee, she knew the rules of a good brew, inside out and backward, the friendliness of being the neighborhood barista without getting too close.

Baking? Her mother's artistry in the kitchen bred true. Tina loved creating, finessing and developing great recipes, the kind that make people smile.

Family?

A chasm in her heart tore open again, a rent that should have healed long ago, as she approached the side door.

Family eluded her. Romance crashed and burned around her. She'd thought…

No, she'd hoped—

It would be different with Max. She'd fallen for him hard, and that was as much his fault as hers, because he'd led her on deliberately.

She drew a breath, blinked back tears, planted a smile on her face and walked back inside, determined. Today was Charlie's day. A Campbell holiday, through and through.

And she'd promised to help them through the busy holiday season, but come January?

Brockport or Spencerport, here I come.

Mrs. Thurgood hurried into the hardware store late the following week. "Tina, I had to see you! I've just gotten the lease for the apartment under yours, and I'm so excited to be your new neighbor!"

Tina couldn't deflate the joy on the elderly woman's face by saying she'd be leaving soon. Happiness shone in the widow's eyes, her smile, the very way she walked. She gave Mrs. Thurgood a big hug, then took a step back. "Now, what about moving day? Do you need help, because there are a bunch of us who would be glad to step in. Zach and Luke both have trucks, and Seth's SUV would hold a lot of stuff."

"That's the nice thing," the old woman explained. "The furniture is staying, and I don't think we need a truck for my clothes. I'm not bringing the bulk of my stuff with me. I figure next summer I'll head back to my place and go through everything, clearing things out, donating this, tossing that. It's easier to do when the weather's nice," she added, as if the reason she'd let things pile up was weather-related.

"Sounds good." Tina patted her hand, wishing things could be different, knowing it was impossible. "And I'm happy to come help."

"You're busy enough." Mrs. Thurgood leafed through a few paint chip cards, her gaze sharp. "Mrs. Benson said I should pick out new paint for the living room. If I drop it off at the apartment, her son will paint the walls on his day off and we're good to go."

"Take them out on the step," Tina advised, pointing toward the front door. "The color is more true in natural light. But it's cold out there, so don't take too long to decide."

"I will! That's a right good idea, Tina Marie!" Mrs. Thurgood hurried outside as Sherrie came through the back door, holding a magazine high.

"This book is filled with great nursery ideas."

"Awesome." Tina turned a fake but bright smile her way.

Sherrie looked close, then moved in and looked closer yet. "What's wrong?"

"Nothing." Chin down, Tina accepted a set of wrenches from a customer and ran them through the scanner. "That will be $22.47, please."

"Nothing?" Sherrie made a face, waited until the customer had checked out, then stepped in front of Tina. "What do you mean nothing? Of course there's something wrong, I can always tell, that's why you can't possibly leave because we've got this, this..." She waved her hand back and forth between them. "Connection thing. And it's not right to mess with stuff like that, Tina."

"We do have a thing," Tina admitted, but then she made a face at Sherrie. "And I'm still leaving. I have to, Sher." She drew a deep breath and lifted her shoulders. "But not for a few weeks and we'll get the nursery done first."

Sherrie stared at her, then glanced around the hardware store. She paused, listened, then sighed. "Max is gone."

"I don't want to talk about this."

"When did he leave? And why?"

"He left on Thanksgiving, and I have no idea why. End of conversation," she warned as Mrs. Thurgood bustled back through the front door.

"It is downright cold out there!" Mrs. Thurgood plunked the paint chips down and pointed. "Vanilla

Latte Romance, right there. I think that would be lovely in a living room, don't you, Tina?"

Right now the word *romance* was enough to put Tina over the edge, so she moved to the paint mixer and pried open the can of pastel tint base.

"Of course, it's kind of plain, but I can spruce it up with some pictures, don't you think?"

"Pictures make the room," Sherrie agreed. She looked hard at Tina, but no way was Tina about to bare her soul in front of Mrs. Thurgood, or anyone else for that matter.

"Just one gallon, Mrs. Thurgood?"

"That's what the landlord said, so I'm following directions."

She smiled as she said the words, and when Tina walked the can of paint out to Mrs. Thurgood's car, a middle-aged woman carrying a bag from the local deli raised her brows in approval. "Aunt Elsie, let me put this back here." The woman took the can of paint from Tina and tucked it into the trunk. "We can drop it off at the apartment. You should be ready to move in within a week." She turned toward Tina. "I'm Elsie's niece, Rachel. She told me she needed to make some changes and I came to town to help her."

"Oh, goodie!" Mrs. Thurgood said the words with false enthusiasm, as if none of this was her doing, and yet...she had little choice but to do it.

Tina understood that too well, and was just as annoyed by the sudden turn-around in her own life.

Which is understandable at her age, her conscience berated. *At yours? Ridiculous.*

"It's nice to meet you." Tina stretched out a quick hand to Mrs. Thurgood's niece. "And thanks for coming to town to help Mrs. T. She's a favorite around here."

"Family's important," Rachel replied. She tucked the grocery sack into the trunk and helped her aunt into the front seat. "Have a nice Christmas if I don't run into you again."

"You, too." Tina said the words, but the thought of nice Christmas seemed anathema, and that emotion shamed her. She had a lot to be grateful for, she knew that.

But she'd gotten all tied up and emotional over Max, and having him disappear from her life?

It hurt.

"We need a painting date." Sherrie greeted her as she came through the door, clearly determined.

"Right after Christmas," Tina promised. "Everything slows down that week, even though the park lights are still going then. The store will be quieter and I can sneak away for a day."

"Excellent!" Sherrie hugged her and left.

She placed a call to the Realtor once Sherrie had gone home. "Myra, it's Tina. I think I'd like to take a ride to see those Brockport and Spencerport locations fairly soon, but I don't think I can do it before Christmas. We're shorthanded here at the hardware store, and—"

"No worries!" Myra's voice sounded like so many others, alive with Christmas cheer.

Blech.

"December is pretty much wasted when it comes to

doing deals," Myra explained, "so you go ahead and have a merry Christmas—"

Tina had to hold herself back from explaining the unlikelihood of that possibility.

"And we'll see them in January. That way the hardware store is quieter and I'll have time to make the drive with you."

"You don't think the locations might rent or sell by then?"

Myra's calm offered reassurance. "Well, they could, but it's unlikely. And the way I see it is if it's meant to be, it will be."

"Que sera, sera."

"I love that old movie!" Myra's voice pitched up. "How did you hear about that at your age? It's ancient by today's standards."

"It was a favorite of my mother's," Tina replied. Saying the words made her remember her mother playing the classic movie, loving the suspense of the story, and the melodious tones as Doris Day sang the old lyrics. "She used it as my lullaby when I was little."

"I did the same thing," declared Myra. "The babies loved it, such a sweet song. But most don't know it now."

"I do."

"Call me after Christmas," Myra reiterated. "We'll plan a day in early January, unless things change between now and then."

"They won't. I can guarantee that." Tina said the words with all the finality they deserved.

Myra laughed. "Another thing I've learned over the

years, Tina… You wanna hear God laugh? Tell Him your plans."

Meaning God was in charge, first, last and always.

Tina had a hard time with that scenario. It seemed each time she tried to let go and let God take charge, something went awry. In this instance, that something was the broken heart she'd been nursing since Max had disappeared a week ago.

No call. No word. No email, no text.

Nothing.

As if Max had fallen off the map completely.

His mother had taken it in stride. She was Jenny Campbell, a woman of faith and grace.

Tina?

She wanted to go a few rounds with a punching bag, and not one of those big, heavy body bags, no, sir. The light, hanging-high variety would do, and she'd pummel away at that thing until she wasn't mad or disappointed or sad anymore.

Ever.

She crossed the street near the end of the day and entered The Pelican's Nest through the kitchen door. Han brightened the moment she stepped inside. "It's like old times again! Three nights this week make me so happy!"

"Me, too." She pulled out a clean apron, and began setting plates for orders. "It feels good to be in here, working with you again."

"It feels right because it is right." Wisdom deepened the cook's lined face. "It was wrong to have you gone from this place. I like this better."

Ryan came through the short passage leading from the dining room to the kitchen. He spotted Tina, stopped short and stared, then spun on his heel and walked out.

Tina turned toward Han. "He hates me."

Han shrugged. "He doesn't know what he feels, I think. He spent too much time listening to his father, and all he heard was how you ruined their business, ruined their lives. And you did none of this," Han reassured her as he grated cheese over a fresh pan of lasagna. "But Rocco always needed to blame others. You were an easy target. Now, we can fix this."

He sounded so sure, so certain.

But could they fix things?

Laura came into the kitchen and gave Tina a spontaneous hug. "I'm so glad you're here tonight. I was just going to call you and see if you could come over. We just got a reservation for a senior citizens bus tour. They're coming to see the lights before they do some shopping in the village. Then they're gathering here for a late supper at seven forty-five. I don't think we could manage it without you, Tina."

"Then it's good I'm here."

Laura moved closer. "What's wrong? What's happened?"

"Ryan is rude to Tina and makes her feel bad." Han minced no words. "He needs to be polite to anyone who helps. All of the time."

"You're right," Laura admitted. "I'll talk to him."

"That might make it worse, Aunt Laura." Tina shifted her attention toward the door. "He's already an angry kid. He lost his father six months ago, he's working all the time and doesn't appear to like it—"

Laura acknowledged all that with a nod, but said, "That doesn't give him the right to be mouthy and rude, Tina."

"But that was the example he lived with for so long." Tina scrunched her face and shrugged. "I'm hoping that time will help heal him. That if he's around me, he'll see that I'm not a terrible person."

"This has not worked so far," Han reminded them. "And Tina has been here many days to help. Ryan should be polite to all."

"I agree." Laura turned back to Tina. "The days of our family treating each other poorly are over. And I'll see that my son understands that, Tina."

The back door slammed shut, which meant Ryan had been in the doorway, listening.

Laura's eyes darkened with worry. "When I see the anger in him, it reminds me of his father."

Tina couldn't disagree. "But he looks like my dad, Laura. And there wasn't a kinder, more generous man than Gino Martinelli."

Laura acknowledged that with a look outside toward the cemetery. "I go to their graves sometimes, Tina. To apologize. To beg forgiveness. But it's too late, of course, and they died hating me, thinking I was a terrible person."

"They were angry, yes, especially at first." Tina shrugged and shook her head. "They felt betrayed because they trusted you with the restaurant, with me, and when you let me go, Dad was too sick to do anything about it. So he was sad. But mostly they thought you married the wrong person, and that Rocco wasn't good for you. And I agree. But they never stopped loving you, Aunt Laura, and they did forgive you before they died. And the first thing my father would say if he heard you now?"

Laura lifted her chin, wondering.

"He'd say head over to that church and get right with God. Because He's the only one we ever need to please."

Laura swallowed hard. One hand gripped the other, tight. "I haven't gone to church in a long time."

"No time like the present to start." Tina smiled at her. "If you want, I can go to the early service, then come here on Sunday and you can go to the later one. That way the restaurant is covered and we both have church time. And then I'll work at the festival booths as scheduled."

"It's a very sensible plan," Han told Laura. "How blessed are we to have a church right across the street?"

Laura looked from one to the other. "I'd like to try that, but not this weekend with the festival craziness on top of everything else. Maybe next weekend, okay?"

It was a start. "Good." Tina nodded agreeably as she grabbed two new orders off the wheel. She handed them to Han as she prepped the plates, but she couldn't erase the anguish she'd seen in Ryan's gaze. He wasn't just angry, although that would be bad enough. He looked wretchedly sad, and seeing that look on her young cousin's face broke her heart. She didn't want her presence to deepen his sorrow, but Laura was right. Ryan needed to find some level of acceptance, and she hoped it would be soon.

The night proved to be as busy as Laura had expected and it was late by the time they closed things up. Tina walked home, missing Max, pretending not to, and half dreading the busy Main Street Festival weekend. She'd be up well before dawn, baking in the restaurant kitchen, getting a head start on a frenetic day. No major snowstorms were expected to mess with the festival, and that was a blessing right there.

She approached her door and sighed. She was surrounded by a Christmas village, lit up and sparkling against a thin layer of fresh, white snow, but her little apartment seemed bare.

She'd been running back and forth between the hardware store and the restaurant, barely stopping for breath, leaving no time to make her little apartment festive.

Because you don't feel festive, her conscience reminded her. *You're mad at yourself for falling for Max, you're mad at Max for leaving and you have no real clue what you want to do with your life. Can't we go back to the "let go and let God" idea? Because it was a good one.*

Life without a firm plan? Without a goal? Without a schedule of events?

The very thought made her antsy.

But then she paused with her key in the lock, turned and looked around.

What had all her perfect planning gotten her? An estranged family and a burned-out café.

Despite her devoted scheduling, life had turned the

tables on her. Sherrie's face came to mind. So happy, so excited about the upcoming birth of her son. But she'd sat with Sherrie for long hours after her earlier miscarriages. She'd held her hand, taken long walks and prayed for Sherrie and Jim.

She hauled in a deep breath and scanned the old café site from her stoop.

Life didn't come with guarantees. Maybe, just maybe, she needed to let go more and plan less. She glanced at the clock tower, saw the time and hurried inside to catch some sleep, determined to adopt that mind-set more fully on Monday.

After the insanely busy Main Street Festival weekend.

Chapter Eleven

A tiny *ping* against Tina's window disturbed her sleep. She rolled over, glared at the clock, saw the middle-of-the-night hour and went back to sleep.

Ping! Ping! Ping!

Hail? Freezing rain? A sleet storm?

Her brain pictured and discounted each of those possibilities as she squeezed her eyes shut and thumped the pillow into a better position. The repeated noise came again, sounding like pellets, lobbed against her window. She pried one eye open and peered at the night sky through her front window.

Starlit with a waxing crescent moon.

There was no storm, and barely a cloud in the chill, December sky.

So what woke her? Groggy, she hauled back the covers and crept to the window. Beyond the short space of Overlook Drive, the town lay quiet and still. The main holiday lights of the town-wide Christmas festival went dark at midnight each day, but the arched streetlights of

Main Street still glowed. The white twinkle lights robing the village trees brightened the long, winter night.

All is calm.

All is bright.

Until another rain of pings pulled her to the other window. Careful, she tipped the edge of the curtain swag back to glimpse what was going on.

Max Campbell stood on the sidewalk below, gazing up.

He pegged a few more tiny stones at the glass. She flinched, and that tiny movement gave her away.

"Tina!" He'd spotted her. His voice was a loud whisper, one she intended to ignore.

"Tina Marie..." His voice came again, not quite so softly. Did he know the apartment downstairs was empty, or did he not bother to worry that he might be waking innocent people from a badly needed night's sleep?

Like her.

"Tina, I'm trained at breaking and entering as needed, but I don't want to spend the next five years in jail. Come down and open the door. Please?" He added the last as an entreaty, and if he was trying to be funny, well...he failed. And go downstairs and open the door for him after his little disappearing act that broke her heart into a million Max Campbell-loving pieces?

That wasn't about to happen. Not in this lifetime. She closed the curtain, put in a pair of cheap but effective earplugs and went back to bed.

Morning would begin their two-day festival of fun, food and frolic. Vendors set up heated tents along Main

Street, and the high school opened its doors for cottage-style shops. Homemade pies, breads, jams, scarves, woolens, candles and art… Craftsmen from all over Western New York, Ohio and parts of Canada gathered to sell their varied wares this second weekend before Christmas. In less than two hours she needed to have the restaurant ovens cranking out baked goods. Rainey McKinney was doing the same on the farm, and Lacey Barrett would supply apple fritters, fried apple pies and glazed cider fry cakes.

Knowing how crazy the weekend would be, and how busy her past two weeks had been, the last person she wanted to see right now was Max Campbell.

Untrue, untrue, untrue!

Tina hushed the internal chastisement and curled up under the covers, ready to ignore everything in favor of a few hours of sleep. Whatever Max had been doing, whatever his vitally important role in the world was, she didn't care.

So there.

"Tina."

She turned from the double oven in The Pelican's Nest kitchen when Max called her name the next morning. Her flat expression said she wasn't one bit happy to see him. "You're back."

Her cool tone said his rapid disappearance put them back at square one. He had no choice but to own this guilt. Procedure dictated that he had to follow orders and maintain radio silence, but now he was back, and this time? He was here to stay, even if it took a while to convince her of that.

"Yes." He moved forward, but she waved him back, away from her domain.

"In case you haven't noticed, the entire town is busy this morning because it's day one of our Main Street Festival weekend, so I have a lot to do. In ninety minutes, people will be streaming in from all over. We have shuttle busses coming from the south end of the lake every quarter-hour so we don't over-tax the parking up here. Your mother is running the hardware store—she could probably use a hand there, and as you can see, I'm swamped."

"Tina, I know you're angry with me," he started, but she pivoted sharply, shot him a look and shook her head.

"I'm not. I'm angry with me because I knew better, Max. And that's not your fault, it's mine. I should have left well enough alone. Blame it on sentiment, hormones, whatever you'd like, but I'm over it."

"Over us?" He took a small step closer, encroaching.

"There is no 'us,' Max."

"I disagree."

"Well." She slid one tray of old-fashioned sugared Christmas cakes out of the oven and slid another tray in, set the timer and turned. "It's not up for argument. I'm glad you're around to help your parents. They're definitely more relaxed when you're here, and that's good for both of them. Now if you don't mind—" she indicated the door with a cool glance "—I've got work to do."

The chill in her voice matched her remote expression. He wanted to stay and state his case, but a public forum during a crazy busy morning probably wasn't the best choice.

"I'll see you later, then. And Tina?" He waited until she turned his way once more, her face void of expression. "I didn't have a choice about staying or leaving or talking about my assignment. I couldn't tell you or anyone else what I was doing, and that's how my life's been for the past ten years." He raised his shoulders, hoping she'd understand. "But for the first time ever, I wanted to." He turned and strode out the door, letting it click softly behind him.

He walked across the street to the hardware store, went inside, punched a back room cutting block several times, then sighed.

Tina wasn't just angry.

She was tomboy spittin' mad, and that meant a bouquet of flowers wasn't going to fix this. He'd only done his job, and done it well, but having to disappear when he'd gained her trust betrayed her growing faith in him. Knowing her history, he understood.

But that didn't change the bad timing, and Max's track record didn't gain him any points.

He manned the first floor of the store for the day while most of the action was in the streets of the lakefront town. People milled about, some dressed in Dickensian costume, mobs of families, carolers, and a horse-drawn carriage ride that took people up and around the old cemetery and through the park before bringing them back down into town, ready to shop and eat.

This festival hadn't existed when he was young. The

whole thing was new, busy, saturated with people and goods, and totally Christmas-themed. A huge red-and-green arrow pointed to the back door of the hardware store, emblazoned with the words Jenny's Country Cove. His mother had taken domain up there for the day, because her old-fashioned housewares store was the perfect go-to site for reasonably priced country and Americana-themed gifts. Streams of people came in throughout the day, taking the stairs to the second-story shopping space, buying bags of country-themed items. They'd broken sales records by midafternoon, and that level of business commanded respect.

No wonder Tina was run ragged.

It wasn't just that he was called away at a busy time. He'd left others holding the bag, leaving them to make good on his promises.

A town-wide family festival, a marvelous cooperative endeavor, and the person he most wanted to share it with wanted nothing to do with him.

Mrs. Thurgood stopped by the store an hour before closing time with a small sack of roasted nuts and a little bag of Tina's sugar cakes. "I brought you a treat," she exclaimed. She handed over both bags.

"I couldn't, Mrs. Thurgood," Max protested, but the old woman wasn't about to hear any such thing.

"You can and will," she insisted. "I wanted you to know how much I love the light display in the park. Butch would have loved it, too. He'd be so tickled to have his things out like that! At night, they light up so perfect that I don't think it could be better, Max. And that's what I wanted to talk to you about. You know I'm moving, don't you? This week, actually."

Max shook his head. "I wasn't aware."

"Oh, that's right, you've been gone." Her expression said that had slipped her mind. "Well, I'm moving into the place below Tina's. It's just freshly painted. I used Vanilla Latte Romance from right over there." She pointed to the paint chip display on the far wall. "And Tina's going to help me hang pictures to make it homey."

Of course she was, because Tina was about the nicest, most helpful person on the planet. Not that she realized that about herself.

But Max did. "It will be beautiful, Mrs. T."

"Thank you." She smiled up at him. "But here's the thing. I'd like to donate all those Christmas decorations to the town, if that's okay."

It took a few seconds for Max to get the gist of what she was saying. "All of them? Mrs. T., that's thousands of dollars' worth of decorations and lights. Are you sure you want to do this?"

"Absolutely certain!" Smiling, she reached up to pat his cheek. "You know, you remind me of Butch."

"I do?"

She nodded. "Tallish, broadish, kind of strong and square. My mother used to say he was 'barrel-chested' and that was a good thing in a man. You know, Max..." She looked off to the left for a few seconds, then drew her gaze back to his. "I was real mad when I lost him. Real mad. I was mad at God, at Butch, at the flag, at just about everything that came around. And I could not get over it for the life of me."

"But you did."

"Because your mama came and saw me regular. She'd stop by and bring me a piece of cake or a slice of pie or a dozen cookies, always saying she had this bit left over. Now, no one in their right heads thought anyone raising seven kids had a bite left over, but as she kept doing that, I stopped being quite as angry."

"Time?" Max suggested.

Her expression said yes and no, but her words went further. "Prayer, more than anything. And those little visits, Jenny Campbell stopping by to chat. She never minded the clutter or the dust, she just sat down, happy as could be, and let me talk until one day she grabbed my hand, gave it a squeeze." Mrs. Thurgood wrapped her hand around Max's and pressed lightly. "She said, 'Elsie Thurgood, if any of my boys grow up to be half as tough, faithful and courageous as your Butch was, I will consider myself a success at motherhood.'"

That sounded exactly like his mother. Warm, affectionate and able to look beyond the chaos and the clutter of life.

"When I saw you come home, I knew," Mrs. Thurgood added.

"Knew…what, exactly?"

"That she was right," Mrs. Thurgood declared. "With all the problems in the world, one good man *does* make a difference, Max. A big difference. And I see that man in you, just like your mother saw it in my Butch."

His heart melted.

He'd watched men die. He'd watched as they gave up their lives for their country, fallen in a new kind of war that broke all the rules.

He'd stood at funerals and weddings, he'd held the children and babies of fellow soldiers, but this old woman's words, going beyond the obvious and seeing the heart and soul of the soldier within?

That meant the world. He reached out and hugged her. "Thank you, Mrs. Thurgood. And I do believe I can eat a few of those cakes, after all."

"Well, our Tina made them, and they're worth every penny we pay for them. Such a treat each Christmas!" she exclaimed. "And now if only we could find a way to keep her here..." She slanted a bright look of interest his way.

Max half laughed, half groaned. "That will take some doing. She's not all that happy with me right now."

Mrs. Thurgood waved a hand that said Tina's anger was no big deal. Clearly she hadn't seen the steam puffing out of Tina Martinelli's ears that morning.

"She's been crazy busy for two weeks straight, and what that girl needs is some old-fashioned courting."

"I can't disagree, but in case you haven't noticed, we don't live in or near the courtship capital of the world, Mrs. T." Max swept the view of Main Street a quick glance.

"The *Kirkwood Lady* has their holiday dinner cruise going on," she replied. "And I just happen to have two tickets right here." She stuck two rectangular pieces of cardstock into his hand.

"My father said these were mighty hard to get." Max

tipped a grin down to the older woman as he scanned the printed admissions. "How'd you score these tickets, ma'am?"

"That's for me to know," she sassed back, smiling. "One way or another, you talk our Tina into getting on that boat with you. Nothing like a peaceful dinner for two, surrounded by Christmas lights, to show a woman how you really feel."

"Thank you." He reached out and gathered her into another hug. "This is very nice of you."

She waved it off as if it was nothing, but Max knew better. In a small town like this, folks pretty much knew one another's financial status because they all shared the same nosy mail carrier. Mrs. Thurgood wasn't poor, but she had little put away for old age, and now she had to move out of a home that was already paid-off and into an apartment where she'd have to pay rent, utilities and medical bills?

Max was pretty sure she'd fallen on some tough times. Still, he knew better than to embarrass her. He tucked the tickets into his pocket as a small crowd of customers came down from upstairs while another group went up.

Ryan's obvious misery made Tina sad.

She'd waved it off with Laura, but the reality of the teen's frustration bit deep.

He avoided the kitchen when she was in it. He averted his eyes whenever he could. And when they did make eye contact, he was quick to drop his gaze.

She'd advised time, but his animosity weighed heavy

on her shoulders. Why couldn't they be normal, like the Campbells? Why couldn't they shrug off drama from this day forward and get on with things?

She trudged home at the end of a long day, but when a group of carolers came out of the church parking lot, singing of angels and stars and newborn kings, her attitude softened. Mary and Joseph had faced multiple hardships. They'd done all right.

They believed. They took strength from their faith. Ryan's got no such basis.

She understood what a difference faith made. And while Laura seemed to think coming back to church was a good idea, Tina didn't fool herself that Ryan would willingly tag along. At least the uptick of business at the restaurant kept him too busy to run around with the little gang of troublemakers he'd befriended last summer, and that was a big plus.

She let herself into the apartment, climbed the steps and glanced around.

Her mother's favorite ornaments were carefully layered in big, plastic totes. Her prized collection of village pieces were wrapped and tucked away in similar fashion.

Every other year she'd pulled the totes out and spread the decorations around. This year she hadn't bothered.

Because you're having a pity party? Or because you're just too busy to think rationally?

The former, she decided. The thought shamed her. In a world where so many did without, she was blessed.

She'd unpack those totes tomorrow night, she decided. She'd fill her little place with light and love and laughter, a perfect ending to an amazing weekend. And not once would she think about Max Campbell, working half a block away at the hardware store.

She curled up on the bed and turned out the light, determined to keep Max out of sight and out of mind, but knowing he was back, and wanting to talk with her?

Made forgetting about Max an impossible task.

"Hey, Dad? Wanna take a ride in to check out the park lights with me?" Max wondered aloud a little after eight that night. His father had been at home alone all day, a surefire way to drive the older Campbell stir-crazy. "I want to make sure we don't have any blown bulbs or bad strings and it's easier with two of us."

"It's cold," Jenny warned from the kitchen, but the look she sent Max said she approved the invitation. "Make sure you guys have hats and gloves."

"I'm on it, Mom."

"I'll get my coat." Charlie lumbered from the living room chair, grabbed his thick shearling-lined coat and accepted the hat and gloves from Max with a smile. "Let's get this done."

"You and me."

Max drove into the village, stopped at the edge of the road's descent and sighed.

The town splayed out before him, glorious in the full spectacle of Christmas lights. Beyond the town, Park Road offered a spectacular backdrop of brilliant color. Festive lights ringed the lake, a circle of holiday splendor reflected in the waters below. And along the western shore, the *Kirkwood Lady* cruised quietly on its nightly holiday dinner cruise.

The effect of water, lights and color made for a stunning display.

"I've loved being a part of all this," noted Charlie softly.

Max fought a lump in his throat.

Was this the last time Charlie would see the beauty he helped create?

In God's hands.

Max knew that. He believed it. He understood the frailty of man. But he didn't have to like it.

"We can park up top and walk down the western slope," Charlie suggested. "That way we're not disturbing folks as they drive through the display."

They took the outer road around town, and Max did as Charlie suggested. From this higher vantage point, the lights played out from a new angle, but the only lights he noticed this time were two small squares on Overlook Drive.

Tina's windows, lit from within.

She'd had a long day, and he didn't dare approach her now. Tired and cross weren't the best conditions for heart-to-heart conversations. And her self-imposed timeline gave him a few weeks to wear her down, although it was easier when she was by his side in the hardware store.

She'd be helping there again, once the festival was over. And he'd spotted Tina's name on the church committee to distribute Christmas baskets to needy families the following week, so he'd boldly added his name to the list.

"We've got a bad string here," Charlie announced as they moved through the display.

Max noted the location in his phone.

"And you'll need to fix the reins on the reindeer," Charlie noted. "They're blinking on one side and not on the other."

"Will do."

Taking opposite sides of the narrow park road, they examined the lighting display, away from the stream of cars. Between them they noted two other spots in need of tweaking, but all in all, the lights looked great and they were three weeks into the display.

"Well done." Charlie high-fived Max as they reached the end, but then he took a seat on a tree stump and breathed in and out, not gasping for air, but none too comfortable, either.

"Dad." Max dropped low instantly, concerned. He took his father's hand and gazed into his face. "You okay? Should I get help?"

"Winded is all. Give me a minute. Not used to walking much these days."

Max prayed that's all it was, and when his father's breathing eased, he nodded uphill. "I wouldn't object if you brought the car down here, though. Your mother keeps warning me not to overdo it, then I do exactly that." He slanted a grin to Max, a smile that alleviated some of Max's worry. "Mostly to get a rise out of her because otherwise she's way too bossy."

"I'll get the car."

"I'd appreciate it."

Max hurried up the outside of the lighted display, through the trees. The park show required one-way traffic. That meant Max had to bring the car around the long way. He worried each minute, thinking of his father, out of breath, sitting on a stump, alone at the bottom of the park slope.

When he finally swung into the small parking lot at the park's southern tip, his lights picked up a group of people, hovering around the spot where he'd left his dad a quarter hour before.

Adrenaline surged.

Max bounded from the car and raced up the short incline.

Zach Harrison turned and spotted him. "Hey, Max. It's nice you guys were able to make it over here tonight."

Zach's tone and expression said two things. First, that Max needed to calm down. Second, that everything was okay, and Max was overreacting.

He took a deep breath and walked up to the group, pretending nonchalance. "How we doin'?"

"Good!" The lights to their left brightened one side of Charlie's face, leaving the other side in shadow, but the visible side looked all right. And his breathing sounded normal. Charlie looked up at him, made a face and swept the gathered group a look of pained patience. "The minute someone says the word *cancer*, you can't breathe crooked without everyone sending up a panic flag." He softened his expression and smiled up at Max. "But I'm glad you went to get the car. These treatments might help slow the beast inside, but they slow me down, too." He stood and waved to the lighted park surrounding them. "We did okay, though. Right?"

"It's beautiful, Charlie." One of the guys from the town highway department grinned his approval.

"The best ever," added an unknown woman. "I think these old-fashioned displays really help focus on the spirit of Christmas, the reason we celebrate. I like that it's not a techno-show of lights anymore."

Charlie thumped Max on the back. "That's the kid's doings. When everything fell apart, our soldier got things back on track."

"Great job, Max!"

"Thanks, Max."

"Not bad." Zach fake-punched his arm, only it wasn't all that fake. "And remember, they're giving the trooper exam in February. You've got my vote, Max."

"I appreciate it. I think." Max made it a point to rub his arm. "But right now I'm going to focus on running Campbell's Hardware until Dad feels up to doing it himself. With no more side trips," he promised his father. His commander had made it clear that Max was officially off the books for the remaining few weeks of his current military contract. "You guys are stuck with me."

"Good." Charlie hugged him, and while Charlie had always been a hugger, this embrace felt different. As if he was ready to hand over the reins.

Max hugged him back. While the small crowd dispersed, he and Zach walked back toward the car with Charlie. "How'd you gather the crowd, Dad? Did you fake a heart attack? Call for help? I'm gone fifteen minutes and you managed to throw a party in the woods."

"My fault," Zach admitted. "I was doing a quiet patrol, saw him sitting there and pulled off. Before you know it, folks spotted us and wanted to pull out of line for the lights and talk to Charlie. I think we made Jake Menko's job hard tonight. He's on duty to keep things moving steady."

"Oops." Charlie pretended to look guilty, but failed. "It was kind of nice, seeing folks out here. I spent a lot of nights checking lights in years past. And Max, I mean it when I say this is the best display ever."

Max accepted that with grace. "I'll let Mrs. Thurgood know. She's pretty proud of her son's part in the whole thing."

"A deserving tribute." Charlie shook Zach's hand and climbed into his side of the car. "Thanks for hanging out with me, Zach. Kiss that baby boy for me, would you? And bring him around to see me."

"We will," Zach promised. "He's had a cold, and Piper is insisting we can't make you sick."

"She's right," added Max. "Dad might be ready to take more risks, but tell Piper thanks for being sensible."

"Oh, she's that all right." Zach grinned their way. "Focused, driven, sensible, bossy...and really cute."

"A town trait," Max muttered. He could take each of those words and apply them to Tina, and the fact that she was mad at him meant he needed to campaign in earnest. What better time than Christmas to win true love's heart?

He waved to Zach, backed the car around and exited

the lower end of the park. As he passed Tina's place, her lights blinked off. Two dark windows stared out, mocking him.

Resolute, he hung a right and headed toward his parents' house. He had Tina's table and chair project to finish before Christmas. And once Tina was back to work on Monday, it would be harder to avoid him. In the meantime? He and his men had completed Operation: Mistletoe overseas, a mission that rescued two young women being held hostage by extremists in western Asia. The success of that endeavor said his skills at covert operations ranked high. Now?

He had every intention of launching a successful Operation: Tina much closer to home.

Chapter Twelve

"Tina! How are you doing?" Zach Harrison's sister Julia stopped into the sprawling festival food tent Sunday afternoon. Her two boys, Conner and Martin, gazed around the tent with hungry expressions.

"I'm good, Julia." Looking down, Tina focused on Zach's two little nephews. "And I have a Christmas cake with your name on it, Martin. You, too, Conner. If it's okay with Mom. Have you been good?"

"Very." Martin nodded with the seriousness of a six-year-old. "Conner was kind of a baby over at the ring-toss game because I got more rings on than he did, but then he said sorry." Martin's face said a simple apology didn't quite make up for pitching a hissy fit in public.

Tina fought a smile.

"Well, you took two of my rings, so that made me madder than mad." Conner glared at his older brother, and Tina had the distinct impression that before too long, Martin wouldn't be nipping anything from his younger brother, because Conner had almost caught him in size already, despite their two-year difference.

"Did not."

"Did so."

"Did—"

"Stop. Both of you. Or no cake. Got it?" Julia directed a no-nonsense expression their way, a look that said the boys better shape up.

They did.

"Here," she said as she handed over a deep box to Tina. "I was told to give this to you."

"Because?"

Lacey Barrett began to help the next customer in line, giving Tina a moment to step aside. She opened the box, stared inside, then turned, puzzled. "It's a crèche."

Julia nodded. "From the Holy Land."

"Olive wood." Tina grazed a finger across the burnished wooden surface, confused. "But who?" Tina hauled in a deep breath as realization hit. "Max."

"The man certainly has good taste," Julia noted as Lacey handed each of the boys a tree-shaped sugar cake. "I saw it on display at the high school, and then Max stepped up to the vendor, quiet and calm, plunked down a fistful of money and said, 'This is the kind of Nativity set a family hands down for generations.'"

A family hands down for generations.

Tina's heart pinched tight.

Family. Her small family, mending. Maybe?

His family, so strong, so loving, being torn by serious illness. And Max, sending her a beautiful, touching gift of Christmas, a hand-carved Nativity from the very land Jesus trod long ago.

"I think you like it." Julia smiled and Tina flushed.

"It's stunning. It's…" Words failed her.

"It's the kind of gift a man gives a woman he loves," Lacey noted once her customer left with a small box of apple fritters and two tins of cakes. "Looks like someone is staking a claim, Tina."

"Or has too much time and money on his hands," she replied, but the old-world glow of the polished wood called to her.

Was she being too stubborn, not letting him talk, unwilling to listen? Weren't these the traits that got her family into trouble? The long silences, holding grudges, stepping back?

A clutch of people came in, and business stayed steady the rest of the afternoon. By day's end, when the last of the baked goods had been sent to the homeless shelter in Clearwater, Tina was bone tired. The short walk home, carrying the box holding the beautiful carved Nativity, gave her a few minutes to think. To pray.

She was stubborn as a mule sometimes.

The gift in her hand reminded her of Mary's willingness to say yes to God. A young woman, asked to do the impossible, to carry the Son of God.

Mary said yes and changed history.

Let not your heart be troubled...

The promise in John's Gospel offered eternal life, but asked for belief. Was she careless in her belief? Did she voice it, but not live it?

Sometimes.

That thought troubled her, and as she moved up the walk, her gaze was drawn to her entrance into the house.

A thick fresh wreath decorated her door. Festooned with bright red ribbons, clusters of berries and white twigs, the wreath looked like Christmas and smelled like a fresh walk in a piney wood.

A card hung from the wreath, and Tina pulled it out, then stepped closer to the light. "It's always more fun to come home to a cheerful door. Merry Christmas, Tina. With love, Max."

She scanned the area, half hoping he'd be there.

He wasn't.

She placed her hand against the lush wreath, bright and welcoming, the velvet-soft scarlet bows nestled against spiny evergreen.

Traditions.

A traditional wreath.

A traditional Nativity.

Could he be wanting the very same thing she craved? A new normal with her? A chance to begin a new branch of the Campbells?

She went inside, climbed the steps and pulled out her phone, then hesitated when the screen flashed on.

She needed to be sure. Not about her own feelings. His disappearing act made her quite aware of how hard she'd fallen, how much she cared about Max Campbell.

What she needed more than anything was to be sure of *him*. And that required a little more thought and probably more prayer.

She reopened the crèche box, dusted a small side table and set up the beautifully glossed wooden Nativity.

Timeless and prayerful, the image of that first cold Christmas touched her heart. Mary had said yes to a contentious request, then Joseph vouched for her when he could have turned his back and walked away.

He hadn't. He'd trusted. He'd believed.

And that was something Tina needed to do more fully.

Max smoothed his palm over the finished patio tables, satisfied.

They'd been knocked around in the fire at Tina's cafe. Not burned, just singed, but smoke and water damage had joined forces against them. He'd dried them out, sanded them down and applied fresh summer-toned paint to each one.

He'd variegated the chair spindles, mixing and matching yellows, greens and blues, until the final cheerful effect saluted nice weather and waterside dining.

Would Tina love them?

He hoped so. More than that, he wanted her to have a piece of the business she'd worked so hard to build. Something tangible to show her investment of time and effort.

Four tables and sixteen chairs, a salute to her café. And to her. If she forgave him long enough for him to give them to her.

He glanced up at the clock, disappointed.

He'd hoped for a phone call tonight.

He knew Julia had presented Tina with the glossed

wooden Nativity. He'd gotten her Mission accomplished! text late that afternoon while he'd finished the last of Tina's chairs.

And Tina would have discovered the wreath he'd fastened to her door a few hours ago.

Still no word.

Stubborn? Or wary?

Both, his brain reminded him. *With good reason. She's been hurt before and doesn't have a whole lot of reason to trust people lately. Take it slow.*

The reminder hit home, but the last thing Max wanted right now was slow. He craved the dream he saw before him, just out of reach.

Tina. A home. A family. A dog. Maybe two dogs.

He grinned as Beezer nudged open the door of the garage workroom. "Hey, old guy."

Beeze yawned, eyed the chairs, then yawned again.

"Time to head in?"

The dog's head bobbed in understanding, his tail beating a quick rhythm against the table leg.

Max led the way out, turned to shut off the light and gave the tables one last look.

Beautiful. Bright. Winsome. Like their owner. Now, if he could wear her down enough to bring joy back to those pretty gray eyes?

He'd be a happy man.

"When's Tina due in?" Earl asked Max shortly after noon.

In forty-two minutes and twenty-nine seconds.

Saying that would make him sound more desperate than a guy should ever admit to, so Max shrugged. "She's on the schedule for one o'clock."

"Then I'll wait and take my lunch once she gets here." Earl lifted a box of parts and carried it to the repair area in the back room. "I'll break down Dan Hollister's snowblower in the meantime. Darn fool things cost an arm and a leg, then don't work when you need them most. I'm a plow man," he advised Max, and let the door swing shut behind him.

I'm a plow man.

Max grinned.

He'd been away from country-speak too long. Military conversations tended toward concise speech, rarely more than was needed. Right now he wanted time to pass quickly, counting the minutes until Tina walked through that door.

The store was atypically quiet. His mother had predicted that the rush of weekend shopping would give them a day or two of quiet time to recover, and Max busied himself with reorganizing the upstairs shelves. Displays had been jumbled over the hectic weekend, and his mother's life would be easier if she could walk upstairs with her little scan gun later that day and order new stock automatically. Her task would be simplified if everything was back in order.

"Max?"

Tina's voice, behind him. He turned slowly, tamping emotion when what he really wanted to do was grab her up, kiss her like crazy and set a wedding date for soon.

Very soon.

Stifling rampant emotions, he faced her. "I didn't hear you come in."

She shifted her gaze to the wide country stairs. "I just wanted you to know I'm downstairs. That way you can finish up whatever you need to do up here."

Polite. All business. Matter-of-fact. But he didn't miss the fact that she had actually come upstairs to deliver the message when she could have simply called out from below.

And that slight difference meant Tina Martinelli was maybe yearning—just a little—to see him.

The realization put him instantly in a brighter mindset than he'd been minutes before.

He stepped forward, crowding her space. "Excellent."

She moved to go back down, but Max blocked her with an arm against the near wall. "That's it?"

"Yes." She gave him a look that said he might be wise to move his arm.

He had no intention of doing any such thing. "Really?" He edged closer, just close enough to see his breath ruffle her short hair. Close enough to watch her eyelashes flutter as she dipped her gaze. "Nothing else you want to say to me, Tina Marie?"

"Probably nothing that won't end up with me in jail. Men that take off for weeks without even the courtesy of a simple farewell or a note that says 'see you soon' don't deserve a lot of leeway when they finally show up again."

He acknowledged her words in a straightforward fashion. "The army's pretty tight on the 'need to know' rule. They called me up on coded orders with radio silence. If I could have said goodbye, I would have. I promise."

She scowled, but her frown didn't look quite as intense as it had three days ago, and right now he'd take any hints of improvement he could get. "How about allowing me to make it up to you? I have tickets to the hottest gig in town and there's no one else I'd rather spend Saturday evening with than you, Tina."

"We have a hot gig in town?" Her arched brow said he must be thinking of another town because the terms "hot gig" and "Kirkwood" weren't exactly synonymous.

He grinned. "The *Kirkwood Lady.* Six-o'clock departure, a three-hour cruise with dinner, dancing and Christmas lights."

"How'd you get hold of those? They were sold out months ago."

"Well-connected." He hiked his brows to underscore his words.

He saw her weakening resolve when she lifted her eyes to his. "I have to help deliver Christmas baskets Saturday morning, then I'm working here in the afternoon."

"There may have been a slight schedule change," he replied. "I'm helping deliver the baskets, too, so Mom said she and Luke could take care of the store all day. That way you and I have a day off together."

"You rearranged my schedule for me?" She stood as tall as a five-foot-two woman could and glared up at him. "What makes you think you can do that, Max Campbell?"

He smiled. "Because my mother loves both of us and

wants nothing more than to see us happy. If that means giving you some time off so I can court you properly, she was all for it."

"Max—"

"We don't have to hash everything out now." He stepped back, giving her an out. She wasn't in a big hurry to take it, but then a customer came through the parking lot door, which meant Tina had to go back down. She started down, paused and glanced back up. Her over-the-shoulder look said he'd made up some serious ground, and that was something to be thankful for. "We've got time, Tina."

Max said they had time.

Did they? Tina wondered on Tuesday afternoon.

They did if she gave up the idea of investing her eventual insurance money somewhere else in January.

She pulled on her hat and gloves, tugged on her warm coat and walked through the park. The displays weren't nearly as eye-catching in the daylight. The combination of merry lights and darkness made them pop each evening, but strolling through them, seeing the work and time the men had put in, made her nostalgic for Kirkwood and she hadn't even left yet.

What is it you want?

She knew that answer straight off. To be happy.

What's stopping you?

Her first instinct was to list the bad things that had happened to her, but then she mentally grabbed a hold of her herself.

The only thing stopping her from grasping hold of happiness right now was her.

She turned and studied the village streets below. The snow had melted, and the dry pavement looked out of place for December, but the full parking lots, the sight of people moving here and there, a town alive with Christmas…

She loved that.

She raised her gaze to The Pelican's Nest.

She didn't just like working in her father's old kitchen. She loved it. She loved partnering with Han, the familiarity of old recipes, the connection to her parents, though they were now gone. But in their old restaurant, surrounded by childhood memories, she felt as if they were with her still.

She stared at the aging building.

It needed help, and Laura had no money. The whole place could use a good makeover, but Tina understood the downward dip of midwinter business. Laura was worried that she wouldn't be able to hang on until the busier spring season, and Tina agreed. It took a busy spring, summer and fall to make up for long, cold winters.

What if you combine forces?

The thought scared and elated her.

Would Laura think she was nuts? Would she even entertain such an idea?

Tina puffed out a breath. It frosted instantly, a tiny cloud of white, drifting upward.

May our prayers rise up like incense before You…

The frozen breath reminded her of that sweet, old prayer. Could she make this step forward? Should she?

God did not give us the spirit of timidity, but a spirit of power, of love and of self-discipline.

Timothy's verse hit home. Yes, she had a tendency to charge forward. Act first, regret later.

But this? Approaching her aunt about a partnership? This could be the full circle she'd yearned for. Faith. Family. Forgiveness.

She threaded her way through the park displays and headed toward the restaurant. It would be quiet now, a good time to catch Laura. She walked in, ready to present her idea, and found Laura in tears.

"What is it? What's wrong?" Tina crossed the few feet quickly. Laura snatched up the restaurant phone in one hand and shoved a piece of paper at Tina with the other. While she dialed 9-1-1, Tina scanned the brief note.

Mom, I've thought about this a lot and I know you'd be better off without me. I'm not a good person, not anymore. I'm sorry, Mom. So sorry. I love you, and I'll miss you, but this is the only choice I have left. I've been trying to get better, but nothing's working. Please forgive me, okay? —Ryan.

The chill of Ryan's words froze Tina's heart. She didn't wait to hear more.

There was only one person she knew who could figure out how to get to her young cousin and save him. And that was Max Campbell.

"Max!"

The desperation in Tina's voice brought Max running from the front of the hardware store. "What's happened? What's wrong? Is it Dad?"

She shook her head, eyes wet, a scrap of paper clutched in her left hand. "It's Ryan. He's going to kill himself, Max."

Mixed emotions climbed Max's spine. He scanned the paper, grabbed Tina's hand and raced across Main Street to the restaurant.

One look at Laura's face said she believed her son was capable of keeping his promise. "Laura, do you know where he might be?"

She shook her head.

"Has anyone checked the house?"

Again she shook her head, her voice struggling for words. "I was just there. I left Carly here to make salads for tonight—" she nodded toward the afternoon waitress "—and ran home for a few things. When I got back here, I found the note."

"You didn't see him, Carly?"

The middle-aged woman shook her head. "Not a peep. I'm sorry, maybe if I'd seen him—"

He'd gotten a forty-minute start. Where could a kid go in forty minutes? A kid who didn't drive?

Max's phone rang. He started to ignore it, but then he saw Luke's number. He answered quickly, staring at Laura while his brother spoke, then nodded, grim. "We'll be right there."

Fear claimed Laura's features. She reached forward and grasped his hands. "It's Ryan, isn't it? What's happened?"

"He's on the interstate bridge, threatening to jump,

but Luke says he's hanging on for dear life and that's a good sign. Let's go."

They piled into Max's car. He drove quickly, following the curve of Lower Lake Road. The bridge came into sight once they rounded the point at Warrenton. A full contingent of lighted rescue vehicles said first responders were on-scene in full crisis mode.

"Max. Laura. Tina. Good." Zach Harrison moved forward, his expression taut. "He's scared, he's shaking and I think he's getting tired, which means his grip could slip."

"Let me talk to him," Laura insisted. "I think I can—"

"He wants you." Zach looked beyond Laura to Tina. "He says he needs to talk to his cousin Tina."

"Me?" The idea that Ryan wanted to talk to her during his crisis seemed ludicrous. The kid hated her. "Zach, I—"

"Tina. Please." Laura turned her way. "If he wants to talk to you, then please..."

"But—" Tina looked at Max. He met her gaze and shifted his to Ryan, standing on the bridge's narrow edge.

Max wanted her to do it. And she trusted him to understand a crisis situation. Crises were his forte, weren't they? *God, don't let me mess this up. I don't know what to do or what to say, and I don't even know this boy. Help me. Please. Give me words.*

She started forward, then a flash of inspiration hit. She turned back. "I need you two with me."

Max's wince said that might not be a good idea, but Tina stood still, adamant. "Laura is his mother, and

Max, no one is better skilled at emergency situations than you. Please."

The trooper commander hesitated, then nodded his okay.

Max moved to Tina's right. Laura flanked her on the left. Quietly, the three of them moved forward.

Strong emotion twisted the boy's face when he saw them. He stared at his mother, then at Tina, and began to cry.

Laura's face crumpled.

Max was just about to call a retreat when Tina took a seat on the cold, hard bridge. "I'm here, Ryan. Ready to talk. But it's wicked cold, there's sleet in the forecast, and I'm scared that you can't hang on much longer, so do me a huge favor, okay? Climb back to this side. Have a seat. And we'll talk about whatever is going on, but I need you to be safely on this side of the bridge or I honestly won't have a clue what's being said, because I'll be worried to death about losing my only cousin. I have two relatives left, kid. You and your mother. I'd like to grow old with both of you, if you don't mind."

His eyes widened as her words registered.

He stared at her, then his mother, then Max.

Max appraised the situation. He wasn't close enough to make a grab for Ryan, and Tina's action would spawn some sort of reaction. But would it be the reaction they wanted? Needed?

God, I know You're there, I know You're with us, and right now, I could use some of that spiritual common sense I'm usually so proud of. Because here, at this moment, with the approaching storm pumping up waves on the lake?

I'm scared.

Ryan gulped. His fingers moved. He studied each hand, contemplating his choices. Moving slowly, Max and Laura lowered themselves to the ice-cold bridge deck and faced him, waiting.

"It's your turn." Tina met the boy's gaze and didn't mince words. "Climb on over here and let's talk. Are you okay to climb back over, Ryan? Because if your hands are cold and you need help, we'll help you."

Max decided then and there that if he ever had a need for a negotiating team in his future, Tina would be on it. Her eyes, affect and tone stayed calm and neutral, offering the kid the lifeline he needed.

Ryan stared at her, gripped the rail tighter, then pushed up. One leg came over. At the top of the rail, he faltered, and for a long series of seconds, he looked like he might fall, but then he pushed down hard against the railing and brought his second foot up and over.

Max's heart soared.

This tiny leap of faith said Ryan didn't really want to die. What did the boy want?

Max had no idea.

"Thank you." Tina nodded toward the bridge deck. "It's cold, but it's the best I've got, kid. So what's going on? What's got you this upset that you're thinking about throwing away God's most precious gift? Because frankly, Ryan, that would break my heart."

"You."

Tina's steadfast expression faltered, but not for long. "Because I've been helping your mom?"

He stared at her. Guilt and anguish fought for his features as he faced Tina straight on. Max looked from him to Tina and back, then spoke softly. "Did you burn Tina's café down, Ryan?"

Ryan's face shadowed deeper. Tears streamed down his cheeks. His mouth crumpled and his jaw went slack. "I was with the guys who did it." He leaned forward after the admission, crying, his narrow back shaking with cold and remorse. "I didn't mean for them to burn it down, I thought they were just messing around. I knew Mom was running out of money and I thought—" He choked back a sob, then swiped a damp glove across his face. "I thought everything that happened was Tina's fault."

"Oh, Ryan." Laura's face reflected Ryan's anguish. "Honey, I—"

"Don't tell me it's okay." Ryan's voice rasped harshly. "I could have done something. I could have called the fire department, I could have tried to put it out, I could have…" He drew a deep breath and sighed, then shifted his attention back to the water. "Done something. But I didn't. I ran home, went to bed and acted surprised the next day. And then Tina turns out to be a real nice person and I ruined her life."

Tina started to speak, but Max held up a hand. "May I?"

She nodded. "Please."

He faced Ryan more fully. "My best friend died when I was eighteen."

Ryan met his eyes, listening.

"I was with him that afternoon. He'd been drinking. Acting stupid. I knew he was drunk, I knew his girlfriend had been drinking and I was mad that they were being so foolish. I got disgusted and left." He hauled in a breath and shrugged. "It made me so mad that years of friendship were being washed away by a bottle of vodka, and I stormed off. I could have called his mother. I could have told his father." He shook his head. "I didn't. I went home, went to bed and the next morning I found out my buddy Pete and his girlfriend had been killed in a boating accident while I was sleeping. For nearly fifteen years I've carried that weight with me, Ryan. Wishing I'd called someone, alerted someone. Wishing I'd made better choices, but you know what?"

Ryan kept his eyes locked on Max. "What?"

"Here's the amazing thing about life. We generally get a second chance. And if we make the most of that opportunity and learn from it, we can turn the bad into good. But—" he directed a look toward the roiling water slapping against the cold, gray bridge "—not if we're dead, kid. Yeah, you shouldn't have spouted off about Tina, and you could have made better choices along the way, but when I went to see Pete's parents they reminded me of something. They said kids make mistakes because they're kids and that God understands kids better than anyone else. He knows they're a work in progress."

Reality broadsided Tina as she listened to Max's story.

Ryan and his gang had burned down her café. He and his buddies deliberately set a fire to destroy her business in an attempt to destroy her, to make her leave Kirkwood Lake.

Anger and regret vied for attention. Her hands clenched, envisioning the group of miscreants, torching ten years of hard work and dedication.

But Ryan's look of abject sorrow pushed her beyond outright anger.

He'd lived in a house surrounded by mistruths and slander. He'd been raised to think she was the enemy. And in a way, an in-your-face move like putting her coffee shop in the shadow of The Pelican's Nest made her the enemy.

She reached out a hand to Ryan.

He stared at it, then her.

"Ryan, we can't change the past. But together?" She swept his mother a look then returned her attention to Ryan. "We can run a wonderful business. But a family business should be run by family, kid. And more than anything else, once we get things squared away, I want you in. You. Me. Your mother, running the restaurant the way it should be run. What do you think?"

Laura held her breath while Max watched quietly. Ryan stared at Tina, then his mother. Disbelief shadowed his face, but then he started to creep forward, the cold, slippery bridge and his chilled limbs fighting the action. He made it over to them, and then clasped Tina's hand, tears still streaming down his young cheeks. "I think yes."

She clutched his hand, then pulled him in for a hug that Laura shared.

Max cleared his throat. "Why don't we head back?

It's cold out here, and we've got a lot of good people who probably want to go home. Or at least climb back into their warm cruisers."

"You're smarter than you look, Max." Zach smiled at Max as he and Luke approached them. He led Laura and Ryan to a waiting ambulance that took Ryan to Clearwater Hospital for a mental health evaluation.

Tina and Max followed in Max's car.

Deep compassion for Max filled Tina, heart and soul.

Ryan's jaw had softened as he listened to Max's story. Max's confession had turned the boy's expression from grief-stricken to almost hopeful.

She looked at Max, really looked at him, and realized she'd judged him unfairly for years.

He'd shouldered unnecessary guilt a long time. How tough it must have been, living beneath a self-imposed cloud, wearing a mantle of blame. No wonder he avoided the Sawyers and stayed away.

Coming back must have been torturous, but Max did it because he knew his parents needed him. Their need trumped his badly placed guilt.

Her heart stretched wider, watching him.

She'd misjudged him. She'd taken what she saw as a kid and mushroomed it into undeserved resentment. And in spite of that he'd been nothing but kind to her. Gracious. Caring.

Loving?

Regret speared her because she'd cut him down pretty thoroughly since he returned from his final mission. And a man like Max, brave, daring, charismatic and caring, deserved someone who didn't make rash assumptions. Someone who could stand up to the test of time, not turn tail and run.

Seeing him here, in action, baring his heart to save a young man's life, she felt pretty undeserving of the brave and true soldier to her right.

But—

If given the chance again?

A tiny spark of warmth inside allayed the bitter cold metal beneath her, because if Max was willing to give her one more chance at that gold ring of love?

She'd never be foolish about taking it for granted again.

Chapter Thirteen

"Well." Max shoved his hands into his pockets while they waited for Laura in the hospital lobby. Ryan would have to pass a short series of psychological tests to prove he wasn't a threat to himself or others, but then he'd be free to come home.

Tina looked up at Max and patted the seat beside her. "You could sit."

"Sitting makes me antsy."

"And yet you sat on that bridge today, looking like you weren't freezing from the ground up and like you had all the time in the world."

"Just following a good example." He slanted a smile down to her.

"I was scared to death," she admitted. She reached up and shoved her hair back behind her ears. "My knees were knocking, my hands were shaking and all I could think was that the minute I opened my mouth, he'd know I was more afraid than he was. Only, you know what?"

Max raised one beautiful, thick, dark brow.

"All the fear disappeared the minute I started to talk to him. It was like God heard my fear and dissolved it. I felt..." She groped for words, then shrugged. "Like a peaceful blanket got laid on my shoulders. Weird, right?"

"Not weird. God."

God.

Calming her. Helping her. Laying peace on her heart.

A rising trust swelled within her. Trust in God, in His path, in His timing.

"You were amazing out there, Tina. When you sat down and challenged him, I wasn't sure what he was going to do, but you made all the right moves. I was so proud of you."

Her heart melted at his words, his expression. "Max, I didn't know that stuff about you and Pete that day. I knew you were there, but no one ever let on that Pete and Amy were drinking. And I thought you were a jerk for never coming around again."

He shrugged like it was no big deal, but Tina read his eyes. She stood, crossed the small space between them and reached up to kiss his cheek. "I'm sorry I doubted you. And I'm sorry you carried that guilt around for all those years. It broke my heart to hear you talk about it."

He sighed, staring off, then shifted his attention back to her. "It's taken me a long time to face what happened that day. I've avoided coming home, I've avoided the water, I've avoided my family, all because I let guilt eat me alive. It was stupid." He waved off Tina's protest with an easy hand. "Hey, it's better now, so I can admit it was stupid to let it go so long, and that's why I'm so glad Ryan came clean. Because guilt makes for a real lonely partner in life."

Laura's approach halted their conversation. She reached out and hugged Tina, then Max. She wasn't crying. In fact, she looked strong, able and energized, more so than Tina had ever seen in the past. "I think he's going to be fine."

"Yes?"

She nodded to Tina, then motioned both of them to sit. They did. Laura leaned forward and clasped Tina's hands. "I need to apologize to you."

"Laura, I—"

Laura gripped her hands tighter. "Let me say this. I know you and I have made progress, but Tina, our actions, mine and Rocco's, messed up more than our business. They messed up our son and ruined your café. Forgive me, please. Forgive us. And when you do that?" She offered Tina a small smile of entreaty. "I have a huge favor to ask of you."

Faith. Family. Forgiveness. Tina squeezed her aunt's hands. "Yes, I forgive you, and I'd like you to do the same for me. Resentment and revenge aren't good examples, either. Now, go for it. Tell me what you need, because that's what family is for."

"Take over the restaurant so I can take care of my son."

It took Tina several seconds to register Laura's request. "Laura, I—"

"Ryan's going to need some time, some therapy, and he needs to have a hands-on parent. More than he's had the past several years because, even before his father died, we were too busy working to do right by our son.

On that bridge today I prayed, Tina. I prayed for the first time in a long time, and I told God I'd make better decisions if He gave me a second chance."

"And he did." Tina squeezed her hands lightly, understanding.

"Yes. So I know it's a lot to ask, and you probably think I'm crazy."

"First, you're not crazy at all, and I can totally see the Holy Spirit at work in this whole thing and I'm never going to question His timing or methods again."

"Huh?" Laura looked from her to Max and back.

"I was coming to the restaurant this afternoon to see if you'd like to become partners."

Laura's jaw dropped open. "You were?"

Tina nodded. "I'd been praying about my choices, and I realized that I'm happiest here, in Kirkwood Lake, working in a kitchen. So why not do it in your kitchen? The place where I grew up?"

"Are you serious?"

Tina sent a teasing glance to Max before bringing her attention back to Laura. "I'm generally way too serious, it seems, but in this instance, serious is good. So what do you think? We could partner up, you get more time off, and we build a café corner on the west end of the restaurant with my insurance money?"

Laura gripped her hands. "The best of both worlds."

"For both of us."

"Oh, Tina." She grabbed Tina in a big hug, a hug that said home and family and forgiveness rolled into one beautiful embrace. "This is perfect. I'll have time with Ryan and an income."

"And I don't have to move." She tipped a quick look toward Max, wondering what he thought of all this. Would he be delighted to have her in Kirkwood or had she totally ruined the beautiful chance at love he offered?

He stood. "Laura, are you staying at the hospital?"

She nodded. "Yes. Until they release him. I want him to know that I'll be by his side as long as he needs me."

He faced Tina more directly. "Then we better get going, because you have a restaurant to open in the morning."

Tina gave Laura one last hug. "Don't worry about anything and keep your cell phone charged in case I have questions. We'll have a lawyer draw up the legal stuff after Christmas, so for now, just relax and take care of Ryan."

"I will. And Tina? Max?"

They turned as they headed for the door.

"I don't know how to thank you enough."

Max met her gaze. "Right back at ya. Good night, Laura."

A crazy but fun week, Tina decided as the dinner rush wound down on Friday evening.

Max and Earl had pretty much taken over at the hardware store, Seth's daughter Tori was going to help there on weekends, and Tina and Han had been running The Pelican's Nest for several days. She'd planned menus, logged orders and checked food quality as vendors made deliveries to the kitchen door, loving every minute. The best part?

She felt like she'd come home after a long time gone.

She hooked the clean pots into place as Ryan walked into the kitchen. "Tina?"

She turned, surprised, because she hadn't seen him since they'd released him from the mental health evaluations a few days before. "Hey."

He came forward, a little nervous, but not stricken, and that was a huge improvement. "You look better."

He rolled his eyes as if that was an understatement. "I feel better. A lot better. Would it be all right with you if I came back to work?"

"Oh, my gosh, yes!" She grabbed his hands. "Yes, please! I missed you like crazy tonight, we were slammed from five o'clock on. It was downright insane for a couple of hours."

"You don't mind me being here?"

This time she stepped over the personal boundary lines and hugged her cousin for the second time since he was a preschooler, riding his Big Wheel up and down the driveway of his house. "I will absolutely love having you here. Family business means just that, Ryan. Family."

Laura stepped in behind him. She smiled at Han behind Tina, then clasped Ryan's shoulder. "We were just discussing that, and how we want this place to be like it used to be. The kind of spot that welcomes travelers and boaters and locals. Where everyone feels at home."

Her words reflected Tina's memories. Her parents had forged a delightful business just that way, by welcoming all who came through their doors. "When can we sit down and write up a schedule?"

"Monday," Laura answered. "I know you've got things going on tomorrow, so Ryan and I are going to work with Han and the girls to cover things, and then we'll go to the later service on Sunday if you can come over here after the early service and relieve us."

Laura and Ryan, going to church. Spending time together, rekindling faith. Planning with her as they reconstructed a Martinelli family business. Joy soared inside her. "That would be great. You sure you don't need me tomorrow?"

Laura smiled and shook her head. "Last I heard you were helping at the church—"

"In the morning," Tina countered.

"And then tomorrow night you have a date," Laura finished. "Max wanted to make sure things were covered here so you couldn't cancel on him."

"He said that?"

Laura grinned as she turned to go. "I believe his exact words were 'It took me weeks to get her to actually accept a date with me. Let's not give her a window of opportunity to wiggle out of it.'"

That sounded exactly like Max. Quick, funny and blatantly honest.

She turned the key in the lock a few minutes later, waved goodbye to Han and turned back to Laura and Ryan. "I'll see you guys Sunday morning. And thank you both for making tomorrow night possible."

Ryan waved it off as if it was no big deal, but Laura grabbed Tina in a big, motherly hug, then stepped back and cradled Tina's cheeks in her hands. "Have fun, okay?"

A day off. A day with Max. A day to help others with Christmas and then relax as the *Kirkwood Lady* trolled the lake's perimeter, listening to Christmas music and eating fine food.

Her heart did a silly skip-jump in her chest as she returned Laura's hug. "I will."

"On the eighth day of Christmas, my true love gave to me…" Max intoned the old carol as they delivered the last boxes and baskets for the day. He climbed into the front seat of the church van and kept right on singing.

"You're really starting to get into this small-town Christmas stuff," Tina teased. "I expect this Christmas is quite different from last year's holiday."

Max considered that as he turned up Lower Lake Road. "Last year I was stashed in a Middle Eastern bunker, pretending to negotiate the release of accused political prisoners who were actually bargaining chips on a badly skewed administrative gaming table."

"Did the negotiations work?"

Max sent her a "what do you think?" kind of look. "They rarely do."

"Max." She leaned closer, almost kissably close, and laid her hand on his arm. "I'm sorry."

He shook his head. "Don't be. We got them out. Over the years I've learned that negotiating with terrorists generally falls under the 'no positive outcome' scenario. So we learned to go in and spring folks on our own."

"You rescued them?"

He nodded. "Safe and sound. One of them got married six months later and last I heard they're expecting their first child, a daughter, in about four months."

"Max." Tina tightened her grip on his arm. "That's wonderful."

He shrugged off the praise. "Just doing my job, Tina." He got out and walked her to her door, even though she argued that he shouldn't. "I'll see you tonight. I'll be here for you about quarter to six, okay?"

"Yes."

He looked down at her and let the intensity of his gaze wish for a kiss, but then he smiled, winked, stepped back and moved to the car.

It took every bit of willpower she had to not run after him and demand a kiss. The only thing that held her back was sheer and total embarrassment.

But the thought of kissing Max, of having an evening with him in a romantic setting, put her pulse in high gear.

The hours dragged on forever.

She tried reading, then ended up throwing the book across the room. She turned on the TV, knowing there was a weekend-long Christmas movie marathon on her favorite inspirational station, but seeing the happy glow on the heroine's face made the afternoon seem way too long.

She dressed with care and was ready impossibly early. That way she had plenty of time to wonder if her sour attitude had ruined whatever chance she and Max had.

He's taking you on a cruise tonight, her inner voice

scoffed. *I think he's making all the right "I'm still interested" moves.*

She wanted to believe that, but did her overreaction mess things up? Then and there she decided that if Max was still interested…and she prayed he was… she'd work harder to be the best partner he could find, a loving and committed wife.

The doorbell rang.

Max.

She stood, slipped on her coat, scarf and gloves and moved to the stairs. The boat would be warm, but the walk over? Another thing entirely. She went down the steps, opened the door and paused, then sighed. Max stood in full dress uniform, looking way too handsome, strong and commanding. "You clean up nice." She tried to keep her words casual but he read the expression on her face and grinned.

"When a guy's working overtime to impress a pretty girl, he's got to pull out all the stops."

"About that?" She turned once she pulled the door shut behind her and faced him square, ignoring the chill breeze off the water. "I'm impressed enough, Max. Just the way you are."

His smile deepened, and he leaned in, brushed a too-light kiss to her mouth and held out his arm. "That's good to hear, but for tonight, you still get the full deal. Mrs. Thurgood assured me that's the best way to a girl's heart."

Mrs. Thurgood.

Tina smiled. With Jenny Campbell and Elsie Thurgood tweaking things, there was little room for failure.

Walking to the dock with Max, Tina clung to his hand. The glorious lights of the village and town spread out before her, then ringed the lake like a circle of hope. A stream of traffic to their right aimed for the lighted park display, while tourists from all over the area milled the streets, snapping pictures and frequenting local businesses.

Drawn to the light.

The duality inspired her. From now on she would grab hold of the bright things in life: faith, hope, love and charity. With so much to be grateful for, old shadows would be banished forever, just like they should be.

She preceded Max onto the boat, and felt a rush of pride when folks greeted them as if seeing them as a couple was a wonderful thing.

"This way, please." The dinner hostess directed them to a linen-draped table. Tiny electric tea lights brightened each Christmas-themed centerpiece. Sparkling twinkle lights outlined the boat's frame, making it a traveling decoration during festival evenings. Bad weather had kept the boat moored a few nights back, but tonight the air was clear, if cold, and stars shone above with no snow predicted.

Tina sat down, smiled at the Gundrys across the way, then stopped, amazed, when Max Campbell dropped to one knee before her.

The entire cabin hushed, straining to hear. Tina was pretty sure that the loud beat of her heart would make that impossible. The sight of Max before her, gazing into her eyes and holding her hand?

Breath-stealing.

He grinned.

And suddenly warmth and longing nudged nervous and excited to the side. This was Max…

Her Max…

About to declare his love.

Or so she hoped.

He gripped her hand tighter. "Tina Martinelli, I know I'm making a spectacle of myself right now."

The other diners in the small cabin restaurant laughed and clapped.

"And I know you don't normally like to claim the spotlight, but on this occasion, I wanted everyone to know exactly what I was doing. And what I want. And that's to have you as my wife, Tina Marie." He paused long enough to let the words sink in. "To marry me. Grow old with me. Have some cute kids." He leaned in as if sharing a secret. "I do believe we've already discussed how many, but as I said then, I'm open to negotiations."

Tina couldn't help but laugh, and the rest of the boat laughed with her.

And then Max turned serious. Beautifully and romantically serious. "I love you, Tina. I didn't realize how much until I was called away last month, and if I had any doubts about a change of career, leaving here—leaving you—was the hardest thing I've ever done. So if you don't mind marrying an ex-army officer—" he withdrew a small box and flipped the top open "—I'd be honored to be your husband, right here in Kirkwood Lake."

Her heart lodged somewhere firmly in her throat,

forming a lump so tight she couldn't force a word around it. Not long ago she'd watched as her hopes, dreams and aspirations burned to the ground, certain that her time in Kirkwood was over. For weeks she'd allowed the dark thoughts to cling tight, but in God's own amazing way…

In that perfect timing Reverend Smith liked to talk about…

Her life had changed and new dreams awaited her.

She reached out, hugged Max, nodded and fought tears. And then she kissed him, right there in front of a boatload of people, applause and shouts ringing in the moment.

"Is that a yes?" he whispered in her ear, his breath tickling her cheek, her neck.

"It is a total, unequivocal yes!" she whispered back, and when he kissed her again, she thought of a lifetime of Max's warmth, his strength, his faith and his humor—

And knew God had things under control.

Epilogue

"Hey. How's she doing?" Max tiptoed into the pink-and-green nursery the following Christmas Eve. "She seemed sniffly when I left this morning."

"Oh, she's fine," Jenny told him. She lifted the baby to her shoulder and snuggled her close. "Babies get sniffly for no good reason just because everything about them is miniaturized."

"Hard to believe it's been a year since I came back," Max whispered. "So much has happened..."

His mother's eyes filled instantly, remembering. "The way of life, isn't it? The good Lord gives and He takes away."

Max sank onto the window seat beside the glider rocker. "I'm glad Dad got to meet her."

Jenny's nod said she agreed wholeheartedly. "He was thrilled to have a namesake."

Mixed emotions tightened Max's throat. "Charlotte Grace Campbell."

"Charlie." His mother smiled up at him through her

tears. "And if your dad saw what you did with this year's light show, he'd be pleased as punch, Max."

"You learned from the best," Tina said as she crept into the room, bent and kissed Jenny's cheek, then did the same to Charlie's. "And as she grows up, we'll fill her with stories and pictures and beautiful memories of the grandfather that made all of this possible. And how God's timing worked so perfectly, bringing you home." She smiled up at Max and touched a finger to his cheek. "Bringing us together..."

"I think his patience might have been tried just a little on that part," Max drawled, meeting his wife's gaze.

She blushed. "Okay, that was all me, but then bringing Charlie just in time to meet her grandpa." She smiled up at Jenny and didn't try to hide the tears in her eyes. "That meant the world to me. To see him hold her. Talk to her. I might have been stubborn about going my own way before—"

Max cleared his throat to show he wasn't about to disagree.

She acknowledged that with a slight grimace of guilt, then added, "But for the first time in my life I saw God's hand in all of this. Giving me the family I always longed for, bringing me Max and Charlie, even in losing big Charlie." She raised her shoulders and touched the baby's soft-as-silk cheek. "As hard as that is, somehow it seemed like we'd all be okay because God gave us one another as He called Dad home."

Max's heart went tight, then soft.

They'd lost so much when they said their final goodbyes to Charlie, but when he looked around this room...

His daughter's bedroom, with his mother holding her ninth grandchild and the nighttime candle glowing in the window…

He saw Tina's words come alive.

God had given and God had taken away, but he was blessed with so much more this year. A home, a family, a new life in Kirkwood Lake…

And a series of tomorrows, blessed by God.

He bent and kissed his mother's cheek, then his wife's, before he went downstairs to heat up the famous Martinelli red sauce. Thirty years ago he'd been a dirt-streaked kid dumped on Social Services four days before Christmas.

Now?

He was part of one of the best families on earth and despite life's ups and downs, Max Campbell couldn't be happier.

* * * * *

"Are the *kinder* okay?"

"Yes, they'll be fine." Uncomfortable with his small intrusion into her family, she said, "Kevin had a bad dream and woke us up."

"Because of the rain?"

She wanted to say that was silly but, glad she could be honest with Michael, she said, "It's possible."

"Rebuilding a structure is easy. Rebuilding one's sense of security isn't."

"That sounds like the voice of experience."

"My parents died when I was young, and both my twin brother and I had to learn not to expect something horrible was going to happen without warning."

"I'm sorry. I should have asked more about you and the other volunteers. I've been wrapped up in my own tragedy."

"At times like this, nobody expects you to be thinking of anything but getting a roof over your *kinder*'s heads."

He didn't reach out to touch her, but she was aware of every inch of him so close to her. His quiet strength had awed her from the beginning. As she'd come to know him better, his fundamental decency had impressed her more. He was a man she believed she could trust.

She shoved that thought aside. Trusting any man would be the worst thing she could do after seeing what Mamm had endured during her marriage and then struggling to help her sister escape her abusive husband.

"I'm glad you understand why I must focus on rebuilding a life for the children." The simple statement left no room for misinterpretation. "The flood will always be a part of us, but I want to help them learn how to live with their memories."

"I can't imagine what it was like."

"I can't forget what it was like."

Normally she would have been bothered by someone having sympathy for her, but if pitying her kept Michael from looking at her with his brown puppy-dog eyes that urged her to trust him, she'd accept it. She couldn't trust any man, because she wouldn't let the children spend their lives witnessing what she had.

LIEXP1119

When a police detective stumbles upon a murder scene with no body, can the secret father of her child help her solve the case without becoming the next victim?

Read on for a sneak preview of Holiday Homecoming Secrets *by Lynette Eason, available December 2019 from Love Inspired Suspense.*

Bryce Kingsley bolted toward the opening of the deserted mill and stepped inside, keeping one hand on the weapon at his side. "Jade?"

"Back here." Her voice reached him, sounding weak, shaky.

He hurried to her, keeping an eye on the surrounding area. Bryce rounded the end of the spindle row to see Jade on the floor, holding her head. Blood smeared a short path down her cheek. "You're hurt!" For a moment, she simply stared up at him, complete shock written across her features. "Jade? Hello?"

She blinked. "Bryce?"

"Hi." He glanced over his shoulder, then swung the beam of the flashlight over the rest of the interior.

"You're here?"

"Yeah. This wasn't exactly the way I wanted to let you know I was coming home, but—"

"What are you doing here?"

"Can we discuss that later? Let's focus on you and the fact you're bleeding from a head wound."

"I…I'm all right."

"Did you get a look at who hit you?"

"No."

A car door slammed. Blue lights whirled through the broken windows and bounced off the concrete-and-brick walls. Bryce helped her to her feet. "Let's get that head looked at."

"Wait." He could see her pulling herself together, the shock of his appearance fading. "I need to take a look at something."

He frowned. "Okay." She went to the old trunk next to the wall. "What is it?"

"The person who hit me was very interested in whatever was over here."

Bryce nodded to the shovel and disturbed dirt in front of the trunk. "Looks like he was trying to dig something up."

"What does this look like to you?"

"Looks like someone's been digging."

"Yes, but why? What could they possibly be looking for out here?"

"Who knows?" Bryce studied the pile of dirt and the bricks. "Actually, I don't think they were looking for anything. I think they were in the middle of *burying* something."

LISEXP1119